Letters to Nobody

ALSO BY JEAN M. GRANT

A Hundred Breaths
A Hundred Kisses
A Hundred Lies
Seeker
Silent Creek
Soul of the Storm
Will Rise from Ashes
And coming soon:
Chasing Roses

Letters to Nobody

JEAN M. GRANT

DEDICATION

To my aunt Frances, whose own writing of grief letters
inspired this story.
To librarians everywhere—you are superheroes! Thank you
for fostering a welcoming space for all.
And, to Kerry, whose unwavering persistence and love for
her community has kept our town's library afloat through
many storms.

Content Warnings
This novel explores aspects of mental illness and grief, and
contains references to suicide, infant loss/stillbirth, and
chronic illness.

One

Helen

"Are you alone? Have you seen it?" Kayley's high-pitched voice resounded from my cell phone.

Expecting a recount of her current drama with a lab coworker, as I settled in to listen to her story, I bumped my desk. The *Librarians Do It Dewey Style* mug full of steaming coffee tumbled onto my keyboard and the pile of new arrivals I needed to log into the system.

I groaned. "Sunny beach! Hang on." I grabbed a pile of tissues and laid my phone down. I blotted the books first.

Kayley didn't pause for a breath, her voice loud despite being off speaker. "Cori couldn't stop talking about the book. Anyway, why didn't you tell me about it? The balls he had to use them! Can we sue him?"

Waiting for my friend to gasp and fall silent with a side stitch, I wiped the spines of two more books. With them salvaged, I moved on to wipe between keys on my keyboard. Thankfully, my desktop survived unharmed. I had zero budget for anything new. My jeans were a mess. At least my mug didn't break. It was a gift from Kayley, one I hid from most of the patrons, because, well, children's eyes. I liked the feel of it in my hand, though. Maybe I could bring it home today. It always amused Mom.

Kayley repeated loudly, "Hell's bells, Helen! Where did you go? Are you alone or what?"

I retrieved the phone. "Yes, yes. Keep your pants on."

"What pants?" Kayley teased. "I'm sweating like my grandpa's furnace."

"You're going commando now?" I laughed. She was in the third trimester of her pregnancy and probably wearing her usual stretchy yoga pants with a very long tank top and a white lab coat over them.

I grabbed another tissue and blotted my wet jeans, the tissue tearing and getting clumpy. Water would've been easier to clean. Exiting my office, I made a beeline for the bathroom to wash my hands, which were sticky because I took my coffee with cream and sugar.

"So what book are you talking about?" It wasn't unusual for my friend to get worked up over stuff, but this felt different somehow. Goose bumps sprung up on my arms.

My assistant librarian, Billie, waggled her eyebrows over her purple frames at the mess on me. "Don't ask," I mouthed.

"Remember when I suggested you do that thing, and you did that thing, and we thought that was the end of it all? Well, that thing has come back to bite us in the ass."

"Elaborate, please. You've made me do many things." I cradled the phone between my ear and shoulder while washing my hands. Thankfully, I stocked the bathroom with real paper towels, not those cheap brown air-thin ones the town provided. I then made some headway on cleaning my jeans.

"Your voice is echoing. You left your office, didn't you? I told you to be alone."

"Well, if you lower your voice, the entire library won't be able to hear you."

She tsked. "The letters, Helen! He used them in a book. Well, they aren't actually *in* it—but your letters inspired the story for his main character, for sure. They're too alike to be a coincidence."

"What letters? And who is 'he'?" I paused mid-wipe of towel against denim.

No. Not *those* letters.

"We're alone. What letters?" I repeated.

"You're a librarian and haven't seen it? There was an interview with the guy on the *Authors to Watch* podcast yesterday. Mr. Sexy Voice! Anyway, the book came out in June and Cori was going on and on about it." I imagined Kayley's eye roll.

She paused for a beat. "So, I read the thing. You know I don't like fiction unless it's compelling. And my friend, it was. Oh, it was! Anyway, I thought you monitored all the buzzworthy books. Bestseller lists? Son of a monkey, Helen. You need to get out more."

"Hey, wasn't your New Year's resolution to stop bashing my lame dating life?"

"That lasted three weeks."

"I like my life. Kayley, focus. What book?" Tremors entered my voice. A book with my letters? Impossible. They should have been tossed, shredded, never read.

Instead of answering, Kayley continued her diatribe about my less-than-sparkly Saturday night calendar. I dried my hands and crossed the main circulation area, a to-do list flying through my brain—approve overtime requests, check the fall calendar, call the electrician, hound the Capital Building Committee about the roof leak, and pretend there wasn't a rodent issue in my basement and chipmunk condominiums under the flower beds.

On the trek across the worn carpet back to my office, I caught snippets of her words. *Don't be an old lady...need to get laid....*

Elwood Greene passed me, a pile of hardcovers under one arm, his granddaughter Alexis at his side. "Hi, Helen. I'm looking forward to trying the new Graham book you recommended."

I smiled at him. "Hang on, Kayley." I pressed my phone to my chest. "I think you'll love it. He sets all his mysteries on Plum Island, and I know how much you and Maureen enjoyed birdwatching there." I suspected most of the books in Elwood's pile were for reading to his wife. Despite her glaucoma, I couldn't convince her to try audiobooks.

Alexis wiggled beside him. "Pop Pop, I gotta go..."

I pointed to the bathroom in the children's area. "Over there. Need help?"

"No, Miss Wright! I'm four now. Can do all by myself." She hurried away. Elwood's salt-and-pepper beard danced with his chuckle.

Billie could probably hear Kayley's near shriek at the reference desk. I nodded goodbye to the amused Elwood and stuck the phone back to my ear.

"Helen, you're not listening! Get into your office, now! Shut the stinkin' door!"

Not needing an angry pregnant lady on my hands, I did. "Okay, you have my full attention. Enough of my lame love life. Can we return to discussing the letters-and-book matter? *What* book and *what* letters? Not *those* letters, right?"

"Yes, those. *Your* letters. Hestolethemandwrotethemi-nadarnbestseller!" she said in a rush that could outrun a cheetah.

"My—?"

"Let-ters." She emphasized her syllables like an impatient teenager. "The ones you wrote seven years ago. I was there for the first one, remember? And you told me what you put in the rest. I remember, and I'm a master at deciphering subtleties. He was subtle. Like, he didn't paste the letters in or anything. But the similarities are *spot on*. He found them, somehow. Used them to write this Emma character. Her story is your story...or well, sort of. Just read it!"

Could a heart stop with bad news? Mine sure did. Oh wait, there it was. Thudding against my rib cage.

Yes, *those* letters.

Thank God I wasn't holding my coffee anymore.

My silence must have conveyed my shock or confusion, so she carried on. "The grief letters. This man, Gabriel Dennehy, found them and they're now in a book."

"Y-you just said he didn't put them in there." Oh my God, she was confusing me. Or my brain was just working way too slow.

"The jerkface wrote some other letters. He fictionalized them for the story, but there's no mistaking it. Zero doubt. Yours!" Her voice rose an octave with each sentence, and I inched the phone away from my ear.

"Gabriel who?"

"Dennehy."

Was I supposed to know who this creep was? "The letters were unaddressed. Yes, I put them in the collection mail-box outside the post office, but with no return or mailing address, no postage. Those kinds of letters get trashed, sorted out. You had me so paranoid after I did it, I googled.

They get dumped. What you're talking about only happens in movies."

"Or books," she corrected.

"You're mistaken, Kayley."

My letters were supposed to have been cathartic, cheaper than therapy. One reckless night, while hopelessly sad over my good friend's death, I'd written the first one. Then another, and more over several months. The letters helped me heal. I'd written them not only to Adalyn but to my ex, my baby, my dad, and even to Mom. And then I'd deposited them all in the blue mailbox because it made it feel more real to send off my grief to my lost loved ones instead of writing about it in a journal and boxing it away. In the moment, it'd cleansed my soul to send them off.

I counted my lucky stars that only Kayley knew about them.

I gulped. "Okay. What book?" I couldn't believe I was buying her conspiracy theory.

"*Letters to Nobody.*"

Ah, that one was on the new release display. Nothing seemed off about it. "I haven't read it yet. Kayley, I know you're stressed about work, and the baby coming, and Aaron's start-up..."

"Read it tonight if you don't believe me!"

"Okay, okay." I'd bet she was pacing. My legs itched to move with hers.

Even if someone *had* found my letters, there wasn't a novel in them. Sob fest. End of story.

The local postal workers destroyed them, most definitely.

Denial raged within me. Denial and I went way back. We were frenemies.

"Maybe it's similar, but I'm telling you, it's not—"

"Read it. *You* will see the similarities," she urged. A beeper sounded through the phone. "Gotta go. The centrifuge is done, and I won't let Cori touch my samples. Talk tomorrow. Read it!"

Well, fine. It's not like I had anything else better to do tonight.

The abyss within me where I buried all the grief released a bubble that rose to the surface with a pop.

Kayley's pregnancy hormones were driving her nuts. My letters couldn't have inspired this novel. This had to be a coincidence.

I hurried to the book display and searched for *Letters to Nobody*. The e-book and audiobook had mile-long waiting lists on Libby, so I was amazed to find the hardcover edition. The exquisite cover showed a melancholic woman clutching a letter as others floated away, carried by the winds of time. The back flap held no photograph of the author above his bio. He lived in New England.

I would read the book tonight and appease Kayley's imagination. This story wasn't about my letters. No way.

After fighting with the persnickety front door of the library at closing time, I walked briskly home. In twenty minutes, I was crunching up the pebbly driveway past my car. I missed Dad's old, beat-up truck and our jaunts down country roads. When he and my stepmom hit the road for warmer weather last year, they sold the truck, which, as Brigette put it, was one of his "unnecessary belongings sitting around."

Floorboards creaked as I padded through the foyer, depositing my backpack by the side table, and clicking on lights. "Hey, Gifty. I'm home."

The tinkle of dishes sounded from the kitchen. "Hiya, Helen. Back here. Mary's already in bed."

"Be right there." With a kick, I closed the heavy door, its moan filling the open space. My job and home mirrored one another—old library, old house, old bones, old soul. Mom had transferred the deed for both buildings to me last year. I deposited *Letters to Nobody* on the office desk to read later.

At the sink, Mom's home health aide offered her chipper grin, though smudges of fatigue encircled her kind eyes. She blew her breath and re-pinned wisps of graying black hair. "She had a good day. We took a short walk through the neighborhood. She insisted on picking tomatoes and zucchini in the garden. Hope you're ready for all this fall canning. The raspberries have taken on a life of their own. The apples will be ripe soon. Time to get saucy." She shimmied her hips.

A matching laugh bubbled in my throat. "Love your spirit, Gifty. What would I do without you?" I grabbed a towel. "I'll dry."

All the same, I wasn't feeling the jam- and sauce-making this fall. It used to be a Mom thing, but she couldn't help anymore. I'd freeze most of the raspberries and crate some apples to bring to the farm for their market.

Gifty gave me a hip bump and scrubbed the last mug, despite our new dishwasher. "Mary does well in the garden with me for now. We've got a groove. But..." She thinned her lips in reflection. "We might need to teach you more. She had me sweating today. Didn't you call the repair person for the AC?" She dabbed at her forehead with a clean towel, her dark skin glistening with sweat.

My pulse flittered, then settled. Seven years after my return, I still wasn't ready for the house's responsibilities and woes. "Sorry. I forgot." I couldn't afford the repairs right now.

"You'll need the heat on soon enough! The gardens have loved this last burst of summer, though, yeah?"

"Me, too. I love early fall."

Gifty flicked her chin toward the coffeemaker. "There's fresh decaf for you. I left jollof rice in the fridge."

I gave her a squeeze. "You spoil me."

"It's nothing. Auntie Eunice's recipe."

I'd given up telling Gifty she didn't need to make the coffee or wash the dishes or bring us food, since these were not in her job description. "Did Mom have tea before bed?"

"Naturally. I steeped it with dried lavender." Her phone chirped three consecutive times. She sucked her teeth. "Evans. Algebra may be the death of us. I thought I was done with this type of math after college."

I snorted. "Who actually likes algebra?"

"Exactly."

Money was tight for Gifty, with Osei unable to work due to his back injury, so suggesting they hire the tutoring services of Kayley's husband, Aaron, wouldn't be the best idea. "He likes chess, right?"

"Can't get him away from it."

"The chess club meets every other Saturday at the library. One boy there likes to help other kids with math."

She wagged her pointer finger. "Oh, I like where your brain goes. I'll have Evans stop by the library. The boy needs a good push sometimes." She glanced at her phone.

"More like a shove." She typed a response, then pocketed her phone. "The daily log is on the clipboard. See you next week."

"'Night. Say hi to Osei for me. I'll bake him my world-famous raspberry scones this weekend."

"Well, don't you know the way to his heart! Now you know why he married me." She winked and gestured toward the fridge on her way out the door. "Remember to eat something, okay?"

Even though Gifty said Mom was doing fine tonight, I looked into her bedroom. Her window was open, carrying the evening katydid serenade in on a breeze. Mom snored softly under a light duvet.

I fixed a late-night decaf with extra cream, grabbed a pre-made salad in a Mason jar, and reheated the rice, my kitchen smelling of ginger, garlic, chili, and other invigorating spices. In the office, I clicked on the desk lamp and deposited the food and mug. A bite of jollof rice hit my taste buds in all the right spots. I opened *Letters to Nobody*, its binding already loosened from being read by many patrons.

Propping my feet on the desk, I read until long after the coffee was cold. I could finish a three-hundred-page book in a night if I set my mind to it.

Which I did.

This was good. Too good. Dennehy had seen into my heart. And the story wept.

Not the same way I had, writing my letters. The griefs Emma wrote about in her letters were different, and so were her joys. But there was no mistaking the likeness. The woman in *Letters to Nobody* was not a figment of Dennehy's imagination, no matter how hard I tried to convince myself while reading.

The woman in the story was real. She was me.

Two

Gabe

The subject line in Laurel Krane's email snarled at me.

Local Book Tour

"Chill, Gabe," I told myself, reading my agent's bolded list of reminders and suggestions.

Laurel had pressured me to schedule a national tour. I wanted to keep it smaller. Our compromise was a tour in Massachusetts this fall, and a small-scale national tour that would run in the spring. With the book's success unanticipated, there had been no marketing budget. Laurel scored a deal post-release as sales numbers soared. Doing a book tour after it reached bestseller status wasn't unheard of. So here we were.

Somehow the grass didn't seem greener on this side of the fence. With success came the headache of accounting. Dad once tried to explain the details of financial management in "Gabe-speak."

I liked to pretend a bully in class had come up with that term, but my gut told me my father invented it.

"A shoebox for your receipts, Gabriel?" he chided during our last phone call. "Learn the bookkeeping software I suggested. There's a step-by-step tutorial. If you had taken more math classes in college, you could be here, at the firm, not writing books that—" A deep exhale sliced through the high I had been riding.

—*are a waste of time.*

—*are more of a hobby than a respectable career.*

—*only paupers and dreamers, not real men, write.*

Then he went on to say: *Settle down. Get married. Get a proper job. Stop flying all over the world.* Dad's advice got old, fast.

At least he hadn't mentioned my actual first book, an awful sci-fi that burned up before liftoff. In stark contrast, I'd already earned out my advance on *Letters to Nobody*. When Dad eventually handed the phone over to Mom, she cried into the earpiece with pride.

I tapped my fingers on the desk, sipping the Guatemalan blend. Not only did my purchase support a fair-trade enterprise, but the coffee reminded me of my travels as an investigative writer. That job had its perks, though the paycheck wasn't one of them. Thus, accounting had never been an issue. One needed a good income to have something to account. Was *account* a verb?

I closed my email inbox, ignored the blank screen in my writing program, and opened an online dictionary. Okay, *account for*. I returned to the blank screen, grunted, and closed that, too. Money management aside, the catch to the awesome deal Laurel scored me? A book two...to be written while on the local tour. That threw a wrench into my other plan with the tour: find my mysterious letter writer.

Could I tour, write book two, and search for M.H. all at the same time? Talk about multitasking. That skill was low on my assets list.

I removed the pilfered letters from my desk drawer. I mentally pushed aside Laurel and marketing demands, Dad and the accounting, and the editor's desire for a first draft manuscript in a few months. Focusing with several fast blinks, I shuffled the stack to bring one worn missive on top. I read the last lines, tracing the cursive with a fingertip, though I had memorized each letter by now, seeking a hint about who the writer was and where she lived.

I removed the dandelion that had been tucked inside a tissue. The letter to her mother had held the pressed yellow flower. None of the other letters held tokens, just this one. I ran a finger over the delicate stem and ray florets.

I needed to summon my inner Sherlock Holmes. Digging was what I did best, after all.

What was I missing? The letters had to hold clues.

M.H. was how she signed all five of them.

M.

Emma, as I'd renamed her in my book. Perhaps it stood for Molly? Mary? Maggie? Megan? Was H the beginning of her last name or middle name?

As I read her words, my mind bolted like a dog let off the leash in a meadow, sniffing the source of a scent. Every sentence, every word held significance.

I miss you, dear heart. I'm sorry I couldn't help you more. I'm so sorry. May we meet in the hereafter, may you forgive me.

Besties for life and beyond,

M.H.

The honestly stated emotion said so much.

In an age where people begged for attention on social media, the letter writer didn't. Instead of shredding or burning these private letters, she had put them in a mailbox. What mindset would cause a person to do that?

The author had to be a woman around my age. She mentioned the death of a baby and that sorrow felt raw, recent. Intuition told me this wasn't an older woman grieving losses from her youth. She mentioned sharing funny memes with her bestie. Even Mom shared weird memes with me but M.H. and Adalyn sounded like teen friends by the language and references. Memes in general were modern, which made me think these were newer letters from a younger person.

However, back to point one: the letters themselves. Who wrote on paper nowadays? Was I in love with a seventy-year-old replaying memories of days long ago?

No. M.H. was from here and now. I felt it in my bones.

The chair's base creaked with the movement as I rocked, urging the queasiness in my stomach to abate. My head spun. I flipped open my notebook. Who was I to judge a letter writer when notebooks and legal pads were my way, too? I loved pen on paper. On a new page, I jotted down what I did and didn't know about M.H.

First, the locations that seemed significant in her letters, anything to guide me to *where*. Marco had been working in a central Massachusetts postal facility when he found the letters.

Next, clues to guide me to *who*.

I described the paper. The letters were on simple stationery with borders of green vines and white flowers. It had a gift shop or specialty store feel, but for all I knew it could have been mass-produced and sold in every shop from here to Honolulu. My good contact in paper sourcing had turned up nothing when I showed him one of the blank pages M.H. had wrapped each letter in. She probably didn't want anyone to read a line through the envelope. And here I'd read all the lines in every letter.

Next, her writing: cursive. That didn't tell me much because learning cursive had been part of the curriculum when I was back in elementary school. I was no expert, but it looked feminine.

The biggest nugget: the story of how the letters landed in my lap.

Marco refused to go into details beyond confessing he'd pocketed this pile of dead letters from the USPS facility. My longtime friend didn't want to get in trouble. I obliged his *Don't ask, don't tell* policy, as much as it nagged me to not know more. Two years ago, Marco had seen my despondency over writing, my "Gabe Rut," and had given me the letters for inspiration. I guess he saw something in M.H. that I might connect with. He said they had moved him, and Marco was not one to be taken in by emotions much.

Not only had her letters held heartache and longing, but also sweeter and more joyful memories. The fact that she was hurting, but found happiness, even if small, and held on to persistence in the face of struggle? That hooked me. My first reaction had been compassion for M.H.'s pain. It then morphed into inspiration.

But the letters did more than inspire: M.H. saved me. I mean, I wasn't hanging out on some cliff ready to jump, but my spirit had been tiptoeing toward the edge.

She felt true and raw on those pages, admitting feelings that she might not say aloud. M.H. was genuine, and that's what I connected with, and what readers looked for. If she could find the light in the darkness, then Emma would do that: she would have heartache, but she would give others a chance to crawl out of the dark.

In writing Emma's story, I changed the painful details of M.H.'s letters and focused on the happier moments. Instead of the loss of a baby, Emma had a false-positive pregnancy, which had given her hope after a hard time with her soon-to-be ex-boyfriend. Emma's mother recovered from her illness. Emma's friend may have suffered from depression, but she ultimately got the help she needed. I couldn't put M.H.'s heartache out there. Instead, I wove the silver linings into the story: the sea glass, the dandelions, the icicles on the rail trail...the fond moments she held with each of these special people she wrote to.

I fell in love with M.H. through those joyful memories she shared, the depth of heart she revealed.

Once I had the protagonist developed, I needed to figure out my plot.

It turns out the USPS has a process for tracking down senders by reading contents of mail—hence the premise of *Letters to Nobody*. It was the perfect plot.

My spin on it: instead of postal workers in the Mail Recovery Center connecting letters with their intended recipients, the protagonist pair, Emma and Declan, are detectives in an obscure unit reassigned to a quiet field office, like a low-stakes *The X-Files*, and they need to solve a cold case via a stack of anonymous "dead" letters all written by the same person. Inspired, Emma begins to write letters to herself as she works through some struggles in her own life.

It was sweet, a bit mysterious, but not gritty, and very romantic. I had become a softie. It was a stretch...but it worked. My books sold faster than we expected.

None of this was an excuse for what I did. Reading letters not addressed to me was a crime. Not a heavy crime, but one nonetheless. Marco had tampered with mail, and I was an accessory.

Shoving my moral dilemma and possible legal liability aside, I gently folded the top letter, slipped it into the torn and faded ivory envelope, and placed it and the others inside a drawer, shutting them in the darkness of my desk.

Massaging the back of my neck, I plodded to the kitchen. An alert whistled on my phone. The interview with the Boston Public Library was in two hours.

I reviewed the T schedule again. My new place in Newton meant fewer transfers. I typed another reminder into my phone. On my travels abroad, I employed guides or relied on company-provided transportation. With adequate prep work, my challenges didn't hinder me. Dyscalculia, with its difficulties around spatial processing, went with driving like peanut butter went with pickles—not well. Public transit was far easier, but the T and bus only went so far. I'd need to drive on this upcoming small-town tour. How else could I track down the letter writer?

Finding my M.H. was worth the driving, the headaches, the dizziness.

My M.H.

Delusional, Gabe. She isn't yours.

Laurel planned for twenty stops in six weeks, starting around Springfield and working east toward Boston. My stipulation was a week-long mid-tour break in Sanders Mill. In the center of Massachusetts, it was an ideal spot for a little R and R. Plus, I could branch out my search.

Returning to my desk, balancing a plate piled with a turkey sandwich, cucumbers, and potato chips, I perused the open file on my laptop listing the towns I wanted to visit in addition to Laurel's itinerary. Detours had to fit my criteria: all in the under-ten-thousand population range (I just had a sense M.H. lived in a smaller town) and in proximity to the old Central Massachusetts Railroad. That former rail line ran for nearly a hundred miles from Northampton to Cambridge. The town could also be somewhere along the old Boston, Barre and Gardner Railroad, which ran south to north. I had drawn a triangle on the map to give me a rough estimate of my search area. Like the Bermuda Triangle.

It was a crapshoot, but I had to try.

My phone rang. I swallowed a bite of sandwich and swiped. "Hey, Laurel."

"Get the schedule?"

"Right here. Heading to the library soon."

"How's the writing?"

There it was. The elephant in the room. More like five elephants, shoulder to shoulder. This room was getting crowded: deadline, writer's block, legal liability and ethical guilt, and of course the question of M.H.'s whereabouts.

"Gabe, I need the manuscript by the end of January if we're to get it into the editorial schedule. We're lucky they're fast-tracking it. This could be a series, you know."

I knew. And never planned to go beyond one book. Why again had I agreed to this? "I'm working on it."

A semblance of a second book sat in a folder on my computer. Like, a few sentences. Without new letters as inspiration, how could I write book two for Emma and Declan? I was back to where I was two years ago...alone, hungering for a vision. Feeling like an outsider looking in at the world, instead of being part of it.

Part of me needed to find my muse. Another part needed to find a way to make things up to her, the real woman whose story I had taken. And a third part needed—or at least *wanted*, very strongly—to know that real woman, to see her face to face.

I needed to find my M.H.

Three

Helen

"He's in love with her," Harper Prescott said, as if she were in no mood for an argument.

My ears perked up at the discussion at the library circulation desk.

"Not possible. She's fictional," Brenna argued, working the attitude of I *know everything*.

"Oh, stop cappin'. You know you think it, too. And she is real." Harper's voice, usually one I could hear from afar with its distinct sugary enthusiasm, sounded deflated today. A book met the counter with a jangle of a wrist bracelet, and Harper huffed. "It's like a real-life message in a bottle thing. Like that really old movie? At least nobody dies in the end of this one!"

Billie said, "That movie was also a book, ladies."

"Huh?" they said.

I bridled a smile at the *save me* look Billie gave over her purple readers. Her tolerance for teen hormones and moodiness was low. I loved their spirit. Kids in the library meant life in a library. Years ago, at the Boston Public Library, I'd handled my share of little ones as the children's librarian. Sometimes I missed those days. Seeing teens here getting books instead of staring at screens made me happy.

Billie told Harper, "The likelihood of finding so many bottles with messages all from one person is best left for Hollywood, girls."

Harper yawned. "It is possible. In my stats class, we discussed—"

Billie brandished her hand. "You win, dear. You won when you said stats. Are you checking that out?"

Harper slid the book across the desk with her pointer finger, then turned her attention to her phone after it beeped. "Yes. The wait for the e-book is just too long. Can't you get more or something?"

"I'll get right on that."

"Need help?" I came to Billie's side, a stack of YA books in my arms. We couldn't keep the *Dragon Saga* on the shelves. I'd submitted another request to Overdrive for digital copies.

"Harper wanted to start a book club for this novel, Miss Wright," Brenna said. "We can't agree on whether it's based on a true story or not."

"Book clubs can discuss both fiction and nonfiction. Memoirs are popular, too."

Brenna gagged with her eyes. "My mom reads memoirs. She's always crying when she does. Who wants to hear about an old lady's miserable life?"

Harsh, kid. I didn't argue that there were plenty of inspiring memoirs on our shelves by non-old people. These two teens probably saw me as old, and I was barely into my thirties.

Billie bristled. "It's a novel. *Fiction*." She checked out the books, mumbling under her breath as one label didn't scan, and she had to hand-type the barcode.

We'd spent the entire summer re-cataloging with new barcodes, yet our scanner was eternally glitchy. Add a new one to my growing list of needs.

"Exactly," Brenna agreed, a victorious glow in her eyes. She fussed with her hair, sweeping it up into a loose bun.

"Oh, Helen, Kenny called again." Billie tapped the note beside the computer.

I'd been avoiding the electrician ever since our elevator failed inspection. That repair was going to cost six grand. Last year, the sprinklers were a surprise of four grand. Fun times in Sanders Mill Public Library!

I turned back to Harper and Brenna. "Book clubs are a great idea—" My mouth clamped shut.

There *it* sat.

I shuddered internally. *Not that thing.* I had purposely re-shelved *Letters to Nobody* with outdated books in the nonfiction section. I hid it between old cooking and scrapbooking handbooks. Two other copies found a new home under my desk, making a great footrest. I would not censor the novel completely. I could, however, make it harder for a patron to locate.

Apparently, not hard enough for two teenagers.

There was no stopping a bestseller.

I slid out an antacid from the roll in my pocket and crunched on it. "Perhaps it's not the best choice for a teen book club, since it lends itself to an adult audience. How about the *Dragon Saga* and...um..." My mind numbed when I attempted to name some books trending on the bestseller lists.

Harper tapped pointed fingernails of alternating claret and navy, the high school colors. Her scowl mirrored her mother's when she got riled. She had the same dark hair as Miriam, though hers was longer and wavy in that youthful style. Today it looked messy. Was the rolled-out-of-bed look "in" again? Deep circles framed her eyes. And not a hint of color adorned her usually made-up face. Was it first-week-of-school fatigue? I bit my tongue to keep from asking if something was wrong, even though the vibes were there.

Stop reading into things again, Helen. Not everyone is Adalyn.

I had been hanging out in the pit of despair all week because of Gabriel Dennehy. His book unearthed feelings I thought I'd banished seven years ago. The book wasn't fiction to me.

Harper continued, still half looking at her phone, "This book's perfect. I'm getting this copy for another girl who wants to read it, since Brenna and I have already read it twice. The author's from Massachusetts. He grew up in a small town near Springfield. In an online interview, he claimed he found inspiration from his local travels, though he's traveled abroad, too."

Give me a break. *More like inspired by the town he read about in my letters.*

"I think Emma was an ex-girlfriend. Maybe he met her while covering a story or he met her somewhere else," Harper said with a conspiratorial lift of her eyebrow. "The fan groups online have theories that he actually got the story from real letters. That he found them."

Brenna rolled her eyes. I popped another antacid into my mouth.

"How could all those people be wrong?" Harper pressed.

"You can't believe everything you read online." I'd done some googling, too. Apparently, Harper wasn't the only fan who suspected Dennehy took this story from real life. At least Billie and Brenna were on Team Fiction.

Harper asked, "Didn't a train run through here at some time? We have the rail trail now. It sounds like our town, like Sanders Mill."

I allowed a deeper smile—the patient librarian smile. Inside, my stomach soured. Too quick for her own good, Harper was clearly on a path to something great if her mother didn't stifle it.

Even Brenna caved to the idea for a moment. "Maybe it's North Prouty? They have that old train station."

Harper shoved her phone into her back pocket. "How large is our town?"

A week had passed since I read this cruddy book, and my mind couldn't stop reeling, unable to deny the truth. I forged ahead in this conversation anyway. Lying went against my grain, but some lies were necessary. "It's fiction, girls. He obviously researched small towns like ours and modeled one after them. There are hundreds of towns along the old rail lines. As for the letters, it's illegal to read another person's mail. Nobody would *really* do it and then write a book about it. It's a realistic, but fictional story. Emma and Declan, the cold case and field office, the letters, they're all made up."

Billie returned to cataloging the interlibrary loan items without another word.

Harper persisted. "I read about it online. There's this postal facility in Atlanta which used to be called the Dead Letter Office, and it now has a new name, Mail Recovery something. Unaddressed letters or packages with missing information get sent there and employees try to reconnect them with the owners or recipients. Maybe certain letters get sent on to the FBI. Like what if this author had a source or something? They even do like auctions of the old stuff that nobody claims, like the bigger packages—"

"Got it. Let's get you on the calendar." I opened the library planner on the computer. "Our population is about nine thousand, by the way."

She smirked. "Nowhereville. Like in the book."

The grimace parted my lips before I could stop it. Harper didn't notice or care. "When would you like to schedule the group?"

With the redesigned and upgraded website, an effort by a local teen working toward extra credit in a computer class, scheduling was now online, and the library was out of the twentieth century. Much easier for promotion...so long as our computers didn't crash again. Clicking open September's tab, I told myself a teen-led event was good for us. One suggestion proposed at the latest Library Board of Trustees meeting was to explore youth activities. After acquiring a grant for our children's programming, Stan suggested a popcorn and movie night. This book club would also be a good activity for kids.

While Harper and Brenna discussed dates and times, my thoughts tumbled to other tasks in my planner—remind the kindergarten about their field trip, set up a day for the preschool to visit, and talk with one of the high school English teachers about their feedback on the summer reading list. "Keep them coming" was Mom's motto.

Triumph glowed in both pairs of young eyes when they finally agreed. "Saturday afternoons—most of the girls have cross country meets early in the mornings."

"An all-girl group? Maybe pick a book that might appeal to everyone?" I offered. *Not this awful book. Any other book!*

"Nope," Brenna huffed. "Girls only. How amazing would it be if it *were* real? The more Harper pushes for it, the more I believe her. Emma...she feels real. She's so sad. So lonely."

"A little pathetic," Harper chimed in, typing the date for the book club into her phone.

Wow.

"Is that really a thing?" Brenna asked.

"Is what a thing?" Even though the scheduling was complete, and I had plenty of work to excuse myself for, I found myself sucked into this conversation.

"Can people open letters like this? Or is it really illegal?"

"Yes, it's illegal."

Since last Friday, I'd read everything I could on the USPS website, just like Harper had apparently. The mail underwent sorting at the local post office first, and they sent improperly addressed or undeliverable mail to central processing centers in each state. There, postal workers classified the mail into categories and sent the dead mail—which could not be matched with a sender or recipient at state level—to the Mail Recovery Center in Atlanta for further assessments. Thank goodness they'd changed the name. Dead Letter Office sounded morbid.

Then again, two of my letters had been addressed to the dead.

Pathetic sounded about right.

Somewhere in the process from mailbox to post office to central facility to Atlanta, Dennehy had gotten ahold of my letters.

"Do people even write letters anymore?" Brenna asked, not looking up from messaging on her phone.

"Some, yes."

In high school, inspired by a nineteenth-century ancestor's letters we'd discovered in my attic, Adalyn and I had written messages in code and mailed them to each other. Stamped and all. We incorporated the idea into our Mystery Book Club by creating a cipher to share with the group. Winners got a small trinket we purchased with our allowances.

There was something intimate about receiving a letter instead of an email. To wait for its arrival. To tear it open. Paper smelled good. Felt good in my hand. Growing up with a librarian for a mom, who had at one point still used the card catalog, I found all formats of the written word invigorating—letters, birthday cards, thank-you notes. Adalyn and I had bonded over this shared love.

I cleared my throat. "So, Saturday's good. You can have the small room downstairs. How many do you expect to attend?"

"At least ten? I want to hang flyers and put it on social."

The delicate hairs on my neck prickled. *It's for the library.* "Sure, Harper."

If Mom's motto had been "keep them coming," mine was "it's for the library." Like all bestsellers, *Letters to Nobody* would ride its course, then disappear into the shadows of yesterday. For now, we needed this activity. Especially now. A glutton for punishment, I moved from one painful topic to the next. "How's your mom, Harper?"

She wrinkled her forehead. "Fine. Always busy. Need me to tell her something?"

I wanted to tell her, *back off, lady. Leave my library alone.* Did the old saying about keeping your enemies closer really work? "Tell her I said hi."

Harper nodded and the girls left.

It's for the library.

With the budget cut this year—again—I contemplated other growth opportunities and scribbled a few ideas on a nearby sticky note.

Whenever the town fell into hard times, the Select Board threatened to defund the library. As if that wasn't enough, Miriam Prescott would not relent about the possibilities of selling the land the building sat on and developing it for new houses. Though Howe Builders had their eyes on multiple properties in town, the library land's beauty and acreage made it a desirable target, and the financial offer reflected that. I unclenched fists. Could a person overdose on antacids?

Penny-pinching was my middle name since coming home, but I could only be so frugal. Miriam's offer would make a world of difference for Mom's care.

But I would not sell. Sanders Mill Public Library was one of the handful in our state that was privately owned—by my family, since my great-great-great-grandfather Joseph founded it—and publicly funded. I worked with the Board of Trustees to govern it. If we lost town funding, I couldn't financially maintain it on my own, and my hand would be forced. However, any sale decision would have to go through me as much as the board. It was...complicated. But manageable, so far.

Between Miriam's efforts to shut us down and Dennehy's book, I wasn't sure what more I could take. If experience had taught me anything, it was that I could expect to take another wallop from life. What would it be?

Four

Helen

The answer to my rhetorical question showed up while I sat at the kitchen table before my Saturday shift. I opened an email from someone named Laurel Krane.

Subject line: LETTERS TO NOBODY Book Tour.

The groan escaped before I could nip it. At least I didn't have a mouthful of juice to spew over the screen.

"What's wrong?" Mom rested her reading glasses and the crossword puzzle on the butcher-block island. The penciled-in letters were more chicken scratches than alphabet, but Mom was stubborn. She said the crossword app I installed on her tablet made her dizzy. I unclenched my jaw. At least the mouthguard I wore at night helped my headaches.

"Nothing." I clicked open the email. My pulse pumped wildly in my neck with each word. I used to get palpitations from stress. Now I got panic attacks. Mom usually picked up on it, despite any attempt I made to keep her comfortably ignorant, but right now she was struggling to squeeze honey into her tea.

I took it from her and poured the right amount in. Mom stirred, the fragrance of cinnamon invigorating my senses.

Mom seemed fine—clear eyes, no hunch, no knotting of fingers, none of the pain indicators she tried to hide from me each day. "Need your morning dose?" I asked.

"Not yet. Thanks, sweetheart. Miriam bothering you again? You seem upset."

I looked at her blankly.

"My nerves might be damaged, but my brain cells are functioning, Helen."

"It's a work thing." I tapped restless fingers on the countertop.

Mom pushed out a "mmm," then pulled her sweater closer with a visible shiver despite the pleasant room temperature.

I told her, "Nan will be here at eight, then we'll tackle the garden this afternoon when I get home. I bought more jars for canning the zucchini mash."

She sipped her tea. "Okay. But maybe you should..." She stopped. "It's Saturday. The ladies can help me. We enjoy a rainy night in."

I heard what she'd kept herself from saying. *Go on a date. Do something other than be a homebody here and hide in your books there.* She was as persistent as Kayley.

Instead, my mom shifted in her seat and her topics. "I'm hoping the ladies bring croissants today. They'd be perfect with your raspberry jam."

My jaw tension released further with the thought. "Weather's been good this year for raspberries. The harvest's busting at the seams. You worked your magic again, Mom."

"Nah, it's the magic seaweed and fish fertilizer Coop recommended I use. Smells like death but works wonders."

"Ah, Coop and his Magical Fish Juice."

Rosy color crept across her nose, and it wasn't because of another hot flash. Mom and Ronan Cooper would make the cutest couple. Like Mom, I once caught Ronan chatting with his plants. He and Mom loved to reminisce about their years in high school together and felt passionate about keeping our small town strong and community-positive. She sipped silently, her attention returning to the cross-word puzzle. The pencil shook in her unsteady hand.

I scowled at the email. To decline such an opportunity—a bestselling author on a small-town book tour—would be nuts. The library needed this press. Never mind that it was thriving when it came to usage. Budget was a different sto-ry. Miriam's claws were so deep into the Finance Commit-tee that she convinced the Select Board our situation was dire, though I did all in my power to show them otherwise. I managed on what we were given. Granted, we had over-due repairs, and lacked step-up raises, and would need to increase our hours to accommodate the rising community population...

It was only September, but budget time was around the corner. I'd need to cross a hundred fingers and toes for my request for funds to float.

Just...float. That's all I wanted right now.

My stomach knotted. I'd have to ask for another warrant article in the spring, for extra funds to be given by the town vote. By the graces of state funding that came during the pandemic, we'd been able to replace our two defunct furnaces, but that money was gone.

It was too early to be popping antacids, but my fingers itched to reach for the roll of them in my handbag. I rose and topped my mug off from the coffee pot instead, though coffee was awfully acidic, and not the best choice either for my rising blood pressure. I pretended to be busy cleaning up breakfast while my mind raced.

Every time the town reached a budget impasse, the library was first on their chopping block. Never the police or fire department, school district, or "more important" departments. The town apparently had a short-term memory. They'd forgotten we hosted the vaccine clinic, served annually as a voting location, and opened our doors when others didn't. They'd forgotten that virtually every department used our space!

Despite those close calls, the library's pulse still beat. It was the heart of our community.

I had decades of budgets at my disposal. My predecessor was notorious for astute bookkeeping and maintaining a community presence. I should know, for that person sat beside me. Mom had been a robust librarian until illness ravaged her body seven years ago. Building on her experience, we always made it work. Maybe something this big—the book signing—would get the Select Board's attention, get them to finally see just how pivotal our library was.

"What next?" I mumbled aloud.

Mom sneezed, her flaxen hair coming loose from its pins and falling to her shoulders. "What'd you say?" She fixed one of the pins with some effort.

I shook her question away and slid the box of tissues over.

Mom cast the *Really, Helen?* expression at me and resumed her scribbles. "Miriam?"

"Who else?"

She pursed her lips, taking a long moment before speaking. "Lorraine was chatting with me about her grandson the other day."

I stiffened, but my brain welcomed the change in subject. "Oh?"

"He has a disability. Dyslexia, I think. Or was it dysgraphia?" She chewed on the eraser end of her pencil. "Nan's daughter mentioned Tessa also deals with—oh, I forget the name—anyway, Nan's granddaughter has been having a hard time. I was thinking...in my day there weren't many parent support groups. I'm sure Nan's daughter and Lorraine's son would appreciate such a thing."

"You're thinking the library could be a location for a parent support group?"

"Naturally. Times have changed since I ran the show, but people still need a place to gather with like minds. Not everyone wants to advertise their problems on social media. People like being with people."

"That's a good idea, but I already have lots of groups using the meeting space."

Mom said, "Well, what do you have in mind?"

"Not sure. Something bigger that gets everyone's attention." I shrugged. "Still, small strides are better than no strides and I won't say no to any group that wants to use meeting space. Could you ask Lorraine or Nan to come see me? The effort would need to be spearheaded by community members and whatever groups they're involved with."

I thought of other nonprofit or even for-profit groups that could use our space. Kayley's husband, Aaron, ran a tutoring program and had outgrown his current home office. He was a long-term substitute math teacher at the high school and offered after-school and tutoring services. He was shifting his focus to non-academic needs, too, like time management, self-advocacy, and independence. Maybe Aaron could use the library space.

I had until the annual meeting in May to get my act together if I wanted additional funds above my usual annual budgetary request. Now wasn't too soon to start. Small towns had interesting processes. I prepared my budget in the fall for the following fiscal year, which began in July. The approval process was a joint effort between the Select Board, Finance Committee, and town administrator. And they usually always came back to my request asking me to trim it.

The annual town meeting was where the magic happened if we needed to make special purchases or requests. Departments submitted these as warrant articles to be voted on by all citizens. I would need to request my extra funds at that meeting if the Finance Committee didn't approve my budget. Which was likely.

Surely, I'd get people who wouldn't agree to vote our library into nonexistence. The library was a Sanders Mill staple, rich in history and resources. Wryly, I asked, "Have any connections to get Miriam off the ballot as the town moderator?"

"No." She added, "I had a Miriam in my day. Thankfully, *he* moved after a disgraceful scandal."

"If we only had a scandal. Miriam will step down when hell freezes over. Pierce Howe is champing at the bit to get our land so he can slap up more overpriced homes. Miriam's in his pocket, I'm sure of it. I'm so tired of people turning a blind eye." She and Pierce were probably in bed together literally, though both were married. "He's been pushing for a special town meeting this fall to get the Planning Board to approve more building permits."

I stared at Laurel Krane's email again. If I couldn't get the Finance Committee and town behind me, the library's life and legacy would end in May. I couldn't voice that in front of Mom. But she was no fool.

She hadn't begged me to come home to rescue her. That decision had been mine. If she could keep the library afloat all those years, so could I.

"Maybe Miriam's idea for a regional library on land in North Prouty isn't a bad thing," she said.

My jaw dropped. "Mom? You can't be giving her idea any stock? She wants to bulldoze our library and flatten most of our old-growth forest, build these McMansions, then force the other district libraries to close by whatever means possible. With no more small-town libraries left, she then proposes building a giant regional library on that old farm property in North Prouty." I made air quotes. "A one-stop library and media center for all." I made a face. "It's an empty promise. She would need all five district towns behind the vote. When have all five agreed on anything? Plus, how would state aid work? It's more complicated."

"Some things are meant to—" She didn't finish her thought.

Be let go? Let die? How could she suggest such a thing?

I clenched a fist in my lap. "Hadley-Wrights don't give up."

"You've got that face."

"What face?"

"The one where your forehead is all scrunched. What do you have there?" She pointed at the computer screen. "This isn't just about Miriam and the library."

I shut the laptop. "Nothing. It's Miriam."

Mom lifted a fair eyebrow. I was an awful liar when my brain was fried. I dropped my spoon and mug into the sink. "Oh. A few of your books came in." I withdrew two hardcovers from my bag. "The memoir, and the new suspense by Harriet Chisolm."

Smile lines appeared around Mom's baby-blue eyes. "Great. I'll sit on the porch this afternoon and read. Don't worry, sweetheart. Miriam won't shut it down. You're creative and resourceful. I survived Ned the Nag. You will survive Meddling Miriam."

If only Miriam was the sole problem.

Mom glanced at her crossword, then back up at me. "Weren't you working on something with the Historical Register? Whatever came of that?"

I grimaced. That process—seeking historical protection of the library—had stalled too often. Whenever I started researching it, I hit a wall. "We need something substantial about the building or land. I can't seem to find anything noteworthy."

She said, "It's worth a shot to dig through the old records again. Maybe get someone to help you?"

"I'll do that."

For now, I had the small things to focus on.

I took a deep breath and reopened my laptop. First up, getting some positive publicity for the library. The fancy New York agent's email included all the pertinent details for Dennehy's tour. With a few taps of my fingers, I replied nicely, agreeing to host him next weekend. The signing could bring a highlight in the local paper, and I could confront the thieving author. I would take any win I could get at the moment.

Let's see what you have to say for yourself, Gabriel Dennehy.

Five

Helen

The following Saturday, a fog rolled in worthy of the Cape, drifting and definite. An overcast morning wasn't a bad omen because I didn't believe in superstitions. In the central hills of Massachusetts, fog liked to linger.

As for the fog covering my head, it would hopefully dissipate with Gabriel Dennehy's departure.

Coffee percolated in the library's ancient urn brewer at a snail's pace, so I ran upstairs to finish prep work. *There's nothing fancy here for you, letter thief.*

Billie set up the tables. The publisher had sent the signage ahead, and the sandwich board was on the sidewalk. Our library might be understaffed, underfunded, and old, but we ran a well-oiled machine here, me and my motley crew of Billie, Stan, and the handful of hourly aides and volunteers.

The printer whirred, the scent of toner infiltrating my nostrils. We were a bit behind because it had jammed yesterday.

I readjusted the plastic displays on the counter while two volunteers folded extra printouts. To my surprise, Dennehy's promo material excluded an author photo. I wondered why. Soon he would arrive, and I'd see his face. I felt as torn as a roughly handled printout—yes, I wanted this publicity for the library, but also, ugh, Dennehy.

He was supposed to be here fifteen minutes ago. Had he gotten lost on the Pike?

My stomach gurgled, and not from digesting breakfast. My cruddy nerves wouldn't calm down, despite Kayley's countless assurances this past week that nobody knew I wrote the letters...that he fictionalized the hell out of them, so much so that only she and I really saw the truth. But saw it we did.

After combing his book for similarities, we made a long list. I was about ninety-five percent sure Dennehy had been inspired by my dead letters.

I wished Kayley could be here. I needed her moral support, but she had some timepoints to run in the lab today.

"Cupcakes?" Billie peeked over her glasses.

I smacked my forehead. "Shoot. I'll be back."

Across the street to Barb's Cafe I went, munching on an antacid, my mind running faster than my legs.

One of Barb's regulars, Mack, greeted me with a hand flourish from his usual Saturday morning corner. "Good morning, mademoiselle. How's the front?"

"Busy. I'm here for cupcakes," I responded, smiling at his nickname for me. Mack had served in the Korean War, and afterward, traveling across Europe, he'd met a French woman he proclaimed was my spitting image. I never asked him to elaborate, as I was hoping I didn't remind him of a love affair. He had an affectionate but not inappropriate glimmer in his eyes each time he kissed my hand in greeting.

"Keep him honest, Louie," I said to his partner in crime, who sat beside Mack.

The quiet one, Louie winked from below his black veteran's cap and took a hearty bite of a jelly donut. A rogue blob of red jelly dripped on his t-shirt.

"I expect you guys to visit today," I told them as I handed Louie a napkin.

"Always, for you," Mack said with a wink.

I went to the line.

As I waited, I tapped a foot on the pink-and-brown-checkered linoleum and picked discreetly at my teeth with the corner of a napkin, wishing I hadn't eaten a poppyseed bagel for breakfast.

Barb spotted me and tilted her head. I followed her gesture to grab the order from the side counter, just a few steps away from the main line. "Be right back," she said in a whoosh of a breath before I could chide her to take it easy. She hadn't allowed a minor heart attack last year to slow her down.

"Lucky," a man said beside me. "I've been in line for five minutes."

Though I nearly jumped from my shoes, I responded with a perfunctory smile to the stranger, who looked like he had stepped out of an L.L. Bean catalog. His sun-kissed olive complexion matched his casual attire. He swiped a hand through his sandy-brown hair, which reminded me of woven waves of flax, honey, and caramel.

I found my voice. "I already paid. Just picking up. Don't despair. The wait is worth it. Saturday morning is Grand Central Station here, though."

"Duly noted." He cast a wary glance at the door as two customers joined the line. "Can you recommend a good flavor?"

"All of them. Barb roasts her own beans here. Caramel pumpkin is the flavor of the week. Everyone's already on the pumpkin craze and it's only September."

"Pumpkin nation," he teased. "Labor Day comes, and it's pumpkin everything."

"No such thing as a pumpkin season where I'm concerned." I shoved a chunk of my curls, overjoyed with the abatement of summer humidity, behind my ear while raising an eyebrow. I placed his accent as New England, without the distinct depth of Boston or Worcester.

Barb was taking forever, and I was taking way too long thinking about this guy's geographic origin, along with how nicely his flannel fit his shoulders. In Kayley's words, *a good specimen.* God, my mind was a wreck today, which was not helped by a scarcity of dates.

Wondering nervously if Dennehy had already shown up at the library, I pulled out my phone. No text from Billie yet.

The L.L. Bean guy's phone rang, and instead of swiping it to silent, he took it.

"Hey, Mom. Yeah, just got here." He chuckled. "The drive was fine. The other stops were good." More listening. "Halfway. Yeah, I'll call you back tonight. I'm in line and gotta run." He looked pleased at something she said, that genuine warm-and-fuzzy kind of expression. "Love you, too."

I felt the guy's eyes on me as he moved closer to the register. I asked, "You visiting?" The cider and chili festival at the mountain was this weekend, though it usually only drew a local crowd. The mountain's ski shop also ran a sale.

He gave a subdued nod. "For a week."

Barb returned, minus the cupcakes. "Sorry, the fridge is on the fritz."

I waved her away with a laugh, not needing any explanation about machines crapping out. "Weather's good this week," I told the man as he moved one more spot in line. "You from the city?"

"Newton."

"Ah. I used to live in Watertown." That felt like a century ago. "No Newton accent," I braved. Boldness helped distract me from my nerves. "That one is pretty distinct."

Sure, tell yourself it has nothing to do with his handsome face or how his jeans fit snug to his frame in all the right spots.

"I'm originally from near Deerfield, in the western part of the state. I grew up in a small town like this."

"That explains it. Usually, I can place the Newton accent anywhere."

His chestnut eyes smiled at me, and sandy waves fell over his forehead with his nod.

I was about to ask what brought him to our town when Barb emerged with three boxes.

"Thanks a million." I peeked through the transparent top of one. Each mini cupcake had a fondant topper. "Cute. Teeny-tiny books. Love 'em."

"Only for you, my dear. Have any of your zuke mash to spare? Folks've been asking for it. And I have a thumbprint cookie recipe for your jam. If you have any zucchini to spare, my zucchini chocolate chip cookies have been a hit this month."

"I can bring more jam, mash, and zukes next week."

Barb held up a finger, already zipping back to the kitchen. She shot words over her shoulder. "I have the day-old bagels and rolls for you to bring to the food pantry, too. Hang on."

Izzie, the clerk at the counter, slid a coffee toward the handsome out-of-towner. He offered his credit card.

"Cash only, sir."

"Excuse me?"

She tapped a nearby sign. "Minimum for cards is ten dollars."

Two twenties poked out from his wallet, but his fingers hovered on the bills, hesitation wrinkling his forehead. "How about I add something? What do you recommend? A muffin?"

"The pumpkin muffins are good. Total is $8.85 with one of those."

He turned to me. "Can I buy you a coffee?"

Getting transported in his eyes for a moment, I stumbled out, "I'm all set, thanks. My coffee's brewing across the street."

He turned back to Izzie. "Make it two muffins, please."

"Now you're good."

He laughed. "Thank goodness. I forgot how much cheaper food is away from the city. Credit is easier to reconcile," he explained to me, though I hadn't asked why the fuss.

"I save my cash, too. Cards give reward points." I had yet to redeem the miles on mine—when would I have time to travel, anyway?—but that was beside the point.

He swiped the card in the reader. "Hey, you said the pumpkin here is to die for. Have a muffin. I can't possibly eat both."

"They freeze well. Thaw on the counter for twenty minutes."

"I don't have a freezer at the inn."

"They'll keep for three or four days," Izzie offered. "And Mr. Cooper's inn has a communal fridge for guests if that's where you're staying."

"Good idea." He looked around, his hands full of coffee and a bag of muffins. "Can you tell me the time? I'd check on my phone, but...." His feathery eyebrows curled and a hint of early wrinkles—handsome ones—appeared around both eyes.

He retreated from the counter, taking a mindful sip of the steaming coffee. "Need help with those?"

I rebalanced the boxes. "No, thanks. You've got a bag of muffins yourself. Also, it's"—I gestured to the digital clock behind us—"nearly ten."

"Thanks."

Barb appeared with a large brown bag of day-olds.

The man reached for it and slid his wrist through the handle. "Here. I'll help you with those. Handles are much easier."

I didn't say no to the offer, as the three cupcake boxes were a balancing act, and I'd need to cross Main Street. "Thanks. I'm not far."

He held the door open using his hip.

I readjusted. For mini cupcakes, they grew heavy fast. Or was it the conversation with this admittedly charming, intriguing, and *okay, okay*, gorgeous man? Nothing ever came from a meet-cute in a coffee shop except for in romance novels. Even that hack Dennehy didn't put one in his book. Emma and Declan were coworkers.

"I work across the street. No car."

"I'll walk with you. You in there?" He flicked his chin toward the town office building as we waited at the crosswalk.

"Library."

"I'm heading there, too."

My delight fizzled. "You're here for the author event?"

He nodded. "Yeah, I'm—"

His words were cut off by a truck honking. It was Tyler Goodwin, a local Rotary Club member and avid thriller reader. "Hey, Helen," he said with a wave out his window as he drove past us.

I smiled hello, and settled my pulse, which raced at being suddenly honked at, even if it had been done in friendliness.

I took slow, deliberate steps across the street. This man had come all the way from Newton, and he was staying over at the inn. *The book made all the bestseller charts.* I wanted to throttle the inner voice that kept reminding me of the fact.

He got the library door for me, adjusting the leather shoulder bag he carried, too.

A horrible idea occurred. Was the issue with the credit card because he needed to keep track of expenses for a business trip? This guy couldn't be... No. Not him. Oh my God, no.

I pushed out my question with a voice trembling to match my gait. "Thanks. I never caught your name?" I tried not to cringe as sweat dribbled down my brow. *Don't say it, don't say it.*

There was that knee-wobbling smile again.

"It's Gabe. Gabriel Dennehy."

Gabe

I caught a cupcake box before it slid off her pile.

"Slippery spot," she mumbled with a nod to the puddle at her feet, then a glance up at the roof's drain. "It's been on the fix list for two years."

"Glad I could save the cupcakes. And you. Slippy spots don't like me either."

The crinkle creasing her forehead smoothed, and with her free hand she managed the door. "Thanks. You're the author? Mr. Dennehy?"

"Gabe."

A flash of something I couldn't put a word to glowed in cornflower-blue eyes.

"Sorry I almost smashed these," she said.

"No sorry needed. By the looks of them and the smells in the cafe, they'd taste great even smashed. All you need is a fork. You work here? Are you the librarian, uh—" Remembering words, people, and faces was my forte, but my mind blanked. Until I recalled the amusement I'd felt reading her name because it was perfect for a librarian.

"Helen Wright. Yes. Helen's fine."

Wright. Right. Write. It was cute and so was she.

A subtle blush joined the strawberry freckles skipping across the bridge of her nose. A curl, its blonde hues highlighted by her complexion, fell into her eyes. She blew it away with a huff of what I presumed was frustration. She wore black dress pants and a lovely teal sweater that hugged her curves. A unique pendant that looked like some sort of sea glass with amethyst accents hung from her delicate neck.

I wore—yikes, a flannel button-down, a white t-shirt, and jeans. *I'm a dope. Should have gone with the tie, oxford shirt, and some chinos but they needed to be washed back at the inn.*

Distracted by all this while juggling the two paper bags, my shoulder bag, coffee, and a cupcake box, inside the vestibule I knocked into a box of canned goods and a cardboard sign reading *In lieu of late fees, please donate to Sanders Mill Food Pantry.* The sign fell.

I attempted humor as I brushed off my pride. "No slippery spots here. My usual two left feet."

With a nudge from one of her own feet, she propped the sign against the wall. "I see a right and a left." She released a strained chuckle and took back the cupcake box. "It's okay. This sign is always falling. You just reminded me that I need to find a way to hang it."

We reached for the inner door of the vestibule at the same time and thumped shoulders. "Sorry. Again." My depth perception had apparently left the building. This was par for the course with dyscalculia; it meant constant work to re-master key life skills around movement as well as numbers, clocks, and schedules. The clumsy gait made for adventurous travels. Dad was right—I should have picked an easier career.

"You okay?" I asked.

She rubbed her shoulder. "Right as rain."

"I'm..."

"No need to be nervous. We're small potatoes for you. I'm sure you'll do well, Mr. Dennehy."

If it only was nerves. For all I knew, my crooked smile matched my crooked gait, but I summoned my journalist charm with some effort. "Just Gabe."

Her face remained unaffected. "Let me show you where to set up after I drop these day-olds off. Our large meeting room is downstairs, and judging by the number of cars already here, I expect you'll have a good turnout."

A charged sensation fell off this woman like an electric storm. I didn't need much of my investigator's skill at reading people to see she was irritated. Had I said something stupid? What was this weirdness I felt coming off her? What had I done to deserve that?

You stole letters and used them for your own gain.

Guilt. It wasn't her. It was me. Afraid someone would find out during my tour. But ever since I fell for M.H.'s vivid words and got pulled in by her grief on pages meant for nobody to see, I'd contemplated trying to find her. The book signing was a cover. And adoration wasn't the only emotion propelling my search.

I didn't exactly have a plan for if—when?—I found M.H. Would I beg forgiveness? Issue a public apology? And if she required it, would I pull the plug on book two? Tell Laurel I was done? Quietly disappear from the limelight and forget it all happened? Or...or what? If I was being honest with myself, I didn't know.

Helen greeted others at the front desk, dropped the brown bag behind the counter, and then gestured to another set of stairs leading to the lower level. The aroma of brewing coffee trickled up.

And you brought your own, moron. I wasn't used to being catered to.

I was a nobody.

Laurel had taken care of everything for me. She arranged with the publisher to send a box of books, bookmarks, flyers, and swag to each of my tour stops. This experience was a far cry from my first book tour, which had comprised of me schlepping my stuff everywhere and begging bookstores, cafes, and libraries to allow me to hold a signing. I'd spent most of the time talking to the store owners, my only customers being friends or those who pitied poor, starving writers.

Thank goodness for Laurel. Most authors handled their own marketing, hired assistants, or outsourced it to a PR consultant, but with my *very* understanding agent, all I had to do was program my phone, manage the car ride, and show up. I knew her eagerness to help me was partly due to her publicist background, but also due to her benefitting from my success. I'd already hired a virtual assistant this summer upon her recommendation. With royalties soaring, I could afford it. But this all felt surreal. Me? With an assistant?

A year ago, I was eating instant noodles and hoping to pay my rent on freelance travel writing and a part-time newspaper column. Now, not so much, though I still came home to a quiet apartment each night.

A cluster of teenage girls giggled and spoke in loud whispers. I shot them a grin as I weaved through the people scattered in the downstairs lobby, keeping up with a briskly walking Helen Wright. As a kid, I learned that a smile hid the awkwardness inside.

"Your following is here," Helen said, her voice cooling to icy.

Maybe she'd had a bad morning or was peeved I was a few minutes late. "I'm not into this sort of thing. I can barely manage my website and social media pages." I tapped a finger on the lid of my coffee to-go cup.

"This way." She pointed.

We shuffled into a kitchenette beside the conference room, where a counter was lined with plates, fruit, coffee cups, and all the fixings beside a gurgling brewer. My empty hand gave way to restlessness.

"What can I help with?" I stepped closer while staying careful, not wanting another collision.

"We've got it all handled."

I put down my coffee and took the cupcake boxes from her. "No, really. I like to help. These events make my head spin." Leaning in closer to whisper, I caught a whiff of something citrus, maybe lemon, maybe from her shampoo. "I'm usually the one putting others on the spot."

"Oh?"

"I was or, well, I guess I still am, a journalist."

"Ah..." She turned her attention to yellow sticky notes near the coffee urn, reading each one and tossing it in turn into a recycle bin, seemingly checking off to-dos. "Let's bring all these refreshments out to the second table in the conference room."

I envied her organization. I used my app for a zillion reminders and still forgot things. And that's when I *wasn't* being distracted by something like her presence.

She gestured for me to follow her into the large room, which was decked out with rows of chairs facing a table that was covered with my swag, piles of books, and the whole nine yards. I hated reading aloud for an audience, especially a romantic scene, but it came with the package deal: read, answer questions, sign books. And the scenes everyone wanted read were the romantic ones.

We deposited plates, cups, and sugars on a side table.

"Does this work?" She gestured to the room.

"It's great. Thanks."

We returned to the kitchenette. After washing my hands at the sink, I lined the cupcakes on platters as neatly as I could. "Nice flowers." The spray of colorful flowers reminded me of the kind the landlady kept by the mailboxes in my apartment building.

"Thanks. Dahlias from my garden. We'll bring that vase out, too."

"They're beautiful. Is it a hobby of yours? Gardening?"

She waved a hand. "Not me. Gardening is my mom's deal. Canning and cooking are more my thing."

"Oh, that explains the zuke mash."

She looked at me, perplexed.

"I heard you and the cafe owner talking about it."

"Oh, yes. It's what I do in the fall. Jams, sauces, pickled veggies, and soups. We get a surplus of tomatoes and zucchini this time of year. I combine them with secret spices to make a salsa-like sauce."

I followed her, toting more refreshments, back into the large room. "Living near the city, I get homesick for this sort of thing."

"What thing?" She paused in laying out creamers and stirrers.

"Grabbing fresh flowers for my mom—though she and my dad live out of state now. Gardens. Farmer's markets. People knowing people's names like at the cafe. The scent of fields. Small-town libraries." *Post offices*, my conscience reproached. I shoved a hand into my pocket. "I miss the small-town lifestyle. I can walk to good markets near my place, but it's not the same as home, ya know? Anyway, that's why I wrote the book...to connect with my roots." *Admiration for the mysterious M.H., your muse, had nothing to do with it? Liar*, the admonishing saint within continued.

Helen smirked. "Don't tell me you miss the smell of manure?"

"No. But it stimulates memories, doesn't it?" I teased right back.

"Suppose so. You haven't lived until you can tell the difference between pig and cow manure."

We both laughed.

"Was it a specific town that inspired the story?" she asked.

That was the eternal question. Every town thought they had been *the* town. "I modeled the book's setting after my hometown."

Who was I kidding? Certainly, the town I'd created was fictional, but it was based on a real place, and that place wasn't mine.

Whoever M.H. was, or had been, she'd left few clues to the location of her home and heartache. Halfway through the tour, and with no luck in the previous towns, my hope had started to flounder. All I had to go on were some clues from the letters: small central town, the rail lines and trail, a cafe, cemetery and mountain nearby, a playground mural, and a few other typical Massachusetts town hallmarks.

Helen drew her gaze away. "I enjoy the slower pace of a small town, too. I moved back here a couple of years ago myself."

I wanted to ask what brought her home, but with how frayed her nerves seemed, it might not be wise. "Thank you for all this."

Finished with the setup, she crossed her arms in front of her. "Just doing my job. I'll be upstairs. If you need anything, let me know."

"Thanks, Helen."

She smiled, tight-lipped, but it didn't blunt the edge persisting in her voice and demeanor. "You're welcome, Gabe."

Six

Helen

There he was.

As Kayley would probably say: Mr. Mesmerizing, working his charm on attendees. He grinned, shook hands, and signed books. And yes, he did have a sexy voice. One that sent goose bumps rippling down my arms.

I watched him in action through the glass wall of the downstairs vestibule. The conference room was packed. We'd run out of seating during the earlier part of the event where he read a scene from the book and answered questions. Now the book-signing line snaked outside of the room and past me.

I could not believe the man who'd read my intimate letters was under the same roof as me. And the kicker—I was fantasizing about a real-life coffee shop meet-cute before I learned who he was. *Sunny beach!*

How did you steal my letters, Dennehy? More important, why did you? I wanted to snap at him. Instead, I'd clammed up.

I pinched the bridge of my nose. The discovery of what happened to my letters had not only dredged up emotions, it had me reproaching myself. How I had screwed up. How I had been so naïve to think my letters would fall alongside the *Dear God* and *Dear Santa* letters. In the trash can, right?

"Right," a voice agreed.

I dropped the stack of books in my hands at the sound. I'd been bringing them to the freebie cart in the vestibule when I stopped to gawk at Gabriel Dennehy and his slew of fans. I looked over my shoulder, hoping to see the person the voice belonged to. If my inner thoughts started talking aloud, I'd have to check myself into the nearest hospital.

Harper bounded past, clutching her signed copy of the book to her chest. "Hi, Miss Wright," she repeated.

Whew. *Wright*, not *right*.

I crouched to retrieve the fallen books. "Hi, Harper. How's it going?"

"Sooo good. How awesome is this? He's here!"

Awesome, indeed. "Have you considered the next book for book club?" I wasn't going to get sucked into more Dennehy conversations.

"If only Gabe—Mr. Dennehy said we could call him that—wrote another book. Like a sequel?" In contrast to her tired appearance the other week, a fresh glow filled her complexion.

I roused a sugary smile instead of unleashing the curses begging to be released. After depositing the free books onto the top shelf of the cart, I said, "I'm sure you'll have no trouble finding a comparable book in the YA section or new release shelves."

"I'll see what the other girls say. We'll discuss his sequel after it comes out." She walked up the stairs with a lighter-than-usual gait, and it lifted my spirits a bit. Before today, she'd seemed off. Even depressed. Perhaps it'd been the pressure of starting high school, but I'd be lying if I said her disposition hadn't triggered internal alarm bells on more than one occasion. Part of my job was to watch and get to know my community. I was here to support and help. Increasingly I'd been thinking that meant saying something to Harper, or, God forbid, her mother.

Maybe I was overthinking it.

Just as I was feeling relieved about Harper's behavior turning a corner, a group of teenagers poured out of the meeting room. One of them, Dylan, rolled her eyes and pointed up the stairs at Harper's vanishing shoes. Dylan used to hang out with Harper. As another girl in the group took out her phone and texted something, Dylan leaned in to read it and then laughed while gesturing at her former friend again.

My heart couldn't help but ache a bit. Teen girls could be mean. Or was I reading into things here again?

With another hour left of the book signing, I decided to get back to work.

In my office, I blew through emails even as a tug-of-war raged in my brain: my tasks versus how I should get Dennehy alone and rake him over the coals. I moved on to updating the website and social media accounts.

"Hey, I'm the woman who wrote those letters," I practiced in a whisper to myself. "You're a jerk for stealing them."

My phone buzzed. This time I was smart enough to not have coffee in my hand when I swiped to answer Kayley's call.

"How is he?"

Sure, no hello to me. "Here."

"Did you confront him? He sounded *schmexy* on that podcast. Does the rest of him live up to the voice, or to his creepy thieving ways?"

"He's our age."

"Hottie or gargoyle?"

"Why does that matter?" What could I say? Despite my anger with him, Gabriel Dennehy was nice if first impressions were any judge of character. Friendly. Handsome. Down to earth. He was nothing like I'd imagined, but even wolves could hide in sheep's clothing.

"Son of a monkey, Helen. I need real details. If I didn't have this grant deadline, I'd be there. Snap a photo and text me! Gah, the boss. Later!"

Click.

Time disappeared as I kept myself busy with cataloging, creating new barcodes, and weeding through the stacks of new arrivals on my desk. I printed updated information from the Massachusetts Historical Commission about the National Register and shoved the paperwork in a folder. Until I had something historically significant to substantiate my claim, it wasn't worth pursuing. One part of the building was old enough, but it had been renovated. Other than the eighteenth-century section of the cemetery that abutted the property, I had nothing to put on the paperwork to support why the library needed protection. I pulled out a sticky note and jotted a reminder to contact Joe from the Department of Conservation and Recreation. He'd said something about old-growth forests and wanting to give talks about them. I wondered if there was any legislation for protecting this land. Protected land meant a protected library.

There'd be no more beautiful forest behind the library if Miriam had her way with it.

I jotted another note to contact the local outdoors club to bushwhack the trails. They loved community service, and they could do it this fall or in the spring.

Work done, my thoughts ping-ponged back to Dennehy and the book.

How had he gotten his hands on my letters? Had he worked in a mail processing facility? Did he have connections here in Sanders Mill? Did he think the letters *were* fictional? Maybe the true story behind him finding them could settle my contempt. There had to be a reason he took them. I tried, honestly tried, to find the good in all people. For example, Dennehy used mostly the good memories I shared in those letters. He hadn't exposed all my pain for the world to read about. In Emma's story, there was no suicide and no stillbirth, two heartaches that I knew I wrote about in my letters. Yes, there were some similarities, but the kinds of tragedies other people in the world had, too. Thinking about this made me doubt everything again. Maybe *Letters to Nobody* wasn't based on my letters. Maybe Kayley was wrong and only seeing what she wanted—and I had joined her on that crazy train. Maybe my memory of what I'd written in those letters was wrong. Maybe Harper and the fans also just wanted the story to so badly be true, too.

Gah! A frustrated groan rumbled in my chest. I needed answers. I needed to confront him.

"Psst, Helen...earth to Helen..." Billie stared over her purple-rimmed glasses.

"Hmm?"

"Have you seen the time?"

My stomach growled. I forgot lunch, again. "Guess I need to help him pack up."

"You okay?"

I waved my hand and grabbed my water bottle to fill at the bubbler. "Just tired."

"Is your mom doing okay?"

"She's good."

"I mean..."

I rapped two fingers on the desk while staring off at nothing. "Right as rain." Everyone meant well with their inquiries. Whenever I went into broody mode, people assumed it was about my mom. Her chronic pain hadn't flared this month more than any other month. The symptoms of her postherpetic neuralgia due to a bout of shingles seven years ago waxed and waned. Her vision suffered, and she had repeated skin infections, plus a partial facial paralysis, a small droop below her right eye.

Her PHN was why I'd come home.

"Okay." Billie eyeballed me incredulously.

Heaviness lingered in my legs and chest. "Really. She's good," was all I could offer. "We've been up to our elbows in gardening stuff all week."

Billie said, her voice sassier, "If you won't help that handsome man, I will."

"Going for the younger guys, are you?"

"Hey, watch yourself, pet. I'm only ten years older than you. Life begins in your forties." She lifted dark eyebrows and gave me a teasing bat of enviably thick lashes.

Forties? I couldn't even handle my thirties right now. "I don't think Hardy would appreciate you eyeing up another man. Imagine the scandal."

Billie tucked a pen behind her ear. "I've got a hall pass for certain hotties. Besides, the Mill loves gossip, as we know." She laughed to herself.

She and Hardy were as solid as any relationship could be. It was enviable.

Billie tapped the computer screen at the front desk. "Side note, foot traffic was good today. I had the teen volunteers do a headcount as people came and went. Jaxon reported two hundred fifty-eight."

"Wow. We've never had such high attendance except for the Holiday Fair. We can't even get this many at the town meeting."

"Know any other famous authors? Might be exactly what we need to keep Mrs. Claws out of our hair."

The nickname made us both grin mischievously. For years, Miriam had filled in as Mrs. Claus at the Holiday Fair. She hid behind selfless volunteering, an affluent founding family, manicured nails, perfect business suits, a powerful lawyer husband, and a train of allies on the Select Board and Finance Committee, but she didn't fool me. "Mrs. Claws won't be sinking her nails into our library if I have anything to say about it."

"I was serious. Have any other author connections?"

I shrugged.

"Go butter up Mr. Dennehy. See who he knows."

Butter him up? More like unleash my wrath upon him. Except the longer I avoided him, the more I talked myself out of it. Damn Dennehy for making such a good first impression this morning!

Billie added, "Book more signings like today, and she won't have anything to use against us."

I wished I could share her optimism. "Usage is not enough to sway the committees. My biggest hope right now is for the town to fix the leaky roof." And our door. And scanner. And rodent issues. And elevator. And for Miriam to leave me alone. And for Dennehy to...

"Fat chance," Billie said. "They won't fix it until it caves in and injures somebody." She shook her head. "We're plugging a sinking ship with our fingers."

My life had too many sinking ships. Mom's care cost a lot, and I was drowning. If I lost my job because the town closed this library, I'd have no insurance. Would unemployment be enough for us? If I took the offer from Howe Builders before Miriam forced our hands, it would more than cover Mom's care for a long time. The idea was a pebble in my shoe. How could I even contemplate selling the land and see Billie, Stan, and others unemployed, our town with no library and my family's legacy erased? No, it was my responsibility to keep this ship afloat. But was I fighting the inevitable? A slow death was still a death.

Billie squeezed my shoulder. "It'll be okay. We'll manage. Oh, I heard from Craig that the town wants to use the large meeting room downstairs for employee training."

I opened the planner on the computer. "When? We have the blood drive coming up."

"Don't worry about it. I'll check in with him and schedule it, and I'll tackle the Miriam issue." A smirk tugged at her lips. "You go tackle that delicious man."

I covered a cough. She was as bad as Kayley. "Billie." I glanced over my shoulder at the few patrons near the circulation desk.

She tsked and gave me the *who, me?* face.

"Mrs. Claws can stick it," I whispered.

Then the devil herself strode through the front vestibule, designer sunglasses perched above her forehead. My ears burned as Miriam marched to the circulation desk. If the building had hardwood and not carpet, her heels would have clicked.

"Where's Harper?"

She clacked her square-edged French manicured nails on the desk. Her pencil skirt and lavender blouse fit her short, curvy frame as if tailored specifically for her. She'd probably come from an open house or real estate showing. Impatience crouched in leopard-like eyes—always watching, ready to pounce when the moment presented itself—below a dark brown fringe of bangs.

Billie moseyed over to the new release display behind Miriam and made a not-so-kind face at our nemesis's back.

"Good morn—afternoon. She left a few hours ago."

"How was the signing?" Miriam puckered her mauve lips. Her phone buzzed with a message, and she seemed already done with me.

I stuck out my chin. "Great. You should visit before he finishes."

Just don't buy a book.

I imagined over two hundred fifty of our town locals leaving the library with a signed copy, hurrying home to read *my* story. Would some of them put it together? Would they find out that the inspiration for Emma was their librarian? Thankfully, to the best of my recollection, none of my letters mentioned people or places in detail. No last names, and if there had been any identifiable locations, Dennehy had transformed them. Most people would not put two and two together. Only Kayley and Mom knew the details of my losses that year well enough that they might glimpse them past the changes he made. I saw the books Mom read because I was the one who brought them home for her from the library; so far, no *Letters to Nobody* on her nightstand.

Even if nobody else saw it, I saw the truth. The swaps were obvious to me. It was still my story, though well masked. And dammit, beautifully written. I swiped at a tear, surprised by the wave of emotion rolling through me.

"Miriam..." Sasha Connors said, popping over.

Miriam looked up from her feverish tapping of thumbs on screen. "Sash. How's Liam?"

The two chatted like they were besties, though Miriam was that way with everyone. As if we were back in high school, everyone either feared her or idolized her. I busied myself, pretending to sort things on the desk.

Nemesis here, nemesis downstairs, nemeses everywhere.

I really had to go downstairs.

I had to confront Dennehy. Never mind the townspeople, would *he* figure out it was me? Doubt slithered into my panicking thoughts. What if Kayley and I were wrong about this? If I confronted him, would I just be making a fool of myself? Maybe I needed to get some proof first.

Where the hell had my gumption gone? Here I was, talking myself out of the confrontation already.

Sasha waved to Miriam. "See you next week."

Miriam looked in my direction, spun around, but then made a strategic pause. I knew those Miriam pauses. My stomach clenched, waiting for the impact.

"See you at the town meeting in two weeks, Helen."

Then she was off, leaving a spicy perfume scent in her wake. What town meeting?

I turned on Billie, my mouth hanging open. "What the—" I snipped my own words as a mother and preschooler approached, a mountain of books in the boy's hands. "Hi, Kaden. Stocking up for the weekend?"

He bobbed a curly-haired head, his bright eyes laughing at me. "You're so silly! This is for the whole week, Mzzz Wright!"

His mother added with a tap to *The Known Gnome*, "He loves these books. Thanks again for getting the series in."

"Always our pleasure."

After they left, I clenched my teeth, then stopped, knowing the ricochet effect it would have. "I thought Craig shot down the idea of a special fall meeting, pushed all requests off to spring?"

Billie was already pulling up the town's website. "Maybe Miriam's getting to him, too."

I clipped my growl. The Finance Committee was one thing, but now Miriam's promises enamored the Select Board and our town manager, Craig Browning. Only the Select Board could call a special town meeting. "There goes my hope of waiting."

A few clicks later, Billie said, "The meeting's scheduled for two weeks from now." Earlier than our normal November. She skimmed the information. "No need to have a coronary, Helen. Nobody's getting shut down at a special town meeting. Some departments might just be making their usual requests and Craig caved. Hey, we should ask for those tables and chairs we've needed for a hundred years now?"

Her attempt at levity wasn't working. I grimaced. "Probably too late to put in the request."

"Nothing bad will come from this meeting. If an article of closure were ever to be presented, it would never pass, Helen. Never. I doubt they can even get enough support to put such a ludicrous article on the May town meeting warrant let alone the fall one."

"Never say never. And if she can't do that now, then what is she up to?"

Billie shrugged, equally nonplussed. "Take it one thing at a time, pet. First work on your budget, then let's see what

Mrs. Claws does at this special meeting, and *then* we can worry about May."

I trudged downstairs, my heart hammering.

I could only handle so many crises at once.

First, the library. Before the special fall meeting, all I could do was gather supporters to speak on the library's behalf so whatever the hell Miriam proposed wouldn't get a green light.

In her heyday, they called my mom Rabble Rousing Mary. Could I follow in her footsteps? I could see the May meeting now—Miriam's co-conspirator Pierce Howe stocking the middle school gymnasium bleachers with his cronies, all instructed to fight for the cause, even if they didn't agree with his effective monopoly on building in our town. With their jobs at stake, nobody dared speak against him.

Howe even looked the part of a hungry predator with his unkempt, graying black hair and beard. I dug my nails into my palm.

This fall meeting was a blip. That's all. My focus would be on May. Find proof of historical relevance of the building or land, build community support, and prepare my request to fill the budget gaps I expected.

As I turned a corner downstairs, I nearly collided with Warren Lawrence.

"Oh, Helen. Didn't see you." Warren grinned, pushing his thick glasses up to the bridge of his nose. He held a copy of Dennehy's book under his arm.

Him, too? "No worries," I said. And a grin from Warren? What fed this bubble of happiness?

"Eloise loves this man's book. She found it in the large print section by accident. She was determined to read it even in the small print. Mr. Dennehy brought large print copies. He even signed it." An upturn of his lips revealed...teeth.

Warren had teeth. I'd never seen them before.

I couldn't believe the word "charmed" occurred to me to describe Warren Lawrence.

Dennehy had enraptured them all. I would not remind myself of his efforts with the cupcakes, nor his endearing lopsided smile, or sweet eyes—one of them squinting a hair more than the other when a grin creased his face...

"How kind of him," I mustered. Warren continued beaming. This was too bizarre for me. Had the entire town gone crazy over Dennehy's book?

"The posters are still up, by the way." His usual dour frown replaced the fleeting smile.

And just like that, the grump had returned. Okay, I wasn't in the twilight zone, as Mom would say.

"Library policy and The American Library Association allow us to hang the posters, Warren, due to freedom of expression. Feel free to look at the library policies we have posted by the front desk and on our website."

The historical war propaganda posters a local collector offered to display had provoked the more conservative population in town. Going beyond Rosie the Riveter and Uncle Sam, they'd included Soviet depictions that espoused Communism. Now was probably not the best time to draw controversy with Mrs. Claws breathing down my back. I added, "You're welcome to display opposing viewpoints if you possess such posters. Or anything, really, if you submit the proper paperwork and it's reviewed by the board. This has nothing to do with politics, only art and history."

He grumbled under his breath along the line of "We'll see," but carried on his way, shaking his head toward the display in honor of Banned Books Week.

I trudged onward to the meeting room, reminding myself that fighting ran in my bloodline. Alice Foster Hadley had been a rebel at the turn of the twentieth century, an early suffragette seeking political, educational, and professional equality. Her letters had ironically inspired my letter-writing fiasco. I didn't think I mentioned Alice in my grief letters.

I reached the nearly empty table by Gabriel Dennehy. "Sold them all?" I covered my despondency with a sweet voice, or at least one I hoped sounded sweet.

"Most of them. I'm surprised. I haven't done this well at the other locations. The magic of Sanders Mill?" His eyes twinkled.

Ah, on to my second battle. "It's like you said. The book reminds many people of home. Some think you wrote it about our town."

Last night, Kayley and I had talked about my three options. One: confront him now based on my suspicion, and risk embarrassment at best if that suspicion was wrong. Two: before confronting him, gather more proof that he actually used my letters—and if I was lucky, have him trip up and admit it. Or three: leave a trail of breadcrumbs that I was the letter writer and make him confess after having an epiphany. Gabe did seem like a kind man; surely he had a conscience in that pretty head of his, and I could prick it to reform him.

In my rational mind, I leaned toward confrontation. One quick convo and this could be all done. Yet doubt sank its teeth into me. Maybe they weren't my letters. I'd written them in a frenzy, pulling from a deep well of grief. Without a photographic memory, it's not like I could remember my exact words. Two recent bestsellers emerged on the charts earlier this year, eerily similar, one written by an author in

Canada and one in the United States. Both claimed they were original ideas. Could his book and my letters all be a strange coincidence? Instead of getting him to confess, all I would do was make an ass of myself and expose myself even more.

Here I was again, shriveling! My gut told me these similarities were more than happenstance. For now, I'd pursue options two and three. I'd gather proof that he stole and used my letters, and I'd leave a trail for him to give it away...like make him walk right into admitting he stole them.

But what would that trail look like?

He had said he was going to be in town for a few days, right? Yes, it was the gutless way, but my heart could only bear so much.

He said, "I definitely see some similarities between Sanders Mill and my hometown of Pratts Junction."

"How many stops have you made so far?" *How many more people have read my story?* I gathered the remaining books.

"This is my fifth in two weeks. My halfway half-time before the next five. I heard the mountain nearby has nice trails. Might go check it out."

He had to be tired from hours of signing and talking and smiling, yet here he was, charisma on full blast. *Stay on target, Helen.*

I had to spend time with him. That was the answer.

My fingers itched. Where were those antacids?

As he placed a few hardcovers into the box, the movement stretched his shirt, teasing at defined biceps. So what? He was fit. Even liars could be hot.

Look away. Look away. I did. The books were the only thing nearby to focus on. The cover was stunning. This didn't help. "The mountain has a bunch of good trails for every level. Too early for the foliage, though. Some yellows. It'll be a few more weeks until peak color."

"September is a great month. The humidity is gone, bugs are gone, and it's the calm before the winter storm."

Speaking of coincidence. "I love September, too. A busier season for us here. Kids in school, fall meetings, planning for the holidays..." I drew my gaze back to his.

Was he assessing me, too? *Good, look into these eyes, Dennehy. See who you stole from.* Time to gather intel. "Why are you doing a local tour across Massachusetts when you could do something bigger?"

He folded the tablecloth. "The national tour is in the works, but I want to say thank you first to the people who inspired my book."

"Oh?"

That's it, Helen? I would need to ask Kayley for more advice on *how* to get the truth out of Dennehy, whether through teasing or intense interrogation.

He didn't respond as my antsy fingers drifted over the table. The cupcakes were gone and the coffee nearly empty. I gathered stray creamers, stirrers, and sugar packets. He followed me around, by picking up cups here and there. Volunteers—Trina and Cammie—came in and began stacking chairs.

"How did you feel inspired?"

"City life was getting to me, so I went back to my roots. I love a good small-town book. The story just...came to me."

Came to me? Bullshit.

"...Now with the success of *Letters*, I hope to move closer to Pratts Junction. Or find somewhere in the central hills. I like this part of the state." He scrubbed a hand on the back of his neck. "Anyway, I thought I owed it to the people to do a tour they could easily attend, ya know?"

We cleaned the rest up in silence. I lobbed napkins into the trash can. "I've got this handled if you need to go." The wimp was winning within me.

"No rush. I'm famished. Can you recommend a good place to eat? Better yet, I could use the company."

I almost dropped the heavy coffee urn mid-wash. "Me?"

He flashed that smile, crooked and charming.

Yes, I was already calling it *that smile.*

"You know the town. I'd love to ask you a few questions about it."

He drew closer, his nearness both unnerving and something else. I thought of Wes, my ex. Not of how I hurt him because of my pain, but how I'd felt for him at the beginning, fluttery and breathless—

What had gotten into me? Yes, Dennehy was friendly. Yes, he was sort of famous. He was also slime. Slime! He'd stolen my letters. Exploited me.

My stomach rebelled with a thunderous growl. Traitor. I busied myself with drying the urn. A meal would be a great opportunity to shoot questions at him. Maybe I could text Kayley from the bathroom to compile a list of what to ask. "I do know a place, but..."

Mom. Use Mom as an excuse. You always do.

The glimmer in his brown eyes faded as he expected my words.

"Sure. I'm hungry, too," I relented.

To Wes

I left.

I've apologized a hundred times. A hundred times too few.

The chasm between us deepened and grew wider with each moment, each day, after we lost Olivia.

The rail trail reminds me of you. Today I walked it alone, retracing past steps, past regrets. Remember the part with the icicles? Beautiful, icy edges which melt in the sun.

I loved those walks. Serene, the occasional dog-walker or cyclist passing by. The twenty-foot-high rock walls flanking the gravel path where the train tracks once ran. Water trickles down and moss and ferns blanket them. Green and lush in summer, it transforms to graceful white pillars in the dead of winter. On these walks now, all I see are icy blades, like the one I used to drive us apart. All I hear are the sounds of equipment from the housing development being built nearby. Most of the land remains protected, but how much more of the forest will be cut down? So much has changed in this town while I was away.

Wes, I miss both of them—Addy and our daughter—so much.

First our baby girl got her angel's wings. Then my best friend after her. I couldn't come back from it. I fell apart. I couldn't save either of them.

I wonder if Olivia would have had your green eyes and my straight nose, my wild hair and freckles, your love of music and sense of humor, my love for reading. Would we have stayed in the city? Maybe she'd join us on the world travels we just never got around to.

Losing her unhinged me. And our "us" had only just begun.

When I saw you, I saw our daughter, and my heart would not allow me to separate the two. I also felt you blamed me for *losing her. I know that's a foolish thought. I didn't cause her stillbirth, but there was something about the way you looked at me after... Though the doctors cleared us to try again, how could we?*

Others told me it wasn't my fault. I couldn't believe them but nodded along anyway. They didn't know the guilt I harbored for not doing it all perfectly. That one time I pushed myself physically on a hike, or that one missed prenatal vitamin, or that extra cup of coffee. Stupid, I know. But I still blame myself.

The pain tore me up inside. I'm sorry I left. We could have fought through this.

Now, I walk almost daily, even to work. It's a lonely walk, with the ghost of us beside me. I visited Addy's and our daughter's graves this week.

I'll always love you, Wes. I can't return to the city. I know you're still living there. My mom spoke with your mom—you know how they are—and I heard you found love again. Does she remind you of me in any way? I wonder if you two will have children. I can't help but feel a little jealous at your new love, your new life.

One day, perhaps I will find love again, too. This time, I won't push him away.

Mom always tells me to find the light in the dark, so I'm trying to find the silver lining in this all. Heartache means there had been some joy in it, right? It wasn't all bad. Never. In fact, we had so many good moments. I've been blessed to find love. Not everyone gets that experience.

I remember the crazy all-nighters studying in our dorms at UVM, our bike rides along Lake Champlain, our camping adventures with leaky tents in the Mad River Valley...and the European tour of architecture and art and music and wine we daydreamed about even on our tight budget. Perhaps we would have gone there on our honeymoon.

I remember our cramped micro-apartment and evening chamomile tea; I only drank it for you. The little espresso machine you bought for me, with Italian instructions we never quite figured out. Your back rubs, our game nights, me reading poetry to you, "grocery Sundays" when we purposely took the long way home.

I knew I had loved you the first time I brought you home to meet my parents. You took life in stride. We laughed so hard that my ribs hurt! You loved me so hard, it took my breath away. You bundled up for our first rail trail walk, although it wasn't that cold, only autumn. Oh, the autumn! Everyone comes here to leaf peep like the rest of New England. The orange, and yellow, and red are nature's gift, like a painter created this masterpiece around us. A masterpiece that crunched beneath our boots and smelled like freshly fallen leaves.

Then came winter—when our walks were sometimes muddy, sometimes icy, sometimes blanketed in snow. Those icicles the size of a person! I loved to witness their freezing and thawing as the winter transitioned into spring. Each visit, the icicles looked different. As sun hit the rock walls, water dripped, growing them further. And that one part where the water trickled down in little rivulets behind a sheet of ice—we always stopped to listen.

Remember that time we forgot our boots and trudged through snow two feet deep? Snow found its way into every crevice of our clothes! We had a fun time warming up afterward.

I love you, Wes.

And I'm sorry I left.

You *will always have a place in my heart, but it is time I move forward, in life, in love, in healing.*
Forever in my heart,
M.H.

Seven

Gabe

"Mind if we walk? The Mill Grille is around the corner, and luckily for us, they're open all day. It's only—" Helen paused at the front desk and glanced at the clock. "—four o'clock. They make delicious burgers and sweet potato fries."

"Sounds good. I like walking." I placed my box containing the few remaining books on the desk. Exhaustion from too much people-ing reverberated in my chest, neck, and legs.

Helen hesitated, tapping a restless finger against her thigh. "Billie, you good to close?"

The assistant librarian smirked. "Good ol' shiny here"—she patted her pocket—"might need a retraining. Been a while since he's seen daylight."

"Shall I walk you through a tutorial?"

A story lay in their salty banter, and I leaned in.

Billie pushed her glasses—which upon closer inspection, were printed in a leopard-spot pattern—to her forehead, then bounced her finger over puckered lips. "Let me try to remember... Stick the shiny thing, pointed end, into the door, give the door a good heave with my shoulder, don't let the roof collapse on me in doing so..."

"Har, har." Helen shifted her sights to me. "She amuses herself, doesn't she?"

"Indeed."

"I'll put this box in Helen's office," Billie said.

I returned her nod. "Thanks. There's a pre-paid return slip in the box, too. I'd like to donate another copy to your circulation."

Crinkles appeared on Helen's brow. "Thank you for that."

Despite her professionalism, the edge had returned to her voice. Had I pissed her off in some way? The thought was a nagging gnat in my mind. Maybe she was just having a bad day.

We exited, and Helen paused outside the door, a musing look on her face.

"Am I keeping you from work?"

She adjusted a light vest over her sweater. "No. I'll come back for my things after we eat."

I lifted an eyebrow. "And to double-check that everything is okay?"

"Caught me." A nervous laugh trickled out of her hard façade.

We strolled past a huge green lawn with a gazebo sheltered by giant oaks. At a granite war memorial, we veered left toward a gas station and traveled down Maple Avenue past an apartment complex and pizza shop. Newer-looking granite curbs and sidewalks with red-brown cobblestones enhanced the town center. Sanders Mill held a nice small-town feel, a strangely familiar one.

"Old towns always feel like home," I said. "I appreciate the history in our state, don't you?"

"I do, too. This way." She pointed, and we turned onto another street.

A few birches lined the sidewalk, their pointy yellow leaves flapping with a wind gust. I absorbed the tranquility: no traffic, blaring horns, barking, people shuffling, or blinking lights. This was what I needed. This tour had me seriously considering moving away from the city. Country living meant more driving and less walking, but seeing as I'd successfully navigated the trip so far, perhaps I'd be okay with it. "I love the colors this time of year, just as they get ready to turn. Plenty of red on the maples already."

Her tone softened as she said, "Fall is our best season. Boston was lovely, but the leaves never turn like they do here in the central hills. I walk past this giant maple tree on my way home. I love to track its changes through the seasons. Soon the leaves will be bright orange and red. Against the backdrop of an old rock wall, it's breathtaking."

The joy in her voice lifted my stride. Everyone had a tender spot. Helen's seemed to be nature's beauty. Maybe it wasn't my presence that set her on edge. Was it the event? Stress from all the people coming and going and the setup?

There was something I couldn't shake about her, a weirdness like my mind was trying to connect pieces of a puzzle but couldn't. I was probably just hungry and tired. My hand, cramped from all that book signing, was sure tired. I directed my focus to a patch of uneven sidewalk. I never understood how I did well on mountain hikes, but sidewalks tripped me up, literally.

"The drawback to living in the hills is the winter," Helen said. "Aside from those first few cozy blankets of white, I could do without it. Don't get me wrong. A fresh layer of snow reflecting shimmers of sun in the morning hours..."

I finished, "—is like a million sparkling crystals."

There was the smile again, teasing its way out. She tucked hair behind her ear. "You seem to like nature, don't you?"

"Perks of the job. I travel a lot." That sounded haughty, so I said, "Before I got into writing novels, I traveled for a lot of my journalism pieces. Focused on investigative projects."

"Ah..."

I wasn't sure my clarification helped. "Anyway, yeah. Snow can be pretty when it first falls."

"Driving in it isn't fun though."

"True. I'm glad I do most of my work from home now and use public transit to get around. I'd hate to deal with snow delays on the Pike. And I wouldn't know what to do behind the wheel in a fishtailing car."

"Didn't they teach you that in driver's ed?"

I swallowed. "If only. I didn't get my license until I was twenty. I failed the test twice."

"Really?"

"It's a long story."

Soft eyes that reminded me of summer, that bright cloudless blue, stared back.

She released a "hmm," then said, "My commute is a one-mile walk. My biggest obstacle is weaving through any puddles on the library carpet from our leaking roof as I walk to my desk." She motioned toward the tavern down the road. "There's the Mill Grille."

My stomach gurgled in anticipation at the scent of char-broiled burgers and fried deliciousness. I held the door for her as we entered. Light music played and a dozen early customers filled booths of the cozy dining area. Two young men sat at the bar and cheered for a college football game on the television.

"Hi, Helen. Two?" the hostess asked.

"Yes, please," Helen confirmed.

The hostess led us to a booth in the back beside a hand-painted mural depicting a fall forest and railroad.

As it had on our walk here, Helen's gaze wandered, not settling on one thing. I followed it to the framed black-and-white prints of the town's early heyday.

"Tell me about Sanders Mill."

She gave a shaky laugh. "This is about it. Town center."

"There's always more to the story than what first meets the eye."

She shifted in her seat, lowering her eyes to read the menu. "Spoken like a novelist."

"That's the journalist coming through."

She flashed me a glance before continuing to peruse the menu, though I bet she had it memorized. "What type of things do you write about on your travels? These investigative stories?"

A server came by and put two waters on our table.

I skimmed the menu's offerings, then looked up. "I focus on the story *within* the story. That's the gold nugget for me. I'm not there for Everest. I'm there to talk to the Sherpa who's climbed the mountain twenty times despite his fear of avalanches, because he needs to feed his family. Or the woman who is trying to keep her family's reef tour business operating." I ran a hand through my hair.

"That makes perfect sense. My mom's an artist. She focuses on the story behind the picture she's painting. She loves history and the human element. Instead of just painting let's say a picture of a farm and barn, what we see with our eyes at first glance, she homes in on the wheel ruts in the ground, or the tired woman turning the light out after a hard day's work. Speaking of history, if you want to know more about the stories behind the photos, check out the Sanders Mill Historical Society."

"How about the local librarian?" I said with a wink and a sip of water. Shoot, that sounded wrong. She *was* worth checking out, though. I gagged on the water and knocked a fist on my chest. "I meant..."

She looked concerned for a moment, and then, once I'd cleared my airways, she said sweetly, "I know what you meant. You can pick my brain."

The server arrived, a tablet in hand. "Ready to order?"

We ordered tomato, basil, and mozzarella hamburgers topped with caramelized onions and a balsamic drizzle, with sweet potato fries on the side.

"A side of honey, please," Helen asked the server.

I lifted an eyebrow. "Honey?"

"I like to dip the fries in it. It's weird, I know."

"No, not weird. Interesting. I love ketchup with everything."

"What would you like to know about our town? I know about its history. Too much, probably. The cataloger in me can't resist." She blinked, a gleam dancing in her eyes.

Target achieved. "Anything. My college degrees are in history and journalism. Take me all the way back." I rubbed my hands together and we shared a brief smile.

"Well, there was this big bang..."

Once we both stopped laughing, she said, "You really want to know?"

I nodded.

"Okay. Well, four founding families—Sanders, Prescott, Hadley, and Estabrook—negotiated a deed with the Nipmuc Nation, who were part of the Algonquian people." She pointed to a set of painted portraits on the rear wall. Early settlers, the Nipmuc people, and farmland stared back at us. "We have books at the library if you're interested—though they're biased, written by the white settlers. I'd recommend speaking with local people descended from and involved with the Nipmuc Nation. I can connect you with someone from the tribal council."

"I'd love that. In-person interviews are my forte."

She continued, "We haven't cataloged the books on the history of the town. They're in a personal collection in our library's history room. Like most of Massachusetts, many places around Sanders Mill—ponds, rivers, mountains, streets—have Native American names. Here, mostly Nipmuc. The Nipmuc people named our local mountain, Wallaneag, which means *fisher cat.*"

She took a breath, and I leaned in, enjoying the story.

"Anyway, as time went on, the usual colonial history followed—unrest, wars, entitlement. During the nineteenth century, it's alleged the Underground Railroad had stops in this region, though we have little proof, mostly rumors and family legends. Secret rooms, old artifacts dating back to the time. It's all hearsay. For all we know, the hidden rooms were for smuggling or something else, and the artifacts are just old relics. Anyway, the most notable abolitionist and suffragette of that time was Abby Kelley Foster, and her influence was south of us in Worcester. Then real railroads came through. Some of the tracks are gone, but an interconnected trail system remains going east and west. You have rail trails out west, right?"

"Yeah, there's a nice one from Pittsfield up to North Adams."

"Then this farming community transformed into a mill town, hence our name. The trains and mills are gone now, but farming has hung around. We're a place where rural meets suburbia. We even hosted a Smithsonian exhibit a few years ago, *Rural Americana.* Got a grant out of it and everything. Was a big deal for our little library."

Holy smokes. Had I landed a research goldmine in Helen or what? "I love the early stories, the untold gems, the ones that don't make it to the history books."

"The story in the story," she reiterated.

My heart skipped a little. "What about you?" I licked my lips as the server delivered two iced teas.

Helen sipped. "Me?"

"Your history. Any gold nuggets in there?"

"Oh. Nothing exciting. My family goes back generations to the founding settlers, Hadley on my mom's side."

That jogged my sometimes-unreliable memory. "I noticed a sign over the common room in the library that read *In Honor of Alice Foster Hadley.* A relative of yours?"

"Mm-hmm." She played with the straw in her drink, ice clinking. "The town founded the original building in 1860, and my great-great-great-grandmother Alice became the librarian shortly thereafter. My mother was a librarian, too. You can say it's in our blood."

"Original building?" The one we had seen looked old.

"Alice Foster Hadley died in a tornado in 1910 and her husband, Joseph, commemorated her life's work by erecting a new library on his own property in 1912. There's an entire book on the tornado in the library. F5 rating. One of the largest in our country's history."

"Wow. What about Abby Kelley Foster, the leading abolitionist you mentioned? Also a relation?"

"Maybe a distant relative of my ancestors. It would be a weird coincidence if they weren't related, since they lived at the same time and in the same county. But our family pedigree knowledge stops at Jacob Foster, Alice's father, born in 1820."

My brain was going to burst if I didn't write this information down. I took out my palm-sized notebook from my leather bag. "My memory sucks. Is it okay if I take notes?"

"Really?"

"Like I said, I'm a sucker for old stories. So, the library was on Joseph Hadley's property. Did he deed it to the town?" I jotted down as much as I could remember from our conversation up to this point.

She moved in her seat, but said, "We have a family deed and endowment. The library is publicly funded but privately owned. Only a handful of libraries are like that in the state. We have twenty acres of old-growth woodland behind the main building. It's prime development land," she added, the delight in her eyes fading. "Aren't you quick. Most people don't stop to think to ask if a library is publicly owned. They just assume it."

Both intrigued and feeling bad for hitting a sore spot, I tried humor. "I'm not always so quick. If you want to slow me down, just give me a basic math problem."

"Oh?"

I swallowed a thickness in my throat as the server returned with our meals. Once she departed, and the silence was too much, I put my notebook and pencil aside. "I have dyscalculia. It mostly presents as issues with math...but it goes deeper than numbers getting jumbled in my brain. People wrongly think it's the dyslexia of math. Math is the tip of the iceberg. There are also visual-spatial deficits, so I stumble with things like organization, schedules, directions, short and long-term memory. I'm clumsy. I constantly need to re-teach myself simple tasks. Even driving is a challenge."

"Oh...I see." She blinked, a flutter of soft brown eyelashes, as she opened her napkin and laid it across her lap. "Didn't mean to pry. I'm not familiar with it, honestly. My friend's husband is a teacher and also a tutor, working with kids with learning and developmental disabilities. He appreciates speaking with adults affected by disabilities. Maybe the interviewer can be the interviewee?"

Something I couldn't pinpoint swirled in the eyes trained on me—not an apology, but maybe hope? The knot that had begun its twist in my chest released. "I'd be happy to speak with him."

She picked up her burger, the balsamic reduction oozing over the side. She licked the sauce trailing down her finger. "I forgot to warn you, these are messy. You'll need extra napkins."

"Delicious," I said after a swallow.

"Isn't it? *Guh.*" We moaned in unison. Then laughed at ourselves.

After that, we ate in relative silence amid the murmur of other people's conversations. How could I broach the subject of M.H.? A comfortable rapport was building between us already. I didn't want to mess that up with pesky questions. In fact, I wanted to know more about Helen. What made her tick?

I swallowed a bite of fry. "You're the first person I've talked with in a while who didn't grill me about my book." That sounded egotistical, though I meant it otherwise. I really was botching it today.

Not looking up, she pushed the sweet potato fries around on her plate and dipped one in honey. "People think your book was based on real life. Our teen book club insists your Emma and Declan are real people."

I dabbed at my mouth. "Did you read it?"

A flicker of interest tipped her lips. "I read it, but I prefer historical fiction."

If she only knew how right people were to suspect this book wasn't totally fiction.

Disappointment probably played on my face.

She leaned forward. "So, what's your story within a story?" She wiggled an eyebrow, and the light in her gaze made me shift in my seat.

"Nothing nearly as exciting as tornados."

"So, Emma...she's not inspired by anyone you met? Not a girlfriend? Declan's not you? He spends the entire book digging into the cold case with Emma. Sounds a lot like an investigative journalist."

"Life lends itself to inspire fiction. I fell in love with Emma from the time I—*created* her first letter," I said, the lie sliding easily off my lips.

"You love your fictional character?"

A self-deprecating laugh escaped my lips. "I suppose. We love to hate our villains. Why can't we love our protagonists, too? Don't tell me you've never fallen in love with a character you've read. Edward Cullen?"

She made a sour face. "Meh. No vampires for me."

"Mr. Darcy?"

Pink spread over the bridge of her nose.

"I knew you'd be an Austen fan."

"How? Am I that readable?"

I winked. "You love history, you're a librarian...natural deduction."

She hesitated for a beat. "What do you have planned during your time here?"

"Nothing. I was going to see where the wind takes me."

She reached for the check, but I grabbed it first. Our fingertips brushed. "I'll pay. I can write it off as an expense." I slipped my credit card out.

"Then I owe you a coffee and bagel or something."

"I'd like that."

The server returned with the credit card receipt. I tapped the pen as the numbers blurred, jagged shards in my concentration. Unapologetically, I explained, "Cash sucks because I've got to do the math, make the change. Credit cards are great for most things, but when gratuity's involved, I ask the staff to do it."

This afternoon I got distracted by the woman sitting across from me.

"How about I leave a cash tip? You sign the check." She glanced at the bill, already pulling out her wallet and laying money on the table. "All set. I feel less guilty about having you pay, even if you can write it off. I'm a modern woman. Win-win, right?"

"Thanks. So...how about a personal tour of the town? You mentioned the mountain?" We made our way to the exit, where I swung the door open. "Ladies first." Without thinking, I placed a hand on her lower back. The brief touch sparked in my fingertips.

We turned toward Main Street again.

Helen said, "Billie and her boyfriend have an alpaca farm and sell woven goods at a boutique down the road there." She pointed past the town hall. "There's an ongoing harvest festival every weekend over at Sanderson Farm. They have a trebuchet competition in October. I used to go as a kid."

"Trebuchet for...?"

"Tossing pumpkins."

"No way! My hometown needs to get on board with that kind of thing! Our biggest landmark is a restored covered bridge. We weren't far from the mountains, though. My family would spend weekends in the Berkshires." I was glad she'd warmed up to me after her initial coolness. I wondered if she'd sensed how much and how fast I was warming to her.

"I love the Berkshires," she said as we turned toward the library. "As a teen, I went to this place near Mount Greylock where you zipline and climb through obstacle courses in the trees. I'm afraid of heights, so once was enough, but my brothers dared me, and I'm stubborn. Only girl. Had to prove myself."

"Oh, I know the place. Turner's Trees?"

"That's the one. What a small world."

"I volunteered there in the summers. It has a special STEM program for school kids."

"Sounds fun."

Our steps crunched on the loose pebbles of a walkway leading around the library. "I hate heights, too. I'd do anything I could that was on the ground, not in the trees. Guided hikes, maple syrup production, education on sustainability, and I'd leave the ropes courses to the jocks. I highlighted the program in one of my first by-lines. I loved it so much as a teen that I now volunteer with the Thrive Center in Newton."

"The Thrive Center?"

"It's a mentoring program for youth. They provide tutoring and workshops on everything from math to cooking to mental health or disability needs. I've taught skills classes addressing dyscalculia." I clamped my rambling mouth shut. Was this a job interview? *Sure, woo her with your resumé, Gabe.* I was supposed to be the one asking the questions. "I sound like a braggart, don't I?"

"No, you sound like a guy who likes to give back to the community. Since you like the outdoors, check out Mt. Wallaneag State Park. This weekend is the cider and chili festival. When I first saw you in the cafe, I assumed you were here for that."

"I love state parks. Been trying to visit as many of the National Parks as I can, too."

We reached the rear entrance of the library, but Helen didn't make a move to go inside. "How many have you scratched off?" she asked.

"Not many. About a dozen."

"A dozen more than me. One day I'll get to some of them."

"None yet?"

She shrugged.

"Hopefully one day you can. I'm not a fan of noisy festivals or crowds, but the one on Wallaneag sounds fun. Might grab postcards, too, if they have any."

"To collect or send?"

"Both. I send one to my mom and keep a few. I have shoeboxes full."

"I save things, too—well, my family does. The farmhouse is filled to the rafters with heirlooms and stuff. I hope to move some of the books onto the shelves I'm having built in my office. My great-great-great-grandparents used to journal and send letters to each other. Oodles of them. There's just something about letter-writing."

Letters? My pulse quickened. "You live on a farm?"

"It's not operational anymore. Mom grows veggies and fruits. We have a couple of chickens who have stopped laying, so they're like pets." She added, "Stop in Billie's shop, Bohemian Boutique. She's got local honey, maple syrup, and all those touristy things. Oh, and funny postcards. Libby's Corner Store has some fun trinkets, too."

We hovered by the door. The rear parking lot was empty. "You said home's not far?" I asked, not wanting our conversation to end. With Helen, I forgot my awkwardness and didn't feel like a reporter. Questions fell off my tongue by habit, but there was something more about her, heady, drawing me in.

"A mile down the road. I'll walk from here. It's still light out."

I hesitated, wanting to offer to walk her home.

What harm was there in getting to know the freckled librarian whose voice was as honeyed as her smile? Pick her brain, nibble her ear? *Dammit, Dennehy.* Where was my head?

There was a familiarity with her. I could easily attribute the feeling to being in a small town again. The local shops, mountain, coziness...all felt like home.

"You all good?" I asked.

"Right as rain. Gotta go inside and grab my backpack. Thanks for the meal. I owe you one."

"How about tomorrow?" My mouth went dry as I chanced again the question she hadn't answered earlier.

"Tomorrow?"

"The cider and chili festival? Want to show me around?"

She slipped her hands into her vest pockets, a puff of breath clouding before her as she fished out a key.

I backtracked like I'd stepped on hot coals. "Unless you're busy. Or don't want to. It's okay. You provided a helpful list of places for me to visit and learn more."

"No. I mean, *not* no. I don't have much going on tomorrow. Sure, I'd love to go with you. Want me to drive?"

"Great." My voice cracked with enthusiasm. "I'm at Cooper's Inn. What time?" I'd need to set two alarms to be ready. I wouldn't mess this up, whatever this was.

"How about twelve thirty? I need to take my mom to church."

"Sounds good. Thanks, Helen. See you tomorrow."

"See you tomorrow, Gabe."

Perhaps she was being courteous to the visiting author, but excitement bubbled inside me anyway. Then I shut the feeling down. I couldn't lose my heart, and my head, to another woman when there was still my M.H. to search for.

Maybe I'd fallen in love with the woman in the letters...or with some imaginary woman I created. It seemed a futile idea to find her, among hundreds of thousands of people in these small towns. What if she had moved away? Died?

All I knew, two years into this journey, was that I *needed* to find her, the inspiration for Emma. Not just because she was my muse, but because I needed to apologize for using her story without seeking her permission. I'd learned quickly that financial security and esteem were not the cure-all for the relentless twitchy feeling inside me. I was still an outsider looking in, not feeling connection to the world.

I'd always regret that I hadn't started this search earlier. Guilt had crept in slowly and surely. Or maybe it had been with me all this time, and it took success to smack me in the face to realize how much I had screwed up. Regardless, I needed to resolve that trespass. And...maybe I needed something more. Because guilt wasn't the only reason I wished I already knew my M.H.

The idea of finding *her* took my breath away.

Helen

I yawned as I entered the house.

From the kitchen, Nan's signature high-pitched laugh was unmistakable. "No, that's his leg. Get your mind out of the gutter, Lorraine."

"Yes, we see!" Mom added to the hysterics. The foreign sound halted my steps. Mom? Laughing? When was the last time I'd heard her laugh or seen her smile without a grimace?

All three erupted in a stronger peal of giggles as I entered the kitchen.

Mom and her friends stood in front of easels. A splatter of brown paint traced her chin. I approached and ventured a side hug. She didn't cringe or moan. Instead, she leaned into me, giddy with delight and squeezing back. It seemed like a good day for both her spirit and pain level. I cherished these days.

"What are we painting, ladies?"

"Lorraine returned from her trip to Tuscany with *inspiration*," Nan said.

"Oh, did she?"

Photographs of exquisite Renaissance paintings and nude statues lay scattered across the island countertop. I glimpsed the drying paintings. "Oh my," I said. I clamped my gaping mouth shut.

"It's his leg," Nan defended.

Ice cubes clinked in Lorraine's iced tea as she leaned forward to get a better look. She pushed her glasses to her forehead, making her short, ashy hair stick up in places. "We believe you, Nan."

My delight faded at the quality of Mom's painting compared to Nan's and Lorraine's. Mom had been a talented artist all her life. Watercolor, pencils, or acrylic, it didn't matter the medium, she was really good. Stunning framed canvases adorned each room in our home. A few hung in the library, too. Most were scenes from our extensive backyard, or the trails and pond on our property, where she'd take her easel in good weather. Billie and Hardy had used her designs to create blank greeting cards and paper pads at their boutique, though now that Mom's pastime had become a past time, the supply of stationery for sale was dwindling.

Her current pieces were beautiful, but not the masterpieces she used to paint. She used to excel at thick, short, and loose brushstrokes and luminous colors to capture light and shadows, emulating her favorite Impressionists. Instead now her colors blurred, her shapes were blobbier, her lines like scratches, and the overall painting was not as smooth as I was accustomed to seeing.

I resisted the urge to wipe the paint smudging my mother's non-drooping side of her face. In fact, the droop wasn't overly noticeable today. Perhaps it perked back up? Did paralysis do such a thing? Nan had suffered an incident of Bell's palsy following a viral infection, and after a couple months with treatment and rest, her face resumed its usual vigor. Could Mom's do the same?

Shingles followed by PHN differed from Bell's, though.

All the same, light glowed in Mary Hadley Wright's eyes tonight. I'd take it any way I could get it.

"Hungry? I can offer chips, cheese, and zuke mash, ladies," I said, shuffling to the fridge. Jars of zuke mash and jam lined the counter, waiting to be labeled and put away in the gigantic pantry off the kitchen. "And I have Coop's farmer's cheese and a baguette from Barb's to make bruschetta."

Today hadn't gone as horribly as the worrywart in me expected. My plan to gather intel before confronting Gabriel Dennehy about the letters seemed to be off to a good start. Did I have the guts to lay down breadcrumbs so he could figure out I was the writer? The man was surprisingly decent and kind. Also sharp.

And sexy.

But never mind that.

I'd get closer to Gabe, and he would let his guard down and—

What? Confess? Grovel? Pull his book off the shelves? Offer restitution?

Going into today, I had been ready for that. Thinking of how he used—or was *inspired by*—my letters, I had been pissed! But, after spending time with him, my flames of rage had reduced to a simmer.

As if she knew I was thinking about Gabe, my phone buzzed with a text from Kayley.

> Where is my photo of Mr. Sexy Voice?

I'd only had a moment to tell her about our pseudo-date beforehand, so she hadn't supplied me with questions to ask him. I did an okay job winging it myself. Tomorrow, I'd have more time.

I texted her back.

> I need more questions to ask him. Call you in a few so we can brainstorm?

> Yes!!

She followed up with a GIF of a couple from a popular TV show making out passionately, and I tucked the phone back into my pocket.

Gabe had been...

Nothing like I'd expected. His presence, his *something*, had eased me. The more realistic side of me did not like that from a liar and thief, but the softer side of me liked him entirely too much. He was sincere and kind and educated. Heat flooded my chest at the thought of seeing him tomorrow.

"I'll grab plates," I decided when nobody answered my question about food. They were all still giggling at their artwork. Artwork that, as I glimpsed it again, had me thinking of how Gabe might resemble a Renaissance sculpture under the flannel.

Despite my softness for the man, tomorrow I would dig deeper, as he liked to say. I'd find the root of his story yet.

Eight

Helen

The next morning, at seven a.m., I donned my compression pants, t-shirt, light fleece, and running shoes and headed off for my daily walk-jog, a short three-mile loop that included the paved paths through the cemetery. My breath puffed before me as my shoes hit country road. Skipping the music today, I tucked my phone into my vest's inner pocket and enjoyed the tunes of a fall morning.

Eugene O'Connell drove past me, the muffler of his rusty brick-red truck rattling when he rode over a bump. He gave a quick wave.

My phone rang just as I pushed through the entrance to the cemetery. I slowed my pace and answered. "Hey, Kayley."

"How about Thai food and pedicures tonight so you can tell me more about Gabe after you go to the festival today?"

"Hmm..."

"You need to get out. Girl time."

"I *am* out."

"*Wogging* your usual route?"

I cringed. "Walking now, since you called and interrupted my wog."

"Correct me if I'm wrong. First, you're at the cemetery, right? Then you're taking Mary to church, then you're going to see Mr. Hot Stuff while working on Operation Truth, and then you'll be jamming with your mom tonight—instead of jamming with that man?"

"I'm that predictable, aren't I?"

"It's why I love you. Anyway, if you won't be curling up with Mr. Honeybuns tonight, I think we need to go out-out, you wild lady. This baby is coming in two months. I need my girl time. My toes look awful, and I can't reach them anymore and Aaron's not great at painting them. And! I want you to dish all about Dennehy! I'll need all the deets after your date today."

I chewed the inside of my lip.

"Well, girl, has he taken your breath away already?"

"Har, har. It's not a date. It's part of Operation Truth, remember? Also, why the heck are you so insistent on me hooking up with him? This guy stole my letters. Or at least we think he did—"

"He did," she affirmed.

I didn't argue, though my doubts had resurfaced last night. "Anyway, I thought you wanted me to kick him in the nuts only a few days ago?"

"I'm allowed to change my mind. I think the book which I am now calling *Ode to Helen* is kind of romantic."

"Stealing and exploiting is romantic?"

She made some sort of throaty sound. "Technicalities. I still think he needs to own up to what he did, but, Helen, this book is like a love letter. Fiction, *schmiction*. The guy is crushing on you, hard. I've read the book three times now. I've changed my opinion about him."

I was going to argue that it was a book about a cold case, but we both knew that was only the external plot line. This book was about Emma. And the idea of it being a love letter to me *did* take my breath away, or at least make it grow uncomfortably short. I took a long inhale.

"Anyway. Even if it's a non-date, I want info! There's a new Thai place near the nail salon. Humor me, girl."

"Your baby is going to enter this world craving crab rangoons and steamed dumplings."

She laughed into the phone. "Please? I want to know all about Mr. Take My Pants Off Dennehy. Billie texted me a photo of him. Now I know he's a good specimen, at least physically."

If I told her to stop with the nicknames for him, she'd persist just to mess with me, so I ignored her.

She noted my hesitation as revealing more than a reluctance to encourage her. "I know you can't pass up Thai iced coffee." In a slightly more serious tone, she added, "Mary will be fine, Helen. One night. Please?"

My toes had been the same polish color for six months now, a chipped and splotchy beachy pink. Maybe I'd go *wild* and do a glitter or something.

"Okay! I'll go. Just stop with this love thing, okay? He found my letters, they inspired him somehow, and he wrote a fictional story. *End of story.*" This was exhausting. Regardless, an unbidden smile perked up my lips when I thought of how Gabe had been. He was...

My brain couldn't find the right word to describe him.

I thought of his touch, ever so soft, on my back as he escorted me through the doorway of the Mill Grille.

"My Mylanta. You *do* like him, don't you? Like, *like him* like him?"

"A little. Dammit, Kayley. What now?"

"Operation Truth, first, okay? Then he can make it up to you."

Oh my gosh, she was all hormones lately. "Kayley..."

She tittered. "Let's review your questions."

"First, I have an idea."

"Oh?"

"I know how he can make some things up to me. And no, not in *that* way."

She laughed. "Do tell!"

"What if I use his help with the library cause? He likes history and has a journalism background. Maybe he can help me find some demonstration of the library's worth to get Miriam off my back. And if I happen to find evidence that he did indeed steal my letters..."

Kayley squealed. I took that as agreement with my plan.

We talked over ideas for a few more minutes. After hanging up, I had questions typed into my notes app and a clearer picture of what I was going to do. Though we'd come up with Operation Truth last night, it was now officially planned. I'd keep talking with Gabe, get proof that he used my letters for inspiration. Once I had it, I'd feel more confident about confronting him.

And in the meantime, he would help me. Gabe had connections. Why not let him dig for the story beneath the story here in Sanders Mill? Sometimes all it took was fresh eyes, especially the eyes of an outsider, unsullied by town politics and familial connections. What if he helped me find the justification I needed to save my library?

I'd consider it Gabe's penance for taking my story. He owed me. Yes, he did.

After doing a few laps on the path around the cemetery, I pushed through the gate to another section. "Morning, Gary," I hollered with a wave to the caretaker by the stone maintenance building. He waved back.

I took the central path that curved around grave markers and headstones dating back to the late eighteenth century. My steps slowed as I reached the Foster family plot, cradled by towering elms and autumn clematis that smelled like honey and looked like white stars.

Adalyn and I used to joke about being related. Kindred sisters. Far distant cousins, in fact. As teens, we'd deciphered our lineages and assisted my mother with updating our family records. We shared the same ancestor, Jacob Foster, born in 1820, the one I had told Gabe about. Adalyn's family tree branched out from Jacob's son, Elton. My side branched out from his daughter, Alice.

All the founding families had plots here. In front of several Spencer and Foster headstones, red flags decorated with the fire department insignia flapped in the breeze. To the left of the Fosters sat the headstone of Michael Prescott, Miriam's ancestor. Of course, their family plot had a six-foot-high obelisk, names carved on each face, towering above the surrounding headstones and perfectly manicured perennials.

I grabbed the nearby watering can, filled it at the spigot, and returned to Adalyn's grave. I ran a finger along the smooth granite, chiseled with lilies and an open book.

"Hey," I whispered.

I never felt silly talking aloud to Adalyn. The distant drone of Gary's lawnmower carried on the crisp wind. The yap of a dog—likely Jenna DeLaria's terrier—drifted over from a path edging the conservation area next to the cemetery.

I watered the flowers, then kneeled and plucked weeds from the shriveling pink and purple petunias. Two black-eyed Susans flanked the stone, and thick, almost-spent catmint carpeted the ground in front of it. A few late season bumblebees buzzed around the fragrant purple stalks. "Hi, buzzy friends."

My mom had helped Mrs. Foster with the plantings here. The gravestone to the left of Adalyn's plot, a solid piece of pink quartz for Winnifred Butler, already had mums and pumpkins placed as decorations.

The mower's hum approached. Gary wore noise-canceling headphones. Even if he saw me speaking to Adalyn and the bees, he never let on.

My emotions cycled often. Today, anger dominated grief. Why couldn't she have listened to me? Why had she done it?

She hid the pain so well. Even after that girls' vacation turned nightmare in Mexico, I thought she'd be okay. Instead of visiting Mayan ruins and enjoying frozen drinks with umbrellas and snorkeling in Cozumel, Adalyn ended up fighting for her life. That harrowing trip to the hospital with only rudimentary Spanish under my belt still haunted me. I blinked the memory away before it grabbed me again. I never truly saw how bad it was, even then. I trusted her, believed her. She had talked the talk. Didn't walk the walk. Many times, she'd return to perching on that edge of darkness.

Until finally, she'd fallen in.

And I had yet to forgive myself for not doing more to save her.

Inhaling deeply, allowing the zingy fragrance of catmint to calm my senses before I hit a downward spiral, I pulled one of Alice Foster Hadley's letters from my pocket.

"You always liked this one, Addy." Carefully, I opened the letter with its worn folds, then read Alice's words to her beloved. I wondered why she capitalized certain words. Perhaps they held a secret meaning between her and Joseph. It seemed that he was away often, and in addition to the poem, she wrote about daily musings or goings-on. He worked as an architect's apprentice on projects across Massachusetts in the late 1850s to early 1860s, while Alice worked on her family homestead, awaiting her fiancé's return. Her poetry wasn't exactly Emily Dickinson, but it captivated me nonetheless.

> "The Clock reminds me of our next meeting.
> At the old Station, slow and fleeting,
> Ticking, tocking, sturdy arm at half-past Ten—
> I will see you then.
> Anticipation for the next Kiss—
> May our meeting at the willow not be missed!
> Its sheltering arms hug the waters of the Pond azure.
> Together like our carved names, mon amour,
> I will speak to you by ink and pen
> Until we meet again.
> Forever your faithful devotee, Heaven's messenger,
> I eagerly await your next Parcel."

I sighed like I was a dreamy teen reading it for the first, not umpteenth, time. I could hear Addy's soft, infectious giggle in my mind, equally lovestruck by Alice and Joseph's romance.

After the poem, the letter became a narrative of town and personal news, including renovations on the farmhouse. Joseph's letters had offered fewer striking words, only explanations of his projects, but steadfast affection came through. Their conversations transported me back to a time when letters bridged distance.

Their young courtship bloomed into a half-century of love. When I finished recounting Alice's memories about sneaking off with Joseph Hadley to unmarked wooded trails on the grounds where the library stood, I released another blissful sigh.

"What a love story. I'm such a sentimental sap, aren't I?"

My phone vibrated, jarring me to the here and now.

Please don't be Mom.

Shame punctured that thought.

It was a text message—from Gabe. I forgot I had given him my number.

Relief hit me.

> Looking forward to the festival today.

I sent a smile emoji back.

I stood, brushed freshly cut grass off my knees, and turned around to head home to take Mom to church.

Nine

Helen

I fluttered restless fingers on the hymnal in my lap. Father Patrick was a younger priest, animated in his homily, but today my mind was adrift. I took the bread wafer and dipped it in the wine as we received Eucharist, assisting my mom all the while. My finger twiddling became foot tapping as we waited to extend our greetings on the way out of Mass.

I yawned.

Sunday was Mom's day to get out and socialize, so I wouldn't rush her along. We shuffled closer to Father Patrick at the door as Phyllis, the oldest woman in the congregation at ninety-three, droned on to him about the next potluck. "...too many of those hippie vegan dishes, Father. Maybe a sign-up sheet would work. My corned beef with cabbage is always a favorite."

A genial smile was glued upon the priest's fair-skinned face as he offered his calm attention to Phyllis like he did with all his flock. "That's an idea."

Mom shifted, released a painful gasp, and would have lost her balance if I hadn't been holding on to her elbow.

"Let's go." I was already ushering her past the throng of people in the entranceway of the church.

"I-I need to say hello to Father Pat—" Mom's voice broke.

The first few times I witnessed her searing pain, it tore me up. Now, it was triage time. I'd work fast before she succumbed to it. "You need to get home and take your meds. You skipped this morning, against my—"

"Enough. Let's go," she snapped.

"Have any oxy with you?" We had depleted the supply of painkillers I carried in my handbag for her. I did a quick mental review—Mom's antidepressant and anti-convulsant were full, and she just finished another round of steroids. Only the oxycodone was awaiting a refill. She used it sparingly.

"No."

"How bad?"

She grabbed the side of her head. "A six."

"Okay." I guided her to the car. At least the pain level was not an eight or nine. I could manage a six without a call to the doctor.

"Face?"

A shake for no.

"Back?"

Mom grimaced, a sharp V diving down her forehead, confirming the location of her pain. She settled into the passenger seat with a shaky whimper. This morning, I'd applied a lidocaine patch to her lower back.

Filling the heart-racing silence on the short drive, I said, "I've heard good things about acupuncture. Even Dr. Boyne suggested—"

"No." Mom puckered her lips, rubbing a hand on her cheek. Wavy gray hair came loose from the bun at her nape. She *had* looked better today, the night in with the ladies having done her good. Her skin, though scarred from old blisters on her neck and side of her face, had held a healthy radiance this morning. Now she'd grown pale and sweat beaded at her brow.

"The needles won't hurt."

"No needles." She shivered.

I bit my lip. There was nothing worse than trying to help a person who didn't want it. What was that quotation? A *man convinced against his will is of the same opinion still.* Was that Benjamin Franklin?

I'd learned that lesson with Adalyn. Now with Mom.

Throbbing, burning, and an aching cacophony struck her whenever it pleased as damaged nerves sent chaotic signals to different areas of her body.

Over the years, I'd read every research article I could get my hands on. Most times PHN lasted for a few months to a year after shingles erupted, rarely for years after. My mom fell into the unlucky minority. Even the specialist at Brigham and Women's Hospital in Boston found her chronic pain perplexing.

Mom had been trying various existing therapies with no success. Dr. Boyne said his clinical trial was going to get the green light soon, and he anticipated being able to start enrollment by next year and Mom matched the entry criteria. For now, he was doing what he could with already approved treatments.

I guided her out of the car and up the front steps. The uneven footing had her racked with shakes that vibrated into me as I held her elbow.

"Let's get you to the couch." I maneuvered her through the front door and grabbed a quilt. She swatted it away. I dropped it beside her on the couch all the same. She experienced rippling chills and heat flashes with the slightest change.

Her cheeks were taffy pink, and angry crimson splotches skated down her neck. I got to work, first giving her the oxy.

"Need a new patch for your back?"

"Not right now."

After I readjusted her position with two pillows, she pulled the quilt onto her lap.

Setting the kettle on the stove, I eyed the open Merlot on the counter. I could use it. But even one glass gave me a wicked headache.

As the hall clock chimed twelve, I assessed tea options. Chamomile and turmeric? Peppermint or lavender? Or the magical combo of lemon balm, organic valerian, ginger, and cinnamon? That was her favorite for pain spasms and sleep. I lifted the canister and filled a tea infuser with the leaves and spices from that mix.

After a half hour, her pain settled some. I replaced the lidocaine patch. Tea consumed, and meds kicking in, she finally loosened her tense shoulders and reclined on the couch. She breathed regularly. I loosened Grandma's quilt to prevent overheating.

The grandfather clock chimed twelve thirty.

Mom opened one cat eye. "Didn't you have somewhere to be?"

"I can skip it."

She tapped my hand with ice-cold fingertips. "No. All you do is take care of me. I-I..."

"It's okay."

She swiped damp hair from her forehead, her skin sticky with sweat.

"Be right back." I hurried to the bathroom and returned with a dampened washcloth.

"It's not okay," she said as I dabbed her forehead. "Call Nan or Lorraine. They want to frame our paintings from yesterday. I have barn boards they can repurpose. Your dad had set them aside for me in the shed."

Dad. *Harrumph!* Where was he now? He was great until life got hard. "You need a nap."

"I'm not a toddler and you're not a nurse."

Ouch. That truth stung. My eye twitched.

"It's Sunday. Nan and Lorraine have family things." I shook my head. Why had I suggested the festival to Gabe? I'd have to cancel my time with Kayley tonight, too. "You need rest. You can frame the paintings another day. Be right back."

I finally had a moment to look at my phone. Two missed texts from Gabe. Shit. I texted him back. And waited.

No response.

I went to the kitchen, out of hearing range, and called Ronan Cooper. "Hi, Coop, Helen Wright here."

"How are you, Mary Helen? How's your mother?"

I said the same tired lie, "Good. Umm, I was supposed to see Gabe Dennehy today. Something came up. Can you send my apologies? I texted him but he's not responding."

He knew what *something came up* meant. "Can do. He went for a walk. I'll let him know when he returns. Need anything? I can swing by—"

"No, we're all set. Thanks. Have a good day, Coop."

"You, too."

As my adrenaline vaporized, I returned to Mom. My limbs relaxed with the letdown. I could use that valerian tea, too. "All set."

She blinked droopy lids. "Good, you'll go?"

"No. I canceled."

Her eyes shot open. "For crying out loud."

I turned away, brushing wetness from my eye. "I need to run to the bathroom. I'll be back."

After a change into more comfortable jeans and a sweater, a dab of teary eyes, and a centering breath while I clenched tight hands on the lip of the bathroom sink, I returned to the living room. She had fallen into a light sleep. Good. Valerian for the win. I repositioned the fallen quilt. Forget the wine or tea, today called for coffee.

I turned on the coffeemaker. My legs buckled at the table, but I caught myself with a chair—okay, my shin caught the chair. I pressed my palms to battered eyes. Took two of Mom's elderberry gummies. While the coffee brewed, I lathered lavender lotion into my eternally dry knuckles and fingers.

Twenty minutes later, halfway through my second cup of dark roast, as the knot in my skull subsided and I filled in Mom's missing answers on the crossword puzzle, the doorbell rang.

Lorraine stood there, a glassware dish in her hands, steam emanating from the edges of aluminum foil.

I leaned against the doorjamb. "Hey. What are you doing here?"

"Your mom called. I'll keep her company. You need to shoo, darling."

I shook my head. Of course, Mom had used the landline in the living room while I stepped away. Outwitted again. I suspected that this meal had been intended for someone else unless Lorraine kept a conveyor belt of casseroles in her oven. "Really, I've got this, Lorraine. It's your family night," was my meager protest, but she never took no for an answer.

Hiking an eyebrow over an undeterred gaze, she pushed her way inside with her wide hips. She might be short, but she was strong in mind and body.

I followed her.

She turned to me. "I mean it, Helen. Go, do things that thirty-year-olds do."

I chewed my lower lip. "Okay. I'll be back in a few hours—but I've also got plans tonight with Kayley. I can cancel those—"

She heaved me back out the open door with a hip bump and a shove of my handbag into my chest. "Nonsense. Go see your girlfriend, too. Call or text if you need me."

"Lorraine..."

"I know, I know. I'm a godsend. Have fun!" Lorraine shut the door before I could second-guess myself further.

Shivers tingled in my scalp as the caffeine hit my bloodstream.

I'd fix my hair and face in the car. If I didn't leave now, I'd never go. I had to follow through with Operation Truth. And I was...kind of looking forward to being with him. I hated this tug-of-war in my brain, this fraying at the edges of my fighting spirit. Damn him for being so nice!

I turned the car on and shifted into drive before I could chicken out.

Over an hour late to our proposed date time—no, this was not a date—I pulled into the gravel parking lot at Cooper's Inn. A few jars of zuke mash and raspberry jam rolled in the back seat with the sharp turn. I had forgotten to give those to Coop last weekend.

My phone finally pinged with Gabe's response to my previous text. I wrote back, letting him know plans changed again. He was going to think I was a nut. After one more swipe at my face, and thankful for my travel cosmetic bag I kept in the glove compartment, I grabbed the jars for Coop and strode to the front door. A stomach cramp hit me mid-stride. I breathed through it. Why was I nervous?

Oh.

First, I hadn't gone on a date in years, not since a horrible setup by meddling Nan and Lorraine. Second, this man stole my letters and exploited my emotions—or at least I was ninety percent certain he had. Third, my faith in Operation Truth was less than resolute. Fourth, I liked him despite it all. Sunny beach.

"Not a date," I whispered, my arms full of glass jars.

Ignoring another spasm while juggling the jars, I fiddled with the funky latch of Coop's front door. I had to give up and knock, catching a jar before it slipped to the porch boards. Why hadn't I put them in a bag? Why? Because my mind was a zone of chaos.

Coop appeared behind the screen. "Oh, Mary Helen. Lovely to see you."

He helped me unload jars from my aching arms. "Hi, Coop. Sorry for the delay. I meant to bring these earlier this week. They've been rattling in my back seat," I said with a shaky laugh.

"Well, they're here now. And what good timing! I'm all out." He shuffled to the counter, the limp in his right leg more obvious today.

The screen door shut behind me with a loud snap and I jumped. *Calm yourself.*

"Hot sellers, these. Have you thought about expanding beyond the jams, apple butter, and zuke mash?"

"What do you think about soups? We have butternut squash and tomatoes. Thought I may try my grandmother's recipes."

"The ones Mary used to make for the festival? Those were lip smacking." He rubbed his lean belly with emphasis.

"Those are the ones. Passed down through the generations—a butternut sage soup and a tomato bisque." I leaned in conspiratorially. "Do you know our secret ingredients for the butternut soup?" I knew my chitchat was me stalling.

"Oh...what?" He waggled furry eyebrows below salt-and-pepper hair that blew wherever the wind took it. Coop was like a skinny Santa Claus. He put anyone's mind at ease with smiles and a belly laugh. The grin creasing his weathered skin nearly reached his eyes—one blue, one brown.

He used to tease me when I was a girl and say each eye had its own personality. I always stared in awe, as the heterochromia only added to his breezy charm. If Coop were a salesman, I'd buy snake oil from him. Or, oh, solar panels. Those salesmen were relentless. But Coop? I'd buy all his potions. And he seemed eager for my family kitchen's magic secrets. I said, "Nutmeg and apples."

He rubbed his hands together. "My mouth's watering. Soups would be fabulous for our winter guests. How much do I owe you?"

I tallied, and he wrote me a check. Well, no more stalling. "Turns out my plans changed. I'm here to visit Gabe." My phone was silent. "Has he returned from his walk?"

His blue eye sparkled with mirth, while the brown eye peered with seriousness. "Not yet. Was headed toward the town center but asked if you came by, to text him." He tapped a finger on the countertop, intricately made from local wood shaped into leaves and branches. Coop was a stellar carpenter, and I always found myself drawn to the inlaid woods of the countertop.

"Feel free to sit on the porch swing and wait. It's a nice day."

"Thanks."

"Anytime. Tell your mom hi from me." Now both eyes twinkled. Lorraine and Nan really needed to spend their matchmaking powers on Ronan Cooper and my mother. The man's crush was clear to almost everyone in town, except Mom. When she and Dad divorced, she'd sworn off men forever.

Like mother, like daughter. I'd done the same after Wes, yet here I was, waiting to go on a non-date with Gabe, my letter thief.

"Will do. She'd love a visit, too. Thanks, Coop."

Trying not to psych myself out, I went to the porch, sat on the swing, and texted Gabe.

Ten

Gabe

Duh, Dennehy. The post office wouldn't be open on a Sunday. This travel schedule threw a wrench into my circadian rhythm. After getting Helen's message about canceling, I shot off a text back to her, and then went to the post office, which wasn't far from the inn. Since they were closed, I scoured the grounds, looking for any clues that this was the town.

I eyed the outside mailbox. Had this been the one—the one M.H. put her letters into? Did anything look or *feel* familiar? I'd done this inane act of assessing and pondering at each of the post offices I'd visited so far, like some great cosmic power was going to strike me with lightning when I was in the right spot. Dumb. Staring at a small 1950s-era brick building would not give me answers.

After many towns, I'd perfected my spiel: I was a journalist visiting towns that could have inspired the book. No lie in there.

However, my rising popularity made inquiries challeng-ing. There was no fighting social media. If someone rec-ognized me while I was attempting to investigate my own book's inspiration...they would think I was a glorified nut-case. But I wasn't that big of a name, nor face yet.

Maybe it was time to shift tactics. My research contact, Lucas Herrera, was an esteemed investigative journalist with good cred. Desperate for information and getting nowhere with my other paper expert, I asked Lucas to inquire about the paper with a few of his connections who were specialists in paper dating and forensics. He was also going to dig around online for the paper source. Each of M.H.'s letters had been wrapped with a second blank page. I couldn't give him a page with the ink or writing sample without disclosing what I had done, so he only had the blank paper to go on. He was good. He didn't ask questions. It should have been enough. But so far, no news from Lu-cas.

I dragged a hand through my hair. Pounding pavement was fruitless. Fools did stupid stuff. I kicked at a patch of grass, then pulled out my phone to set a reminder to return tomorrow to speak with someone. Oh! I missed a text from Helen. And my earlier response had not gone through. Doh!

She was waiting for me at the inn. My heart did a little somersault. I picked up my pace to get back.

Helen

Watching Gabe's return, I swallowed a lump in my throat. Why was I nervous? "Hey," I said, meeting him at the bottom of the steps.

He stumbled on the uneven sidewalk, and I looped my arm through his. My forwardness surprised me, but I relaxed into his reciprocated grip. His gentle squeeze of my forearm sent shivers to my elbow.

"Hey," he said, tearing his gaze from his feet. "I can climb mountains, travel the world, but silly cement slabs trip me. Some days it's like my brain freezes." Fine lines rippled across his forehead.

"That's got to be frustrating." I didn't discount his struggle nor belittle it by trying to relate it to one of my own. I know I hated that, personally. "Sorry I'm late. Still interested in the cider and chili festival?"

The tension dissipated from his face. "Definitely."

"I'll drive."

On the ride, Gabe asked questions about this and that, while I jabbered about events and notable hallmarks of our region. I felt like a tour guide, but I was following my plan of laying out tidbits about Sanders Mill that could connect my letters to his Emma's letters. If I shared, and he put the pieces together, he might slip up and reveal his realization in his expression or behavior. I could rock this—those were Kayley's words.

"We have a blood drive this week," I said in response to his question about upcoming events at the library. Now *that* wouldn't bring me closer to the truth of Emma. I was rambling.

Freaking nerves. Date nerves.

Not-a-date.

"When? I'm overdue to donate."

"Wednesday afternoon." We finally found a space in the crowded lot.

We headed toward the lodge, our shoes kicking up dust on the gravel parking lot. Gabe peered at the ski runs, delight curving his lips. "Sweet view." The sun feathered its hues on the knolls left to run wild through the offseason.

We glided through the crowd that had gathered near the entrance. The aroma of cider and everything apple perfumed the air. Mingled with it, I inhaled cinnamon and greasy fried food.

I could have fun.

Not a date.

We reached the ticket booth, and Gabe slid his credit card into the attendant's hand. I didn't protest. Though we hadn't walked arms linked or anything, my skin felt abandoned, craving the momentary contact we shared at Coop's.

"My mouth is watering," Gabe said, angling toward the first of the vendor trucks.

"My stomach is gurgling. What first? Hot cider, cider beer, apple cider donuts, apple fritters, oh, apple whoopie pies. That's a new one."

Gabe skimmed the offerings at the truck, Over the Top Apples. "All of the above?"

I pointed toward another truck. "There's chili and chowder. Maybe we start with that, then work our way toward the donuts and pies. If we walk around here enough today, we can burn the calories."

"Good plan."

We grabbed two bowls at Chillin' Chili, each sprinkled with shaved Parmesan cheese and topped with a slice of crusty bread. We found a spot at an open picnic table. A live band played folk rock as people of all ages walked across the grassy lawn at the base of the mountain's slopes. It was Hallmark-nice.

"A-plus," Gabe said after a swallow. "Chunks of sweet potato. Black beans. Good combo."

Heavenly basil garlic bread from Barb's Cafe hit all my happy places. I'd recognize her bread anywhere. "I better not get used to this."

"To what?"

I dipped the bread into the chili. *Dating.* "Eating out. Two days in a row."

"I prefer home-cooked, too, but cooking for one gets lonely."

I bought a moment with a hard swallow at his not-so-subtle glance at my naked ring finger. "I cook for two. Mom lives at home with me." I scooped my chili, avoiding the uptick of his eyebrow. "She became sick a few years back. Easier for her to live with me."

"I see. That's a lot to take on for somebody your age."

Oh, he was good at the art of getting answers. "I'm not *that* young. Thirty-two. You?"

"Me? Thirty-three."

Well, we'd established our ages. My turn to ask questions. "Does your family still live in Pratts Junction?"

"My parents retired to North Carolina. My brother lives on the West Coast, so they divide their time between here and there."

"My dad's down south, too. Myrtle Beach. My two brothers live out of state. I'm the middle child. Just me and Mom here. We're homebodies. Though traveling is never far from my mind. In books, of course," I said with chagrin. *I travel in books?* Well, I did. I hadn't been anywhere since that horrible trip to Mexico with Adalyn.

"You're the magical middle."

"Yup." I spooned another mouthful of chili.

"To be honest, I would prefer being a homebody over traveling. My freelance work has slowed down since the novel's release. I send my parents photos and postcards, as you know. Speaking of which...you mentioned shops in town to visit. Are they open on Mondays?"

I chewed, swallowed. "Should be."

He withdrew his phone-sized notebook from his back jeans pocket, flipped it open, and read aloud, "Alpaca farm, the boutique, historical society, smashing pumpkins..."

"All good choices." I pointed to the notebook. "Why not an app on your phone?"

"Helps me remember stuff. I write scenes for my novels in notebooks sometimes, too. Write articles on a yellow legal pad, of all things." He crinkled his brow. "I use like a million apps already. But writing boosts my memory when it fails me. Which is frequent. I need to re-read things multiple times. When I write, I remember. I also like to feel the words flow from my fingers." Boyish charm lit his brown eyes

I laid down my spoon. "Know what's funny? I like card catalogs. Libraries don't use them anymore. Ours sat in the main circulation area when my mom was the librarian, when I was young, and even by then they'd gone out of practice, but she kept it around as long as she could, kind of like this relic to remember the past or something. Everything is digital now. I wonder—where did they put all the card catalogs from libraries across the country? Were they destroyed or kept as artifacts, or are they like chic retro décor now?"

"Never considered it. I have an old apothecary chest I use to store spices in little tins in the drawers. Bought it at a flea market."

"That's inventive."

He finished his chili. "What's in your card catalog?"

"How do you know I still have one?"

His lips curved in a flirty way. "Because of the way you talk about it. I bet you're not one to toss the sentimental things, especially if your mom likes them, too. Am I wrong?"

I felt giddy with this conversation. Did he know he had this effect on people? Or it was just me? Or was this his journalist charisma? "Got me. It's nothing fancy, though. I once saw a tea shop somewhere that used an old card catalog for teas. Cute. Like your spices. Mine, it's just the old cards. Sad, isn't it? I could redesign it and use the drawers for storage, or for my mom's sewing threads and needles or her art supplies, but I..." I pulled a face. Mom seldom sewed or painted anymore.

"Like the history?"

"Hmm?" His gentle question drew me back from the sad thoughts about Mom. "You can say that. I keep it in the storage room. I even have an old microform machine."

"What's microform?"

"Come on, you don't know about them? Microfiche and microfilm?"

He stared blankly.

"I'll show it to you sometime. Sort of like old filmstrips. People copied images and newspapers on films or on this stuff called fiche before computers came along. You'd probably find my house a bit of a museum, too. My mom's doing. Old farm, and lots of journals, genealogy charts, books, knickknacks..."

Letters. Don't say letters. Letters from Alice Foster Henley, which inspired me to write my own stupid letters.

He rubbed his round chin, which was speckled with light brown whiskers. Chewed-down nails tapped his skin. He stared up at the cloudless blue sky as if pondering a memory. "I think I learned about microfiche a little in college, now that you mention it. A course on outdated technology." He laughed softly, teasingly. He squinted from the sun, his cinnamon-hued irises almost dancing with glints of light.

Even his laugh was sexy. Dammit.

He added, "I'd love to check out your fiche."

We held our looks for a long moment, and I swallowed.

Gabe eyed the running ski lift. "Wanna take a ride to the top? I'd love to see the view from there. I know we both aren't fans of heights, but I can handle a ski lift as long as I don't look down. And if there are no steep grades on top."

"Sure. The view of this region is nicer from far away. Believe me. Sometimes I feel too close to it." I let sarcasm slip into my tone.

"What do you mean?"

I nibbled my lip and waved an explanation away. "Oh, the usual small-town drama. Meddling busybodies. Politics."

"Now you've piqued my interest."

We stood and walked to the nearby trash can to throw away our bowls and spoons.

"It's a long story." I ducked a hand into my pocket for an antacid.

"I've got time."

We reached the loading area of the lift. The chair was a quad. Hmm... Sit far apart or near? We placed our feet in the marked spots on the cement platform, waited for the chair to swing around, and planted ourselves in the middle as if the wind had shoved us together, leaving a few inches between us. Gabe fell into me with the forward motion of the chair. I held a firm hand on his forearm as we swung down the handlebar.

"Heights hold no power on us," he whispered.

I inched closer. "If you say so."

"We'll protect each other."

"On a twenty-foot fall?" I said, the words whooshing out of me as the lift took off and my stomach dropped. To me, that was the worst part. "Never liked roller coasters either."

Don't look down.

I did. Instant woozy head. "Ugh..."

"Me neither. It took one scary flight to develop a genuine fear of heights. Climbing in the trees in the Berkshires is one thing—we're harnessed and have loads of padding on—but a near-crash landing is another."

"That would rock my confidence, too. I've only flown a few times." That came out more pathetic than I wanted it to sound.

"The bigger passenger jets I'm cool with. This flight had been on a fixed-wing prop plane. Short runway surrounded by gigantic mountains. And the runway, no joke, angled upward. Scary weather. High elevation. Once you start the descent, there's no turnaround. All so I could cover a story about a nonprofit group of trekkers at the base camp of Everest. Never again. No more adventure journalism."

Everest? Gabe had been to freaking Mount Everest? I'd hardly been out of New England. My one and only international beach trip—a nightmare. Could I ever summon the courage to travel again?

I almost snorted. With what money?

"Do you still fly to places?" I focused on the thick green trees flanking us, anything to prevent me from either looking down—making me more woozy—or into Gabe's piercingly gorgeous brown eyes—making me a different woozy.

"When necessary, with...don't laugh—"

"I won't."

"—meditative exercises, a prescription from my doc, and calming music."

"If I had a bad landing, you'd have to drag me on a plane again, nails digging into the ground. Bet those views and that experience were out of this world, though." I cemented my dangling feet to the foot bar to give myself a sense of safety.

"Once my stomach settled, yes, the view was worth it. Mostly. I can't eat mac and cheese anymore after I saw it coming up on the runway once we landed."

I swatted his shoulder. "*Eww*, thanks for the visual."

He brought the conversation back to me. "Do you have a dream vacation?"

"Europe. Sounds cliché..." I shivered, inching closer to him to absorb his body heat, to feel his nearness, to feel irrationally safeguarded from falling. I stopped denying it was a date once we got on the lift. My heart could let loose a bit, pretend I wasn't upset about the letters. Gabe made it too easy to like him.

He waited for me to continue. "I want to experience the culture, learn the history. Walk in castles, see masterpieces, eat food in Italy, hike the Alps, everything. I've always wanted to go." Rather, I was supposed to go with Wes on a honeymoon that never happened after a marriage that never happened after a baby that...

I swallowed that lump, fast.

"One day," he said in a near sensuous whisper.

Another check on the scorecard of Gabe Dennehy. Sexy voice. Kayley had been correct. She'd melt into a horny puddle if she met him in person.

Restraint was my strong suit, though. "One day," I repeated.

In the descending chairlift, Harper Prescott rode alone. She was busy on her phone, face turned down. I tried to wave when she unglued her eyes from the phone, but she stared at the valley below for a moment, her gaze distracted by something or someone, and then went back to her phone. My look followed her as she hopped off the seat and trudged to the ski lodge.

"What's wrong?"

"Nothing. A teen I know... She's..." I frowned. "Probably embarrassed to see an adult wave at her."

"I bet they think you're a cool librarian."

"You and your compliments today. Do they teach you this?" Did he know I had this internal scorecard going?

"Who's they?"

I waved a hand at nothing. "College, in your journalism classes. To say all the right things."

"Nah. This is—" He seemed to search for the word. "—me and you, fun. I'm on break, remember?"

"So you say. You seem very invested in learning about our town."

"It's appealing. So are its stories."

We locked eyes. I analyzed his face...every inch. The line of his smooth jaw. The light brown stubble that danced down from chin to throat. The tiny lines around his almond-shaped and inquisitive eyes that squinted from the sunlight. The crooked smile. I finally broke from his hypnotic look.

We absorbed the vistas in silence for a few minutes, me gripping the handrail the entire time. I started jabbering. "The ride down is less scary. Seems counterintuitive, but that's what they told me last time. Maybe it's because I can see far away, see the horizon, and here we have the summit ahead. Or maybe it's because the seatback has a slight recline, so on the way down, I can't see the ground directly below me. The few times I've taken the lift, it's better on the way down, so there has to be something behind the theory."

"Let's tell ourselves that."

A soft wind stroked my face, and goose bumps hopped across my skin again despite the temperate day. "I forgot my jacket."

"Sit closer. Been told I'm like a furnace."

Don't I know it. The vision of warm toes against my naked thigh under a thick duvet invaded my mind. Sunny beach. Where had that vision come from? "Does that line work on all the ladies?" I quipped.

"If only. My brother used to set me up with dates, but he quit trying when he moved to California. Women...don't like to stay. I travel a lot." He scrubbed a hand through his hair. "Well, I used to travel a lot. I've cut back this year. And I like it."

Pink blossomed in his olive complexion. Who would not want to wait at home for him?

I swear someone had tainted my chili with a love potion. What was wrong with me today? I cleared my throat. "Pesky friends and well-meaning family. I've had my share of setups, too. The only way to date seems to be on apps or maybe a lucky encounter at a bar."

We reached the top, and as Gabe lifted the handrail, my heart thumped extra beats with the spike of anxiety. Falling was an absurd thought. Fluffy grass teased below us. Then the sturdy platform. I leaned in closer, even putting a hand on his knee. In return, he gripped me around the shoulders.

"Got you. We'll keep each other upright," he said with a breathy laugh.

A hop and step and we were on the landing.

"Whew. I prefer hiking up the other face of the mountain," I said. "If I fall, it's on my butt and on the trail, not twenty feet down."

We wandered around the area by the lift and ski patrol hut, Gabe whistling as he took in the view. He scanned the large wooden sign painted with the ski trail map. "I bet it's nice in winter. I'm not a big skier. The whole coordination thing."

"Me neither. The whole falling thing."

We shared a laugh. In fact, my cheeks hurt from smiling.

"Not sure how this can compare to Everest base camp," I said.

"Equally stunning in its own way. I love the central hills," he said. "Round, worn down with time and the elements. They hold stories greater than the most jagged peaks."

Gabe was a deep thinker. *Come on, sweet talker, give me a tally mark on the cons side of this pros and cons list.* Letter thief—check. Could his hundred good checks make up for that one big, bad one?

I shoved my hands into my jeans pockets. "Want to see the summit? They renovated the top with a tower. Gives a three-hundred-sixty-degree view. On a clear day like today, we can see the Boston skyline."

A brief hike brought us up. People meandered here and there, the mountain teeming with enthusiasts enjoying the September weekend. A group held binoculars and cameras.

"That's the Mountain Watchers Club. They track migration of hawks, vultures, eagles, and falcons here. They did an event at the library once."

"Sweet." Gabe tented hands over his eyes and squinted.

We walked up to the tower platform. He ran a finger along one of the four displays illustrating the mountains and landmarks in each direction. He took a few pictures of the distant mountains in New Hampshire with his phone.

"I used to hike here with my mom. There's a newly paved road, so we drive to the summit now."

"She has a hard time getting around?" Gabe joined me at the railing facing New Hampshire's closer mountains.

My shoulders tensed, and I forced myself to lower them again. I hated that sharing meant opening veins to the past. But if it also meant getting some sort of answer from Gabe about the letters, so be it. I had written a letter to Mom, after all. A letter he read and used for inspiration for his book. "She has postherpetic neuralgia. She had shingles a while ago. A rare case, the doctors say. PHN is usually temporary after shingles, but hers stuck around. Her damaged nerve fibers send confused pain messages to random parts of her body. She had minor paralysis in her face, but it's better. Her balance is wonky. She has repeated skin infections. We manage, but we never know when or where the pain will strike..." My words drifted away on a wind gust. "Sorry, that was a lot there."

He squeezed my hand. "A lot for you, too. I'm sorry."

I squeezed his hand back. I missed touch.

As we descended the tower, Gabe bumped into Fred Wheeler. "Oomph! Sorry."

"Oh, hey, Fred," I said. Of all the people to run into, it was Miriam's right-hand man on the Finance Committee.

His eyebrows lifted, then fell. "Helen, how are you?"

Fake niceties were Fred's talent. I played along, seeing his two children with him, both regulars at the library. They bolted ahead to the viewing platform.

"Good, and you? Lovely day today." It was all I had.

"Yeah. Good day to enjoy what the mountain offers." He removed his hat and swiped sweat away from his receding hairline. Replacing the cap, Fred turned to Gabe. "Hi there. Have we met?"

Gabe stretched his hand out to shake. "No. I'm visiting. Gabe."

"Nice to meet you. You've picked a pleasant week to come." With a nod of his head and a gesture to his kids, Fred scampered up the platform.

We walked the trail back to the ski lift. Gabe asked, "Do I want to know? What's his deal?"

"Finance Committee. He's...let's say he is not on Team Library."

"Oh?"

"Touchy subject."

"Sure. Didn't mean to pry."

A smile tugged my lips at his sincerity. "No worries. Small towns. Big-ego politics. Budget cuts."

"I've got listening ears if you want to talk."

"Thanks. Maybe later this week?" My heartbeat quickened, and before I lost the nerve, I said, "Over coffee?"

I could not believe what I just did. I asked him on a date. To get him on Team Library. To get him to work to make his theft up to me. To get him to work with me, and not just work... Hot damn, my insides were warming way too much around him. I cleared my throat. I was for real doing this. I was all in.

"I'd love that."

On the way down, the view was breathtaking. We sat extra close in the seat, cups of steaming apple cider in our hands from the waffle hut at the top. Sunlight glimmered in Gabe's eyes and highlighted waves of sand and honey in his brown hair. A gentle breeze ruffled it, and I was envious of the wind.

What had I gotten myself into?

Eleven

Helen

Monday came, accompanied by my least favorite time of the month—bills. Not just household bills, but invoices for the library, too. I nibbled on an apple cider donut procured from the festival yesterday, sipped an Earl Grey with a splash of cream, and stared at the balance teetering on zero in my checking account.

Nickel-and-diming was my middle name. When it came to our personal finances, I had most costs covered. Mom qualified for government-provided healthcare on top of her Social Security deposits, and the house was in my name, so it wasn't listed as an asset for her disability payments. However, every year I fought the state insurance program until my sanity was razor thin, reapplying for premium assistance and getting physician notes to explain why my mom was still sick. They'd save us both a lot of trouble if they filed her condition as permanent. But I made it work. Dad had her listed as a co-owner on a percentage of his retirement savings, but we couldn't touch it for a few more years, not until he retired.

With a groan, I slumped my forehead to the desk. I wanted to scream, to hurl my frustration across our property, let it ricochet off the trees and skitter across Wompi Pond. The scream would likely boomerang back and thump me in my skull.

I massaged my temple. I had quite the imagination sometimes. Reminded me of the silly stories Adalyn and I would write as kids. Then I wrote silly letters.

I sucked my teeth in frustration.

A bounced check I'd written to the home health aide service. An overdraft fee. No, wait, two overdraft fees. With clicks of the mouse, I transferred funds from my dwindling savings account into the checking.

Just for kicks, I scanned my retirement accounts. Those would remain on the upswing as long as I kept contributing. No lottery ticket was going to rescue me. Every stinking time I reconciled the bills, I pondered Miriam and Howe's offer to buy the library land—all of it, excluding our personal home and property that abutted it. Then I shooed the thought right out of my headspace.

My eyes glossed over as I read numbers in columns. By the time I finished a few hours later, I'd paid everything to keep us afloat until my next paycheck, organized paperwork, and made notes of Mom's upcoming appointments.

I ate another donut to mentally prepare myself for the next task—the library budget.

I started the process early in the fall. The proposed budget first went to the Finance Committee in January, then to the Select Board for final approval in the spring.

I clicked open the spreadsheet. At the last interdepartmental meeting, the Finance Committee asked us all to cut our budgets by ten percent. Ten percent didn't seem like much to larger departments, but the cut brought us below the minimum level required for state aid. Basically, we had to *have* money to receive money. If I didn't file a waiver, our library would lose its certification status, and with it, reciprocal privileges with other libraries. Our residents wouldn't be able to check books out from other towns' libraries, we'd have to cut staff and cut hours to save on paying wages and utilities, and it would pretty much kill us. Not immediately, but a slow death.

I swear, some years I used sticky tape to hold the budget together. I needed another meeting with the Capital Building Committee about the leaky roof.

Could a person's head implode?

An hour later, having exhausted my mental energy for the day, I shuffled to the porch to check on Mom. I carried a tray with two iced teas, pretzels, Swiss chard tahini dip, bell peppers, and cheddar cheese.

"Hey," I said. After serving her and doing a quick assessment—she seemed comfortable in her lounger with a book—with a whoosh and a sigh I flopped into the accompanying Adirondack chair Dad had built. I propped my slippered feet up.

"What's wrong?" she asked, dipping a pretzel in the dip.

"Crunching numbers for home and work."

She muffled a moan. "Sweetheart, I'm sorry. I'm a..."

"No. Don't finish that sentence. You're my mom. This is our home, Mom. Ours. I've got this. This is our library, our land." *Our everything.*

"Maybe I should call your father again—"

"No. Don't bring Dad into this." I dug into my hoodie pocket for an antacid. Last time I'd spoken with him, Dad had been bragging about a 1950s car he purchased and refurbished. *Fine, relive your youth.* Once upon a time, his hobby had extended to fixing the Hadley homestead.

He had been the cool parent, jet-setting across the planet on one auditing job or another, bringing me back keychains from each location. I'd linked them together and strung them up around my room like Christmas lights. Where was he now? Not here, that's where.

Mom munched on a pepper. "What if I call Ryan or Dan?"

"Mom...Ry's got kids to take care of, and Dan is knee-deep in his thesis and has student loans coming out his ass."

"Mary Helen." Her pinched features showed her disapproval.

I swallowed the lump in my throat. "No. I've got this."

She heaved one of those tired, resigned mom sighs.

With a clenched hand, I rubbed my throat, wishing the acid would go away. I sipped tea.

"What if I try new designs, get stationery created again for Billie's shop and Libby's Corner Store? Maybe we can solicit the other mom-and-pops in North Prouty and Fraser? I want to do my part to help. My hands have been steadier. I've enjoyed using the watercolors and charcoal again."

"Sure, Mom."

Why not? Let her help the way she liked. "The special printer upstairs works. I've got cases of cardstock, envelopes. You create, and I'll print." These efforts would be like setting up a lemonade stand to buy a new car. But if it meant Mom was happy doing something she loved, then it made me happy.

Mom took a long sip of her iced tea. "I heard the news."

"Which?" My heart flipped for a moment. Was this about Gabe's book? Had she read it? I closed my eyes and leaned back on the chair.

"Meddling Miriam. Need help to prepare anything for the town meeting next week?"

"I'm okay. Already reviewed the warrant articles. Not much I can do at this point. She's proposing the creation of an ad hoc committee via the Planning Board."

Mom raised a brow with my groan.

"Their purpose is to determine"—I made air quotes—"the importance and longevity of the current library versus the benefit of the proposed regional center. Pretty much: small town vs. regional. To keep or not to keep."

"Just another pointless committee."

I sat up and leaned over the tray to scoop big bites of tahini dip with pretzels.

"What's your game plan?"

"Well, first off, I'll be speaking to Craig soon to work on the budget and our goals. It's possible Miriam has influenced him, too. She seems to have her claws in everyone with her hairbrained ideas."

"A town manager isn't the be-all and end-all. And I like Browning. He's fair and impartial."

Where was Mom's drive, her passion? She seemed so...acquiescent these days. "The Finance Committee is not."

I stared at the backyard to recenter myself. Bumblebees buzzed near the raspberry bushes and the marigolds lining the vegetable garden. Birds fluttered around the feeder, riding the draft of a windy afternoon.

"Besides speaking to Browning about your budget, what else do you plan to do?"

I rattled off the list I'd come up with: speak to every committee to rally support, request town funds at the spring meeting if my budget got denied (which it would), arrange more events, speak to the school district superintendent about reading programs and other school-led initiatives, arrange the DCR visit to educate about old-growth forest, create a community education campaign on understanding small-town government, and dig into our historical archives to find anything I could use for the Historical Register application.

"We already donated the bootlegging artifacts we found in the old root cellar to the Sanders Mill Historical Society, but none of them were deemed significant enough to register the property with the Historical Register. *Dime a dozen* sort of thing, though they appreciated them."

I didn't tell her yet about recruiting Gabe to help with some of this. Maybe because the more she knew about Gabe, the more likely she'd know about his book...and make the connection.

Mom asked, "Do you think the town may be receptive to a vote for the Community Preservation Act again?"

"The public has shot down that idea twice. They don't care that the surcharge is matched by the state. Many see it as new taxes, not as community protection. And it gets messy because our land isn't town land. I don't know."

"Well, you've got a solid plan, but, hon, try to not get yourself worked up over this. I know it's easier said than done. I know you have it in you. Be a marathon runner, not a sprinter."

"Miriam is a long-range planner," I said.

"So are you."

A storm spiraled within me. Saving the library was important for the community, our employees, and for my family's legacy. But frankly, I needed this job, too. For the money, for the insurance. Though my degrees qualified me for other vocations at corporate or academic libraries or even in book preservation, I didn't want to change jobs or move again, not with Mom's health issues. And I would have little luck finding employment at a school library since most in our district were run by parent volunteers—all the more reason to keep our town libraries!

I could work as a substitute teacher as the district was always in need, but the pay sucked, and the job lacked insurance.

"Mom, for real here, can they do this? Take the property away? We have a trust."

Mom munched on pretzels. "I don't know." Fatigue strained her voice. "The next question is who is going to help you? Who's in your court?"

I had to wrap up this conversation. I squeezed the bridge of my nose to regain focus. "At least Rohana Reddy on Finance. Miriam's got the other four members cinched tight. The Select Board has been understanding about my needs, but Miriam's got a better hold on them, even though she's technically supposed to be impartial."

Mom moaned, and when I gave her a concerned look, she waved my worry away. "Fine, fine. You're always fussing over me. Wish you'd fuss over yourself."

"I'm fine."

We two Hadley-Wright women were anything but fine.

"I know our land has Miriam seeing dollar signs in her sleep, but why not shift her focus to the *available* properties in town? They won't bring in as much money, but they're substantial and easier to obtain. It's almost like she has it out for our family."

Mom finished the last of her iced tea. "I suppose that goes back to my mother and Miriam's grandmother."

"Not Grandma Barnes?" My grandmother, Helen Barnes, had been my namesake.

"Yes, her. My mother didn't like to talk about it. I'm not clear about what happened. I think they were best friends at one point. There was a man..."

I rolled my eyes. It was always a man! "Grandma Barnes was a fireball. I could imagine her taking on big, bad Serafina Prescott in a fight. But, even so, Miriam has this vendetta against the entire Barnes-Hadley family all over some romantic war between our grandmothers?"

"Could just be the pressure of being a Prescott."

"This is all to please her parents?" I remembered them from when Miriam and I were in high school, always pushing her to do, be, and accomplish more. She was the class valedictorian after all.

"The things children do for their parents..." Her voice trailed off.

Hint duly noted, Mom. She and I were nothing like Miriam and her baggage! If my mom even attempted to end this conversation with another "Mary Helen, go back to Boston," I'd scream.

"The Prescotts and Hadleys go way back in this town. I like to think it was amicable for a long time. Joseph Hadley worked as an apprentice under Michael Prescott."

"I read about it in Joseph's journals and his letters to Alice. He and Michael seemed to be on good terms. Joseph spoke highly of him."

I felt a pang of nostalgia for the long-ago harmony in Sanders Mill.

Mom shifted in her lounger, the old thing creaking with her movement, though her frame had grown slighter since her illness.

We sat in silence for a while as the afternoon waned.

Just when I thought Mom was asleep, she spoke up again. "Nan told me something the other day..." She paused. "Never mind. Gossip. Pay no heed to it."

I leaned in, intrigued despite myself.

She adjusted her quilt. "Supposedly Miriam and Pierce Howe are...well, er, involved in more than a shared interest in land."

I blinked. "They're both married. That's a silly rumor. She helps him develop a new neighborhood and that helps boost her public image. I've heard she has her eyes on a state Senate seat. Positive community growth under her advisement looks good to voters."

"Sometimes, though, it's not political. It's personal. Why is she in such strong cahoots with him if they aren't..." She lifted her eyebrows.

Heat flooded my cheeks, not from the idea of Miriam and Howe having sex—*yuck*—but with the idea *of* sex. It'd been ages. Nothing serious since Wes. Gabe's face jumped to my mind, and I shifted in my chair, tingling sensations traveling to my extremities. Now was not the time to daydream about him. *Him.* Of all people. Yesterday was nice, but I had a mission, well, two of them—Operation Truth and the Save the Library.

"Remember when Coop was the town moderator?" I sipped the last of my tea, urging the burning acid of frustration down, down, down, and moving the conversation away from the library and my own issues.

"He always had the dirty farmer look." Mom laughed.

"He asked about you yesterday."

"Oh?" A blush reddened her complexion, usually a sign of impending pain but, this time, perhaps the opposite. Could Mom be sweet on the old guy, too? Sixty-five wasn't old. Perhaps I needed to bring her to visit his farm stand.

Instead of her setting me up on dates, I could set *her* up on a date.

Mom continued, a gleam in her eye, "He'd stagger into the meetings, exhausted to the bone, fingernails grimy from work, probably aching from head to foot, but dressed in his simple gray suit. Tall. Dominating presence. A farmer who probably was up to his elbows in manure only hours before a meeting. Fitting, too. From shoveling poo to moderating poo."

I laughed, the image a comfort on fried nerves.

"How was the festival?" she asked.

I stirred a spoon in my empty glass, the metal clinking against two remaining ice cubes. "Good."

"Going out again?"

"Not sure."

As if on cue, my phone buzzed not once but twice.

> Want to grab that coffee?

Gabe followed it with a coffee mug emoji.

A tiny glow within cheered me on to respond. Instead, I dropped the phone into my lap and wrung my hands.

Mom stared at me with as wide a smile as her exhaustion allowed. "Go. I'll be okay."

"Gifty doesn't come on Mondays."

Mom plucked my cell phone from my lap and began tapping the screen. "Mom!" I reached for it, but she gave me a whole lot of shoulder, surprisingly spry today.

"Yes. You should definitely go."

"Mom..."

"Oh, I'm not texting him, hon. I have boundaries." She handed it back. "I asked Lorraine to come over."

My phone rang a moment later. I answered and gave Mom a heavy eye roll. "Hey, Lorraine. That was Mom. You don't need to—"

"I'm on my way," Lorraine said.

I disconnected. "She's on her way."

It began to sprinkle, so we went inside. I texted Gabe back. It was time to recruit him to my cause. No more procrastination.

> Interested in seeing the history room?

> Definitely. I'll meet you there. When?

> An hour?

Once Lorraine arrived, I grabbed my laptop. I'd work in my office while letting Gabe peruse the stacks.

Let's see what this investigator could help me scavenge from the historical troves.

To Dad

You left.

When we needed you most, you left. Without a look behind you.

I sat in the back of the church this week, with Mom too sick to attend. I sat near an exit in case I got a call from her and needed to leave.

The homily spoke about forgiveness. As regret and pain carve places within my bones, I sit here wondering how I can forgive you for not staying when times got hard. For not helping when she had given so much of her life for you. Sometimes I hate you. Sometimes I miss you. If I love you, it's from a sense of obligation. Not that you would understand what it's like to fulfill an obligation.

Where were you when Wes and I lost the baby? When I needed help to pay for tuition? What about when Ry got kicked out of his place? You wouldn't let him come back home. Bet you didn't know he spent a few weeks in a shelter. If Mom had known, of course she would have taken him in! But no, he had gone to you, his father. If he asked me, I would've found room for him in my tiny apartment. Thankfully, he's turned himself around. I bet he gets married soon. She's good for him.

I really do try to work on forgiveness.

When I was young and your work took you around the globe...I saw your efforts. You did your best to provide in the way you knew how. I remember getting excited about what keychain I'd add to my growing collection linked around the room. Did you know I had over a hundred from different cities, states, and countries? You did what you could do. All the chains you gave me were not enough to bind you in place when I needed you, though.

Maybe I'm more ashamed than angry. Because when times got tough, I left, too. I'm like you. I also left a person I loved. Out of weakness and fear. It's too late for me to return to him. Too late for you to return to us, but you can be a part of our family again. You owe it to Mom.

There you have it.

As I did with my other letters, I suppose I need to find the silver lining. Mom taught me that. She's a strong woman and I hope she will be okay facing all these health challenges head-on.

Not all my memories are tarnished by pain. Some glow. Like sea glass. I loved our beach trips. We'd search for those sea-polished shards, our own little scavenger hunt, while the boys built cairns or sandcastles, and Mom painted pictures of the seascape.

Pavilion Beach in Gloucester was my favorite because it was blanketed in rocks. I just had to look down, poke my fingers around, and turn up lovely smooth pieces of white or brown sea glass. I remember sifting through the sand at Rockport at low tide. Oh, and Nantasket Beach—we'd venture there in the late winter, bundled up, in boots, to look for any gifts the ocean churned up after winter. I loved pink sea glass the best, and Mom loved the blue and teals. You loved green.

Like tears exposing raw emotion, wetness makes sea glass shine anew. Sunlight glints off broken pieces, beacons within the gray. Battered by time, tossed by the sea, they become worn and smooth.

Life can put us through the wringer. Do we become smooth and shining pieces of glass or remain broken, pointy shards?

I haven't been to the beach to look for sea glass in years. Maybe I need to return. Maybe if you come back to visit, we could go again. Will you come back? As time eases my resentment and pain, I hope that anger will fade away and

this battered soul will come out worn but smooth, gleaming in the sunlight.
     M.H.

Twelve

Gabe

Defeat punched me in the gut as I left the post office. Hard-asses. Even with my most charming shtick, nobody was saying anything. At all.

I shot off another text to Lucas. My friend's quick reply twisted the knot in my belly further.

> Not sure my contact for forensic analysis is gonna work out. No luck with searches on the paper style and design either. Will keep looking.

A soft drizzle matched my mood. I grabbed two hot teas and some pastries from the cafe. Despite my eagerness to get to the library, I put each foot down carefully. *I will not slip; I will not fall; I will not spill these hot drinks on myself.* Even having walked this route the other day with Helen after lunch, my brain had already reset. Every stinking time. Like a computer. *The dreaded blue screen of death. Restart. Wait for the memory to kick in. Processor running like molasses.*

To top it off, Laurel had texted me again this morning to check in on the status of book two. Spoiler alert: what book two?

I dropped off the cardboard tray of teas and bag of pastries on a bench in the front of the library. The rain lessened to a mist as I nosed around the library grounds, waiting for Helen. Seeing her would lift my spirits.

A snaking footpath meandered around the building to bring me to a remarkable view of woodland in the back. With the fog curling among evergreens and oaks, the landscape gave off such serenity, even on a gray day, that I had to sit on a bench beneath the shelter of a red maple to take it all in.

My phone beeped. I swiped the reminder away and, after another moment's respite, returned to the front of the building. Instead of pacing, I wiped the surface of the front bench with my jacket sleeve, then sat. Nearby, a memorial stone protruded among spent flowers. *Adalyn Foster Memorial Garden.*

Adalyn?

As in *the* Adalyn?

The sight of her name hurtled me to M.H.'s letters. Adalyn wasn't a common name, not now, at least. Maybe they recently updated the stone to commemorate a prominent citizen from the nineteenth century? I pulled out my notebook. Foster wasn't a founding family here, but Alice Foster Hadley was one of the first librarians, and a distant ancestor of Helen's. And then there was Abby Kelley Foster, the abolitionist. Was Adalyn related to either of them? This memorial stone could be for an Adalyn Foster from two hundred years ago.

But M.H. did mention such a stone for an Adalyn in her letter.

I typed Adalyn Foster into my search bar on my phone and waited, but my phone was slow. Must be a dead zone for Wi-Fi. I'd google Adalyn Foster tonight and see what I came up with. I'd also ask Helen more about her ancestor Alice. I had a lead, even if landed by dumb luck. That's all that mattered.

I stood and paced with my notebook in hand. My fingers itched to read the letters again. Scanned copies remained at home on my desk and the originals were at the inn. It was a weird compulsion to bring them with me, but it's like I traveled with M.H. on this trip.

I skimmed my notes.

Alice Foster Hadley. Tornado 1910. Founding librarian. Husband, Joseph. Alice and Joseph = Helen's great-great-great-grandparents. The library and property under a family deed, publicly funded but privately owned. Twenty acres. Prime development land. Founding families—Sanders, Prescott, Hadley, and Estabrook. Abby Kelley Foster—distant relative?

Action items—read about town history, dig into Helen's family tree. What's the development deal? Library at risk?

Thoughts spun like a hamster on a wheel.

This could be the town.

I shivered.

Around the corner of the building, brakes shrilled as the driver parked. A minute later, Helen approached. "Hi there. Hope I didn't keep you waiting long." Despite looking a bit tired, her beauty was unmatched. I liked her wavy hair that fell just right on her shoulders, the pink freckles on her nose, and the glow in her blue eyes.

"Not a problem. The view behind the building is incredible. You okay today? You look beat."

Through a yawn, she said, "Nothing a nap later can't fix." She pointed to behind the building. "We have a few trails back there, too."

"Would you mind if I walk them later this week?"

"Have at it. They're overrun, though. Watch out for poison ivy. The local outdoors club comes and maintains them, but not until October. Even though our exterior maintenance falls under the scope of town budgets, the trails are my responsibility. A fun Catch-22 to owning all this land."

"This front area is pretty. The stone here—" I pointed to the memorial. "—was this someone famous from the town? Another librarian?"

The look in her eyes softened. "Nobody famous. Just someone who loved the library."

I followed her to the door, grabbing the tray with the two hot teas sitting on the front bench. "Got you tea. Barb says hello."

"Thanks." She took two tries on the key and lock. "Rusty. On the endless list of repairs the town needs to address. God, sometimes this key feels like an anchor."

The door groaned open, and I followed her inside. The lobby area and circulation desk were illuminated through high skylights. She took a sip of tea and shivered. "Ahhh. Need me to turn up the thermostat? I keep it low. Costs..."

"I'm okay. Got layers on." I held out a bag. "I brought two pumpkin turnovers from the cafe."

"I had one of the apple cider donuts this morning." She flashed an infectious smile. "Okay, two. Maybe later. Barb's treats are rich."

"I might put on five pounds this week from the food alone," I said.

"Me, too, if you keep pushing pastries on me. But I won't say no." She flicked on lights. We set down the teas and treats on the circulation desk. "What would you like to see? I have some meetings to prepare for and I can work here in the fish bowl."

"Fish bowl?"

"Librarian lingo." She pointed to the office behind large glass windows, then to the room across from it. "The history room is there. I can leave you to it. Search the stacks in the back, too. We have glass case displays of artifacts provided by the historical society."

"Anything off-limits?"

She lifted an eyebrow. "Free range. Be careful with old bindings." She led me into the room. Small, it held books almost overflowing from the shelves, old maps on the walls, and a bust of some notable person. The overhead light flickered twice.

I was too busy listening to instructions to pay attention to my proximity behind her, and as she turned around to leave, we nearly collided.

I grabbed both her arms and allowed my touch to linger before letting go. "Sorry. Thank goodness we set down the drinks!"

Her eyes held mine a moment before her gaze shifted to my mouth. "No worries. I'm a whirlwind. Always shuffling around."

"I like a good shuffle." I drew back a step with a flare of arm and leg and winked. "Though my dance moves aren't the best."

My words and movements teased out a subtle curve of her lips. After giving me the rundown of what was what on the bookshelves and desk in the room, she left for her office. "If you'd like, bring in your tea, but keep it away from the older books."

"I'll leave it out there. Never a good idea to have liquid near books...or computers."

"Don't I know it." She lifted a brow, both inquiring and sympathetic. "And you do?"

"One computer, one first-edition book."

"Painful."

Plus, leaving it out there gives me an excuse to come visit you.

Before long, I lost myself in the research. The narrative of the town's history was cut and dry though. Where was the history that had *not* made it into the books? The story within the story: my guiding principle, which I had given to my character Declan in *Letters to Nobody*. Art imitating life and all that.

I tapped a pen against my notebook. No Adalyn in any of these books.

I walked light-footed to the desk. I didn't want to disturb Helen.

She flashed a friendly wave from behind the glass window. I sipped cooled tea. As much as the rush of new information propelled me, a rumbling of unrest percolated in my bloodstream. The battle between the two emotions, eagerness and—was it guilt?—gave me a moment's pause.

Marco assured me he'd take full responsibility if the truth came to light, but I would never betray my friend. Marco had a wife, a life. If confronted, I would say I found the letters. I alone would face the consequences. But I had no idea what those might be. Would I pull the book? Would I tell Laurel? The world? Would I hope that M.H. would say, "Hey, it's okay"?

She harbored unwarranted guilt over her baby's and Adalyn's deaths and the loss of other relationships. It was heartbreaking.

From Helen's office, Elvis Presley's voice crooned, his "Return to Sender" shooting shivers down to my toes. Of all the songs. I mumbled to myself as I went back to research. My mind circled back to my goals: find M.H., apologize, declare my admiration for her, and offer restitution in some shape or form...in that order.

Was it admiration—or love?

I shook my head. Too muddled with thoughts to ponder it more.

I flipped through a book published in the 1930s, the pages thick but delicate with age. Beside the book sat a framed black-and-white image of the destruction from the infamous 1910 tornado. A laminated newspaper clipping tucked into the pages read:

Sanders Mill mourns the loss of forty-three people from the June 1 tornado. Town offices and the library, which stood since 1860, and the local school were all destroyed. Funerals are scheduled this weekend at St. Peter's Parish and neighboring North Prouty churches. Notable community figures were among the deceased, including Alice Foster Hadley, age 70, the librarian. She leaves behind her husband, Joseph Hadley, and son, James, daughter, Mary, and grandchildren.

The rest of the list was disheartening. A dozen children died.

Later, Joseph Hadley donated over twenty acres of his fifty-acre property to the rebuild of the school and library—which by the looks of it had been renovated again since then—including a natural area crisscrossed by trails. He later gave another chunk, about twenty-five acres, to the Sanders Mill Conservancy, making that section untouchable. By the sounds of it, Joseph's remaining property had been about five acres, which was where Helen's home and apple orchards remained.

Helen had referenced a Finance Committee member—the man we'd run into on the top of Mount Wallaneag—not being *on Team Library*. An approximate picture of what was going on formed in my head.

I cleared my dry throat. Again, my limited scope was causing me to guess. The thought of digging out information about Sanders Mill and now the library energized me. This woodland would be worth a lot to builders. This could be material for a newspaper article; certainly, it was in the public's interest to know about these issues.

If, a big *if*, I followed this trail of information, I'd need to be mindful of whom it affected...and get full permission this time.

I stood and stretched the kinks in my back. Another thirty minutes had passed. I went out and drained my tea and took a bathroom break. On my way back, I heard the sound of a soulful Patsy Cline, and Helen's groans resonated. A few slipped curses. Something about a librarian muttering like a sailor caused me to chuckle.

I knocked on her door. "Hey. Lively tunes. You're a bit of an old soul."

She dropped a pencil, then ran her hands through her curling locks of strawberry and honey, and I wanted to be her fingers.

"Yeah. Mom's favorites became mine, I suppose. Patsy, Elvis, and Johnny try their hardest to help me get through the misery. This town meeting may be the death of me."

"Sorry to hear that."

Sticky notes in neon shades adorned her large monitor. She pulled a fresh note off a pad and wrote something, then stuck it on the desk on a folder pile.

"Got a thing for sticky notes?"

She crinkled her nose. "Necessity. I like outlines and spreadsheets, but the notes are visual reminders."

Slightly hidden behind the teetering pile, a simple wooden picture frame sat on the desk. I snuck a peek. The photo was of Helen, younger, with a woman the same age beside her. Maybe a relative or friend? Framed and hanging on the wall above it was a lighthouse made from smooth glass and flat pebbles.

I pointed to the lighthouse art. "That's creative."

"Thanks. My mom made it for me with sea glass I collected with my dad."

"Cool." Her monitor displayed a spreadsheet, something far less appealing. "Budget problems?"

"You can say that."

"Does it relate to the issue you mentioned about housing developments?"

"That long story requires refreshment. I've got a Keurig downstairs. Need another? We can make tea, coffee, cider, or chai. I have juice in the fridge."

"Maybe a decaf coffee. Don't want to be buzzing all night. Hang on. I got something for you." Her smile had disappeared, and I missed seeing the little crinkle in her forehead and subtle dimple in her cheek when she turned her lips up. So, as she grabbed her sweater off the back of her chair, I tore off a sticky note from the larger of her notepads.

A few folds later, with her watching me all the while, I handed her the yellow origami bird.

Her face lit up and there they were: crinkle and dimple.

"Cute. That's a talent I've never mastered. Didn't inherit the artist gene from my mom." She placed the origami bird right next to a mug beside her monitor.

"Origami keeps my nervous fingers busy and helps my brain, I think." I pointed to her screen as we exited the office, lines and numbers in the spreadsheet making my cranium ache just from a glimpse. "That—that is an art."

"I was reviewing the budget I need to present to the town manager before an upcoming meeting. Come. Caffeine—or decaf in your case—first." She motioned for me to follow her downstairs. In the small kitchen area, she clicked the coffeemaker on and dropped in a one-serving filter cup while the water heated. She twiddled her fingers on the counter. "My budget is bare bones. We're one of the lowest-funded departments in town, second only to the Council on Aging. A huge chunk of the annual budget goes to the schools. Like seventy percent. Then there's public health, public works, public safety...and we get the scraps. I get pushback when I try for step-up raises or added hours, though the state requires them." She blew out a sigh.

"That really sucks. It's a shame the town doesn't understand how important the library is to the community."

"Yeah." She pushed buttons, and coffee trickled into the cup. "To them, we're *obsolete*. Like a dinosaur. We all know what happened to them."

"They're not threatening to shut you down, are they?"

"When are they not threatening us with a shutdown?"

"That bad?"

She crossed her arms and leaned against the counter. "Yup. Do you know much about small-town government?"

"Honestly, not much. I took a US Government course in college but didn't learn much about small towns."

She swapped coffee cups and set hers to strong. She pulled out sugar and cream while it brewed.

When we were all set, she gestured to the larger meeting room. "I'll tell you about it on our way."

"Our way to where?"

"Something cool to show you."

"Oh, a hidden passageway?" I teased.

"I wish."

As she steered me down the hallway, turning on lights as we went, she explained the drama surrounding the library, the heat put on by the town moderator, and the contention over the land. "What's Miriam Prescott's deal?"

"World domination?" She pointed to a basement stairwell. "This way. Miriam's proposal is to make a larger, regional library in North Prouty, our bigger neighbor. Turn this land into a residential community. Her compromise is to keep a 'beautification area' by retaining a parcel of wooded land."

"And you don't want that?"

"Well, I'm all for conserving land, but her proposal would mean tearing down our library, and now residents would have a farther drive to the regional one. It's more complicated with budgeting when you have multiple towns involved. What if all the district town libraries close and the new regional one doesn't happen? Plus, having a library in a town is beneficial. Increases property values. As for her true motive? I've heard she wants to run for the state Senate. Doing all this 'community improvement' sure looks good on a résumé." Pain laced her words.

"Then this is just one step upward on her political ladder?"

"I would say so. She exploits the fact that she's descended from a founding family. Name is everything here."

"Helps you, too."

She agreed with a shrug. "People know names, but they forget the history of this building and town. The library kept people employed during the Depression, and it's offered job fairs over the decades since. It was a vaccine clinic during pandemics past and recent. Regardless of weather, we try to be open to provide a warm or cool refuge. A safe place to explore the world of books, connect with others. People can print things for free, use free internet. Parents connect with other parents. We've hired teens from a nearby behavioral health school to help with projects. We're a resource of knowledge and community." Her voice became more impassioned with each sentence, and now bitterness entered it. "Miriam conveniently forgets how I allow the Select Board to use a space here. After years of the cable committee—which records all the Select Board meetings—operating here rent-free, they're finally paying their cut of the electric bill. They have a whole studio set up on the lower level. I had to get town counsel involved. People forget."

"People will remember when the time comes."

"I'd love to have your optimism."

I paused as information churned in my mind. "Is she in Howe's pocket? You mentioned her being tight with the builder."

"More like his bed," Helen said.

"Ah..."

"Rumors only. Regardless, I could never use Miriam's personal affairs against her. Not my style. I can't fight dirty. Gotta focus on hard facts. Strategize. Galvanize support. She can't force me out directly, legally. But she can—"

"—make the library not seem an important asset anymore?" I finished for her.

"Exactly. We have a special town meeting next week. That's why I'm pushing this budget prep. I need to justify it all."

Without thinking, I gave her shoulder a squeeze.

She released a soft sigh and didn't step out of my touch. "People will vouch for you."

"One can hope."

"What can I do to help?"

"Funny you should ask that, because I have a job for you." My heart actually fluttered.

With a jingling keyring, she unlocked a storage room door. We entered and the familiar musty scent of *old* filled my nostrils. Dim lights showed stacks of old books, boxes, discarded computers, signage, furniture, and a computer that looked 2001: *A Space Odyssey*-esque.

"A microform," she said with glee, pointing to the odd contraption. "I suppose it's not as cool as I promised. Interesting, maybe. Definitely historical."

The tight quarters forced us to be close to each other, not that I minded. She didn't seem to, either. Remembering how she'd softened under my shoulder squeeze, I was emboldened to brush a hand against her waist. "Reminds me of my brother's old arcade machine in his basement. He's got Pac-Man and Asteroids on it."

She laughed. I liked it.

"Let me plug it in. Don't worry, it won't beam us up to space." She laid her coffee down on a box a safe distance away.

We took two chairs around the desk. She opened a compartment in the metal cabinet that vibrated with the sound of decades-old drawer guides. "What do you want to see first? Space Invaders or Pong?"

"I'm more of a Frogger guy."

Fun as our easy banter and laughter was, I considered seriously what I'd like to see on the machine. "Any films on the tornado?"

"Were you reading about it upstairs?"

"Yes. Fascinating resource collection in your history room."

"Tornado it is." She thumbed through a lower drawer. "Do you write for newspapers, too?"

"Used to. Layoffs. Local papers merged into regional ones. Everything is accessible online, too. Daily newspaper delivery is dwindling these days. No more newsprint on your fingertips. And now AI is taking over where it shouldn't."

"My mom insists on still getting the local paper, *The Pioneer*. The subscription has gone through the roof, so we only get the Sunday edition." She grimaced, but then her frown disappeared when she found the film box she was looking for.

"Newspapers merging is similar to this regional library idea." I tapped my chin. "Similar but different. Libraries serve a unique function in a community. Several functions, like you said. They're much more than words on paper or paper in bindings. There's life here." I wasn't saying it to impress her, but I'd be lying if I didn't acknowledge the satisfaction I got from seeing the gleam in her expression. "Maybe I should have been an archaeologist. Digging into things. The closest I've come is scaling ladders to cliff dwellings and ducking through passageways in places like Mesa Verde National Park and in Mayan ruins."

Something changed in her look. It went from bright to dimmed. "Mayan ruins? How were they?"

"Just as you could imagine and more." I downplayed it, sensing there was something else going on behind that pained expression. "Have you always wanted to be a librarian?"

"Long ago, I wanted to be a teacher, but books won my heart. I used to be a children's librarian."

"I've always loved libraries, too. I used to meet my tutor in the library. I also loved to curl up with a book in a corner chair until closing time. Words have always been my thing."

She tilted her head to the side, giving me the brightest of smiles. "I'm glad you have happy memories of libraries."

Pleased I made her beam, I peered over her shoulder as she sat in front of the machine.

"Some resources are only available on film or fiche, no matter how much modern digitalization goes on. I'll skip the history lecture. Don't want to put you to sleep. Come, sit."

As she swapped spots with me, I deliberately brushed against her. Her hair fell into her face at the momentary shuffling, and my fingers itched to tuck a strand behind her ear. She allowed my touch, even leaned into it a bit, her back slightly rounding.

I took the film box, our fingertips touching a moment longer than needed. Waves of warmth flooded my veins. We were alone. Alone-alone. I could kiss those strawberry lips.

I opened the box, nixing that thought—momentarily.

"Sparing you the boring details, film and fiche are read on the microform. Got that?"

"What's the difference between film and fiche?"

"Films are here, in the cabinet, and are on reels, like old movies. The fiche are flat films in envelopes."

"Got it."

She sat beside me, our shoulders touching again, hips and thighs comfortably close. I'd take any chance I could get to touch her. A hint of citrus—perhaps her shampoo—teased my nostrils when she leaned in, opened the box, and showed me how to load the film.

"Mount the reel on the square peg and feed the film into this shoot until it's under the glass." She let me take over while she spoke. "Hit the load button. Then the text appears magnified on this larger screen. You spin the film with the dial to go forward or reverse, or you can rotate it with this knob. And there is this knob for side to side." She leaned in closer, pointing, demonstrating, then laughed. "This is ancient, right?"

"Maybe we *are* archaeologists." I fed the film fast and it whirled. We laughed again. "Whoa!" The blurry images swayed before me as I twiddled. "Reminds me of when I was a kid in home ec class and the pedal on the sewing machine. Vroom."

"I remember that. We sewed gym bags in seventh grade. You?"

"Don't laugh."

"Never."

"Aprons."

She laughed.

"Hey! It was for my mom." I caught myself leaning in so close, my breath was on her neck. I inched back. *Play it cool, Gabe. What are you? Sixteen?*

"To use the fiche, you pull this handle, and the glass top pops open. Load the fiche, push in, and it's a similar process of viewing, but you move the glass viewer around instead."

I fidgeted with it, amazed by this simple and once vital and innovative technology. The symbolism of something that outlived its time was not lost on me. But while this machine sat in a basement under a cover, the library was a vibrant, evolving part of a community. A mainstay.

Soon, the view revealed the news I'd been searching for. "Can I print this?"

"Sure. I stick in this square reader box thing—okay, I don't remember what it's called—and we can take sort of a screenshot. Then we can print it upstairs."

"Sooo high tech." I grinned. "I could spend hours down here." *More like hours with you.*

The upturn of her lips caused the hair on the nape of my neck to rise. As she finished her coffee with a gentle slurp, I imagined how sweet those lips must be from the amount of sugar she used.

She said slowly, "Well...so, I was wondering if you could help me."

I rested a hand on hers. "You name it."

"I have a million tasks on my Save the Library list. One is to dig through our archives and try to find something to support me putting in an application with the National Register of Historic Places."

"That's smart. What are we looking for?"

"That's the kicker. Anything. Something about the building or land that would qualify it for legal protection."

I skimmed the criteria listed on a webpage she pulled up on her phone. Association with significant events, persons, and a lot more historical jargon.

"It's a long process. I gotta get the ball rolling now."

"Then consider me yours for a few days. I can talk with the historical society, too?"

She scrunched her face. "Miriam's friends are there. They're no help."

After we cleaned up, I leaned in close again. "Dinner tonight?"

"I'd love to, but I need to get home to my mom."

"Walk tomorrow? Show me sights? And we can check in on all this after I do some digging online?"

She nibbled her lower lip. "Sure."

We closed the storage room and climbed a different stairwell to the main floor. I followed her, eyeing the swish of her bottom with each step.

I picked up my pace to walk beside her. "Pretty art," I said, trying in vain to distract myself from thinking about her bottom, curvy hips, and the sculpted thighs in her skinny jeans. *Chill, man.*

I stopped walking to focus on a random watercolor, ushering all that horny energy away with willpower. It had been too long. Far too long.

A garden scene. White picket fence. Old country house. My breath caught from the nearness of Helen and my racing thoughts.

"Thanks. All local artists," she said with a glance over her shoulder.

The painting in front of me was signed M.H.

Thirteen

Helen

"Helen! Hey, Helen!" a voice called from the library parking lot.

I spun around as the neighboring First Congregational Church bell tolled seven times. It was Tuesday and I'd gone home to check on Mom before returning for my meeting with the Capital Building Committee. "Hi, Rohana."

Waiting for her to reach me, I crouched to pluck a weed poking through a sidewalk crack. The town could spend fifteen thousand dollars to hire a team to re-assess the safety of a traffic light—which didn't need replacement—but couldn't budget the expenses for edging, weed treatment, and pest control here. I had run out of sighs. Mom, Nan, and Lorraine led a group of friends to come help with some of it at least.

"Glad I ran into you." Enviable dark hair bounced on Rohana's shoulders with a nod and a huff as she caught her breath. The humidity never affected her silky waves the way it blew mine into a round frizzball in summer. She came closer, lowering her voice. "I need to talk to you."

She held my gaze with her usual direct focus. The kind that peeled back the layers of guilt and grief I'd built up over the years like a seasoned cast-iron skillet. In a way, she *had* seen right into me, when I went to see her on my mom's insistence and to my utter embarrassment. And I, um, ran. Blamed my busy schedule.

I had never mentioned the letters to the psychologist, but we discussed my pain associated with Adalyn, the baby, Wes, and even caregiving for Mom. Just my luck, Dr. Reddy—or as she said in our first session, "Call me Rohana"—had recently received an appointment by the town moderator—good ol' Miriam—to the Finance Committee. Talk about awkward.

Rohana sputtered, "M-Miriam's setting you up to fail. You can't go to the committee with your requests."

"Why not?" I wiggled my fingers in my pocket, ready to pop an antacid. "How do you know what I'm requesting, anyway?"

"Your board minutes are public record. Miriam asks me to review all the boards' meeting minutes. Listen, she's already gotten to the Capital Building Committee. Jacobs, Elmsworth, and even Hecksley."

"Hecksley?" My hope sank.

"They're going to not only turn you down but use your request to support the argument that the building needs to be shut down, and the proposed regional library is more beneficial."

"That's asinine. I have a leaky roof! They didn't balk when the fire station needed roof repairs last year. The roofing company did a shoddy job replacing our roof. If you remember, the Capital Building Committee approved the company, not me. Those useless decorative things"—I hitched a thumb toward the roof—"have rotted beneath. I cannot—will not—have water falling on my books, carpets, or patrons! And I can't have the HVAC on the roof potentially falling through and hurting somebody."

"Exactly. It's a danger. Thus, their stance."

"Give me a break. This is their *job*. To keep buildings up to code."

Rohana's thick eyebrows knitted together. "You're preaching to the choir. But this is exactly why Miriam thinks it needs to be shut down."

I caved, took an antacid. "Over a roof?" With the nervous hand lodged in my jeans pocket, I finger-thumbed the antacid roll while crunching on the one in my mouth. "The other buildings in town get paid their due respect, get the proper upgrades. Why can't I get mine?"

She rested her hand on my forearm. "I'm telling you what I've heard, and what I know. Go in there with your demands. Make them listen. I'll do my best to keep the Finance Committee neutral."

I breathed through my nose. "Thanks, Rohana. I appreciate it."

"Be careful."

"I will."

Rohana's dark eyes went to the pocket that held my fidgeting hand. "You doing okay? With your mom and all?"

"We're good. We're both good."

The jerks denied all my requests. I grumbled under my breath, not paying attention to where I was walking, and smacked into Gifty's son.

"Oof." His notebook thumped to the worn carpet near the circulation desk.

"Oh, Evans. So sorry. How are you?"

He picked up the notebook which had *Algebra I* scribbled on the cover. I almost cringed, remembering I had promised Gifty I'd check into tutoring options for him. I owed her. She was a lifesaver.

"Good," he said. "My mom said you have a chess club here?"

"Yes. They meet on Saturday mornings, every other week. This week is an 'on' week. Ten a.m. in the Hawthorne room downstairs. No need to register. Drop in."

"Okay, great."

I pointed to his notebook. "Algebra isn't fun, is it? Never could wrap my head around all the expressions and inequalities. Don't get me started on exponents."

He scuffed a sneaker, half holding my gaze. "Yeah."

"There's a boy in the chess club, Todd. He loves math." I left my statement open-ended. His eyes lit with understanding. Good. Gotta let teens think something is their idea.

A bright look as beautiful as Gifty's crossed his face. "Thanks, Miss Wright."

I crossed my arms, pleased with myself. "No problem."

Evans scurried down the wide stairs, a lightness in each step.

Chess.

That was my answer. I had to anticipate Miriam's next moves. I scratched my head, trying to remember the rules of the game Dad taught me as a kid.

Open with smart moves. That strategy wouldn't work. I was in too deep to reflect on my mistakes.

Don't give away pieces unless you have a plan. No way could I sacrifice one for the good of the whole. Miriam would get none of my pieces!

Adapt. The opponent will always counter move, foiling your plans. How could I evaluate and adapt?

Corner and attack the king—or queen. Miriam and Howe. It took more than one piece to succeed in checkmate. I'd need to gather my team. Now that, I could do.

Lastly, always protect your king. Never let your guard down.

I rubbed two fingers together, chewing on that idea.

Time to move a pawn with my budget suggestions.

Renewed hope filled me as I returned to my office to finish work.

My phone pinged, and I nearly jumped out of my seat. An unexpected eagerness surged in my belly at Gabe's text.

Walk this evening?

Rain check? Blood drive this afternoon and I need to box up books for the monthly book sale this weekend.

Tomorrow?

Yes.

Can I help with the books?

It's not exciting.

What was I doing? Turning down help? Turning down handsome, friendly help...

Yes, yes I was.

Gifty offered to stay later tonight so I could put in a few hours at the library this evening. Before the blood drive and book boxing began, I left at three for a quick stop by the senior center with food for their supplemental nutrition program. I was too familiar with living on a fixed income.

Wilma welcomed me at the desk. "Hiya, Helen. What do you have for us this week?"

I held up one of the bags. "I'll be canning some soup soon. Got you raspberry jam, and of course, zuke mash. Plus, zucchini bread. Loaves of whole grain bread from Barb and fresh cheese from Coop. Veggies from the garden, too."

We made small talk for a little while, then I saw myself into the kitchen. My spine straightened when I heard the click-clack of familiar heels in the corridor.

I poked a nose around the corner of the kitchen entrance to see Miriam walking into the common room across the hall.

Miriam settled in a seat next to her grandmother. Serafina Prescott had to be pushing ninety-five. Miriam placed a spray of daisies beside her and took her hand affectionately. She pulled the quilt on Serafina's lap closer to her chest and refilled her grandmother's water bottle.

Tenderness filled Miriam's face as the two spoke. She fussed over her grandmother, and I swear Miriam's rosy cheeks seemed rosier. This was not the Miriam I knew who put on a show for any and all. This wasn't another front, an actress lathering on the empty promises for a vote or favor. It was private, it was real. I won't lie and say my mouth didn't hang open there for a long moment before I snapped it shut. Even villains could have a soft side.

Sometimes Serafina mistook me for my namesake, my grandmother. She'd once said something to me about a guy named Walter, then called me a trollop.

I was about to leave when I spied Roberta Prescott's entrance from another doorway on the far side of the common room. She tsked at Miriam as soon as she came upon her.

"Why did you bring her daisies? You know she's allergic." Roberta grabbed the bouquet and promptly tossed it in a nearby trash can.

"She loves daisies, Mom," Miriam said, her voice faltering.

Serafina sneezed.

Roberta pushed past her daughter and wiped Serafina's nose with a tissue. "See? And look at you, Mir. Did you come from a rodeo? That studded shirt and—what is that atrocious thing? A belt?"

"I'm not on display." Despite saying it, Miriam glanced down at her attire, nonplussed.

"No, you are always *on*, dear. You're a Prescott. You're running for office. Every person you encounter could be a voter."

Miriam clenched manicured nails into fists at her sides.

Even in comfort clothes of stylish jeans, complete with her signature heels, she looked pristine and put together to me. If her mother thought this outfit was bad, what would she think of yoga pants or sweats?

"If your father could see you now...well, I'm just glad he can't." Roberta continued to chide her daughter, and my ears burned.

Time to go. I snuck out the rear exit.

I returned to the blood drive as the Red Cross was finishing with their final donors in our large conference room. The staff had set up beds and equipment along the walls, and the front area had chairs and desks. They worked like well-oiled machines here. I greeted the woman at the registration desk.

"Evening, Helen," Shelley said. "We're almost done. Help yourself to a snack at the refreshment table."

"Thanks. How was it today?"

"Good. People love it when you host a drive here. They've got books to read." She shuffled around the table, stacking papers and putting away pens and clipboards. "A few whole bloods to finish and then we'll be out of your hair."

My quick assessment counted three people left, all in various stages of donation. Aside from Mack, munching away on pretzels in the refreshment area, one reclined on a bed, squeezing a sponge ball in her hand, and another sat with his back to me.

Mack held up his apple juice in greeting. "Mademoiselle!"

I waved. "Hey, Mack. How are you?" I fell into the chair next to his, and for the life of me felt the breath whoosh out. I didn't question why I was feeling drained.

"Good. Going for the club. Tried to convince Louie to come, but he faints when he sees blood."

"The club?" I untwisted a cap from a water bottle and sipped the refreshing cold contents.

"The twenty-four club. They're only doing whole blood donations here. I usually donate platelets every two weeks at the main branch in Worcester. I like the ease of coming here, though."

"Wish I could donate."

"Why can't you?"

"Well, first off, I hate needles." Mom and I shared that excuse, lame as it was. "But I've worked through the fear. I don't watch, so it loses the queasy factor." My gaze darted back to Mack after a microsecond's glance at blood bags and vials that were being organized by the phlebotomists and techs. *Don't look.* Like my fear of heights. "I'm anemic, too. Vitamin supplements help, but I've never made the cut when they do the iron prick of my finger. I mean, if it's here, why not try to donate? But I haven't passed that first screening any time I did."

He slurped juice and waggled his eyebrows. "Good for you for trying." He withdrew a handkerchief from his pocket and dabbed at his mustache and mouth. "You do so much already for the community, Helen. I've heard through the grapevine about the upcoming town meeting. Don't let them bully you."

"I won't."

"Leah used to be like you. Hating needles. Except for sewing needles."

"I loved having her help with the bake sales."

He blinked wistful eyes and cleared his throat as he tossed his wrapper in a trash can and the apple juice bottle into the recycle bin. "Heart of gold." He slid his Homburg hat on.

"Have a good evening, Mack."

"You, too, mademoiselle." He nodded goodbye and shuffled away with his cane.

As I sat pondering Mack's late wife and his likely reason for being a donor—Leah's own illness and hospitalizations—a hand slid upon my shoulder and gave me a soft squeeze. "Hey."

Too spent to be startled, I turned to see Gabe. "Hey. Whatcha doing here?"

He sat next to me while rolling down his sleeve, then reached for a box of raisins and a water bottle. "You mentioned a blood drive. I'm a regular donor. I found a time slot on the app."

Ah, so he was the man across the room with his back to me. I should have recognized the well-formed muscles in his signature plaid shirt.

He's a blood donor. Of course he is. These brownie points were getting out of hand. I wanted to hate this man who ripped my heart out and exposed it to the world.

I liked him instead.

My mouth hung open. I covered it with a partially fake yawn. "Excuse me."

"Do you still have books to box up?"

"A bazillion or so to move to the downstairs sale room."

"I can help. Can't lift heavy boxes until tomorrow, but I'd be happy to sort, move things around short of heavy lifting."

"Sure. I'd love that. We have a cart and an elevator."

I said "sure" a lot to Gabe this week. This *sure* was purely heartfelt.

I was in trouble.

Fourteen

Gabe

I arrived fifteen minutes early for our walk the next day and found my signature apology rolling off my lips. "Sorry. I'm always early or late."

"No worries. I'm almost done." Helen dropped the last box into a corner behind the register in the book sale room.

"You seem more awake today. I was thinking maybe I should come here with a turbo-charged coffee."

"Har, har, no turbo anything for me today." As we walked to her car, she added, "It was a good night."

I couldn't help but hope that implied her time with me, too.

Last night, we'd worked on sorting books, moving in a quiet, comfortable rhythm. I'd hold them up, she'd say yes or no or give the cutest face of dismay, especially when I held up one falling out of its bindings. It was nice to just be, to enjoy the time together. I didn't realize until this week how much I missed companionship. With Marco in Atlanta, I hardly socialized other than at writing conferences or book signings or at the Thrive Center. Bars weren't much my thing either.

Eventually, she couldn't stifle her yawns, and I'd encouraged her to go home last night.

Now, as she drove, Helen said, "Where would you like to walk?"

"You pick."

"How about the local rail trail? There are ponds, a Bigfoot sign, and a carved-out section with twenty-foot rock walls. In winter, the ferns and mosses all over them are frozen beneath gigantic icicles. Wicked big."

Icicles? My pulse pumped. Those were in the letters. I crinkled an eyebrow. "Bigfoot?"

She tsked. "Here I thought the icicles would intrigue you."

"Seeing as it's fall, Bigfoot caught my attention first." Okay, that was a fib.

"You're the reporter and haven't heard about our own personal Sasquatch?"

I leaned in, daringly closer to her, but not too close to disturb her driving but close enough to disturb myself. I breathed in her scent. Strawberries today. I bet it was her shampoo or hand lotion. She didn't seem like a perfume type of woman.

"We've even got documented sightings. We call him Eddie."

I couldn't tell if she was joking or not.

"Check the history room." A long breath, then she giggled, unable to hold a straight face.

"You had me for a second."

She blinked at me, her eyes shimmering with humor. "Fatigue makes me giddy. Okay, Eddie isn't real. Instead, there's this giant life-size cutout of a Bigfoot along the trail.

Somebody put it there for fun. Quirky hallmarks in small towns."

"Can't wait to see it. Hey, speaking of small towns, I haven't found anything useful for your Historical Register application yet, but I'll keep looking online after I leave."

Leave. I had to leave. Already. This sucked. "I am, however, thoroughly in the know of who is on what committee and what each board or committee does. Found most of that on the town website. Fascinating."

"More like frustrating."

"That, too. I shifted my focus to reading about the town in the nineteenth century, since we need something old and significant." I paused when she very quietly sighed in frustration. Fighting the impulse to squeeze her knee, I instead rubbed my knuckles against my thigh. "Something will turn up."

"Hope so."

"So, tell me more about Eddie."

She pulled over to an empty parking area that could accommodate four cars. As she explained Eddie's legend, we approached a trailhead sign. I eyed the map of an interconnected rail trail system spanning five towns. Between Adalyn and the rail trail with icicles... I'd hit two on my list of details from M.H.'s letters. And though M.H. didn't strike me as an artist—but her mother was, per her letter—there was the signed artwork at the library with the same initials. Not to mention what I felt in my bones. Sanders Mill was *the town*.

"This way." She pointed right, and we set out on our walk.

I slipped along a loose patch of the trail. A scattering of rocks rolled into one of the flanking drainage ditches as I regained my balance. Helen linked her arm with mine. Prickles rose on my neck at our connection. "Two left feet."

She looked down at my shoes. "I see one right, one left," she repeated from our first meeting. "The trail gets slippery this time of year with leaves and mud after a rainstorm."

Helen squeezed my forearm and slowly released her arm from mine now that I was steadier. Maybe I needed to fake falling so she would hold my hand again. I almost snorted at the inane idea.

After a few minutes of walking in silence, we paused at a granite bench before the large, lake-like pond. I scanned the deep blue water speckled with lily pads and pondweeds. Building equipment hummed, the sounds echoing from the clear-cut area off the western shoreline.

"Wow. I haven't been here in ages." A puff of breath formed before her in the crisp air. She tossed a pebble that skipped across the water, leaving little dings of ripples in its wake. "Used to be all trees." She shook her head and crossed her arms. "Even the land around the trail is no longer considered sacred to Howe Builders. I don't object to people moving to the area, but if we could have town-houses or more affordable senior housing rather than Mc-Mansions with huge lawns that take down so many trees. We have an excellent school district, accessible community services, and we're not too far from the MetroWest area."

M.H.'s letters mentioned building happening near the rail trail. Could I be standing where M.H. had once stood? Or still came to?

My googling the other day firmed up my theory: Adalyn from the letters was likely Adalyn Foster, a young woman who died seven years ago "after a brief illness." I suspected the memorial at the library had been erected for her. She had a small digital footprint, so I wasn't absolutely certain, but my findings all seemed to point toward Sanders Mill.

Helen stepped closer to me. She pointed diagonally across the pond, her face near my shoulder. "See, there, around that tree?"

"Yes?" I drew even closer to her, pretending to move because of the tree's obstruction of my view. The whiff of her hair shot right to my stomach and, err, lower.

"The library's a half mile west, beyond that clear-cut area." She pulled back, the heat rising from her body replaced by a whoosh of cold as she inched away. "Soon, what drew people to this rural area will no longer exist. If the state park and conservation lands weren't protected, Howe would probably be building on them as well."

Words got lodged in my throat. My heart squeezed, and my fingers, for once, did not itch to write it down. Why did I find myself wordless around her? I shook my head as if to dislodge my stupor. *Because all your blood is flowing to other parts of your body.* Even now, I was wondering if the cold would offer another excuse to snuggle with her.

She skittered another stone on the glassy water as a pair of women jogged past us. With a loud exhalation, she dropped onto the granite bench.

"I liked your local pieces the best," she said.

"My local pieces?" I came over to sit beside her, mindful of my footing on the loose dirt slope so I didn't fall on my butt.

"On your website. I read all your articles. Seeing all this here"—she gestured to the clear-cut area—"reminds me of some of your stories. You highlighted eye-opening environmental and cultural injustices all over the world while also capturing the beauty of the people and land. My favorite was 'Ghost Towns of the Quabbin Reservoir.' It hits home. Quabbin isn't far from here."

Her favorite.

"The story always intrigued me." She rubbed her arms. "Your highlight piece gave me shivers. The part about the libraries rehoming thousands of their books to other towns...I felt that, ya know?"

It was still sinking in. "You've read my work?" And it gave her shivers?

She knocked her shoulder into mine. "Of course. Had to read about the world-famous author coming. I do my research, too."

"Thanks. Means a lot to me." I nudged the toe of my sneaker against a scraggly root. "It's one of my favorite by-lines, too. When I was a kid, we visited Quabbin Reservoir, and my mom told me about the four towns that were flooded making the reservoir. It horrified me. I don't care if people were given restitution. These were century-old homes, factories, mills, churches, whole towns...all gone because Boston needed more drinking water. Some streets were at a high enough elevation that a few structures remain. Cellar foundations, rock walls, a town common. Former roads are now trails. Eminent domain hasn't disappeared. Maybe it's on a smaller scale now, but an assault like that could still happen today, just as it did eighty years ago. And the scars are felt to the present."

Machines and equipment droned on the far hill, grinding away nature's simplicity.

Helen nodded. "We boast about being a farming community, but we have half the farms we did fifty years ago. My family's homestead used to be a working farm, but it's been decades since we plowed our last field. We're not literally sinking because of waterways being dammed up, but regional conglomerates boom and replace the rest of us." Anger flared in her blinking eyes.

"I'm sorry."

She sniffed as a breeze swirled past and twirled dried leaves. "Sorry. I'm stuck in my head these days. This 'village development' stuff just takes over."

"I know how that is." A long moment passed. "The Quabbin piece took a lot of digging. Finding the story within the story. I didn't travel far for that one, but it pushed me personally farther."

She poked my knee. "You did a good job. Your digging paid off. Like that interview with the woman, one of the last surviving residents of the town of Enfield, who made a trip to revisit it every year. How she sometimes wakes up in her nursing home thinking she's a little girl, asleep in her bed in the valley."

She leaned over and picked up a smooth, bright pink rock, then held it out for me to see the red heart at the center. "Kindness rocks. They're all over the place. A local scouts group paints them." She traced her index finger over the heart. "You've traveled a lot. Do you have a favorite place?"

Instead of my usual canned answer that I loved every place I've visited, I said, "Guatemala. I traveled into the Highlands—I saw volcanoes, rainforests, Mayan ruins, and a hillside washed out by a waterfall. It's stuck with me. I visited a preschool where they taught Spanish to Mayan children who grew up speaking Quiche. I spent two weeks working with a nonprofit that runs a health clinic and preschool. They're working to empower the Mayan people to run the place without outside organizations and help, eventually. I dug out a driveway, restored a roof, painted furniture, tiled a kitchen. I know, you're wondering how I managed on the roof."

She tutted while fidgeting with the kindness rock. "No, I wasn't. You're too hard on yourself." She looked at me, the rock going still in her hands. "I was wondering if there's anything you haven't done."

"Oh, plenty." *Like kiss you.*

"What did you like best about Guatemala?"

I gave her question some thought. "I loved the people the most. Sure, the scenery was indescribable. But the people used what resources they had. Corn grew in every available fertile spot—and I mean every; whether it was an alley or two square feet between shed and farm stand, if they had soil to plant, there were cornstalks. Oh, and the markets. I've never met a more kind, generous people."

Memory whisked me away. "Rene, our guide and interpreter, was hilarious." I found myself whispering the rest of it, as if saying it aloud would take away the memories somehow. "The eight-year-old girl carrying her baby brother on her back. And the other kids that gathered around and wanted to play with us. I just loved the children. And the trucks loaded beyond capacity with twenty people in the bed traveling up a winding road to the hillside. Or three people squeezed together riding a motorbike. Chicken buses."

"Chicken buses?"

"Old, colorful school buses. They didn't use turn signals. Instead, a guy hung off the side of the bus to indicate turning." I grinned as the images whizzed through my mind, so vivid that I saw them instead of the pond.

"So, you went there for a service project? Not for an article?"

"Another friend suggested I join his service team. Gerard." I scrubbed a hand on my chin, realizing I hadn't seen Gerard in a long time. "He works construction and spends all his vacation hours doing service and emergency relief projects. He nagged me to death until I agreed to go. So I went. I'm supposed to be savvy with words, but I've never written about that experience. I kept a journal. Sounds corny, but it almost felt too personal to share in an article."

Too personal to share. How hypocritical. Caught up in how M.H.'s intimate words touched me and inspired me, I shared too much of her with the world.

That fact pulled me out of myself like a vacuum that sucked up a marble. Woosh. Clattering around in the canister, a jarring reminder of what I'd done.

"What a story. How could you *not* write something so moving? Your writing is...good, Gabe. I'd love to hear about all of it. Especially the Mayan ruins. I was supposed to see them with a friend...but uh, plans changed." Her voice had turned so soft, as if pained to say the words.

"I'm sorry about that." I squeezed her knee.

She pressed her lips together. "Thanks."

We sat for a long moment.

I usually brushed such accolades off, but from her, it felt like it meant something. Helen was different. "Want to see photos?"

"Yes, please."

She leaned in close, hip against hip, and if my hands had not been holding the phone, I'd have scooped one around her waist to draw her even closer.

"You'd love the coffee. I brought ten pounds back with me and got flagged at customs." I inhaled as if I could smell the roasted blend.

I swiped through images. "There's Gerard in a three-wheeled, motorized rickshaw. They're called tuk-tuks," I explained to her. My chest filled with delight as I saw my friend laughing, dressed in his bright yellow shirt and white painter's pants, in a photo of the kitchen we tiled. I vowed to give Gerard a call soon and invite him for dinner.

All this traveling left me empty, with hardly time for friends or a girlfriend. I wasn't exactly a digital nomad, but seeing the world was lonely when you did it solo.

"You're an amazing photographer. It's like I can smell those flowers and the coffee, hear the kids laughing, feel the wind off the lake. Maybe one day I'll get away from this cramped corner of the world and away from small-town drama."

"You will. And everything will work out for you and the library, Helen. I feel it. You'll make it happen. *Ut'z Ipetik.*"

Her eyes glowed. "What's that mean?"

"*All is good,* in Quiche. All will be okay."

She repeated the phrase. "All is good. I like that. Now to believe it."

I slid the phone into my pocket, but neither of us stood.

"I try to find the hope even in hard times. My mom's health issues remain a mystery, but I love her resilience."

"Her care sounds like a full-time job on top of your other full-time job."

A cloud darkened her expression. "She used to paint and draw all the time. Sometimes I think if I could get her out more, go on a trip to see her favorites—Monet or other Impressionists—it would help her. This disease is filled with uncertainty, and I know it's possible that she'll stay at this stage forever, but both of us have hope. The art I showed you in the library, some of it was hers."

"Oh? Which ones?" I tried to hide my eagerness.

"The garden one we passed in the stairwell, for starters."

That garden scene had been signed M.H., but the signature held a different slant and curve than the M.H. from the letters. "I didn't see any signed *Wright.* She doesn't go by Wright?"

"She signs under her given name, Mary Hadley. She and Dad divorced a few years ago, though she always used her birth name professionally. She's made a few prints of her art, and she sells stationery to local stores, too."

The stationery.

Holy. Smokes. There were way too many coincidences for these to not all be related. Art, stationery, initials, the icicle rail trail, Adalyn...

Quakes of intuition shot down my spine. Was Mary Hadley my mysterious Emma? *Not so fast, Gabe.*

Though Marco had "found" them a few years ago, he never elaborated on how old they were. Did he discover them stuck behind a cabinet from decades before, lodged in the shadows with dust bunnies? Did they get caught in the track of an old filing drawer? Lucas seemed to have hit a wall with dating the paper.

But M.H. mentioned GIFs and memes and a Ryan Gosling infatuation. So that letter couldn't have been written before the 2000s. And to be honest, I couldn't imagine many women in their sixties writing those things. The references, the tone, the voice...all were recent. The paper was in decent condition, frayed, but not brown. Though the dead letters had no time stamp, my gut and the few facts I had told me they were written recently, within the past decade. And M.H.'s mother was the artist, unless M.H. also dabbled in it?

Time to call Marco again. No more postulating. I needed all the information that existed.

I shifted uncomfortably, the cold hardness of the granite seat getting to me. Helen must've misunderstood my movement as something else, because she leaned in closer and laced her fingers in mine.

A pendulum swung in my mind.

I needed to find M.H., beg forgiveness, do whatever it took to make amends. After that...I admitted to myself that, however stupid it was, part of me hoped she wouldn't send me out the door as soon as I did. I was intrigued by her, inspired by her...even infatuated with her. Not real love, but admiration. Even empathy. But, I had to admit, nothing deeper. For all I'd learned from her letters, I didn't truly know her. If I had real empathy for her, maybe I wouldn't have used those letters in the first place.

Meanwhile, a kind, intelligent, beautiful, and layered woman sat beside me. And I liked her. A lot. She was also hella sexy. I wondered if her passion carried over into other areas of her personal life...

I squeezed her hand in mine. Helen's proximity added to my foggy brain. She unraveled my guilt and elicited desire. I swallowed, my heart racing as I tucked a strand of her soft hair behind an ear. Something I had wanted to do since our first meeting. She let me, her chin angled up as we faced each other, a tremulous smile parting pink lips. Our surroundings blurred. All I saw was her.

"Bummed to be leaving tomorrow," I said.

"We had a good time though."

"Promise me something." My gaze lowered to a birthmark on her neck, then rose back to her awaiting eyes.

"Promise you what?"

"Pumpkins," I blurted.

Her oh-so-serious expression cracked. She blinked over a puzzled grin. "Pumpkins?"

"Promise me we'll see the pumpkins when I return. Not the Great Pumpkin, but the smashed pumpkins. The pumpkin smash-fest," I clarified. A sweet-as-honey woman sat inches from me with the cutest upturned lips that aroused all my senses. My attention was like a pen connecting the dots of freckles across her heart-shaped face. And I was talking about pumpkins. I was such a dope.

She visibly swallowed, rays of silver sparkling in her pale blue eyes. I could get lost in them.

"You're coming back?" she asked.

My reason for returning wasn't only to continue my search for M.H. "I'd like to see you again. And I want to keep helping you dig for that historical nugget you need to save the library."

There's something about you, I wanted to say.

She whispered, "I'd like that, too."

Now or never, Gabe.

With a hand on her lower back, wishing it were touching bare skin and not layers of shirt and puffy vest, I slid closer to her so we didn't only touch at the thighs but melded together. I felt the immediate softening of her back into my hand. A chilly wind whipped across the pond, sending our hair flying. Her wild locks tickled my face as we drew closer. Closer. So close.

It was a slow-motion movie kiss. Forget about writing romance... It was time to *live* it. I loved squeezing her, wrapping arms fully around her. I skimmed her lips with mine, feeling the chill of the fall breeze upon her mouth. This, this was real. Not a fabrication of my mind. Not an infatuation with a writer of lost letters. As I deepened the kiss, every neuron in my body zapped me with jolts of desire.

She relaxed in my arms, the comfortable, secure intimacy like we had known each other for a lifetime instead of mere days. The tension and anticipation evaporated from my own shoulders as we embraced. She glided fingers to my shirt collar and the nape of my neck. Goose bumps rippled across my skin with her touch. I threaded one of my hands through her locks, wishing to inhale her fragrance, but too focused on the feel of her lips. She parted them more, and my tongue eagerly explored, wanting all of her. My head spun. It was as if she'd painted her lips with a drug that overwhelmed all my senses.

My other hand dipped down to slide under the hem of her vest and sweater, and I traced fingers along her spine, beneath the layers of clothing. Her skin was supple, and my fingers wanted more. So much more. Wanted to bring her back to the inn with me, lay her on the quilt and kiss the tender skin behind her knees, drip kisses down her belly...

I needed the moment to last longer. Much longer. I kissed the birthmark I'd been eyeing a moment before. She purred under my touch.

Footsteps, paws, and a jingle of a dog leash approached from farther up the pebbly trail. I drew away from her like a reluctant iron nail from a magnet, feeling downright dizzy.

We fixed our tousled hair. Uh, how had that happened? Oh yes, my hands. I could still feel the smoothness of her hair on my fingertips.

Without a word, we rose to walk back to the car, hand in hand, my mind a tumultuous spin and my gait lighter even as my heart was heavy. How could I leave Sanders Mill and Helen tomorrow when my entire being screamed not to?

"When will you return?" she asked.

I was glad she couldn't see the color heating the tips of my ears. "A few weeks? Hopefully in time to see the farm with the pumpkin trebuchets firsthand."

"You really have a thing for those pumpkins."

"Not just a thing for pumpkins."

She squeezed my hand. "The foliage will be peak, too."

I squeezed back. *You've already got me* piqued, *Helen.*

All I wanted was to stay here with Helen, kiss her, hold her longer, and enjoy the heck out of whatever this was. Damn right I'd be back. As fast as I possibly could.

Fifteen

Helen

Finding joy.

The theme of tonight's yoga class—which Kayley had dragged me back to after my hiatus the past month—seemed fitting. If only I could stay in that happy place, or at least in the room with my classmates in our flexible poses. My mind wandered to the library conundrum, not focused on my downward dog.

How was I in such an asinine battle? Instead of stewing, I assigned the players in the Library Saga to chess pieces. I probably had the game on my mind because Mom and I were re-learning it the past few nights. It was good for her neurologically and good for my anxiety.

Howe—king.

Miriam—queen.

Planning Board and ad hoc committee—pawns.

Craig Browning—knight.

Finance Committee—bishops.

Select Board—rooks.

Chantelle, the instructor, continued, "Deep breath in for six, out for five…"

I flowed through the sun salutation, each round quickening through the poses from mountain to a final downward dog. My abs would hate me tomorrow. This is what I got for skipping a few weeks. Did anyone even like planks? I exhaled my negative energy.

Kayley exaggerated her breaths, fully engaged in the moment. She cradled her gorgeous pregnant belly while doing modified poses. Back to standing, she had the Madonna-and-child thing going on, hand over heart, hand under abdomen. Earlier this evening she'd moaned about being a sausage stuck in leggings. I thought she looked divine.

Though I appreciated the physical rigor of yoga, my mind never emptied to reach a calm state. Instead, tabling my chess analogy, it propelled me back to the walk on the rail trail with Gabe. Thinking about him was certainly more pleasant than the library shitshow. Maybe embarrassingly pleasant…my cheeks grew hot… Thankfully, everyone else's eyes were closed in meditation.

Oh, that red-hot kiss.

His hands tracing a circle on my lower back.

Fingers threading through my hair.

On to tree pose…

I found a spot on the sunlit hardwood floor, dappled with leaf shadows, to concentrate on. Chantelle spoke in a low, nurturing voice. My lazy eyes shifted to an unfocused gaze ahead of me as I lifted my heel to my thigh. I lurched, losing balance, and started over with a huff.

Next to me, Kayley was sitting with her legs out, wiggling her toes. Her pedicure was cute, pink with blue spots. I didn't have swollen feet either during my pregnancy.

Cravings, morning sickness, bleeding, high-risk ultra-sounds, uncertainty, and then the worst twenty hours ever.

My lips trembled. Happy thoughts, happy...

Gabe. Joy. I was focusing on joy. Dammit, yes I was. His kiss certainly held promise. Butterfly wings flapped in my stomach, blood drained from my extremities, and warmth pooled in my chest. Perhaps this was joy?

I yawned, still tired from a late phone call with him last night.

My brain felt whiplashed from thinking about the library, my grief, and Gabe. Our calls were nice. Too nice. And that kiss...

You're infatuated with the man who stole your letters.

I listened to the birdsong and waves of Chantelle's meditation music.

A different flush filled my cheeks. Not from the heat of attraction, but from my brewing anger at allowing myself to fall for him.

My chest tightened. Couldn't Chantelle crack open a dang window? The spicy scent of her natural oil infuser suddenly lost its intended purpose just as I lost my balance in tree position.

I rubbed my fist against my chest, trying to work the knot out of it. *Let the anger go. Open your mind to forgiveness and understanding. Maybe there's a reason he stole the letters. There's always a reason. Or maybe I am wrong about it*—though that option was losing traction. At this point, even though I hadn't drawn out a confession or concrete proof, my heart told me it was true: he had used my letters.

Ugh! Back to joy.

His lips: delicious. His words: thoughtful. His touch: soulful. At the memories, my knees buckled, and I pretended it was my poor balance again.

We flowed through warrior positions, bridge, and boat. How did these poses get their names? *There, think about yoga. Nothing else.*

At the end of the hour, we settled into our final resting pose that Chantelle referred to as the cherry on top—savasana. Also called "death" or "corpse" pose... I tried not to stare at the cracks in the ceiling as I released the tension from my toes to my head.

Fifteen minutes later, my muscles loosened and my mind far from being clear or rejuvenated, we sat in a coffee shop at the far end of North Prouty. With a spin of a plastic spoon, my caramel macchiato's tiers of white and brown merged, going against the entire point of the layered drink.

"Helen..." Kayley said.

"Mmm?"

"You've been stirring so vigorously, I'm afraid a tornado may pop out. What's up?"

I blushed, caught not paying attention to her latest update on her work project. "Sorry. I'm listening."

"Sure you are. It's okay. If I'm not talking about dolphins or sharks, Aaron's bored, too. Water microbes, filtration systems, and ecosystem breakthroughs don't excite everyone."

"You going to miss it? I mean, while on maternity leave?" I sipped my settled whirlpool.

"I'll go back in a year. I have great maternity leave."

"Did you decide on daycare or something else?" As a child, I hung out with Mom in the library a lot. Books were my babysitters.

"Aaron's had no luck shopping his tutoring start-up around, so he's going to be a stay-at-home daddy for a while until we figure out the moving parts of his plan."

"What about his job at the high school?"

"His time as the long-term math sub is almost over. That teacher is coming back from maternity leave soon."

"That's going to be fantastic, Kayley. He will love it." I tapped my spoon to a napkin. "Gabe mentioned a place called the Thrive Center. Have you heard of it? It's in Newton."

"Sounds familiar. What do they do?"

"Mentoring and tutoring youth. Might be worth a check. Maybe Aaron can pick their brains or something."

"Good idea. He's all about making connections. Let me guess, Mr. Dreamalicious volunteers there?"

I didn't even need to acknowledge it.

I glanced at the time on my cell phone for the sixth time.

"It's not going to grow legs and walk away. Tuck it back in your handbag." She flipped her coppery hair over a shoulder, then batted auburn eyelashes over mossy eyes that could see right through you.

She bit into her muffin. After swallowing, she said, "Your mom is fine. She's with friends. You know she enjoys her girl time."

"Yeah..." We carried on for another half hour about the home renovations Kayley was doing to make room for the baby's nursery, and her meddling mother-in-law. Kayley's energy was contagious as ever, and my troubles quieted themselves.

"Wanna see those carved pumpkins in a few weeks?" I asked. "The annual display on Braun Street?"

"Sure. Though I feel like I swallowed a pumpkin and by then..." Kayley rubbed her belly and made a pout. Her round face was fuller, drawing attention to the riot of freckles scattered across her nose and cheeks.

"You're beautiful."

She groaned. "Thanksgiving can't come soon enough. If I'm this big at seven months, I can't imagine nine."

The thought of that holiday stirred sadness within me. Adalyn died the day before Thanksgiving. Even seven years later, it was hard to celebrate in her absence. The Hadley and Foster Thanksgiving feasts ended abruptly that year. Her parents moved away. Chapters of my life closed forever.

Kayley looped an arm through mine as we walked across the parking lot.

"I can't wait to meet your little pumpkin," I told her.

"Forget pumpkin. This baby is going to be a turkey by the time they arrive."

I forced a laugh. At least the upcoming birth gave me something to look forward to during the Thanksgiving gloom. Maybe holding a baby again would create new memories.

Maybe Gabe would come this year. He said he was going to return soon, but for how long?

"You going to tell me about it?"

"What?" I asked, innocently.

"You avoided all talk of him tonight."

Thank goodness for a dark evening to cover the pink creeping into my cheeks. I clicked my key fob, and we got in my car, Kayley mumbling under her breath. A car had parked too close beside us.

"I can't exactly walk sideways and suck in my gut. What a jack-o-lantern-hole."

I coughed on a laugh. "That's a new one."

"Festive. Okay, Miss Wright who is always right. You're not getting out of this. Drive as fast as you want. I'm not hauling this booty out of the car until you spill. I gave you all night to wallow and ponder. I need more deets. Gabe.

Mr. Sexy Voice. And all his other good tally points, which you've told me about at length." She snorted and waved her cell phone in her hand. "Should I read them off to you?"

"No." I rolled my eyes, though she had a point. I had sent her my list of his pros and cons, and yes, it was in bullet-point format. "What more do you want to know? It's all there."

"What about you, girl? How are you feeling? I don't want lists. I want truths. Do you feel ready to forgive him yet? Or are we back to kicking his nuts? And how is he doing with his penance?"

"Hold up. Too many questions! Forgive him? I thought I was confirming that he really did this and, uh, I was leading him to admitting it?" I had been laying breadcrumbs for him to discover my own identity, either subconsciously or consciously. I wasn't sure.

"Yes, that too."

I exhaled a reluctant breath. "Does kissing him count toward forgiveness?"

She swatted my shoulder as I drove. "You did not! You just sent me a list! *Deets*, please." She rubbed her hands together with a squeal.

I caved. "It was nice."

"Oh, girl, a guy that hot can't just be nice."

A flare of remembrance heated me down to my toes, even warmer than the air coming through the floor vents.

With a gloved hand, I wiped at the fogging windows, then shifted the air vents to defrost. "Bestseller-grade kiss. For real. Is that what you wanted to hear?" I almost snorted at the silly metaphor, then sighed. "People always leave."

Where had that come from? The coffee stung in my stomach, but this time I didn't reach for my antacids. Dad left. My daughter. Then Adalyn. I left, too. Even the former

Mom from my childhood was gone, too. Too much leaving. Too much loss.

Now Gabe. Though he said he'd be back.

"I'm sorry, Helen."

"But...he left. Needs to finish his tour. He probably won't come back."

"No buts allowed unless it's his butt. And, not everyone leaves," she said firmly. "Whatever his reason is for reading and using your letters...maybe it's forgivable." She paused with a wistful sigh. "Maybe I'm a romantic. I believe in happy-ever-afters. Even with all the Miriam baloney, you're happier. Talk to him when he comes back. And he is coming back." She eyed my expression. "And, he's no dummy. He'll figure it out. Either way, you can't start a relationship with a secret hanging over you two."

"A relationship?" I rubbed my nose. My eyes were watery and not from the blasting defrost. "What happened to confronting him?"

"Girl, that ship sailed the moment you started hanging out with him. Have you been talking? Texting? Sexting?"

"God, Kayley."

"Hey, hormones."

"We text or talk daily."

She waggled her eyebrows suggestively.

"You're like Adalyn. Always a romantic."

"I'm sorry you lost her." She tilted her head toward me, seriousness rippling ridge lines in her forehead. "I believe we have people in our lives, sometimes for a moment, sometimes for phases, sometimes forever. I'm your Phase Two. I came to the library looking for those hard-to-find research articles, you worked your magic, and then I worked mine and dragged you off to yoga and lattes—"

"And the rest is history." I rubbed the back of my neck, my composure faltering.

Kayley softened her tone. "You didn't cause her death, Helen. You loved her and did all you could. That hellicious trip you two had in Mexico—her overdose or cry for help or whatever it was, the *Fast and Furious* ambulance ride and dealing with all that bullshit—that was a lot for you, Helen. I'm angry she did that to you. When she tried again here, back home, and you couldn't stop her that time—that's on her. Not you. Do not carry that burden."

I wiped a rogue tear.

Kayley continued. "Helen, you carry so much guilt over so many things. Your dad leaving? Not your fault. Your sweet daughter? Oh, honey, not your fault. There's nothing you could've done differently. Viruses suck, too. You can't stop your mom's illness. You *can* make her comfortable for however long. You're a helper. It's what you do. Think about what is, and is not, in your control. If it's not? Let it go. You're so task-driven, you forget the most important thing of all."

"What's that?"

"Yourself. Your soul. Things can wait. People can wait, but Helen needs to stop waiting. Self-care and all that song and dance."

"Somebody was listening to Chantelle tonight," I said.

"And—" She tapped her temple. "I see a future with Gabe. You and him. But it's up to you if you want to let him into your bubble."

"I've got a bubble now?"

"The invisible force field you have around yourself. You keep people at a distance. I get it. Superficial means no commitment, no emotional investment."

"You broke through the bubble."

"I'm persistent."

I loved Kayley's frankness. "Are you my shrink now?"

"Not a shrink. But I have the gift. My great-aunt was psychic. Said she had visions. I'm a Pisces, you know. We have psychic abilities." She looked at me, deadpan.

Then we burst out laughing, the cloud lifting from my churning mind.

Me and Gabe. A future? I chewed my lip. I couldn't see it in a clear vision, not if our relationship was based on lies or non-truths, but... Maybe. For now, all I could hope for was him returning for the pumpkin festival. It was too early to imagine something long-term, not if I didn't deal with the elephant in the room.

The letters.

Did he take them? And if so, why?

And could I forgive him?

If I did, would he pop my bubble?

To my baby Olivia

Taken.

Far too soon.

Summer fades into fall. A last trip to the beach to collect seashells. I can still feel the sand between my toes, the cold lapping of water against my ankles. I found some pretty pink sea glass just for you.

Leaves flutter to the ground. The beginning of a rainbow colors the trees. Cherry red, burnished orange, goldenrod yellow. I catch a leaf and twirl it in my hand. I walk through the old town cemetery down the road from the library, the crunch of leaves underfoot. How can I describe this smell to you? Your grandmother's gardens explode with ripe vegetables. The scent of tomato leaf oil clings to my fingers.

Cars drive down Main Street. The cafe overflows with energy and cinnamon fragrance. Pumpkin everything. Would you have loved the sweet, yummy goodness that is pumpkin pie? The mountain teems with activity. I take it all in with my new office view. It's so beautiful here.

But you're not here with me, as you should have been. You're not here to feel the sand, play with seashells, pick veggies with Grandma, or jump into a leaf pile.

You were tiny, cupped in my hands. Ten fingers, ten toes. My girl.

Our joy faded to heartache in an instant.

I ask myself—What did I do wrong?

When I returned to work and saw the smiling children, awaiting me with eager eyes and ears...all I saw was you, who you could have been. I saw you and me in the hospital, our first and last moment as mother and child. Everywhere I went, I couldn't stand to hear the laughs, couldn't stand to watch the mothers sharing sweet, affectionate moments with their children or hear them chatting about the sleepless nights and potty training. How could I continue a job surrounded by life that you and I would never be part of?

I had to get away from any reminders of you and take your spirit with me.

Now, the sunshine on fall foliage reminds me of your due date. Dew speckling curved leaves and long grasses, winds rustling. A silent awareness of the transience of life. When I should have been holding a newborn, I was holding sorrow.

I know I promised myself I would find the joy in each heartache, the light in the dark, and put it here...

Okay, I will try.

The first time we heard your heartbeat.

My cravings. If it was orange, I wanted it. Pumpkin, orange slices, crunchy carrots, even cheese curls with that fake powder that sticks to your fingers! Your daddy said you might come out with orange hair! Or be radioactive. Now I'm laughing. He was a nut.

Your daddy and I aren't together anymore, but I know he still loves you. Neither of us will ever forget you.

That first flutter of movement, before anyone could even see that I was pregnant.

The first few board books I got you. Because we knew reading would be in your genes! Then the kicks and rolls and hiccups. Olivia, how you loved to hiccup!

I'll stop there before I get sad again.

I love you, sweetheart.

M.H., your mother forever

Sixteen

Gabe

I called Marco. I had put off this conversation with him for far too long. Dread gurgled in my stomach.

My friend picked up on the third ring. "Hey, Gabe."

"You alone?"

"You caught up in the law, my famous friend?"

I cringed. "Uh, poor choice of words, man. It's about *the muse.*"

Marco was quiet at the mention of our code name for M.H. The screech of a screen door and the thud of steps broke the silence. "I'm outside. Visiting Juliana's mom. Told her the good news."

"Congrats again. You two will be great parents."

"Thanks. We have the ultrasound next week. Juliana thinks it's twins. They run on her side." Half laugh, half a loud breath came through the earpiece. "Okay, what's up?"

"Do you know *when*—what year—the letters were written? Did they come from a blue postal collection box or from the spiderwebs behind an old desk? I mean it.

I need to know." I paced my bedroom. Sanders Mill had to be the town. But was Helen's mom the writer? Or someone else? Adalyn Foster, if she was *the* Adalyn, had been a young woman, which made me think no on Mary Hadley-Wright. And the GIFs/memes thing. I mean, M.H. *had* to be younger, even if a few details had made her sound like she might be old-fashioned.

I'd read her letters so often that it rubbed out all certainty. It's like when I edited a manuscript to death. I got too close to it and couldn't see the forest for the trees.

"Liability, buddy. You know this. We agreed. I'm your magical fairy... And they just showed up. Found them in a dusty corner."

"Bull, man. I'm breaking our agreement."

"No can do. Both our butts are on the line, and with the success of your book..."

I heard pacing on a creaky porch. Then the sound of shoes on gravel, a dog bark. "Chino! Quiet."

I pushed, "When, Marco?"

He released a sigh so strong I swore spit came through my phone. "About six or seven years ago. They came from a central Mass post office, yes. They were newish, okay? Not like fifty years old or even a decade. Like, brand new. Don't know the location. They were sent to central processing, where I worked at the time before moving down here to Atlanta."

I knew it! M.H. was not Mary Hadley.

To my baby Olivia. The baby letter supported this theory. That pain felt raw, recent. Mary Hadley had to be in her sixties given Helen's age. I understood reproductive biology. Plus, M.H. had written to a man named Wes, her fiancé.

Perhaps she was an old soul. My mind wandered back to the sound of Elvis and Patsy crooning in Helen's office, and her sticky notes, or my love of notebooks ... Some younger people appreciated the oldies and old ways.

"Why did you hang on to them for so long before showing me two years ago, instead of just tossing them? Why didn't you just toss them, man?"

Well, now I *was* blaming him. I was getting myself worked up.

Marco sighed, clearly choosing his next words carefully.

I sat on my bed. The letters were splayed across the quilt. A simple "To" and a person—Wes, *Dad, my baby Olivia, Mom*, and *Adalyn*. Five letters that I'd spent so much of my time with. I could relate to some of her sorrows. My dad wasn't the best at showing love. I struggled with loneliness, with being challenged with a learning disability. Though my pains did not compare to M.H.'s grief, I felt her. I heard her. I saw her.

I'd mulled over words, trying to decipher meaning. When he had given me the letters, I grilled Marco on rules and regulations, ones he was willing to share with me. Then I read the dry-as-hell Postal Operations Manual and Domestic Mail Manual to understand everything I could about the mail system.

Guilt was eating me alive. But I could not let this link up to Marco.

Could I go to jail?

Hold up, sport, my dad would say. *No need to put out a fire that hasn't been lit yet.* Nobody was pressing charges. Even if sometimes I thought I might deserve it. A part of me had wanted to confide in my mom. She would know what to do. But how could I tell her that I screwed up this badly? I wanted Dad to be my only disappointed parent.

"Gabe, you need to let it go. Nobody knows. Yes, seven years ago. Yes, new. They made it to the inside of a central Mass post office and through the sorting process. So, I guess they were USPS property. Nobody there opened them. Joe Postal Worker sent them along from one of the town offices. My curiosity got the best of me, and I put them aside with the Santas and Gods at central processing. Then—when I read them, to work on trying to locate her, like we do with that sort of mail before we trash them—her words sucked me in, too. I read them and knew I wouldn't be able to locate the sender. I shoved them inside my desk. Just couldn't bring myself to throw them away. They sat there for a few years. Nobody else there knows or will know." His words held a demanding tone. Marco didn't get irked easily. I was irking him. "You were depressed, man. I thought they would inspire you. I could have easily found them on the street. Nobody knows but us," he repeated sharply.

I countered, "M.H. does."

Always devil's advocate, Marco said, "Your book doesn't mention her, and it doesn't have all the details from her letters. You fictionalized the hell out of them. The likeness is subtle, man. Only a sleuth will put two and two together."

"What about the postal worker who initially found them in the town post office before they got shipped to central processing?"

"Wouldn't that person have mentioned it by now, if they even remembered them from seven years ago? I doubt they would. Hundreds, thousands of parcels of dead mail in each postal office. Millions nationwide. Maybe they're dead, too. Lots of lifers work in the small-town offices. Plus, I was the first to open them."

I heaved a half-hearted "Okay" through the phone.

Marco spirited on. "Here's another idea. She dumped the letters in a mailbox elsewhere. Along one of the city routes with daily pickups. That postal worker who deposited them in the undeliverable bin to send to central processing could be anywhere, not necessarily a small town. We just know they're from central Mass. That's it. Worcester County is damn big, ya know. Lots of ifs. Nobody has come forward to claim them or claim anything about your book."

I took a deep breath before saying, "I think I found her."

"How?"

"On my tour. One place, Sanders Mill—it rings true to the letters. I think she's there."

Marco clicked his tongue. "Then find her, Gabe. Atone. Do what you need to, but, I've got a family here...and I can't. I can't be connected to it." His last words knotted my stomach. "It was a mistake to give them to you."

"I'm sorry, Marco. Maybe she'll understand when I tell her. I can undo this wrong."

"Maybe."

"I won't implicate you in any shape or form. I'll say I found them. Somehow."

"I gotta run, Gabe. Think about it more though, okay?" Before I could answer, Marco disconnected.

No sooner had he done so than my phone pinged. Laurel. I opened the email, knowing what it would say already. *Deadline. Book two. Yeah, I know, Laurel. I know.* Lord, my agent was a patient person. Again, I found myself stuck. Unabashedly stuck. I'd outlined some of the sequel, but I was lost. Writing took time and mine was running short. I had written a few random scenes, but they sucked. The creativity was a dry desert. I didn't respond to Laurel.

Instead, I called my mom.

"Hey, honey. Was just making a care package for you." The sound of pans rattled through my phone. Brewster, their new puppy, barked in the background.

"Mom, I'm not twenty anymore. I can cook and stuff."

"I know, I know, but you just love these peanut butter chocolate kiss cookies. And I wanted to get a head start on my holiday baking and freeze some. How are you, honey? How's the book tour?"

I chatted with her for a few more minutes, but didn't disclose my big, bad, horrible, shitty lapse in judgement. Moms were supposed to love you unconditionally. She wouldn't yell at me about the letters. She'd offer love, compassion. And it would be cowardly of me to unload this drama on her. What could she do, anyway?

Rather than do that, I wanted to tell her about Helen. But I wasn't sure yet how to define our relationship.

"I'll put these kiss cookies in the mail to you, okay? Your dad and I were thinking of visiting in January if that works for you."

"Thanks, Mom. And yes, I'd love that."

Pulling on my coat, I went for a walk, my thoughts turning to the kiss with Helen.

I couldn't wait to return to Sanders Mill.

For the first time in two years, something other than M. H.'s letters pulled me along, even rescued me from myself.

Helen. I needed to see her again.

Seventeen

Helen

The special town meeting had been such a waste of my energy. As predicted, Miriam won in her venture to create the ad hoc Regional Library Site Plan Committee to assess the functionality, needs, purpose, and longevity of the current library while also devising a plan for the proposed regional one. Their job would be to evaluate our infrastructure, facilities, productivity, and impact on the community. Virtually an audit of every working part...to seek a hole, to find a reason for them to shut our doors and build this grand new center. Of course, she loaded the town warrant with verbiage to make it sound like this was a good thing. They made this new site sound snazzy. Bigger. Better.

No mention of Howe's building plan and what would happen to the current library and site.

So, the vote passed.

Whatever. Let them convene. Let them evaluate.

All I could do was look forward to May. Do what I needed to do to prepare for that more pivotal meeting, where I would request funds to bridge our budget gap. That request went to the public. The committees had no say in the matter. If I got the requested funds, my library would live to fight another day.

I tapped my toes to the tunes of Johnny Cash as I finished my work.

"Somebody is especially chipper. Who replaced Helen?" Billie grinned as she came into my office. She pretended to look around for hidden cameras or recording devices.

I turned off my music and powered down the computer. The grandfather clock in the main circulation area chimed five. "I need you to lock up."

Billie feigned surprise with a hand over her heart. "An alien has replaced Helen." She held out her open palm like a crossing guard to stop my protesting. She pushed up her latest glasses—big, round red ones today, to match a fire-engine-red lipstick only she could pull off with her bright grin and enviable cheekbones.

"I'm also taking tomorrow off."

"Saturday? Return her at once, you crafty extraterrestrial." Her laugh reverberated in the small office.

I poked her in the shoulder, then gave her a side hug. "I have company coming this evening, so I need to relieve Gifty and get cooking."

Billie's dark brown eyes sparkled. "Get cookin' with good lookin'?"

She was as bad as Kayley. "Perhaps."

"He's the lucky man. Your food is mouth-watering."

She prodded no further. I picked up the Baked by Barb box holding the deep-dish apple pie and hurried out the main door, the key in my pocket no longer an anchor.

Gabe

With my heart in my throat, I turned the rental car onto the driveway lined with old oaks leading up to the farmhouse. I paused at their mailbox, which was decorated with what looked like hand-painted flowers. Similar to the stationery M.H. had used. I needed to scour the local stores for that stationery or subtly ask Mary about it.

This trip back to Sanders Mill was two things. First, my gut told me this was *the* town. So, I had to locate M.H. and make up to her for everything. How? I still didn't know. Second, I wanted to spend as much time with Helen as possible. I hadn't felt this fired up about a woman I was dating—in a long time.

Wait, were we dating?

Well, I was having dinner with Helen and her mom. And we shared that passionate kiss. And I wanted more. Many more. Definitely dating.

Also, I was eager to help her with the library.

Of course, I'd brought my laptop, too. With the local tour completed, I had more downtime...and a looming deadline. Okay, so three goals. Third: write the sequel.

I parked next to Helen's car. My steps crunched along a walkway covered with fall leaves, and I rang the doorbell, a bottle of white wine in one clammy hand.

Mary Hadley greeted me at the door, her eyes a mirror image of Helen's bright blues, with the same frank friendliness. They placated me immediately. Her wispy gray hair was pulled up and off her neck.

"Good evening, Ms. Hadley—"

"Call me Mary," she said with a gesture inside. She hugged a plaid wrap around her shoulders.

I wiped my feet on the welcome mat. "I'm Gabe."

"Indeed, you are." She winked. "Helen, your friend is here," she gently hollered over her shoulder.

Friend. I had intentions of changing that.

Coziness lured me inside toward the glowing pellet stove in the sitting room. I fidgeted with the bottle in my hands. "Some wine for you."

"Thank you." Mary took it and placed it on the coffee table. She followed my gaze as she clicked off the small flat-screen television tucked in the corner. "Early in the season for the pellet stove, but this old place is drafty. Please sit, Gabe. We have snacks."

I eyed the glass dish with a chunky green salsa and tortilla chips. "Oh, Helen's zuke mash. I've been wanting to try it."

Wrinkles furrowed her forehead. "Certainly unique. Doesn't quite go on crackers. Chips work better for dipping. Don't tell her, but it's not my favorite. I'm not a big fan of zucchini. Cucumbers either. I grow those because Helen likes them in her salads, and we pickle them." She sat in a large, overstuffed leather chair and drew another blanket onto her lap.

"Not even zoodles?" I said, still standing.

"Never got on the trend. Nothing beats homemade pasta. My mother used to make ours from scratch."

Her easygoing chatter settled some of my nerves as I sat. Why was I nervous? Oh yeah, because I made out with her daughter, and I stole letters which just might be Mary's—but really, my intuition told me otherwise.

Helen poked her head in, looking energized and gorgeous. She styled her hair half pinned up and wore a pink sweater with fine-fitting jeans. "Hey, Gabe. Couple of minutes."

"Want help?" I stood, picking up the wine.

She waved to me to sit but grabbed the bottle. "No, no. Almost done. Chat with Mom." She planted a peck on my cheek, which flared with a warmth that lingered long after Helen went back to the kitchen.

I sat again and dipped a chip into the zuke mash, then topped it with a triangle of cheddar. After a bite and a swallow, I said, "I like it. Has kick. I taste cumin or nutmeg or something smoky." I ate another scoop. "Helen says you like to work in the garden. Those apple trees are gigantic."

"My grandparents planted the orchard. The property has been in the family for two hundred years."

"That's a long time. Is the house original?" I cast a glance around the lofty room, admiring the exposed timbers in the ceiling. Another garden painting, its brushwork similar to the one in the library, adorned the wall above the pellet stove.

"Built in the 1820s. The original homestead is located farther back on the property, near the pond. It wasn't more than a few cabins and a root cellar. I haven't been back there in a while—overgrown trails. And that part is technically on the library land."

My radar blipped with the potential—and not just for research. A walk with Helen to check out the old cabin foundations, see what remained in the cellar? Maybe we'd find something to support the library's historical significance. Something from the abolitionist movement, perhaps? The Civil War didn't extend this far north. Maybe something older, eighteenth century or Revolutionary War? A grave of a historical figure? Finding anything was a long shot. It was a true shame that a tornado had destroyed the original library; otherwise, that would be worth registering as a historical landmark by its age alone, if left intact.

I cleared my throat. "Interesting." I took out my notebook but hesitated.

Mary waved a hand. "Oh, please, please. Do write it down. Helen mentioned you're helping her. Not sure if our old cabins and woodland might be any help, but you never know what you can find on a hike through the woods. Too bad we don't have a hidden unpublished work from Alcott or Dickinson." She paused as if trying to remember something, then said, "'We can never have enough of nature,'" quoting Thoreau.

I quoted back, "'I went to the woods because I wished to live deliberately.'"

Delight danced in her voice. "Spoken like an author."

"And you've spoken like a librarian."

We shared a soft chuckle. I was such a geek, quoting a nineteenth-century Massachusetts author with my girlfriend's mom.

Girlfriend?

Helen returned, smiling. "'Books are the treasured wealth of the world and the fit inheritance of generations and nations.'"

"Now that," Mary said, pointing at Helen, "is spoken like a true librarian."

"Dinner's almost ready if we're all done quoting Thoreau." Helen's look fell upon me. "And welcome to our bookish home, Gabe." She lifted an eyebrow and pointed to a book on the shelf: *Great Quotes of the Nineteenth Century*.

Mary said to us both, "Sit, dears. I'll set the table." Without a response—and I bet Mary wouldn't take no for an answer—she rose and departed the room like a feather in a breeze.

"She's having a good day," Helen whispered, sitting next to me on the couch.

I slid closer, leaned in, and kissed her cheek. She had a crumb of something in a knot of hair. I plucked it out.

"I'm glad you're here," she said.

I brushed my hand down her shoulder. "I'm happy to be back."

"How was the tour?"

"Good. The national tour is in the new year. With the pre-launch of book two. If I ever write it. Potential cover reveal and some teasers."

"Book two?"

"Yeah." I swallowed, eager to be done with that topic. "Hey, am I in time for the pumpkin fest?" A gentle whiff of Helen's fragrance—citrus again, mixed with whatever herbs from dinner—sparked other feelings. I let the pleasure of being with her take complete hold of me.

"Definitely. Let's go this weekend. How long will you be staying?" Her fingertips stroked my knee before reaching forward to tidy the chips, cheese, and zuke mash, none of which needed tidying.

"Ronan Cooper gave me an extended-stay deal. I'll be here for a few weeks. I want to help you with the library stuff. I need to do some writing. Brought my laptop in case my muse returns."

"She's missing?"

I splayed my hands out in a poof gesture. "Gone."

Helen tugged at her bottom lip with her teeth. "The foliage is perfect this week. Maybe it will stir your creativity. Mom loves painting in the fall the most. All the colors. Hopefully, you find your inspiration again," she said softly.

She could be my muse.

Could be my *more*.

"Dinner's ready." Mary beckoned from the hallway.

We rose, and I squeezed Helen's hand. She squeezed back.

While enjoying baked chicken, mushroom risotto, roasted carrots, collard greens, and one too many glasses of wine, we talked about upcoming events at the library and about Mary's gardening. After the meal, we retreated to the front sitting room again.

"Oh, the pie." Mary rose but wobbled. "Oh..."

Helen swooped in. "You okay, Mom?"

Mary's hand clung to her brow, and she blew out hard, deliberate breaths. "Seeing spots. Stood too fast. I may need to skip dessert. How about I see myself upstairs?"

Helen shot a look at me.

"I'll be okay here." I lifted my teacup.

Helen escorted Mary upstairs, the old creaking steps a complement to the tick-tock of a clock on the wall.

I padded around the room, admiring Mary's artwork and portraits of what I assumed were ancestors. They shared similar features: soft noses, high cheekbones, round eyes. I ventured to the foyer, then across the hall to what looked like an office under renovation. A massive mahogany desk sat in the middle, with a laptop and a gazillion fluorescent sticky notes on top, which stood out against the nineteenth-century décor—charts, town maps, sepia prints, and black-and-white photos—on the papered walls. This was Helen's own history room, I'd bet.

I was drawn back to the desk. Beside the open laptop were framed pressed dandelions, one yellow in flower and one white in seed, and a few other pressed flowers I didn't know the names of.

I glanced at the paper stack on the desk and saw a floral pattern on the paper at the bottom.

Oh my God. My mind raced as fast as my pulse. That stationery looked like M.H.'s... Maybe Mary had designed it—that would explain it being here. Either way, that was it. That was the stationery.

Creaks on the stairs announced Helen's imminent return.

I moved my attention to a portrait of a stately-looking woman on the far wall. *Elsie*, it read underneath on a nameplate.

"That's my great-grandmother," Helen said from behind me.

"You have her cheekbones." I cast a wave around. "You've got your own history room, Helen." The words came out brighter than I intended, almost cutesy. I took a breath to calm the Indy 500 happening in my chest. I wanted to look at the paper once more...

She said, "I love this room. Used to be my father's office. I'm renovating it, but it's slow. Expensive. Coop said he may be able to help me with some of it." She gestured to the two far walls. "I want ceiling-high bookshelves with a moving ladder. I'm a nerd."

"If I had a big space like this, I'd do the same." I glided over to the next framed work. "Genealogy chart?"

"Mm-hmm. My mom used to update it. I need to add me and my brothers. This is a new version, not the original. She started copying it like maybe eight years ago, after taking some calligraphy lessons, but then she got sick, and that type of handwriting became an effort for her. We just never got around to finishing it. I guess I could try my hand at it."

Helen stood close to me, as if inspecting the chart for the first time.

"Do you see your brothers much since they are out of state?"

"Family gatherings, holidays and such. We text a lot. Ryan is married, has two kids, and lives in Maine. Dan is finishing graduate school and diving headfirst into engineering. The two of them don't always get along. I call myself Switzerland, keeping the peace between everyone in the family, but it's more like Swiss chocolate."

"I hope it's the kind with the sweet and gooey inside."

She smiled. I loved her smile.

"My brother, Corey, is an engineer, too, like yours. I texted him about the trebuchets. He told me to take photos." I turned back to the chart. "This is impressive."

"Mom is the family records and relics keeper on the Hadley side. We have tons of boxes, bins, and trunks upstairs with memorabilia, journals, books, even a Christening gown made by my great-great-grandmother Josephine Brown-Hadley."

Another name that if I didn't write it down, I'd forget it. I fought the urge to snap a picture of the family tree. "Do you know the history of most of your family? Did anyone do anything notable?"

She arched an eyebrow at me.

"For the Historical Register."

"Ah. Nothing more than what I already told you."

I admired the framed pages behind the glass and drew my finger down the pedigree. The first ancestor listed was Jacob Foster, born in 1820. Then came Alice Foster, born in 1840 and married in 1862 to Joseph Hadley. Then came their four children, and son, James Hadley, married Josephine Brown, who gave birth to sons Jonathon, Silas, and Jacob Hadley. Jacob married Elsie Smith, and they had a daughter and son. David Hadley married Helen Barnes. Last, Mary

Hadley and Geoffrey Wright completed the pedigree. Spots were left for Helen and her brothers. My head spun with so many names. I needed a picture!

Instead, I said, "I'd love to explore your trunks." I cleared my throat, considering an alternate meaning of my statement. "You know what I mean. Pedigrees, history, old notes. Maybe something for the register—"

She laughed lightly. "That's an idea. Think we could find something in my attic other than dust bunnies?"

"Maybe." *A dark corner to make out?*

"Want pie?"

"Sure—I hope I have room. Dinner was delicious."

"Barb's pies are the best around. I bet you'll find room."

I teased, "Well, if it's Barb's..."

"Exactly!"

We returned to the front room. As we ate pie, an evening storm moved in, and the house randomly creaked and moaned. A tree branch scraped the window.

"This week's been cold for October. Think we'll have snow?" I asked.

"Mom might flip if we have snow this early. I have the rest of her gardens to harvest. It's supposed to be warmer tomorrow during the day."

I scraped the last bit of Dutch apple crumb into my mouth. "This was great, but I would say the company tonight was better."

She saw me to the door with no protest, but asked, "Pumpkins tomorrow?"

"You bet. Need help with the gardens, too? Give me a task and I'm on it."

"I'd like that. Come by tomorrow morning after breakfast?"

She blinked and then stood on tiptoes and planted a soft kiss on my lips. "See you tomorrow," she breathed, pulling back ever so slowly.

I fought every urge in my body to sweep her into my arms and return the kiss with a hell of a lot more heat. Instead, I squeezed her hand, hoping it relayed my eagerness to see more of her, but not the full extent of my raging desires. "Tomorrow."

Eighteen

Helen

"Holy tomato!" Gabe said like an excited kid as he plucked the cherry and Roma tomatoes off the spindly plants.

I dropped another empty container next to him. "Pull the green ones, too. Mom showed me once how to remove these suckers, right here," I said, pointing to the intersections of branch and stem. "I let it go this year, and before I knew it, I had clusters of tomatoes on the suckers. So holy tomato is right."

"Why remove the suckers?"

I waved a hand, not quite remembering her specific reason. "Encourages the remaining branches to grow more, I think. Some sort of selective reduction for quality. As you can see, I have hundreds of them on suckers and branches. I don't like choosing which lives and which dies. If I were left to handle the garden, the beds would become crowded, and things would die anyway! I'm glad Mom takes the lead on deciding. There's a method to her madness. Mine would be pure madness. It's also why I leave weeding the bookshelves at the library to Billie. She's far better at triage. No guilt. I try to save every last one, even if the spines are broken and pages are falling out." That admission gave me an internal pause. Kind of like with Adalyn, too. I had a hard time giving up the fight.

"My mom used to have a garden before my parents moved south," Gabe said. "She focuses on flowers now, but when I was a kid, she would put us to work in the vegetable beds, weeding or picking carrots or peas. But we caused more mischief than help. Spraying each other with the hose or throwing gardening tools like we were ninjas." He pointed to a heavily laden branch. "You want me to pick *all* these green ones?"

"If a hard frost comes, these tomatoes are doomed. If I store them in a box covered with newspaper or in a window with sun, they'll ripen and taste good for weeks."

"Sounds like you have a greener thumb than you let on." He dropped a handful of cherry tomatoes into the bin, then let his fingers skirt across my lower back. The touch sent all the fine hairs attuned. I popped a ripe tomato into my mouth and dangled another near his. "Want one? Juicy and red. Nothing beats the burst of a fresh tomato."

He parted his lips in response. I fed him, the intimacy of the moment not lost on me.

I watched his mouth chew, then morph into a smile.

We moved through the gardens and orchard—more raspberries, carrots, fall peas, Brussel sprouts, bok choy, eggplant, and apples. "I'll be processing veggies and fruit all week. Mom's friends come over to help. You're welcome to take some back to your place."

We laughed and picked and talked about his favorite trips, my beach weekends with Kayley this past summer. "We even found sea glass at Long Beach in Plymouth and at Devereux in Marblehead. See? I can do my own kind of digging." I winked.

"I've never actually dug for sea glass."

"Really?"

"Really."

"We may need to fix that."

Gabe and I sweated beneath a bright mid-October sun. I cocked an eye heavenward. "I haven't felt this good in a while. Guess gardening isn't my nemesis after all. Good for the soul." I chewed my lip. Good company. "I've tried to cut back each year on how much Mom plants, but she's stubborn. I can't possibly carry this all on my own. We need to downsize the garden beds."

"I'm sure you'll be able to carry on the legacy at your own workable level." He added, the timbre in his voice shooting right down to my toes, "I'd be glad to help."

The idea of what his simple phrase meant unsettled me. It was the kind of offer that could lead to long-term-relationship territory. I wasn't sure if I was unsettled in a good or bad way, to be frank. Like Kayley said, I couldn't keep the secrecy for much longer. I'd laid down breadcrumbs, more than I wanted. Gabe just made it so easy to...just be me.

The other night, Mom and I watched one of her favorite movies, a late 1990s rom-com classic—*You've Got Mail*. The whole time, my brain could not stop seeing the parallels with my own story. Meg Ryan played a woman who needed to save her floundering family-owned bookstore and was carrying on an email exchange with Tom Hanks's character, both using mystery identities. Of course, the truth came out, and it had the happy-ever-after ending. Could I let what I felt for Gabe pave the way to forgiveness?

Each passing day, it became harder to find a casual way to mention my letters to Gabe. I should have just confronted him on day one. Now, it felt too late.

I checked out the sugar pumpkins, turning them to inspect all sides. "Almost ready. I give these to Barb for pies and muffins."

"Speaking of pumpkins, what time is the trebuchet fun today?"

"If we go closer to sunset, the crowds are smaller."

He sipped a glass of tea from our refreshments on the picnic table. "I can't get over the view here." He looked briefly at the rolling hills of green and brown, fringed with younger trees, but then his eyes went back to me and lingered there.

Oh, he was smooth.

I eyed our landscape as we made our way to the raspberry bushes. "We have a maze of trails through this property."

"Your mom mentioned that. Do they connect to the library trails?"

I nodded. "And to one of our oldest town cemeteries. The historical society used to offer 'haunted' tours, and ours was one of the stops. They'd share ghost stories but also embellished stories about the Underground Railroad while taking you to several places supposedly on it."

His eyebrows rose. "They don't anymore?"

"Miriam is persuasive and has seeds planted everywhere. They stopped offering the tours for 'budget reasons,' and because, without any verified evidence, the historical society didn't need to support such 'fluff.'"

"On that...I couldn't gather anything with my online digging. Perhaps we can go back to the history room in the library. But the Underground Railroad isn't very well documented, being secret and all that."

"There's probably nothing on the microfiche or films either because those are mostly newspaper articles, but we can give it a shot. Maybe something was found somewhere, and they wrote about it."

He didn't mention my attic troves again, which was a relief. Showing him Alice's letters felt too personal, and I wasn't sure why I'd suggested it last night. But what if there was proof of historical significance sitting up there in my attic?

Pushing aside that nagging thought, I paused in raspberry picking to pop one in my mouth. "I appreciate moments like this."

My phone buzzed from my pocket. "Oh, I need to take this." I stood, stretching my back. "Hi, Sam."

Samantha was the head of the Council on Aging and had offered to help me talk to other committees about the library's need for support. "Hey, Helen. Good news! Ronnie is on board to meet. And we have Alex and Carter, too."

"Fabulous!" The public works director, police chief, and fire chief? The town got behind anything those three would support or recommend. It was a bit of an old boys' club, but if I could work that angle, I would. We didn't have any Y chromosomes on our Library Board of Trustees currently.

Also, nobody wanted our public safety budget slashed, and their departments, though not on the chopping block, had seen enough cutbacks in recent years that they could commiserate. "Let's plan a date to meet this week?"

We hashed out details and I disconnected.

"Good news?" Gabe asked. He came closer and picked berries alongside me.

"Yes. Working my way through the committees to get support. Still need something tangible for that national Historical Register, though."

"Another date with the history room and microform," he said enthusiastically with a raise of one eyebrow. He made research sound sensual.

"Okay, you win. We'll go back and look again."

I could smell him, a pleasant mixture of spicy body wash and sweat, not the locker room type, but that of healthy exertion. His body shadowed the sun, yet he radiated his own heat. He was close enough that I could just lean up and—

A painful prick plucked me from my fantasizing. "Ouch!"

"What happened? Thorn?"

"No, those are nothing. Yellowjacket." Holding my wrist, I glared at the offender as it flew away. "This bugger has been guarding the berries lately. Probably a nest in the ground nearby. Gah! Little bastard. Hurts like the devil." Flustered, I writhed from the pain.

"He has it out for you, huh?"

Tears puddled in the corners of my eyes with the sting. I gritted my teeth. "Everyone does, it seems."

He bent his head between mine and the growing pink welt on my wrist, catching my gaze. "Let's get you ice. You allergic?"

"No."

"Want an antihistamine?"

"Only if I want to nap. I'll be no good for pumpkin smashing. Ice will be fine."

We hurried through the screened-in back porch, where Mom was sleeping with a book tucked under an arm. In the kitchen, I fell onto a tall chair at the island while Gabe dug in the freezer. He wrapped ice cubes in a clean dish towel and approached. Instead of handing it to me, he turned my palm up and rested the ice on my wrist while cupping from beneath. He didn't let go, standing in front of me, so close. So very close. Thick, honeyed-wheat hair fell across his forehead. Yes, in that romance-movie way.

Where was my head this afternoon?

"I can do it." I made no move to retreat from his hold. Or from his eyes that held me just as intently.

"You do enough already, Helen. Let me help. I like to help."

I blinked frustrated tears. Keeping one of his hands holding both my wrist and the ice-filled towel, he used the other to brush wayward hair from my face. His fingertips held the earthy aroma of tomato leaf. The oils stuck to your skin for hours after harvesting. I might not love gardening, but the smell was an aphrodisiac, almost as good as the smell of old books.

I released a giddy laugh.

"What's funny?"

"Thinking of silly things. How books smell old and tomato plants smell invigorating. I've got a weird nose."

He took my free hand, brought it near his nose, and sniffed our fingertips. "They do smell good. As for books, I like their scent, too. Crisp paper, fresh toner, or musty with age. Not weird. It's nostalgic." He took a deep breath as he leaned in closer, his swallow audible. "I like the smell of your hair. Been trying to place the scent for a while."

"My hair?" For a while? He'd been smelling my hair? I struggled to find words that wouldn't reveal my self-consciousness. "Do you know why old books smell different?"

He skated his fingers from my temple down along my cheekbone. "Why?"

"Has to do with the breakdown of chemicals. I read about it once, long ago. There are the components—cellulose, lignin—which smell like vanillin when broken down over time—ethyl *something*, benzaldehyde."

His gaze was rapt on mine while I rambled. Anything to distract the sting...anything to distract me from kissing him again. His touch paused on my chin as I continued, "As teens, my best friend and I loved to host a book club, and the smell of books...reminds me of her, too. Anyway, it's the cellulose from plants, plus processing chemicals, and the breakdown of these components, that makes for this woodsy scent we book nerds adore."

"It's chemistry?" He lifted an eyebrow, and his touch returned to my hair, playing, stroking. Shivers crept along my scalp.

A fuzzy fog encircled my brain, and I hadn't even taken an antihistamine. He inhaled deeply with his nose pressed to the lock of hair between his fingertips. The shivers spread down my neck to my toes.

"I like a woman who knows her book facts. And I love your scent."

My tongue lost its words. No thoughts in my head.

I was first this time. I bent my head up, and like a rocket launching, pressed my lips to his. He responded eagerly, and our kiss deepened heartbeat-fast.

He tasted like tomatoes and iced tea. The cold towel was no longer at my wrist; I heard a thump as Gabe dropped it on the counter beside us. Lost in the kiss, I was lifted off the seat, scooped onto his lap, my hip and shoulder leaning into his oh-so-lovely chest.

As his tongue explored my mouth, I cupped the back of his neck, keeping him close, enjoying the comfort of his arms around me. Dizziness catapulted me to a place I'd fought since meeting him. I wanted his lips on mine, his arms around me. I wanted more with him.

Gabe traced the waistband of my jeans. A finger dipped beneath my t-shirt, touching the bare skin of my back. It was like that spot had hungered for a repeat since his touch on the rail trail. *Yes, more*, it begged. His other hand sat knotted at my scalp—I imagined the beast I called my hair had ensnared his hand and would not let it go. My own hands ran over his body, feeling the contours of his muscles through his shirt, wanting to undo buttons or rip them away.

This make-out session had to stop soon, or I'd be stripping his clothes off and Mom was just around the corner, on the screened-in porch.

I longed to kiss his chest, see his abs, see all of him.

A moan escaped my lips as his exploring hand traveled north, to the concave area between my ribs and waist, then higher... He brushed a thumb beneath my breast, and I arched into his touch.

The heavy front door groaned open, and immediately after the heartbreaking sound, Nan's and Lorraine's cheery voices drifted down the long front hallway. "Helloooo?"

That's what we get for always saying, "*Just come on in, no need to ring.*"

Gabe and I tore apart. Interrupted, again, like on the rail trail. We needed to find better opportunities and places. I fussed with my tousled hair, snatched the soppy towel, and hurried to the sink, where I busied myself with running water over the single dish in the basin. Gabe cleared his throat and shifted in his seat, grabbing the nearest thing—an apple from the fruit bowl. He spun it around in his hands, a swirling unrest in his brown eyes. Not washing it, he took a bite.

I watched his mouth move. His lip curled up when he caught my gaze.

The Terrible Two strode into the kitchen, each carrying shopping bags.

At least my bra hadn't been unhooked or anything. My front-closure lacy bra was buried in the underused lingerie drawer. Oh, I was pulling that thing out tomorrow.

Nan looked me over swiftly, brown eyes assessing. She was a tall woman, with this regal, all-knowing air.

Lorraine, however, was always the first to speak. She pushed past her companion, even if she was a good six inches shorter than everyone in the room. "Helen, you look flushed. You okay, dear?"

Nan's O-shaped mouth said it all. Quicker to put one plus one together. She nudged Lorraine in the ribs. "Let's put these groceries away and then check on Mary."

I turned off the water and found my lost voice. "Got stung." I held up my welted pink wrist and the dripping towel. "Yellowjackets are back." Overemphatically, I fanned myself.

Lorraine lifted the reading glasses which were slung around her neck on a chain that fell across her ample bosom. "Lemme see. Stinger?"

"No, this type doesn't leave a stinger."

Still munching on the apple, Gabe steered around the high island counter, conveniently shielding the lower half of his body. I had felt his arousal only a moment before. Smart man. I reached for the freezer to get more ice.

Gabe offered his hand to Nan, who stood nearly as tall as him. "Hi, I'm Gabe. Nice to meet you. Need help with the bags?"

She clasped his hand in a shake. "Oh, yes. We have more in the trunk," she said in a soft voice. "I'm Nan. This is Lorraine. How are you?"

He didn't answer her before going out, faster than a teenage boy caught with his hand up a girl's skirt—or in our case, my shirt. The idea of his hand down my pants was...

Ice. I needed ice. Lots of it.

I squeezed extra moisture from the towel before placing it back onto my wrist with a wince. Lorraine and Nan shared a devious look.

"Don't," I said.

They laughed. Despite myself, I laughed, too.

"Love the new do, Nan," I said, drawing the attention from myself.

"Thanks." She ran a hand through the sharp pixie cut of her salt-and-pepper hair and added, smirking, "He's a dear."

Dear wasn't the half of it.

Nineteen

Helen

After helping Nan and Lorraine with unloading groceries, Gabe and I were off to the Sanderson Farm pumpkin event. I drove silently, stewing in uncertainty. Were we dating? Could I let Gabe into my bubble? The more I thought, the more I wanted to pop an antacid. I was hopelessly failing Operation Truth.

So, I stopped pondering and embraced the moment. Today was good. And I wanted to enjoy the heck out of it.

A deep blue sky welcomed us. The farm was abuzz with families and pets roaming among mounds of pumpkins, gourds, and hay. Soon, gusty winds and rains would pound New England, undressing the trees of their color in one fell swoop.

We meandered, devouring spuckie bread sandwiches and apple muffins, purchasing the gourds Mom would like to decorate our dining table with, and watching pumpkins fly high and smash far.

"Whoa!" Gabe said as one was propelled hundreds of yards across the field to smash into pieces against a faux stone castle. "Impressive."

"I know, right? The local school tech clubs have a competition each fall. Engineers, farmers, anyone with an interest and materials, can build the catapults and trebuchets."

A few teens loaded the overgrown and inedible pumpkins into the baskets, countdowns began, and away they went, flying. People cheered and released compassionate "oohs" and "aahs" as contraptions failed or floundered.

"Those are high-flying pies in the sky."

I laughed. "Someone told me that these splattered seeds end up being a new pumpkin patch next year. Or the wild animals eat them. Either way, I guess it's not wasteful."

"Smart. Have you been coming here a long time?"

"I used to come here as a kid with my friend, just to watch, not build. My brother Dan was the mastermind. His inventions took up the entire barn. He and his friends would go dumpster diving for any piece of scrap metal or wood they could find."

"Amazing what they create from lumber and bolts." Gabe took a few photos with his phone.

After the trebuchet action died down, we took a hayride.

"Ohhh...spooky," Gabe said, nestling closer as we bumped over uneven ground toward the dusk-shadowed forest at the edge of the property. The guide spoke about the history of pumpkin tossing and the tiny cemetery hidden in the woods. I shivered as we approached it. How quickly the heat of the day had dissipated. Fall nights required a wool sweater—or a warm man at my side. With his arm wrapped around me, Gabe pulled out his phone one-handed to snap photos of headstones that dated back to the French and Indian War.

"I like to walk through the other cemetery in town," I admitted. "Kind of peaceful in a macabre way."

"I imagine a cemetery can be calming. Especially one like this, far from the noise of roads or crowds. And they hold so much history. I read the inscriptions whenever I visit old town cemeteries. It paints a picture, you know? Who they married, who they left behind, their children, the story of the town—like did it lose a lot of servicemen overseas? Or was it hit by a disease outbreak?"

"Or a tornado."

"Exactly. Once, I saw a cluster of headstones where the inscription was for a husband and wife on one, and then a second wife on another, and a child on another. By the dates, it looked like the first wife died in childbirth, and the man married right away, perhaps to secure a mother for his child. There's a story there for those who visit. It's like conversing with ghosts."

The words rang in my chilled ears. I tugged my hat down farther on my head.

"Want a hot cocoa?" he asked as the wagon drew to a stop.

"Oh, yes. I'll get it."

"Okay." He nuzzled into my neck and gave me a peck on the ticklish part just below my earlobe. An *I'll keep you warm* kind of peck. And the shivers racing across my skin weren't from cold.

"I'm going to interview some of the trebuchet winners." He pulled out his notebook.

His genuine interest was adorable.

I zigzagged through the crowd toward the Sugar Shack. On my way, I saw my least favorite person. Miriam wore jeans and a jacket, not her designer pants and heels, and her hair was hidden beneath a winter cap, but I knew her mannerisms, always assessing her surroundings and competition. She disappeared in the lengthening shadows behind the shack as an amber sun sunk to the horizon.

Know what? I was peeved. I was tired of being Swiss chocolate. With the way Miriam tore me and the library down bit by bit, I felt more like Swiss *cheese*. The line for concessions was short, so it wasn't like I didn't have time to give her a word or two.

I balled my fists at my sides as I headed around the shack. In my head, I repeated the words I'd been saving to spew at her when I had the chance. That chance was now.

On my turn around the rear corner of the shack, I froze.

Miriam had not gone behind the building to avoid people or take a shortcut, as I assumed. She stopped in the shadows. And she wasn't alone.

I knew Pierce Howe by his commanding presence and height. He was one of the tallest, most muscular—beefy—men in Sanders Mill, towering over many with both his size and attitude.

Reflexes had me backtracking, but not fully disappearing.

I couldn't hear a thing because of the rear exhausts blowing greasy scents into the air, but I watched their lips move with heated, snippy whispers. Conspiring. Nothing new about this.

He moved in closer to her. He rested a hand upon her waist.

Wait, *what*?

Not an accidental swipe. His hand lingered. Intimately. She leaned against the wall of the hut. Pierce pressed against her, hips against hips.

As he kissed her, his roaming hand squeezed her butt.

Just as the icky voyeur factor told me to march myself right back to where I'd come from, they peeled away from each other and then he was gone around the other corner of the shed. Back to the crowds.

My feet would not unstick from my spot as my mind absorbed everything it had just witnessed. I needed soap to wash my eyes.

The rumors were true. Both were married to others, yet here they'd been, sticking tongues down each other's throats behind the Sugar Shack. Oh, how aptly named.

Spinning around to leave, I snared my boot on a drainage pipe. A fall on my face was prevented by catching myself on a deep window ledge.

"Oh, Helen...how are you tonight?"

I turned back, thanking my lucky stars dusk hid my awkwardness. "Good, good. Was heading to the bathroom."

Did she know I'd just seen Pierce—*eww*—grabbing her ass? If she had, she hid it well. On her approach, she casually zipped her jacket and shoved her hands into her pockets. "A lovely weekend for the event."

"Didn't see Harper. Did she and her friends build a trebuchet this year?"

My attempt to distract her failed. Miriam's eyes sharpened.

Come to think of it, Harper had been noticeably absent from a group of her friends gathered around one trebuchet and not present at the past few book club meetings. She'd fallen off my radar despite my resolve to watch her.

"No," Miriam said. "She's home studying." She eyed me like a lioness with her prey. "Just thought you'd like to know that the ad hoc committee's work is coming along nicely. Browning will have the report in the new year. However, I heard you've again submitted a budget we simply cannot approve."

What was this *we* business? She was the town moderator. *She* should not have a say in my budget. Zero. Zilch. Nada.

A piece in my chess game with Miriam just tumbled. So much for Browning and any hope of the Finance Committee being on Team Library. Time to re-evaluate.

I pushed my chin out. "I look forward to their report. And to speaking with the Finance Committee," I emphasized.

Miriam closed the space between us. Her dark brows angled sharply into her don't-mess-with-me stare. "The library will be shut down, Helen. Allowing an underutilized, falling-apart building to sit on such important community land is a travesty."

Oh, so your hump buddy can have it? Unable to spit out the rebuttal, I swallowed. "The community does not own the land, Miriam."

"But the upkeep and operation of the library is town-financed."

"Our building is a historic treasure."

"Not officially."

I needed Gabe's help, badly. Tomorrow: history room and microform. And my attic. Anything. "There are other subdivisions for new homes, Miriam. Howe knows this. Nice areas. Why can't you just leave it alone?" Alright, that last sentence came out poorly.

"You're going to regret not taking my offer." She crossed her arms, pinched her lips, and stiffened pompous shoulders. "We'll keep the community strong. We'll have a centralized library and media center in North Prouty, beautiful community grounds here, and new families to support the growth of Sanders Mill. Your building *will* be history."

Well, I fell into that one.

Did Miriam believe the lies she told herself each morning over her kale smoothie? The worst part was that regardless of whether she did, other people would. People would see her not as the person who shut down and demolished the library, but as the liberator who created a shiny new community with beautiful McMansions. She would cut the ceremonial ribbon of the new fancy library as her first duty as senator.

I blinked hard. *Do not cry, Helen.* "Why do you have to tear my home down to b-build yourself up?" Despite my resolve, my voice broke.

"The library's not your home, Helen. And it sits on twenty beautiful, wooded acres. The building's falling apart and requires repairs our community simply cannot afford, not when the money can be better served elsewhere. It's not like we're going to tear down your old farmhouse or take that bit of garden from you."

The painful truths I already knew tore me down further. A tear burned wetly down my face.

She continued her attack, scoffing, "Why would you let it run into the ground and humiliate yourself in the process? My offer still stands. Let the library and its land go, Helen. I know you and your mom can use the money."

Playing the mom chess piece now. Just swell.

My thoughts raging, this battle lost, I swung around and left.

Miriam hollered at my back, "Have it your way."

I dug into my pocket for an antacid but produced only lint. Shaking from head to toe, I returned to Gabe.

He furrowed his brow. "What happened?"

"I-I ran into Miriam." I sniffled, drowning in distress.

He rubbed both my shoulders, looking over one of them toward the Sugar Shack. I leaned into him until my cheek pressed against his chest. His jacket hung unzipped, and his nearness soothed my aching heart. I had no energy left for this fight. At least not today.

He held me close, squeezing with the comfort I needed. After a few moments, he whispered, "You're shivering. Let me grab those hot cocoas and we'll get you home."

I nodded.

"Want me to drive?" he offered as I pulled my head back. He swiped wet hair stuck to wet cheeks.

I wiped my nose. "No. I'll be okay."

"You sure? My night vision isn't great, but I can drive. Really."

It was my turn to hold his hand. His long fingers thread together with mine. "It's okay. I'll be okay to drive."

Once settled in my car, hot cocoa a salve on my raw throat and my tears blotted, I filled him in on what happened.

He listened, eyes turned on me as I drove him back to the inn.

"This feels like high school popularity contests all over again!"

He squeezed my knee. "She fights dirty. You don't."

"And we know who loses in political mudslinging. I mean, she has nothing dirty on me, but she goes around the back way. Gets people who I think care but then are swayed or manipulated by her. Talks trash behind my back. She makes stuff up. Seeing her and Howe? Ick. I could use that, but I won't."

"Because you have a good heart, Helen. You're a good person. I'm sorry you're shouldering this. I'm at your disposal. Use me. Let's research more, okay? Want me to put in inquiries anywhere? I've got random connections all over."

"I really do need your help, Gabe." I turned down the dark roads with blurry eyes. I'd need to take my contacts out soon. Thankfully, I carried spares along with my glasses in my handbag.

"You okay?" Gabe asked as I again wiped my eyes.

"Acid tears. My superpower. The optometrist was astonished by the way they can burn through contact lenses."

He gave a soft laugh. "That's a kick-ass superpower."

I snorted, rubbed my eye, and took a tissue he offered me.

"We'll find something."

I inhaled deeply and shook my head as if to dislodge all the pain and frustration. "Alright. I swear I've looked at every deed and old document a hundred times, though."

"We'll find something," he repeated.

I pulled into the parking lot behind Coop's. "I'll come get you tomorrow. We can excavate the basement's dusty treasures, but my hopes are low. Then later this week, the attic—I have old historical journals and letters there."

Like Alice's letters. The ones that inspired *my* letters.

I was a fool to not tell him the truth sooner. Forget being in a pickle. Now I was in the world's biggest pickle jar.

Gabe unhooked his seat belt. "It'll be an adventure."

"You seem to always find the light in the dark, don't you?"

"I try. It's not always easy. I've found inspiration from others...who can find that silver lining when things are really rough, when life throws the kitchen sink at them, ya know? Want to come inside for some tea? No TV. I read or write at night."

"Is your muse back?" I blew my nose.

"Not yet."

"I should probably go home." My limbs felt like gelatin, my strength fully spent. I leaned in to kiss him goodbye, wanting to rest my head on his shoulder and sleep. Burdens awaited me at home, and I felt like an awful daughter to even refer to the house and Mom's needs that way.

I seized his lips at first for comfort, for escape, but then it morphed into desire. My movement changed to a full-on needy kiss. Gabe returned it with his sweet cocoa tongue until my lips were numb and swollen.

Oh, to be again a straitlaced Catholic schoolgirl who dated bad boys. The sneaking out and the sharing about it the next day with Adalyn. Prim Helen once had her teeny rebellious streak.

Gabe was not a teen crush or a bad boy. He was better. He was a man I really liked and wanted to go into his room with, one I wanted to forget the pain of the world with.

This time, his hand didn't stop at the band or under-wire of my bra. His touch traveled to stroke and then cup my breast.

Now I really cursed myself for not digging out that front-closure bra.

With his other hand, he caressed my neck and hair, doing things I'd only read about in novels. This man loved playing with my hair, and I loved him playing with it. We had to be fogging up the windows.

I was full-on making out in a car, in a parking lot, behind Ronan Cooper's inn. *Could the center console just disappear, please?* I wanted to sit in his lap again, feel his everything against my everything. So, I shifted out of the driver's seat and full-on straddled him. He released the lever and reclined his seat back, giving us room.

Our kisses grew hotter, an aching need climbing my throat to my demanding tongue, and down to my core, which begged me to go inside with him. I unbuttoned the plaid flannel over his t-shirt. I slid my hand hungrily along his abs—perfect, as I suspected—and up to his chest.

His hands fumbled with and quickly unclasped my bra. Mouth found nipple, and I was a goner. I lowered my hands to his belt.

My cell phone beeped from my jacket. Beeped a second time.

I wrangled myself free from our tangled arms and pushed my shirt back down, not caring about my unhooked bra dangling under it. My heart thrumming, out of breath, I said, "I need to get going."

"Stay here with me, tonight."

Our breaths heaved in unison. The look in his eyes seemed to dig into my soul, and it made my thighs quake.

This was not the time nor the place to make poor decisions.

He brushed a thumb against my cheek, then down the curve of my neck, and I closed my eyes, reveling in the final touch before I kicked him out of my car. He brushed ever-so-soft lips against mine in a brief kiss. I enjoyed it way too much.

My phone beeped again. Reluctantly, I fished it out of the jacket pocket. As I read the texts from Nan, my belly knotted.

"Crap! My mom's at the ER. I need to go."

"Want me to come? Is she okay?"

I reread Nan's messages.

"I don't know. No, please stay here. I-I'll talk to you tomorrow."

To Mom

I came home.

I'll be honest. I didn't want to. I liked being away, experiencing freedom.

The memory of the phone call has become a scar with rippled re-growth that itches in the sun. I wasn't here. I wasn't here to take you to the hospital that day. Just like I hadn't been there for Adalyn. Different situations, but all the same. I wasn't there.

The hour drive home was an agony of questions. Stroke? Meningitis? Or something worse? You fainted at dinner. They rushed you to the ER, incoherent, babbling. I had to pull over once to throw up. Once I arrived, I paced the waiting area, shivering from the anxiety that felt like welts across my skin.

Would you be you when you woke up, when they brought me to you? I envisioned it all, what our life would be like. Would you be able to walk, talk, use the bathroom? Would you need long-term care in a facility?

I decided to stay here, with you, for good. I never should have left. Bad things happen when I leave. Bad things happen when I don't answer the phone. No, I didn't cause your illness, but I hadn't been there for you—not immediately.

I never told anyone, but I had ignored the first phone call from you that day. I'd let it go to voicemail and gone about my day. Assumed it was you calling to argue again. You wanted me to fight for my marriage after the loss of my daughter. I was angry with you. How could you understand such a loss? To lose a baby? And I was still mourning the fresh loss of my best friend. And as a result, I missed the first call from you, earlier in the day.

But you hadn't called to argue with me again. You called to tell me you were feeling unwell.

I was a spoiled brat. What if you had died while I was giving you the silent treatment?

You're still you, my mom, the one who loves me unconditionally. But I miss the former you, the former me, the former family.

I always told you it was good for me to be back home after losing the baby, and Adalyn, after Wes abandoned our marriage.

I lied, Mom.

You thought that Wes left me.

I left him.

I can't tell you that truth, not now, not ever.

I was irrational and consumed with grief. I needed to escape the hurt, the constant reminder of what could have been. Returning to take care of you was a fortuitous excuse. I no longer had my daughter, and Adalyn was gone, but I had you to take care of now.

I get angry at God, at the world, at Dad, at your disease, at the doctors, at this gossipy small town. But it's life. You've taken it in stride, handling it with candor and aplomb. I see the bursts of light within you when you're with your friends or in the garden.

Though we're returning to the closeness we held before the losses, before the illness, things just feel different now. But I know this is only temporary. I won't leave you the way I left Wes. I won't leave you like Dad did. I can't leave you again. I lost my sweet Olivia, and then I lost Adalyn. I won't lose you, too.

I'm here for you, Mom, forever.

I inherited your fighting spirit. You have a way to make lemons out of lemonade, so as I sit here writing this letter, I allow myself to drift in and out of happier moments.

I made a new friend a little while ago. I think Adalyn would have liked her. Every week, she drags me to the new yoga studio down the road. She's the one who encouraged me to write these letters, now that I've been home for a year and the wounds—the losses—are still gaping.

I miss going to yoga with you. The doctors say you'll be able to resume some of your physical activity with time. Not sure if we'll be able to do those long walks on the old trails anymore. In the meantime, we can dream big.

I loved our adventures in the woods and meadows. Thank you for nurturing my curiosity and imagination.

We built fairy homes and positioned them in the field, along the pond, and in a hollowed-out tree. At night we'd chase fireflies and collect them in glass jars. We'd pick wildflowers and put them in your plant press. Then we would frame them. Mom, I know I'm not the best in botanical knowledge, but you let me press weeds—white clover, dandelions—and we pretended they were rare flowers only found in our yard.

I pressed dandelions, Mom! I loved to blow on the white puffballs to disperse a million wishes into our yard. We'd count how many breaths it took, and that was how many wishes I was granted.

Of course I tried to blow in one gigantic breath, because I thought the bigger breath, the bigger the wish.

My wish now would be to see you get better.

The yard is full of dandelions today. I can't bring myself to mow them over, so I'm letting the grass get wild and long. Instead, I picked one.

As I exhaled, I hoped the flying seeds would carry my prayers for Adalyn, for my daughter, and for you.
Love always,
M.H.

Twenty

Gabe

I knocked on Helen's door at eleven a.m., once again holding coffee and a box of pastries. We'd texted earlier in the morning. Her mom was stable and back home and they were skipping church today. She'd had a pain incident yesterday in her lower back, combined with an excruciating headache. And she'd been dehydrated and fainted.

I chewed my lip during the long wait.

The clock was ticking on finding something to help the library, and digging in the archives was still our best bet. But this was the wrong time to bother Helen. Maybe she could lend me the key or something? Or...we could postpone.

Just as I contemplated leaving, the door opened. Mary's glowing appearance surprised me.

"Oh, Gabe, hi. Helen didn't say you were coming." She waved me inside.

I stepped in. "How are you, Ms. Hadley?"

"It's Mary. I've been better. I worried Helen sick all night. She's asleep again, upstairs."

"Oh. I should go, then. Let her sleep, let you rest."

"You'll do no such thing. I'd love your company. Plus, I smell Barb's pastries. They're a slice of heaven. Come inside and have tea with me." She gestured to the sitting room. A crossword puzzle, a bowl of raspberries, a glass of juice, a mug, and a tea carafe sat on the antique table in front of the leather recliner. She situated herself within layers of blankets with a hefty moan.

I hovered, uncertain what to do. "Can I get anything for you?"

"I'm all set, thank you." She pointed to the carafe. "Tea? I can grab another mug."

"I have a coffee here but thank you. Would you like your tea heated?"

"Thank you, yes. I see you brought coffee for Helen, too." After I topped off her teacup from the carafe, she added, "Sit, sit. Standing people make me nervous."

I sat reluctantly. "I can come back tomorrow."

Mary dunked her tea bag in and out of her cup, then sipped, orange-cinnamon fragrance wafting to the couch where I perched on my toes.

"No. Please, stay. She'll be awake soon. Usually rises bright and early, but last night was trying on her." Mary assessed me.

I took a hearty swallow of too-hot coffee and almost coughed. "I'm sorry to hear you're unwell."

She released a harrumph. "Never thought shingles would wreak such havoc on my relatively healthy body, but diseases are complex." Tapping her knees, she said, "So, any more finds in your historical research? For the library?"

"Nothing really. We're going to check more resources at the library. I saw your work there. Beautiful. Watercolor?" I chose a raspberry cream cheese pastry from the box and Mary took one, too. Chewing it kept my mouth busy while I gnawed over how to ask the next question without sounding obvious.

"Oh, yes, used to be. A part-time hobby. I paint occasion- ally, but my hands can't hold the brush like they used to."

"Do you stick to watercolor?"

"I've dabbled in acrylic and oils. Ages ago, I used to design notepaper and blank cards or take my easel to the beach, paint while the kids played. Helen loved to collect sea glass."

"Oh, I saw that framed lighthouse art in her office. Your doing?"

She nodded.

"I'd love to see that paper."

"I might have a box or two of it still kicking around here. I'm afraid the art of letter-writing has become a past time to most. I believe your book may bring it back, though."

I stopped mid-bite and put the pastry on my napkin. "Oh? You read it?" Why was I surprised whenever people said they read my book?

"I liked it and loved the premise with the letters. I enjoyed Emma and Declan's journey. Letter-writing is more than an art," she said softly. "People pour their souls into it. In the 1850s and 1860s, my great-great-grandmother wrote love letters to her husband before they got married. We have a collection of them in our attic. Helen loved to read them when she was a girl."

The attic that Helen suggested but kept putting off and the letters she mentioned before. "Oh yes, Alice Foster Hadley."

"Will there be a sequel to your book?"

"Supposed to be, yeah. I've already signed the contract. But..." I scraped a hand through my hair. "Writer's block."

"It will come to you, I'm certain."

I glanced at the stairs through the doorway. "I have a question, Mary." The words came out faster than I could stop them.

Mary evaluated me with a hooded gaze. "What about?"

Do it, Dennehy.

"Adalyn Foster...do you know who she was? I saw a memorial for her in front of the library. Wondered about it. Was she someone else from back in the family tree?" Half lie, half truth. I already knew she was from the recent past. I hoped Mary or Helen could add to the little info I found online.

Her eyes narrowed, as if in pain, and she repositioned herself again. "She passed away a few years ago. She was a very distant relation."

I raked a hand through my hair.

Mary added, "She went to school with Helen."

Helen might know who M.H. was. Facts connected in loose chains. How could I link more? Could I access old yearbooks online? Look for any woman with the same initials?

Despite my eagerness, I said, heartfelt, "Sorry to hear about her death."

The creak of a person descending the steps stopped our conversation.

Helen's sweet voice followed. "Be right there." Then, sounds of steps running back upstairs—for something she forgot?

Helen padded into the room a moment later, sliding her arms into a sweater. Circles hugged her eyes, and her wavy hair looked wild, like the way it had after our make-out session in her car. "Sorry. I slept through my alarm." She yawned and gestured for me to join her in the kitchen.

"Talk to you later, Gabe," Mary said, her perceptive tone quickening my pulse again.

"Nice chatting, Mary."

I followed Helen to the kitchen. She twisted an aspirin bottle and took two, then swallowed a gulp of the coffee I offered. She rubbed her jaw. "I grind my teeth," she said, answering my unspoken question. "Have to wear this ridiculous mouthguard at night."

"Acid tears. Grinding teeth. I sense your superpowers are going to reveal their full potential soon."

She cracked a smile.

"You need more rest. I can help—get groceries? Hang out with your mom?"

She waved a hand. "What I need is to get out of this house. Let's go."

At the library, we divided and conquered. Helen perused a stack of documents like spring-loaded dishes in a cafeteria; remove one, another popped up in its place. I sat in front of the microform again, the whirring hypnotic and certainly better than the sound of a laptop fan overheating, then crashing. I tapped a finger on my chin as the fiche flew past. Or was it microfilm? Shoot, I couldn't remember the difference.

"Careful, Shelby," Helen said. "Don't need to break it. I doubt I can afford its repairs...if they even repair these anymore."

"Shelby?"

"Carroll Shelby, the race car driver. Shelby Mustang. My dad liked old cars, so I did, too. He would take me to antique or classic car shows. I had fun learning the history of each."

"Oh, I see. I'm a Corvette guy. If the thought of getting a car above the speed limit didn't make me queasy." I pointed to the screen. "How far back can we go again?"

"We have films with newspapers dating back to the late nineteenth century."

A few hours passed. I learned a lot about local elections, grocery prices, and responses to the Great Depression and both World Wars as well as the Civil one, and the Spanish-American War. But about how to save the library, exactly nothing. Then it appeared as if the micro-what-ever-the-machine-was-called could read my mind. "Oh, this is interesting." And appalling. The screen displayed an ad from 1858 offering a reward for a runaway slave named Mabel Elizabeth and a picture of the girl holding a ragged-looking home-made doll with a polka-dot dress. "She was a little girl. This is local. From Worcester. People suspected her passing through Sanders Mill." Below it was another ad for an adult runaway slave.

Helen leaned in. "Those could be something...or nothing. Let's print them."

After a few more minutes, she said, with an audible moan, "My brain's fried. Gonna get us some waters. Be right back."

Not finding anything else meaningful to our cause in the historical news, I shifted my focus to Pierce Howe and Miriam Prescott, in favor of uncovering dirt on this troublesome duo.

I switched to the computer, and a few minutes later, Helen came up behind me as I scrolled through articles from the 1990s. I highlighted one. "This is interesting."

"'Local builder sued for fraudulent practices,'" Helen read aloud. "That's old news. Won't help. When Pierce's father ran Howe Builders, he did shady stuff, like burying tree stumps beneath new housing properties so as they decomposed, the foundations cracked or sinkholes formed. Or he built on swamp land, bribing the DPW, inspectors, even assessors. He knew the right people in high places and got off with a slap on the wrist. Pierce has tried to be better about it." She cocked her head as if considering the truth of her statement. "Who am I to say he's not equally corrupt? I try to see the good in people...but it usually bites me in the ass."

"If Miriam and Pierce are in bed together, willing to risk their families and reputations, what's preventing them from making other dodgy deals behind the scenes?"

"Miriam's been upfront with her objective. But...I wouldn't put it past her. I mean, she's having an affair. Who is to say she isn't also doing other worse things." She pointed to a chess game box. "Look." She took the board out and set pawns, knights, bishops, and rooks in the squares. "My dad taught me as a kid. I can't remember all the moves, but I remember the strategy."

I slid my chair closer and leaned in. "Who's the king and who's the queen?"

"Their power lies in each other, but you need to take the king for the game to be over. The queen is probably the most powerful in the game, so I would say that's Miriam, and the king—Howe—can still survive if she is captured. He won't stop building houses if he loses the library land acquisition, so he may be out in *my* game, but he has more games to play. But Howe wants my land to build on. He needs Miriam to help him, as a Realtor and as someone who has cred in this town, to broker the deals, navigate the process. Miriam can move fast on the board. She's a versatile attacker, moving in any direction." She moved the queen around while elaborating. "Howe sits on his throne and waits, lets others do the work for him. He is the most powerful force, technically. I need to knock out his queen from this game—Miriam—to checkmate him. But if they trap me"—she tapped the other king—"it's game over. What they don't know is I've built my team, slowly." She slid pawns across the board.

"Always remaining one step ahead?"

She flicked the queen over, then the king, like they were dominoes. "Exactly."

"You've given this analogy a lot of thought." Crossing my arms, I leaned back, the chair groaning like an old ghost. "Tell me about Miriam the person."

Helen took a long drink of water. "She's married. Obviously unhappily. She runs the local welcome wagon, used to be on the PTO, volunteers on anything 'community' related. She's a well-known Realtor. Her company is on the town welcome sign, and her face is plastered on display ads hooked into the shopping carts at the grocery store. She wants recognition. Miriam touts her founding family a lot, uses it for her campaigns. Name and image mean everything to her. I've seen her with her mother...I feel some sympathy. Her mom is...let's just say unkind. Miriam's daughter, Harper, goes to the high school and attends the teen book club. Sweet girl, but I worry about her."

"Why?"

"She seems withdrawn lately. I think she's being bullied." She rubbed her pointer finger on her throat, and the hint of tears formed in the sides of her eyes. "I-I lost a friend to suicide. So, I'm sensitive to the signs, watch out for people. I'd hate to see Harper go down that road. It's just a feeling. It's also why I hope Kayley's husband, Aaron, can get his start-up going. His plan is more than tutoring. He wants to support kids in multiple areas—academic, social, and mental health. Kids need support before it's too late, ya know?"

I squeezed her hand. "I'm so sorry for your loss. That must have been very hard for you."

She stared at her shoes, and her shoulders drooped. Tears moistened the light brown lashes that fell over her eyes. "I could just be reading into things. It's hard to be a teen these days."

"Have you said anything to Miriam?"

"She blows me off."

I let her sit for a moment. Sometimes just being a presence and letting people be silent and breathe was the best thing. That's what my mom always told me.

She recovered herself and exhaled. "So, what do we do next? With Miriam."

I picked up the queen. "Might be worth looking into her backstory."

"Do you always sound like a writer?" Her pink lips turned up.

"Sometimes. Okay...moving on to the Hadleys..."

Helen crossed her arms and leaned back. "We have the deed to the library. The building underwent substantial renovations about forty years ago, so it's no longer original. I was thinking, maybe our focus needs to be on the land, not the building." Helen removed three of her own pawns from the chessboard. Took away a knight. Tapped an opposing rook. "The forest is classified as 'old growth,' but that's not enough. I've had someone from DCR assess the land, but he found nothing we could use to justify its protection on that front. I can check again though. Unless we find like some ancient, buried treasure or cemetery or dinosaur bones or something, anything... Arrgh!" She gathered the chess pieces and pushed them in the game box. "So much history here, staring in our faces, but none of it is significant." She held my eyes. "Want to hear something awful?"

I tilted my head.

Her voice quivered. "I've been giving the offer consideration. It's a lot of money. I can pay my employees severance. I can set Mom up for life, with good healthcare. Maybe this regional library is an okay solution."

I leaned in and squeezed her hand again. "Don't wave the white flag. Your king isn't cornered. What about the historical stuff in your attic? We could dig through that next?"

"I've read those letters a hundred times."

"Fresh eyes, remember? Plus, there are journals and other things?"

"Okay. Tomorrow? I'm fried."

"Sounds good." The wheels turned in my mind, rotating and stuck in mud. I moved closer and planted a gentle kiss on her cheek. "Let's bag this for the day and do something else."

She chewed her lip as we cleaned up the tottering pile of books and documents. I shut down and covered the microform machine.

"Have you visited the shops?" she asked.

"Not yet. Perfect idea. I need to get my postcards. I didn't on the last visit."

She wiped her eyes one more time and rose. "You're adorable. Dying art, postcards. Like letter-writing."

"You sound like your mother. She said the same thing."

After leaving the library, we strolled through the center of town, Helen's hands nestled into the pockets of her fleece vest. I squinted up at a soon-to-be-setting sun in a graying sky. The leaves had reached peak color—red maples, yellow birches and hickories, and multi-hued sweetgums. The more time I spent in Sanders Mill, the more it felt like home. "Gorgeous evening again. Want to have dinner after we shop?"

"Probably should get home to be with Mom tonight. How about tomorrow after we go through the attic? The library is closed on Mondays. Just FYI—don't get too excited. Old journals and letters aren't likely to give us anything except an image of days gone by."

"We'll find something." When I told Helen I'd been inspired by silver linings expressed by others, it was true. M.H.'s letters had truly left their mark on me, and I found myself leaning toward the optimism end of the outlook spectrum more and more because of her.

And from being around Helen.

She didn't give up. It inspired me.

In fact, M.H. had slowly fallen into the recesses of my mind as I found myself falling for Helen more. I wanted to get her alone and show her how much I thought of her.

We first stopped at Libby's Corner Store, where I thumbed through black-and-white historical postcards. I showed off the cool pictures to Helen—the old Mason's lodge, town hall, First Congregational Church, and Mount Wallaneag—and for each she had a story. She was a walking historical library.

Next stop was the Bohemian Boutique. I grabbed bottles of maple syrup and honey, then made a beeline toward the stationery section while Helen talked with Billie at the register. I wasn't sure how Billie managed both a job here and at the library, but Helen had hinted at her partner, Hardy, running the show here most days. The library was open Tuesdays through Saturdays...which means Helen had taken off yesterday. To be with me.

I eyed her perfect body from behind. Hmm. My mind was definitely not on the task at hand. She caught me staring at her, and a smile ruffled her mouth.

Smiling back a bit sheepishly, I leafed through the small stack of blank writing paper first. Nothing resembled M.H.'s paper. Then on to the boxed note cards. Sure enough, I found a box with Mary's initials on it. The note cards were bordered with the same trellised pattern of vines as M.H.'s letters. My pulse was a ping-pong ball. How many regional stores sold her stock?

"Be right back," Helen called as she stepped out the back door.

Billie rang up my purchases at the cash register. "Oh, Mary's note cards."

I shifted my sights in Helen's direction. She was talking to a burly man who I assumed was Hardy.

Billie caught my gaze and tutted. "Don't fret, pet. Hardy's only got eyes for me. You have no competition." She pushed her teal tortoiseshell-framed glasses to the top of her head and tapped on the register. "Thirty-five dollars and fifty cents."

I handed her my credit card. "Mary's art. Does she have anything else here other than the note cards?" I gambled on a second question. "Does she sell the note cards elsewhere?"

Billie bagged my goods. "Not anymore. She used to work with a printer to make lovely loose-leaf paper with her designs. That went to multiple shops in the area, including mine. Most people want note cards, and with her illness, I don't think she's made much of the paper in, oh, over five years. These are the last of my cards of hers, too. I could order you specialty paper by other local artists if you're interested."

I fidgeted with the collar of my shirt as Helen returned. "Thanks. I'll let you know."

After we walked back to the library where her car was parked, Helen drove me to the inn.

"I've enjoyed our time together here," I told her as we got out, then walked to my room door. "I was wondering...would you like to come see me in Newton sometime? I can treat you to my local favorites, now that I know yours." I held up my shopping bag.

An uncertain shadow fell over her features.

Flipping that look into a smile, she said, "I'd like that. I haven't been to the area in ages."

I ran a hand down her waist and settled it on her hip. "Great."

"There's always something to do in and around Boston. I love the Isabella Stewart Gardner Museum. Used to take Mom there when I worked for the Boston Public Library." She shifted from foot to foot as we stood under the awning over the door.

I wanted to kiss her again, but some weird awkwardness clung to me like static cling. Like when you found a sock stuck inside a t-shirt. Maybe she was just feeling discouraged after our research and depleted from everything with Mary. "That's right. You were a children's librarian, you said?"

"Yeah. I moved back home when Mom got sick."

I stroked her hip, and leaned in closer to her, my mouth close to her ear. "Want to come in for a coffee?"

Or more?

Before she could answer, Ronan Cooper approached. He gave me a nod, clearly intent on chatting with Helen for a second. I unlocked my door and ducked inside to relieve myself of my bags.

Their conversation filtered through the open doorway as I shrugged off my jacket.

"How's it going, Mary"—a phlegmy cough garbled Ronan's greeting—"Helen?"

"Good."

"Tell your mom I said hi," Ronan said, mixed with another cough. "Haven't seen her around as much. She okay?"

"She's good. That cough doesn't sound it, though. Want me to bring Billie's peppermint elixir for you, Coop?"

"If you think it'll help. Hey, been meaning to tell you that folks love the soup. Got more?"

I returned outside.

Ronan's eyes—one brown, one blue—sparkled with friendliness that totally disarmed a person. "Gabe. Enjoying everything here? Perfect weekend for all the leaf-peepers."

"Very much." My ears rang. In his greeting, had Ronan asked about Mary or was he confused when he first saw Helen? She looked a lot like a younger version of her mom, from the wavy hair to the vibrant blue eyes and pale complexion. Or had he called her *Mary Helen*?

She chatted with Ronan while my brain ran a mile a minute. I'd heard wrong. Ronan had been inquiring about her mom.

That had to be it.

Yes, that was it.

Then why did my pulse not slow down? Why was sweat beading at my forehead?

Ronan excused himself. "I should let you get home before you turn into a pumpkin or something. Say hi to Mary for me. Of course, I'll support you. Count me in. I'll talk with others. We'll lead the rebel charge!"

"Thanks, Coop."

Instead of asking her inside after Ronan walked away, I gave Helen a soft kiss on the lips, a different kind of charge zapping me now. "See you tomorrow for our *attic excavation?*" Unease bubbled inside me.

"Sure." She tilted her chin up and captured my lips a second time for a deeper kiss.

Once she left, I hurried to the desk and pulled out scanned copies of the letters from my shoulder bag. I left my beloved originals at home. With my notebook flipped open on the desk, I dug out a highlighter and began my comparison between M.H.'s letters and my notes about Sanders Mill, Mary, and her family.

And Helen. Anything in the letters with similarities to Sanders Mill or the Hadley family, I highlighted. Half of the content stood out in neon yellow after I finished. Granted, many of the facts could apply to anyone in a small town in Massachusetts.

I scraped a hand through my hair. Then, I composed a specific list of similarities:

Silver linings
Stationery—Mary's, also in Helen's home office
Adalyn Foster—Helen's classmate, memorial; distant cousin?
Helen's friend's suicide
Cemetery in proximity to the library
Rail trail (with icicles)
Housing developments

Absent father
Love of reading and art
Ill mother—Mary
Artist mother—Mary
Sea glass
Pressed dandelion—in letter, and some in home office
School mural on playground—check tomorrow?
Returning home (Sanders Mill) from somewhere else/job relocation (Boston)
Children's librarian at BPL, worked with children
Baby?
Cafe and mountain nearby
Hadley-Foster relation—common ancestor, Alice Foster Hadley
Grandma (Mary's?) gardens, tomato oil
"New office view"—library on Main Street?
Helen's two brothers. Ry = Ryan?
Ronan Cooper called Helen "Mary Helen"—?
M.H. = Mary Helen?

I felt like my head was about to explode as I reread the list. Was this mere coincidence? I massaged my temples. What next? Analyze handwriting samples? I'd given up on Lucas's help with the paper.

My chest expanded like the Hindenburg. I didn't need it to combust.

M.H. was not Mary Hadley-Wright or a stranger.

It was Mary Helen Wright.

The highlighter fell to the floor in a soft clatter.

Helen was my mysterious muse.

Twenty-One

Gabe

Yellow light pooled around the journals and books on the attic floor. Helen stood up and stretched, then tiptoed around the pile.

A box jangled as her foot kicked it inadvertently.

"Those don't sound like journals or letters," I said.

She turned the box around to see the label. "Nah, just a gazillion keychains."

"Got a thing for keychains?" I asked.

"Used to. My dad traveled a lot and would bring me back one from each place."

A collection of keychains.

Another similarity to the letters. I mean, how many kids collect keychains from their globe-trotting dad? Maybe some, but combined with the other likenesses in the letters...

My mind raced a mile a minute. Truth stared at me in the face. I had decided last night that first, I would see this project through. Help Helen the best I could. And, admittedly, I wanted to stay and enjoy her company as long as possible. Selfish, I know. Then, I would come clean. Fully. And accept the consequences. Those consequences might involve her never wanting to see me again, but I didn't want her to give up any leads on saving the library if she cut me off.

"Let's bring these downstairs. I made brownies. I need chocolate and it's dusty up here." She sneezed for emphasis.

We gathered the boxes and settled in the living room a few minutes later. I stared at the boxes, hands on my hips. "This is awesome. I'm sure we'll find something of historical relevance here. Sometimes the answer is sitting right in front of you." I watched her expression at my words.

My letter writer sat directly facing me, her heart-shaped lips biting down on a brownie. She'd been in front of my nose the entire time.

I'd wrestled with sleep all night. At first, my insomnia was because of pure delight. I found my M.H.! And I liked her in person as much as I'd liked her on the page. A lot. Like *a lot*, a lot.

But as I stared at the ceiling, my excitement had morphed into worry. Did she know my book was inspired by her letters? And if she knew, did she not hold it against me?

Now, sweat slicked my palms as I considered how to broach the subject. I couldn't just say, "Hey, by the way, I stole your letters, and yeah, the book is based on them. Please forgive me and have my babies."

She held out the plate of brownies. I took one, savoring the chewy sweetness, swallowing all sense of courage with it. "Yum."

"I sneak zucchini in them. Healthy-ish. Less guilt when I eat two...or three."

An hour passed as we pored over the contents of her ancestors' journals and letters.

I wanted to say Alice's "voice" in her writing was like Helen's, but I kept the thought to myself. Instead, I tapped one letter. "Alice's style is captivating. I love her poems."

How do I tell Helen I'm the horrible person who stole and exploited her words? The brownie suddenly didn't sit well in my stomach.

Helen read the paper in her hand, oblivious to the sinkhole in my brain. "I wonder why she capitalized certain words."

"Perhaps for accentuation? Artistic flair?"

She held out a few letters. "I don't see anything earlier than 1855, and the latest is 1862. She was fifteen in 1855 and twenty-two when Joseph finally returned home for good from his apprenticeship. They married, and a year later James was born."

She paused, and it was like something clicked in her head. Her blue eyes grew darker. "Reading them over and over, all of them at once, has me wondering...no, it's silly. I mean, I've read them a hundred times."

I blinked, rubbing unfocused eyes. *God, how I get it!* I'd read *her* letters a hundred times and had been left enamored and confused. "Nothing's ever silly. What?"

She tapped a finger to a crinkly page. "My friend and I used to write mystery letters to each other, using a cipher."

"Like a code?"

"We were goofy back then."

I wondered if it had been Adalyn.

"Look at this." Her hands shook as she handed me a letter and a journal opened to the same date.

I read both but didn't understand her excitement. "Looks like more inventories. Joseph's written loads of them in the early journals that cover his apprentice years. I've skimmed. To be honest, his writing is a bit dry. Alice's writing is more romantic, with her poems and all."

She pointed to one letter. "Look at the capitalized words specifically. Notice anything about them?"

Clock, Station, Kiss, Pond, Two, Ten, Heaven, Parcel.

I scratched my head. "They're all nouns? Wait, 'two' isn't a noun, is it? No, wait, yes, it can be. Like the 'two of clubs.'"

She snorted. "You're the writer and you're overthinking. Just listen as I read it."

She did:

"The Clock reminds me of our next meeting.
At the old Station, slow and fleeting,
Ticking, tocking, sturdy arm at half-past Ten—
I will see you then.
Anticipation for the next Kiss—
May our meeting at the willow not be missed!
Its sheltering arms hug the waters of the Pond azure.
Together like our carved names, mon amour,
I will speak to you by ink and pen
Until we meet again.
Forever your faithful devotee, Heaven's messenger,
I eagerly await your next Parcel."

She read the inventory in Joseph's journal. "Damn. No match. Silly idea. Not a code."

"Station? I know a few railroads went through here, but was there an actual rail station, a stop?"

"Not in Sanders Mill. One in North Prouty, though. Why?" Helen's face did somersaults: excited, bummed, curious. She said, "Maybe their relationship was forbidden by their parents—thus the code. A bit of *Romeo and Juliet*? Alice was a little younger than Joseph. Perhaps the station was their secret meeting spot. But..." She scrunched her face. "My mom never mentioned anything about that. Seemed like all parties were happy with the union."

A lightness filled my chest. "Remember how you said the historical society speculated that the Underground Railroad ran through Sanders Mill? They said the route may have passed through the older part of the cemetery? The dates of Alice's and Joseph's letters would align. And your Foster ancestors might be a distant relation to Abby Kelley Foster, the abolitionist in Worcester. I know you thought there was a chance."

We went back and forth between the letters and journals. Helen shifted in her spot, fingers dancing from one line of writing to the next. "The capitalized letters *do* have meaning, then. Perhaps they stand for times, locations, and people they were assisting? A *Station*—an Underground Railroad stop..."

"Would it be possible?"

"Maybe we're seeing what we want to see," Helen said, rubbing the back of her neck, doubt leeching into her voice. "My hope is in short supply these days. And this is big. Huge."

"Sometimes it's okay to hope. Find the silver lining in it, right?"

Like your letters, Helen. She didn't acknowledge my hint at all.

I swallowed. "We need to contact somebody, an expert, archivist, or consultant..."

She chewed her lip while she searched the web on her phone. A few moments later, she said, "All the common terms 'conductors' used for ferrying passengers were related to railroads or to Biblical locations or terms, like

Canaan or River Jordan. *Heaven* meant Canada or freedom. And *station*—a safe house or location. The letters contain those two words." She continued, her phone shaking with excitement, "*Parcel* meant fugitives or expected passengers. Maybe *Clock, Kiss, Pond, Two, and Ten* are other clues about time and location, or they were used to throw off authorities? A shared code only Alice and Joseph knew. I know where the weeping willow is on the back of the property. The pond, too. There's an old root cellar nearby. The original homestead was back there, then they built the big house here."

"Yes, your mom was telling me about it. And that it's no longer on the homestead part of the property, right?"

"Yeah. That area, around the cellar, is now part of the library's twenty acres. The cellar was used for bootlegging during Prohibition, but perhaps the Hadleys had a secret use even before then."

I tapped Joseph's journal. "I think you're right."

Her complexion was ruddy, her eyes wide. "I wish we had a key Alice and Joseph wrote to their code. This is all circumstantial until we find hard proof. Something physical. But maybe the key was never written down."

"Who was the architect Joseph apprenticed under?"

"Michael Prescott." She cringed. "Miriam's ancestor. Why?"

"Look at this other letter. It's not a poem. Alice says, '*Please do extend my heartfelt gratitude to Mr. Prescott for bringing your letter to me in person. He was a sympathetic gentleman, and I took great pleasure in speaking with him about the work that keeps you away. When he arrived at the Station, he came with a Mr. Smith, another Passenger for whom he bought a Ticket. Glory be to God for their safe arrival! I invited them both for tea and delightful conversa-*

tion before Mr. Smith needed to make his next connection. Mr. Prescott shall greet you with a Parcel from myself. Do be gentle with it, for it means much to me. Forever your faithful devotee, Alice.'"

I smacked my knee, rose, and paced. "This is it, Helen. The connection we need. Proof of the library's historical significance and I think Michael Prescott was involved. If we find something in the root cellar, that *is* part of the library property."

She stood up. "It's a reach, but I wonder if Michael Prescott kept his own journals. Maybe he had the key? Though writing the key down on paper would have incriminated them all," she continued, her words tumbling out faster. "And he was Joseph's boss and had more to lose. So maybe not. But Joseph does speak highly of him as does Alice, and those letters have a few of the Underground Railroad code words. It sounds like maybe Michael sometimes personally oversaw some of the escapee transfers. I'll email the Massachusetts Historical Commission to find out how to get these analyzed. It might hurry my application with the Historical Register along." The brightness in her blue eyes dimmed. "This process can take years, though, Gabe. We'll never have it by May."

"You knew going into this it might get bogged down in red tape, but you have to try, right? Once you have official paperwork in the queue, the town might need to cease and desist until the commission decides. You'll have the townspeople behind you for the vote. And even Miriam, when it involves her family's reputation. You did it, Helen!" I stopped moving and embraced her so tightly she squeaked. I pulled back, the fire blazing inside me. "Are you thinking what I'm thinking?"

"We need to check out the cellar."

"Let's go dig."

Helen

Memory navigated me on the old paths. "Glad we hosed down with the tick repellent. They've been worse lately, even in the fall," I said as I tented my hand over my eyes from the afternoon sun and pointed the way.

"Give me snakes in the Amazon, tarantulas and scorpions in the desert, and bears in Alaska, but ticks—gross." Gabe visibly shuddered and steered clear of long ferns beside the trail, keeping as dead center as possible.

"When Mom's shingles hit, I originally suspected Lyme disease. Boy, was I wrong."

He fell back beside me and brushed a hand along my spine. "I'm sorry."

"When did you go to the Amazon? Or is that a dream trip?"

"In Ecuador, after my Guatemala trip. Remarkable—I fell in love with it and all the other places—Mindo Cloud Forest, Cotopaxi Volcano, and of course the Galapagos," he said with awe. "The islands are worth the hype. Darwin's foundations. Naturalists love it."

Jealousy twinged in my gut. "Sounds amazing. Did you see, oh, what are those weird birds called? Boobies?" Reminded of his hands on my breasts, a flush raced up my throat.

I tripped over a thorny vine and muffled an ouch.

"Blue-footed boobies. There are also red-footed ones," he said. "Plus penguins, sea lions, giant tortoises, iguanas, sea turtles... I scuba-dived below a school of hammerhead sharks. That was a dizzying experience. I had to get certified before going. I prefer snorkeling. Did that with the sea turtles. Much less stressful!"

We paused near the tree with my and Addy's initials. Sunny beach. M.H. read clear as day. I leaned against the spot, feigning a need for rest, and pointed to the fallen log with Alice's and Joseph's carvings. "Check it out."

He followed my gesture. "Directions for the Railroad?"

"Alice and Joseph. That's the tree they carved their initials in."

He ran a finger along the old bark. "Hard to read."

He admired the etchings in wood from one hundred sixty-odd years ago. "Does this mean we're close to the cellar? We already passed 'the Pond azure.'"

"Close, yes."

I headed in its direction. Fatigue throbbed in my muscles, in my soul. I wanted to tell him. To ask him point-blank. But we were so deep into this relationship that it was too late now. I liked him too much. I wanted to pretend he never found my letters.

He caught up to me. "You got quiet there, Helen. I sound like a showoff with my trips, don't I?"

"Nah. Traveling is what you do. My dad traveled a lot, too." The comparison of him to my dad was not lost on me. I waved to the forest. "Apparently, this is what I do. Librarian meets Indiana Jones?"

He rested his hand on my hip, drawing me in close. Close enough for a kiss. His lips skimmed mine. It was chaste, yet the most sensual of them all. I wanted to melt into him as his lips lingered, his breath hot against my mouth. I found my hands tangled in his hair, pulling him closer.

When he paused, I gasped, my heart a freight train in my chest.

Clearing his throat, he glanced around. "Is there any evidence of the original houses here?"

I blinked from a mental whiplash. "They were closer to the pond. Nothing's left of them but crumbled stone foundations. The root cellar was constructed to have a longer lifespan."

We walked another minute and then I saw it. "There." I pointed to the natural hill into which the cellar had been built. The old door had disappeared, but rock supports flanked the entrance, forming a rough arch. Still-green grass carpeted the roof.

Gabe teased, "I wonder if a hobbit lives in here."

The sunlight backlit him and I admired his well-shaped bottom in those jeans, his muscled back, and his hair dancing atop his head like grains of wheat on a windy day.

"Not cozy enough. No fireplaces or sunlight streaming through windows. Solid, though. Families hid in here during the infamous tornado."

"Underground Railroad, bootlegging, tornado shelter...what a history."

"We're not sure of the first one."

"Yet," he said with a wink.

I clicked on a flashlight. "So, we're scared of heights, but the dark and small places...you're okay with?"

"I am if you are."

We entered a dank space barely fifteen feet wide.

Gabe zipped his jacket to his chin. "Cold."

"Root cellars were ideal fridges back in the day. It stays under forty degrees...or maybe just a little warmer, since the door is off now."

"Ever explore a cave?" he asked.

"Once, in upstate New York. You?"

"Mammoth Cave National Park in Kentucky and a few smaller ones through the years."

I tried not to allow envy bubble to the surface, because despite it, I enjoyed listening to Gabe's stories and adventures.

My flashlight beam jumped over the dirt and reinforced timber ceiling, rocks, and metal scraps of miscellaneous machinery. We walked in circles on the packed earthen floor. "Not sure what we'll find." My breath clouded in front of me. "I've heard of Railroad artifacts found beneath floorboards in houses. It's damp in here. Anything might have decomposed. I imagine there used to be shelving."

Moisture dampened my cheeks already. I would have racoon eyes after a few minutes. Waterproof mascara could only do so much. And my hair was a great hygrometer. I tucked a strand behind my ear with a huff. Soon it would be thickening, the waves growing, shorter pieces sticking to my forehead.

Gabe lifted rusty old equipment. We both ran our hands along the walls, over any tool or crate. Some items were newer, a few decades old. I never had time to maintain this area of the property.

"There's got to be ventilation shafts in here, right? Food needs air flow?" he suggested, looking around. "What are these barrels?"

"They're plastic, newer. To collect rainwater outside. They used to be near the library. I have no idea who put them here. Mom, Dad, or someone else."

"Do you think they'd hide runaway slaves in here when so many people had access? Sounded like this was a communal cellar at one point, right?"

"Food was in here. People coming and going. Doesn't sound safe for hiding people to me. But maybe hiding something or someone in a conspicuous place was the magic behind the hiding. They wouldn't think to look in here."

"Hide in plain sight. Yeah."

My shoulders slumped. "I give up. It was a silly thought."

"You? Quit?"

I huffed. Water dripped from somewhere within. Soft plops hitting puddles on the ground. I wrapped my arms around myself, shivers rippling on my skin.

"Let's check the walls again," he urged.

"You want to say you *literally* dug, with dirt under your nails and all," I teased.

"Humor me. Feel around."

"What are we feeling for?"

He didn't respond.

I set the flashlight on the rain barrel, angling it to shine into the middle of the cellar. I started on one side, Gabe on the other. As high as I could reach, I ran my fingers along the wall. Up, down, circle motions. Felt for creases, hinges, latches, carvings, holes...anything. I came upon the occasional holes, spaced equidistant. Shelf supports? "Do you hear the dripping?"

Gabe and I met unsuccessfully at the two barrels. We wiped our dirty hands on our jeans. "Yeah. It's louder here. Give me a hand with these," he asked, reaching for the first barrel.

I repositioned the flashlight and propped up my phone with its light, and we heaved both barrels away from the wall. I shined my phone at the wall. Dirt, grime. Same as the other walls.

I rubbed my fingers through a groove, figuring it was another shelf support. Except— "Gabe? This feels different here. A different kind of hole. Like a long and vertical groove. I can slide my finger up and in it." My heart pounded. "Come feel it."

He did, then moved back to his side of the barrel. "I feel it over here, too. Goes from the floor up about three feet."

I followed the groove as it turned ninety degrees. Gabe and I met in the middle.

"A door," we said in unison.

"Find the handle," he said.

None.

"A closet inside a cellar?" I said, my voice quaking.

He sifted through an old toolbox and came back with a flathead screwdriver. Wedging it into various grooves, he slipped and hissed when he jabbed his finger. Tried again.

My heart ached to see his determination. He wanted to help me save my library so much.

I clutched the flashlight. Gabe had really gotten to me, hadn't he?

I hovered beside him, feeling his anticipation, keeping the light as steady as I could.

A few cracks later, the door popped open. A gust of even colder, clammier air hit me in the face, smelling more earthen than the main part of the cellar. I shined the light with a trembling hand and crouched.

"Goes back...I don't know. Six or eight feet? Not high, either." Gabe bent to go inside, but I stopped him. "Not sure we should. We don't know the stability of the ceiling in there."

"I'll chance it." He froze. "Unless you want to."

"I'll stay here. Be quick."

I kept the light steady as he went in on all fours.

"It's tight in here. Wet. The water seeps in somehow." He thrust his hand out. "Can I have the flashlight?"

I gave it to him and felt instantly freaked out, left with only the light coming through the exterior doorway and my phone. Moments passed like hours. I kept expecting something to jump at me or tap my shoulder.

His muffled voice filtered back to me. "There's not much in here. A small room. No tunnel or anything. I can't imagine how people could hide in here, but I've heard of smaller spaces than this. But..."

Shivers coursed through me. "Gabe, let's come back with more lights."

He scuffled around. Metal clanked and shoes scraped dirt. He handed something to me. A metal cup. Then another thing, both soft and brittle, had some weight to it. An old doll?

Scraping. Heavy breathing. My pulse flaring. By the time he finally emerged, cold gripped me so hard, I wasn't even shaking anymore. "I need air, Gabe."

We emerged into the bright afternoon, and I saw spots, gulped in freshness. Once my vision cleared, I stared at the mug and doll in my hands. The mug looked like tin. The features on the doll's wooden face had disappeared, leaving it expressionless. She wore a polka-dotted dress. No chipped paint, no carvings. Old tufts of yarn sprung out from the head. The dress felt like a tightly woven, but deteriorating cotton—like the kind used for flour sacks.

"This doll, Gabe..."

He eyed it. "Looks like the doll in the newspaper photograph of that little girl. I know." He held an old lamp burner and metal bucket. "I felt around and gathered what I could in this." He set the bucket down and ran his hands through the findings. "Some broken teacups. A comb. Crab claws and chicken bones." A few dirt-covered buttons slipped through his fingers back into the bucket. He pulled out two intact glass bottles.

"Well, someone was in there. And not recently." I inspected the smaller blue bottle, embossed with *Brockton* on the side. "Medicine?" I ran my finger over the raised letters.

Gabe pulled out the larger, round amber bottle. "And this one probably had wine or cider or something?"

"I wonder if this stuff can be dated by experts."

"I suspect so. They can even date the dirt in there. I've read about them doing DNA testing on tobacco pipes to connect the owners with present-day family." He wiped a dirty hand on his jeans. "I think there was a tunnel in the back of that secret space. The rear wall felt loose, not packed like the rest of the room, like there had been a collapse at some point."

"Do you think—?"

His brown eyes lit up. "Each thing on its own—the letters, these artifacts—that doll, the newspaper article—may not point to it, but if we put it all together..."

I bit on a tremulous smile.

"I think we found the Station, Helen."

Twenty-Two

Gabe

After discovering the hidden room behind the root cellar, my adrenaline was pumping. Sleep evaded me again that night. And I could not stop thinking about Helen.

I had a few more stops in town, evidence to gather that Helen was M.H. Then... I would tell her the truth. I owed her that. Before I lost my courage, I texted her to meet me later today.

First stop, the local schools. There it was: a mural painted on a wall beside the playground showing the four seasons of Sanders Mill, just as described in the Adalyn letter. As I checked it off my list in the pocket notebook, I wasn't even surprised.

While working the confession and apology over in my head, I stopped at the town cemetery, though at this point I was just procrastinating. I had already explored the older section of the cemetery that abutted the library grounds, eighteenth-century headstones nearly worn clean from weather and time. Given that Adalyn was born in Sanders

Mill, I expected her grave would be here, too. If not, it'd probably be in North Prouty, where she lived later.

At the entrance of the hilly, well-maintained cemetery, I drifted past manicured hydrangeas and commanding maples clinging to their colorful leaves. Trails went left, right, and straight. I worked my way around. Clouds had rolled in last night, leaving overcast skies. I zipped my thicker coat to my neck, chilled to the bone from the drop in temperature...and from the truth I still fought.

A cyclone of emotions twisted through me: guilt, shame, grief, hope, fear. What if she didn't forgive me? What if I lost Helen forever? But I knew things couldn't continue forever with me keeping this from her.

A woman walking a golden retriever strolled past, greeting me with a friendly nod. I read the names on headstones I passed, but none was the one I searched for and dreaded.

Halfway through my searching, I stopped cold. Helen stood before a group of headstones along the path. She took her phone out of her vest pocket. I gulped, instantly sweaty despite the chill.

She looked up from her phone. "Hey, you. Thought we were meeting up later?"

"I wanted to check out the older headstones, see if any names matched those from Joseph's journals. Unearth more about Miriam's family, too, maybe. You?" Could she see my sweat? The lie burned my conscience.

"Getting my steps in before work. Heading to the library now."

"I'll walk there with you if you'd like?"

She tucked her phone into her vest pocket. "Sure. I'd love the company."

I cast a glance at the gravestone where Helen had been standing.

Adalyn Foster.

Waning yellow and purple flowers, which I'd bet were the asters and catmint referenced in the letter to Adalyn, cocooned the granite, but not enough to obscure her name.

Helen *was* without a doubt my M.H.

Helen

My heart drummed.

He'd just seen me at Adalyn's grave. He *looked* at the engraving. He'd made a weird face! Like the kind you see on someone when they bite into a sour candy.

He.

Knew.

I popped an antacid, the chalkiness a distracting hit. *Breakfast, stay down.* Was he going to say something...or would I finally say it?

We trudged up the incline in silence.

I was tired of this. If I had only confronted him sooner, I wouldn't have fallen for him.

If he wasn't going to say something, then I would. I pried my mouth open to speak.

At the same time, he said, "Helen, I need to tell you something."

He tripped on the loose paver just before the turn into the library parking lot. I knew this sidewalk by heart. He did not. How many times had I asked to have it fixed?

Down he went, and I was too slow to grab him.

"Oof!" His phone fell out of his jacket, along with his small notebook he wrote everything in. The phone made a cracking sound when it hit, and the notebook fell open.

"Dammit! I'm such a klutz." He blew on scraped hands as he righted himself.

I was reaching for him but stopped when I saw the list in his notebook. A highlighted list with words I recognized. *Adalyn. Sea glass. Artist mother. Baby.*

My breath caught. I grabbed the notebook and skimmed the page.

These weren't his notes on the historical stuff we talked about. It was a list.

About me and someone named M.H....

The signature I used for my letters. I remembered that much. The only people who knew I signed the letters that way were me, Kayley...

And my letter thief.

A horrible taste rose in my throat. Blood pounded in my ears. I didn't expect to feel so enraged. I mean, I suspected what he'd done for ages. And I knew he had figured it out when he made that face at the headstone. But anger surmounted nerves now.

Had he known all along? Had he been playing me since day one? Was he using me for the next story like he'd used me for the first one?

He grabbed his broken phone and shoved it in his pocket. Then he saw me staring at the notebook. "Helen...this is what I needed to talk to you about..." he said, his breathing ragged.

"What is this?" I flipped through the pages, my eyes blurring. "All this time, I wanted to believe it wasn't true. That you hadn't stolen my letters." A hiccup came out as I bit back the tears that wanted to fall.

"Helen, I—"

Too furious to let him speak, I shook the notebook, then shoved it into his chest. "These are notes about me." I muffled a sob with another hiccup. My voice was barely audible, a strained, mouselike squeak that didn't sound like me at all. "About M.H. Mary Helen. Me."

"Yes. They are." His brown eyes widened, pleading. "That's what I needed to talk to you about today. I-I didn't know it was you until..." He shook his head, his mouth downturned. "I'm so very sorry, Helen."

"You really had my letters. My...letters..." My knees grew weak as a sharp pain fisted in my chest. I swiped at the tears. It was all true. And I had known this. So why was I reacting this way?

Oh, that's right. Because I cared for Gabe.

He stepped closer, his hand outstretched. I jerked back, hugging myself.

He closed his eyes for a moment and visibly swallowed. "I screwed up so badly. I'm an ass. And I'm so sorry I did this to you. I only just figured it out, Helen. That's why I texted today," he said, sighing so hard it could shake trees. "I've always felt disconnected from the world, even from my worlds I write. But your letters changed that. I began to feel like I was part of something. No longer an outsider looking in. As weird as that sounds. I'd lost my muse, Helen. But then I found her. Or the letters found me. Or whatever. Your words saved me. You. I found you."

I wiped the snot that dribbled out of my nose as more tears fell. "Well, you just lost her again."

I closed my eyes for the briefest moment, refusing to look at his face. Then I turned and ran into the library.

A long day later, my eyes and soul weary from trying to distract myself with work while replaying the scene over and over in my head, I went home. I flopped into the squeaky desk chair in my office.

I leaned back and stared at the far wall at the only photograph we had of Joseph and Alice. The lovebirds who had inspired this entire miserable journey. Alice's fine, fair hair, almost white in the monochrome, was parted in the middle and swept back into a low chignon. She posed in a rocking chair, the one that now sat in the corner of Mom's room, draped with Grandma Helen's quilt. Joseph, tall and lean, stood beside her, his jacket open, a chain to a watch crossing his vest. Though a smile wasn't typical for this era, I could see the hint of one in Joseph's dimples, and the happiness in Alice's subtly upturned lips.

"Why did I write those letters?"

"Because you needed to."

I wiped at wet eyes and found Mom standing in the doorway, an apron on.

With a scratchy throat, I asked, "What?"

"Come, Helen. I made dinner. Let's talk."

I followed her to the kitchen. A stir-fry sizzled on the stove. It smelled delicious, but my stomach had been fighting me all day. The brown rice might help. I served Mom a larger portion and myself a small one.

"Wine?" I asked.

"A splash."

I chose one of the few bottles we kept for company and poured.

"Lorraine's doing?" I pointed to the centerpiece on the dining room table.

"We went to Bern's Farm for the fall workshop."

"She's a good friend." I forked a bite of rice and chicken dripping with Mom's mystery sauce into my mouth, followed by a three-second gulp that emptied my "splash."

After pouring more, I swirled the light-bodied red wine around in my glass. It smelled like cherries and was dry on the tongue.

I'd have a headache come morning if I drank too much. Screw it. I wanted a headache. I wanted the pain to dull the ache in my chest. Is this how Adalyn felt when she self-medicated, drowning sorrows in pills and alcohol?

We ate, me feeling sicker to my stomach with each bite, before Mom asked, "Remember when you had an appendicitis?"

"Yes."

"The worry I felt. I can't explain it. I remember watching over you in the hospital. Then the waiting. I paced the halls. Your father had to calm me down."

"What's this about, Mom?" I didn't want to hear a Dad story right now nor anything remotely sentimental.

"You've done so much for me, Helen. I need you to stop trying so hard. I'm going to be okay. I have my ladies and my senses. A daughter shouldn't have to be this worried about her mom."

I laid my fork down and took another long drag of wine. With a mostly empty stomach, I was already feeling buzzed. Enough that I could forget about Gabe.

"You need to live your life, Helen. You're surrounded by reminders, by grief."

Bubbles caught in my throat, and I coughed. "What do you mean?"

"The library—"

"I thought the subject was off-limits during dinners?" I snapped. I never snapped. I put my glass down.

She drew out slow, hesitant words. "Usually it is. But...you have so much on your plate, how can we not talk about it? And it's a constant reminder of..." She paused and grimaced. "There's the memorial for Adalyn..." Mom sipped her wine and looked me hard in the eye. "Me. Our home. And now this search for historical significance."

"I found something significant!"

"Yes, you did, but at what cost?"

I huffed. "What's wrong with wanting to take care of you? What's wrong with wanting to save *our* library?"

"You didn't have to come back."

"Wes and I...it didn't work out. I lied, Mom. He didn't leave me. I left him."

Silence.

Maybe she already figured it out.

"The baby..." I stopped myself. I was *not* going down that path with its twists, turns, and knots. My heart trembled, remembering my sweet Olivia. She'd been a welcome accident. Born an angel. Oh, God. Through more tears, blubbering, I said, "Mom, I love you and want to help you. I couldn't help—"

"—Adalyn. Helen, there was no helping her. You've got caregiver's syndrome, or whatever they call it. You carry endless remorse over her death. And Olivia's. I'm so sorry you lost her, too. But running away from Wes and Boston and coming here to deal with me...wasn't the answer. Living here, you're stuck in yesterday. I need you to move forward."

I slammed a fist on the table, rattling the salt and pepper shakers. "Dad isn't here, Mom. He left. Nan and Lorraine are friends but can't live here with you. Ry and Dan have their busy lives away from here. Have you forgotten the other night? The ER? Somebody needs to be here for you! I had a great childhood and now it's time for me to reciprocate. I love you and want to help you." My head thrummed. I twirled the now empty wineglass. "I'll clean up." I stood.

"Mary Helen Wright, sit, please." Mom's voice shook, as if she'd used her last breaths on those words. Fatigue furrowed her brow, but concern welled in her eyes. "I read the book. Gabe's book. I know it's *you*."

Wobbly knees brought me back onto the cushioned dining chair. "Mom...it's fiction."

She glared at me, eyes narrowed like blue daggers.

"How did you know?"

"Well, Gabe is a great writer, and it takes a keen eye to see the similarities between Emma's griefs...and yours. That night you wrote a letter with Kayley, I had come down to get tea. I overheard some of your conversation and you spoke about Olivia, Wes, your dad, Adalyn...me. I take it there was more than one letter?"

"It's complicated."

She topped off our wine. "Tell me."

"It all started with Alice."

Her eyes glowed. "Alice has a hold on us, even a century later."

"Adalyn and I loved reading her letters to Joseph. Remember?"

"I do. You two were thick as thieves."

"After moving back home, I was miserable. I lost our baby. Then Adalyn died. Then I left Wes." The pain hitched in my chest as a sob bubbled up.

"And then you were here, taking care of me," she said softly.

"Those love letters messed with my head. I told Kayley about everything, and she encouraged me to write to all of you—Dad, too. To get it off my chest. I started with one and then found myself writing more. But instead of burning them like any sane person would do, I dropped them in the postal mailbox. It felt more real that way. But I didn't put on any address or stamp. I thought they would just get thrown away. And, well..."

My lips trembled and fingers shook as I played with the cloth napkin beside my plate.

"How did Gabe get them?"

I explained what I knew about the post office and central office processing. "Maybe he had a friend there? He didn't exactly explain. However he did it, he found my letters and thought, 'jackpot!'" I said bitterly. "Sure, he changed a lot from the letters, but it still contains just enough, you know? For me and for Kayley to see the connection. You, too." I chewed on my lip. "He knows, Mom. He knows it's me. Today...not until today did we both know." I recounted everything up until today, all of it. Sobs racked my chest. "It..."

"...didn't end well, I take it," she finished for me.

I poured and gulped more wine. My head spun. I shoveled some food into my reluctant mouth.

"I think he came to town searching for his mysterious Emma, the muse who saved him. Me? I can't seem to help or save anyone," I said miserably.

With a frown, Mom said, "Mary Helen..."

I rubbed my nose.

"Well, he found his mystery writer. Me. He pieced it all together. It's all out in the open now. He apologized, but all I did was storm away." I dabbed at my tears with the cloth napkin. "He's in love with the idea of me. The letter writer... He's in love with the fictional person he created in his mind."

"That's nonsense and even you know this. He loves you, Mary Helen. And you love *him*?"

"I don't know."

That was a lie.

The next morning, Billie rapped on the door to my office. "Yes?" I looked up from my cold tea and the soggy bag beside it, and from a dreamland of regret and what could have been.

"We have a problem."

"Great." I rubbed my temples.

"You're going to need something stronger than tea."

I grimaced. "I did that last night." And woke with a wicked hangover that still hadn't subsided.

"Okay, don't say I didn't warn you. Paula from the historical society emailed me." She shuffled books off one chair to another and sat across from me. Oh, no. Billie never sat, always a busy bee, trying to get her ten thousand daily steps.

I wrinkled my brow, bracing myself. "And?"

Billie steadied herself for impact, hands clamped tightly in her lap. "The historical society has moved their event to the newly renovated senior center."

"Wh-what?" I blinked as if I'd heard wrong. "The Holiday Fair? The biggest event of our year? The one where Santa is already booked, and all the vendors, and the gingerbread house contest, and...and..." I wondered if my trash can was nearby. I needed to puke. "Our biggest event. She didn't."

"She did. Mrs. Claws isn't pulling any punches. At least we don't have to watch her parade around in that red dress and white wig, acting sweet as a candy cane."

Another chess piece captured by Miriam.

Twenty-Three

Gabe

Unlike the hazy fog I was accustomed to when forcing writing, today I could barely keep up with my fingers on the keyboard, words flowing like water from a broken dam. I feverishly strung sentences together as soulful melodies thrummed from my phone. My heartbeat matched the music's tempo.

After some time, dizzy and breathless, I slid back from the desk. I cupped my stiff fingers...but, when I took a break, reality shredded me to bits.

I was a horrible human being. I should never have taken those letters from Marco. It wasn't until I saw who I'd hurt that I truly realized how awful my choice to use those letters had been.

I loved Helen. The flesh-and-blood person, not just the letter writer.

I hurt her badly. The breath had been sucked from me when I saw the pain in her face as I tried to apologize. I'd known she'd be angry, and I deserved it, but her words burned like acid. She had opened a line into her soul with those letters, and fictionalized or not, I had exposed her most personal thoughts. I'd allowed my ego, my hunger to write something people would remember, to over-shadow integrity. I had wanted to prove myself worthy of...of admiration, of pride, love, of...worth.

God, I effed up.

I stood and hit the kitchen. My mouth dry, I dug in the fridge for orange juice.

I needed to make up for the pain I'd inflicted upon Helen. My botched apology was shit. She deserved better.

Slow steps brought me back to my desk, and I stared at my computer monitor.

I hadn't been working on the sequel this past week. Sure, I had found inspiration in Sanders Mill. But that second book was still dead in the water. In fact, I was going to try to get out of the contract. Laurel might kill me, but I could not write the sequel. Not now.

Instead, I'd spent all week writing Helen love letters.

In the letters, I expressed in words what I had stumbled over in my botched apology. How she inspired me. How she pulled me back from a ledge. How I loved my time with her. Damn, how I *loved* her. Down to the freckles across her nose and the nervous habit of popping antacids and the little smiles she let slip out when she thought nobody was looking. I sure had been looking.

But Helen needed something tangible. She had recruited me to her cause, after all. Though Helen appreciated the written word, I suspected her love language was acts of service: she needed action, not promises. She did so much for her mom, for her community. She even worried about her enemy's daughter's mental health.

These heartfelt letters were not the answer. I closed out the file and dragged the folder to the recycle bin on my desktop.

I had another idea.

Helen

During the weeks after Gabe's departure, colorful October transitioned to the dark nights and somber brown of November. I missed him.

Anger had won. And he left.

On my best days, I was frustrated, thumping around my office snapping at Billie and volunteers, slamming books on the counter, leaving without saying goodbye, and glumly taking care of Mom at night. On my worst days? I was a sniveling, crying fool.

A leaf blower droned outside my open library office window on a wet November day—the sort of day which made my head itch with a weird combination of allergens and moist air. The sound grated on my last nerve. I sneezed, then took a decongestant.

"Be grateful they're *doing* the landscaping," I whispered to myself. Did blowing the leaves into the woods count as landscaping?

I shot off a follow-up email to the Massachusetts Board of Library Commissioners. Then another to the Massachusetts Historical Commission. I already sent in my request for consideration along with the inventory form weeks ago. It sucked not having the historical society to vouch for me, but whatever.

Next, I composed a follow-up email to Dr. Virgil Gavison, an accredited Underground Railroad expert with the National Park Service, about the letters, journals, cellar, newspaper article about Mabel Elizabeth from 1858, and hidden room and the artifacts we found. He'd not responded yet to my initial inquiry. Time to push more. I read the message ten times before hitting send. Who knew how long the queue was for getting a person on-site? I couldn't even fill out the nomination form until they deemed the property and items eligible. I hoped Dr. Gavison could help speed the process along.

Last, I fired off emails to several small-town librarians who ran private libraries with public funding, to pick their brains for any ideas on how to save this sinking ship.

This week, I'd contacted local shop owners. It was time to put thought into action and raise my army while I waited on the "officials" to decide if my request held water. Everyone I ran into understood my predicament and would gladly vouch for the library. But when the time came...would they? Saying and doing were completely different things.

Once the leaf blower stopped, I clicked open my planner.

First on the calls today—Joe with DCR. I summoned my happy persona and covered a yawn while the phone rang.

"Joe here."

"Hi, Joe. It's Helen."

We made small talk before I got to it. "Is there any way we can protect the forest from developers? I know we talked about it a few months ago, but I thought I'd check in to see if you managed to get more info? You know about Miriam's vision."

"Yeah, I've heard about her master plan. Here's the problem with Massachusetts old-growth forest protection policies—they can change at any time. It would need to be state-owned to fall under those policies, really protected, and sadly, we don't have a lot of land like that as is. They're still contracting out logging of older forests. I hate to envision what it will be like in thirty years."

My hope sank. This was my plan B.

He added, "We can keep on educating the public, but there's not much more we can do beyond that scope. Currently, less than one percent of forests are old growth, so that's a unique thing you got going there. I advise not spending your time or money on this. It could even be to your detriment if you let the state get involved. An education campaign is the best plan. Keep that land private, Helen. Fight for it."

"I am, Joe. I am." It came out a squeak, more like a mouse than the determined fighter I was trying to be.

We chatted a bit more and scheduled a few informative events about the old-growth forest, and he promised to assemble a team to aid me in clearing out the trail to the root cellar. I checked the call off my task list, even if it wasn't what I'd envisioned.

I emailed one of Mom's lawyer friends, cringing with the idea of accruing legal fees. I might go bankrupt and drown in paperwork, but my boxing gloves were on.

A rap on my door knocked me from my focus.

Kayley smiled brightly. "Hey, girl. Let's get coffee."

I followed her, my head spinning.

We snagged the corner sofa at Barb's Cafe, and I sipped my decaf latte, the milk frothy, but the flavor falling flat.

"You know I love you, right?" Kayley patted my knee.

I squinted at her over the mug.

"You've been a crankosaurus for weeks."

I glowered at her, my shoulders sagging. Sliding the mug onto the coffee table, I exchanged it for an apple Danish. Apples made me think of the festival with Gabe. I turned to her and said, "Grr."

She laughed. "Okay, let's take this one thing at a time. First, Miriam."

I groaned.

"Touchy, touchy. Okay, let's table her for a sec." Kayley didn't retreat. Instead, she pivoted—one of her assets. Intense green eyes pierced me. "Gabe?"

The room suddenly felt too hot. He and I first met here. I'd taken it for some sort of meet-cute. "That situation's not any easier."

"Your heart is invested in both problems, but I disagree. I think Gabe is *much* easier. Time to put on your big-girl panties and make the move."

I gaped.

"No, not that. Though I'm sure he'd appreciate *that*." She smirked, then shifted to a serious expression. "The other thing. Talk to him."

"Ugh. I can't."

"He's texted you a few times, hasn't he?"

"Yes. Twice. Wanting to talk. I didn't respond."

She continued, "The way I see it, you have two options. One, give him a chance to apologize properly and make it up to you. Two, completely walk away. You can't keep teetering like this. For your own sanity, pick one, embrace it, and don't look back."

I drummed fingers on my coffee mug. Pumpkin mocha. Gabe liked pumpkin. That's why the flavor didn't hit my taste buds like it usually did. "Kayley, what do I say? 'Hi, *Gabe. I knew all along about you stealing my letters and*

*writing them into a bestselling book. I knew I was Emma
from the moment I read it. I was too chicken to confront you
and instead fell in love with you. And then I let you think
I was so pissed off—okay, I was pissed off—when I found
out that you figured it out."* My voice had risen and drew
attention from other customers. Patty Schlegel stood at
the counter. One of Miriam's friends. Of course, just my
luck.

Kayley snapped her fingers in front of my face. "You love
him?"

"What?"

"You said you loved him, girl."

"I guess I do. I-I love Gabe."

"Sounds like you don't want to be mad at him." Her eyes
widened, then narrowed. "I know this is shitty. What he did
was shitty! And I'm sorry if I've been pushing you to hook
up with him all this time as if none of that happened. But...if
you *do* want to... Or do you want to kick him in the nuts?"

I didn't know if I wanted to do either. Or both. "Don't be
sorry. You...he's...it's..."

"Very complicated," she finished for me. "But..." She
chewed her lip, clearly pondering. "Can I tell you something?"

I sipped coffee. "Sure."

"He called Aaron."

"What? Why?"

"He wants to help him with the start-up. They were
already talking about it before all the shit went down
between you and Gabe. They spent hours hashing out
ideas. He connected Aaron with a few people at the Thrive
Center. And Gabe is donating money to the project—in
memory of Adalyn. He got Suicide Awareness of Central
Massachusetts to sponsor Aaron as well."

I had no words. Gabe was supporting Aaron's SPARK Tutoring project?

Kayley pressed on. "Maybe he's trying to make up for it. He can't undo his mistake, but he can make a difference. You said he apologized. So, the question is...can you accept it?"

"I don't know yet." I finished my coffee.

Kayley squeezed my hand harder, and we sat in silence for a few minutes. Because my bestie knew when not to push too hard, she didn't bring up what I'd said about the "l" word again.

My phone beeped. I looked at it, then shoved it in my pocket. Kayley watched me expectantly. I told her, "It's Gabe. He wants to see me. To talk."

I felt more tears welling, a river behind an old dam ready to break at any moment.

Twenty-Four

Helen

From under the leaves blown on the front porch, I collected the Sunday newspaper Mom forgot yesterday, then trudged inside, tightening my thick wool wrap sweater. "Brr. I smell snow. The skiers will be happy if we get some before Thanksgiving." I flopped onto the sofa in the front room, not ready to face Monday.

Mom whistled, working on her crossword.

"Feeling okay today?" I asked, leaning in for a sip of hot tea.

"Good. You?"

"I'm breathing."

"That's important."

"I scheduled a meeting with one of the library commissioners for early January to talk about all our options, just in case."

"You've got a good mind for this, Helen. You'll make it work. I'm proud of you." Mom squinted at her crossword and tittered. "Oh, the irony."

"What?"

"The answer was *villain*." She penciled it in.

"Did the clue read *Miriam Prescott, town moderator*?"

Mom chewed on the end of her pencil. "How's everything going with the historical expert?"

"It's going. Finally. Dr. Gavison is evaluating the items we recovered and the letters and journals. The MHC scheduled a team to come evaluate the cellar in December to see if it meets criteria. I feel good about it except..."

"It *won't* be too late," she said, shooting down my unspoken worry.

My limbs felt irrationally heavy. "If they find it eligible, then I need to fill out the nomination form, and then it gets presented to the State Review Board at one of their quarterly meetings. The only one between now and May's town meeting is in March. That's cutting it close, Mom. If all the stars align, they'll forward the nomination to the National Park Service." I blew out my breath. "Whew. So many steps that are out of my control. All these *ifs*."

I opened *The Pioneer*. Like letters and libraries, the newspaper was another thing Mom and I wouldn't give up, even after the local paper had been acquired by a Worcester conglomerate. Most news was available online, but I enjoyed the feel of our weekly edition in my fingertips. I knew a few of the journalists on staff, and I submitted announcements for upcoming events. Maybe I was just holding on to yesterday.

Mom did her crossword; I read the paper.

Splashed across the third page read the headline, *Local Letters Inspire Bestseller*. I spilled my tea. As in, all over the coffee table and rug. "What the hell!"

Oh, this cursing was not about the spill. Not at all.

Mom squinted at me above her glasses.

I bounced my fingers against my mouth as I read the entire article about Gabe's book and an *anonymous letter writer* inspiring his story, and that letter writer being from Sanders Mill.

My hands trembled, and the newspaper slipped from my fingers. I wanted to toss it into the pellet stove. "Patty Schlegel."

"Who?"

"One of Miriam's minions. I think she overheard me and Kayley talking."

Anonymous. Thank God. But why? Why? If Miriam knew it was me, why not mention me by name? And what good did this serve her? It didn't help her cause. It just made me feel like a fool. "Is this just to toy with me? Get in my head?"

Mom picked it up and gasped. "Crafty twit. This is low, even for her. Ignore her. And yes—just to get under your skin, sweetheart. Gabe made up a lot of the story. It would take someone who knows you very well to see you in the book."

"Am I being punished for wronging Miriam in another life or something?" Humiliation stole my voice.

My mental chessboard shook with earthquake proportion, but it was still intact.

I would not let this get to me.

I slogged through work on Tuesday.

Thankfully, only a few people came into the library asking for the "book about Sanders Mill." Given the number of people who had attended Gabe's book signing, I suspected many already owned his book and were dreaming up ideas of who the real Emma was.

Needing a breather, I took a walk around back on our newly cleared trails.

Upon my return, my mind no clearer, I found Harper sitting on the bench. She stared down at her hands, crying. I stopped mid-step to turn around and give her space, but the crinkle of maple leaves under my feet betrayed my presence. She wiped away her tears and looked over her shoulder.

I resumed my approach. "Hi, Harper. How's book club going?" I chewed on the inside of my cheek. A lame question and touchy subject, since I hadn't seen her there in many weeks.

Harper sniffled and rubbed her nose. "Fine." Deep circles cradled her eyes.

"May I sit?"

She moved her backpack to her lap. I took it as a yes.

How could I start? My ignored pleas to Adalyn played in my mind. "Is everything okay?"

She gave a half-hearted shrug.

"If you don't feel comfortable talking to your parents, there are school guidance counselors who can help with whatever may be upsetting you."

She flaked pieces off her chipped fingernail polish. "They suck. I can't talk to my counselor."

I pressed on, my fortitude withering. How did any parent of a teenager do it? "If the other kids are bothering you, speaking to your counselor at school should help. There are mediation processes on bullying."

She laughed cynically. "I doubt Mrs. Howe will understand."

"Your counselor is Andrea Howe?" As in Pierce's wife. Well, damn.

She nodded, fidgeting with the hem of her jacket.

"Is there someone else you can talk to?"

"You don't get it."

"I'll listen."

Harper looked up, and against skin that looked gaunt, like she'd just gotten out of the hospital from a prolonged illness, her eyes glowed with anger. "She's ruined my life!"

"Who?"

She tapped and swiped on her phone screen before thrusting it into my face. A social media post with a photo of her mom standing next to Pierce Howe at a grand opening event, "slut" scrawled in red text over Miriam. The post had hundreds of likes and a bunch of nasty comments.

I kept my composure, despite the swirl of emotions within me. "You can't believe everything kids say or let that get under your skin. They're trying to get a reaction out of you."

Harper tossed her phone into her backpack. "You *can* believe it when it's true. I overheard her on the phone with him. Not just cringe but disgusting." She clenched her jaw and gave me a pained stare. "All she cares about is her *reputation*. Her position in this town. Not me, not Dad."

"This will pass. Everything does."

My heartbeat quickened as pissed-off tears welled in the corners of her eyes.

"It won't. All adults do is lie."

My fingertips felt like I had touched a cold glass window in deep winter. The iciness slid from fingers to chest. I hadn't been able to help Adalyn, who suffered emotional wounds into adulthood. I had barely saved her life on that horrible beach trip when she had overdosed...only to lose her a year later.

How could I help Harper, who was fifteen, with so much of her life ahead of her?

"Not all adults lie," was all I could muster, trying to instill hope.

She wrapped her arms around herself. Shadows stretched along the edge of the forest, and their length crept closer as the sun dropped behind the trees.

"Oh? You lied about the letters and the stupid book! I heard it all when Mom and Patty were talking. You wrote those letters, and when Brenna and I talked to you about the book, you flat-out lied to our faces. I thought I could trust you. You. All. Lie," she said through orthodontically perfect clenched teeth.

Before my brain could catch up, Harper stormed off.

The effect started with my throat—the flush of shame, a burning ache with each swallow—then surged to my stomach, my shoulders, my fingertips and toes, the crown of my head. All I'd done was push her away more. I had to undo this.

"Not again," I mumbled to myself on the way home. "Don't do it. Don't do it."

Do it. Do it. Help the girl, my conscience countered.

After a quiet dinner with Mom, I closed myself off in the office and pulled out my phone. Finding Miriam's number was easy. She was a Realtor, after all.

She answered on the third ring. "Prescott Realty."

With my pulse throbbing in my neck, I spoke. "Hi, Miriam. It's Helen Wright."

"Oh." Her disappointment could be felt across an ocean. "Hold on." A pause. Quick steps. Clacking heels crossed stone or tile. A door closed. "Yes?" came out like a growl.

"It's about Harper. I'm worried about her."

"Worried? How? What business is this of yours?"

I opened and closed my mouth twice. I didn't want to betray Harper's trust, but I had to do something. "She's in trouble."

"She's fine. I would know."

"She seems..." Not *disturbed*; that was too gloomy.

Gloom could quickly turn into something far worse. One moment Adalyn had seemed fine, the next she was downing pills and hurting herself in a public bathroom before our snorkeling outing in Mexico. It was supposed to be a girls' weekend to celebrate our friendship. I had planned it. Pinched pennies to save. I wanted us to just be, to let our hair down and share in the moment and that beautiful place.

The door had been locked. She didn't respond even though I knocked several times. An attendant had to break in. We found her on the floor, unconscious. A pocketknife on the floor beside an empty pill bottle. The cut on her wrist had been superficial. She must have passed out before she got too far. The shop owner called the paramedics. I called her mom during the ambulance ride. I had to check her in at the hospital. Get her social security number, insurance info, everything. I don't know how I held it together in the moment.

I had felt so alone, so responsible for her. I had gone into survival mode until our plane landed and she was back at her parents' house.

Then I cried.

I felt angry, betrayed, used. She knew that I would be her life preserver. Had it been a cry for help or the real deal? Even before then, I had felt used. For a long time. I played to her whims. But I thought that this is what friends did for each other. I looked out for her.

Afterward, there were unanswered phone calls. Long periods of radio silence. Disconnection from friends, from me, from her family. While I encouraged her to see a therapist, to exercise, take a class. Reminded her to consult her doctor about her meds. Tried, and failed, to help her.

Harper is not Adalyn, Helen.

I finally said, "She's upset. I don't see her with friends. There could be bullying."

Miriam snapped, "Harper's a moody teen."

"But—"

"Last time I checked, Helen, you don't have kids. And this is none of your business. Butt out."

Pour an entire sea of salt into the wound, would you? I clenched my fist, then dug in my pocket for the antacids and pulled out an empty wrapper. I could not dull the agony rupturing my insides with a chalky antacid. "She needs help before she hurts herself."

"Helen, you'd be smart to back down now. I'll handle *my* daughter."

The knot tightened. I sat there and took her verbal beating.

"You have other pressing issues, Helen—or should I say Emma? Not only will I release the information about *who* wrote the letters, but I will disclose *how* they were obtained. Stealing mail is a federal crime. Dennehy might not look good in a prison uniform, will he? And your little library knowingly hosting a felon's book signing." She tsked. Or was it a laugh?

"What?" *Great comeback, Helen.* My head spun, and I paced the office. "Leave him out of this."

Countermove time. Attacking me was one thing, but attacking Gabe... No. Just. No. Sure, he hurt me, but I would now allow her claws to drag him down in this war, too. And Harper needed help. Her life could be at stake, and I would *not* stand by. I steered this conversation back to where it belonged. "Miriam, Harper knows about you and Pierce Howe. That's why she's falling apart."

She inhaled sharply, to my surprise. "We're collaborating on the housing project. I'm his Realtor."

"No. I *saw* you two. At Sanderson Farm. Making out behind the Sugar Shack. It wouldn't look too good for you, what with you running for office next year, would it?" I felt ill just throwing that threat out, one that I would never, ever follow up on. I clapped a hand over my mouth but could not stop the rage from leaking past my fingers. "I know journalists, too."

Her grit faltered. "Rumors aren't proof."

"Others know about it, too." Loose truths at best. I said firmly, forcing down my raging stomach acids, "If you don't do something to help Harper, I will get the school involved. And if you say one word about Gabe to the press, I will tell them about you and Howe."

"You conniving bitch—" Miriam said, but I cut her off by ending the call.

I found the nearest trash can and threw up.

To Adalyn

You left.

But your spirit remains.

Why did you do it? Why couldn't you give it time, wait for me to help you? I asked you to see your doctor about adjusting your meds. I helped you find a good therapist. I encouraged you to join me for girls' nights. Just me and you—downtime, like we used to have. Movies and popcorn with chocolate chips. I checked in with you every few days.

None of that was enough.

After that vacation from hell...I thought you'd reached rock bottom. I guess not.

So, I've been feeling crappy about everything that's been going on in my world—my baby, Mom's illness, Dad deserting us, and of course you. The trip to Mexico...and also the day I lost you. I hadn't been there for you when you needed me. It wasn't on purpose; I had been in a meeting. And God, Adalyn...I had just lost my baby! I could barely be there for me.

I wish I could hug you again!

Guilt eats at me. If I had responded sooner, would you still be here?

Could I have done more to help you? Was I too caught up in losing Olivia to see your struggles worsen? I hate myself for being angry with you, too. But the day I lost my daughter shattered my soul. And you weren't there to help me get through it. The one time I needed you to be my rock...you weren't.

Then you left us, left me! You stopped fighting.

Anyway...I'm sitting on the couch beside a roaring pellet stove and empty wine bottle. I've got a new friend here. She's *a godsend on many days. She drags me to yoga class. I think I even see my abs now. You'd be proud.*

I know how much you loved to run. Maybe I'll take up walking. My new job isn't too far away from home. Maybe your sprit will be there with me with each step. I still have some of your favorite playlists on my phone.

Anyway, we just watched a very sappy movie. We munched on your favorite snack—homemade popcorn with almonds and chocolate chips mixed in so they melt and get all over our fingers.

Between the movie and snack, my emotions are probably just charged. My friend—she insisted I do not put her name in here—said I should write this letter, let the pain out. I told her how much you and I liked letter-writing. She suggested burning it in the pellet stove after I'm done, but then I thought, why not drop it in a mailbox? It would make me sad to burn a letter I wrote to you. Maybe if I send it off, it'll be like you're not really gone, you know? I can pretend it's just a letter like old times. Obviously, you don't have an address where you are. And we know I'm frugal, so I won't put a stamp on this. But my shoes are on, so I'll just walk to the box and drop it in there. You'll be with me on this inaugural walk.

In fact, I think I'm going to write letters to other people, too. There has just been so much grief this year. Your letter is the first, though.

When it comes to grief, people say "give it time." Bullshit. Time does not heal all wounds. How can loss go away when it feels like parts of you have been carved up and removed? Grief never disappears.

The town has commemorated you. I walk past the memorial stone with its plaque every day. I pluck the dead flower heads from around it. You'd be proud of me, finally starting to get a green-ish thumb.

Mom bought flowers to plant by your grave. You'd love the asters and catmint, a bright yellow flower and a zesty scent to match your personality. You hid the gloom behind sunshine. But I also need a flower to recognize the deep sadness you carried in you, hidden behind a bright façade.

I try to remember the you before it got bad. Before your pain became too much to struggle against. I love you. Always will, Addy.

Remember the old weeping willow way back behind the library, off the trails? When our book club was just us two and we would read under that tree? An escape from reality. Giggle-fests when we read old Emily Post articles on etiquette and called your imaginary advice column Fussy's Mussings.

And how, when we read our family records—those old letters and journals—we became investigators, digging through our histories. We were sisters in spirit and distant-distant-distant cousins.

Our initials are still carved in the old willow, I assume. I haven't visited it since your death. I can't muster the courage to visit your grave yet, either.

Remember when we were twelve and we helped my mom paint the mural on the school playground? The one showing the forest through the four seasons? She was patient with us as we flicked paint at each other and goofed off. I painted the fox, you the black bear. But Mom painted all the rest. Mom misses you, too.

I remember so many things, Addy. Sleepovers. Concerts. Swimming at the lake. Cramming for finals together. Holidays. Talking all hours of the day. Your hunt for the perfect Ryan Gosling meme or GIF. Your bright smile, the real one, on your good days.

I miss you, dear heart. I'm sorry I couldn't help you more. I'm so sorry. May we meet in the hereafter, may you forgive me.

Besties for life and beyond,

M.H.

Twenty-Five

Helen

Billie walked by with a stack of newly labeled books. "Relax. He'll text."

I tapped a pen on the counter, saying goodbye to the last of the library patrons for the afternoon. The day after Thanksgiving was always a slow one. But then, the library had been eerily quiet for the past few weeks. The annual Holiday Fair *should* have been next weekend. Harper's book club stopped meetings, too, and the adult book club took the month off.

My heart hurt like hell.

I kept checking my phone, but not for Gabe's texts. At least not today. He had given up after my last non-response.

I paced downstairs, shutting off lights, double-checking locks. Finally, my phone pinged, and I read the long-awaited message from Aaron.

> It's a girl! Deciding on a name. Mom and baby are doing well.

Kayley's daughter was here on the day after Thanksgiving—a sweetness added to the bitterness of the anniversary of Adalyn's death. I'd been so preoccupied and excited that, although I still carried the grief of Adalyn's passing, for the first time in years I didn't get a chance to put a flowerpot by her grave. I would go tomorrow morning. Instead of crying all day, I had been filled with anticipation, with hope.

I drove home, the night crisp and a dusting of snow on the ground.

I found Mom cooking up a storm. "Great, you're back. Shepherd's pie, Thanksgiving leftover style."

"Yum. Good news—Kayley had her baby! A girl."

"Wonderful! I made a second pie you can bring to Aaron this weekend."

As we ate, I flipped through my notebook, updating Mom on Operation Save the Library. Mom and I had decided nothing was off-limits anymore at dinner. "I have a bunch of local businesses backing me." I rattled them off. "...even the Four Founders Lodge. The Sanders and Estabrook families were all in when I approached them. But the Prescotts? Adamant no." I sighed. "Who cares if I don't have Prescott support? I also have the support of the two churches. You got me the senior center and knitting club." I reached across the table and squeezed her hand. "We have so many voices that will speak and vote for us at the town meeting in May."

Her face glowed with maternal pride. "I knew you could do this."

"Thanks for dinner, Mom. And for listening." I pushed my plate away, too full—too revved—to eat another bite. "I know he'll be busy with the baby, but I spoke to Aaron about SPARK Tutoring operating out of the library. Now that he's got the financial backing, we can start moving forward." At the mention of Aaron's start-up, my heart throbbed again. Gabe had planted the seed, which had germinated faster than one of Mom's seedlings.

"That's great," Mom said as we carried dishes to the sink. "You might get youth support behind you, too. Young voices at town meetings can inspire."

"I haven't seen Harper around. I hope she's okay."

Mom leaned in and hugged me as I scrubbed a plate. "You did all you could."

"I suppose." My shoulder muscles tightened, even with Mom's rare hug, my body unwilling to release the nagging guilt. "No updates from Dr. Gavison, though I check my email a hundred times daily. I met with a historian in North Prouty who knows about some rumored Underground Railroad locations in our area."

So much hinged on this. If the ball could just roll!

Another possible lead—any hidden records of Michael Prescott's—was a dead end for now. But with more digging—Gabe would be so proud—I found an old article confirming that Micheal Prescott was a known abolitionist. Even with this, and the mention of him in Alice's communications, it was still not enough proof of his involvement. I couldn't possibly approach Miriam to ask what she had from her ancestor, not after our last phone call.

Ugh!

Still, things hadn't gotten *worse* after that tense conversation. Perhaps it was the spirit of the season, but she had eased back on her smear campaign. Spirit, ha. More like my threat had worked, for now. She hadn't released any more information to the public about the letters' author. Nor had she made any efforts to bury Gabe in legal charges, that I knew of. No matter how complicated my feelings were for him, I didn't want to punish him as harshly as the U.S. government might.

Mom didn't ask about Gabe. I didn't talk about him either.

On Saturday, I dropped off the shepherd's pie with Aaron, and then I shot over to the hospital to see my bestie.

After going through registration, I stepped into the elevator to the maternity wing.

I didn't expect the grief to hit me so hard. First, it roiled like a low wave, building in my stomach. Then, as the elevator doors slid open, the colorful storks, cheerful sun, and rosy characters painted on the wall made it a tsunami. The sounds of babies crying, the astringent smell of cleaners, bustling medical personnel, whiteboards, bright lights, beeping equipment...

A pain stabbed my stomach as the elevator doors closed behind me.

I'd become a pro at managing hospitals with Mom's illness and getting over the trauma associated with Adalyn's overdose in Mexico. This grief was distinctly and specifically related to the day I lost my baby girl.

This is where women become mothers.

My fingers grew numb, and I dropped the gift bag with its pedicure kit and baby onesies, toys, and bibs. The contents spilled out as it toppled.

Hunched over, I breathed through the memories of me and my sweet Olivia Alice.

I am okay. It is okay.

I would do this. For Kayley. For me.

My lip trembling, I gathered the items and pulled myself upright. Heavy legs brought me to the desk. I checked in, got my visitor's badge, and made my way to her room.

I could do this.

"Knock, knock," I said at the door, finding my voice.

"Come in," Kayley's fatigued voice called.

When I saw her in bed holding her baby, the pain retreated to its sacred spot within my heart. I was going to be okay. Happy tears gripped me. "Oh, Kayley. She's beautiful."

Kayley reached for me with her free hand. "Oh, honey. You shouldn't have come alone."

I sniffled, sitting in a nearby chair. "No, this is good for me. I'm going to be okay."

And for the first time in a long time, I believed it.

"How is Christmas almost here?" Kayley asked as we wandered through a craft store in the mall. Ivy, already three weeks old, was asleep in the stroller.

"No idea." I paused at a box of origami paper.

"New hobby?" Kayley asked.

"No. It's... He—" I still had the little origami bird Gabe made for me.

"Get it for him." She nudged my shoulder.

"But...we're over."

She grabbed a box and placed it into my hand. "You're not over yet."

We continued to the next store, the purchased origami paper assortment like a lead weight in my shopping bag.

"Even though it felt strange not hosting the annual Holiday Fair, and Miriam's been slowly snatching groups from me, I'm okay," I said as I flicked through cute baby sweaters hanging on a rack. I held up one with a purple teddy bear.

Kayley let out a little screech and grabbed it. Despite sleep deprivation, she radiated beauty. But then she asked, "*Okay* okay? Or like, well—" She made a grumpy face. "—Eeyore okay?"

"Decent okay. Even stopped taking my antacids." And my eye twitch had calmed itself.

"I'm happy for you, Helen."

"I have a good feeling about May."

She paid, and we left the store. Kayley pointed to a bench in the food court where we could sit and enjoy a couple of soft pretzels.

"How's mommyhood treating you this week?" I slid a bootie that kept falling off back onto a teeny baby foot.

Kayley yawned and sipped her decaf tea. "Ivy seems to have day and night backward. Thank you for all you've done with Aaron. I can't wait to see the new space."

"His program is going to be a hit. I can just feel it." I dipped my pretzel into mustard.

"I never got to ask you...how was Thanksgiving this year?"

"You were kind of busy. Honestly?"

"Always." Ivy made unhappy newborn squeaks, so Kayley picked her up.

"Mostly good. I got so wrapped up waiting to hear your good news that I got busy, distracted. Almost forgot what day it was."

"That's a good thing?"

"Yeah, it is. I didn't cry this year. The day wasn't filled with all the pain. It held joy—for you and Ivy. I still went to visit Adalyn. Put a winter flowerpot by her grave after I visited you. But I felt...less sad."

I shivered despite the sunlight bathing us through the skylights, then closed my eyes and tipped my head back, allowing the warmth to soothe my fatigued eyes. "Sometimes it feels like yesterday. But it's been seven years. As time passes, the grief loosens bit by bit. Like a scab falling away, leaving only a fading scar. I feel okay. Really okay."

"That's good, honey. Good. You've come a long way. How's Harper? I know you're concerned about her." Kayley shifted Ivy over her shoulder and tapped her back gently.

"I hope my message to Miriam got through her thick head. I don't know anything for sure, though. I still worry about Harper. Ever since Adalyn, I've had this radar for those in trouble. Maybe it's penance."

Kayley cleared her throat. "Not penance. You're just sensitive to it. And that's okay. We've gone over this..."

"Okay, okay. Not my fault. I couldn't help Adalyn. There's this stigma with mental illness, you know? She hid herself, even from me most days. I couldn't see into her brain. And I can't take on the pain or burden of others. It's not my job to help or 'fix' them. Adalyn, Harper, Mom..." I inhaled deeply, grounding my thoughts. "Writing those letters helped me seven years ago. Got the ball rolling on healing. It's been a slow and bumpy journey, but I've been feeling better."

Kayley squeezed my knee.

"And who knows—Alice's letters may just save my library. If it wasn't for her, I wouldn't have written mine, and then Gabe brought my letters back to me—figuratively—in the form of his book, and then he came here on tour and helped me find the Underground Railroad stuff... This all started with Alice and Joseph and now is coming full circle. If Alice only knew how much her words would impact lives now as much as they did then."

"You amaze me, Helen."

"Me?"

"You. I'm proud of you, what you've done despite it all." She paused and stroked Ivy's teeny, tiny nose. "Life sure gave you a kick in the ass but look how you've overcome it."

"Thanks."

Kayley adjusted Ivy to nurse her. "How's Mary? How are the treatments?"

"She seems to be doing okay with them. I'm hopeful. The doctors are optimistic. Though we can't reverse her condition, we can keep it from progressing."

My phone beeped, and I ignored it.

"Oh, girl, you know you need to get it."

"Mom's with Coop today. The man would lay down his cape for her!"

Kayley's eyes widened and her pink lips formed an O. "What? Your mom and Ronan Cooper? Oh, Mary's getting some action!"

I cringed. "Uh, gross. He took her to get our Christmas tree."

"Followed by a kiss under the mistletoe."

I slid a look to my phone. I was waiting for the news. The notification wasn't from Mom.

As I read the email from Dr. Gavison, I whooped so loudly it startled a nursing Ivy.

I bolted upright and my feet did a happy dance. "Oh my gosh! The team has authenticated the letters, journal, and artifacts as historically accurate! And the site evaluation team supports the eligibility of the property! So now I need to bust my butt on getting the nomination paperwork in, and then we wait for the review board in March." The happy dance slowed. "Depending on the number of applicants, it may be weeks or months before I hear a decision. Which cuts it close to town meeting time."

Kayley squeezed my hand while balancing Ivy in her other arm. "It will happen."

My heart fluttered, and I summoned hope from the trench of uncertainty. I held my fingers over spread lips, overjoyed. Then faltered.

"Text him."

"Who?"

"You know who. This is a great icebreaker. Tell him the good news. Then listen to his apology. I'm sure he'll have one. He helped Aaron, after all, and now you."

I stared at my phone. "I ghosted him, though."

"He'll respond. I know he will. Go. Tell him. Now. Don't make me take your phone and do it myself..." She arched an auburn brow.

I knew she would.

My phone pinged again, and I dropped it. It bounced on its side, then went face down. Thank goodness for its case. I swiped it from the floor. "It's Mom." I read the text.

"Should we go?"

"It's Gabe!"

Kayley mumbled as she situated Ivy in the stroller, "I know they call it mommy brain, so I am a bit confused. Was it your mom or Gabe?"

Prickles stung my eyes. I grabbed Kayley's forearm as my voice trembled. "Gabe wrote an article about the library—about our plight and other libraries in the state in similar situations, with budget cuts or threats of closure. It ran in two Boston papers today. A Boston news show just called Mom. They want to interview us! And, well, now we have the historical stuff we can share."

"That man has pull. And he's using it for you. After he helped Aaron and everything. Girl, sounds like he wants to make it up to you."

My hand shook as I reread Mom's text message. A million "buts" ran through my brain.

Kayley softened her tone. "Helen, bestie, wonderful, amazing you. Are you ready to bring him back into your life? Are you ready to forgive him? I love you and will support whatever you decide."

Forgiveness. The word had been floating around in my head for weeks now. Like a puffy cloud that never seemed to go away. "Yes. I am. Forgiving him for reading and using my letters is hard but...I'm ready."

Before I lost the courage, I texted him.

Twenty-Six

Helen

Going to Newton wasn't nearly as hard as I'd made it out to be. Nan and Lorraine agreed to schedule time with Mom, and Kayley said she'd come by with dinner Saturday night. Nan gently pushed me out the door with a wish list of things I'd promised to buy for her from a notable market.

Chest tightening, I wrapped my sweaty palm around the list.

Nan squeezed my other hand. "Helen, she'll be okay. Girls' weekend. Time for you to go see him." She leaned down, patted my shoulder, and had to push me farther off the front porch, my feet feeling leaden. "Don't make me call Lorraine..."

If Lorraine were here, she would heave me over her shoulder and toss me in the car. I supposed she and Nan knew I needed more gentle persuasion today, not forceful encouragement.

"What if Mom has a nighttime issue?" I argued, turning around.

"Gifty's on call. Plus, we'll come by first thing in the morning." Nan tutted and came down the steps with me, wrapping her thick alpaca sweater close over her svelte frame. She was the same age as Mom yet seemed ten years younger. Fresh face, life in her voice, lightness—not fatigue—in her step.

I hesitated by my car door.

"We've got this, okay?" she said once more.

"Okay." My voice cracked.

Newton was an hour away, and Saturday morning traffic was a breeze without commuters. Before I knew it, I was almost there.

Seven years had gone by since I'd last driven to the Newton-Watertown area. Until now, the only reason I had to drive east was Mom's doctor visits. I avoided any excursion Kayley suggested to see a museum or even a Sox game, allowing only some beach days. As I drove along familiar streets, recollections passed through my mind—trips to the grocery store, coffee shops, and bookstores, walks in parks, dinners out, bike rides, visits to historical sites. All with Wes. My old life. I cracked my window, regardless of the cold, to inhale the scents of memory. Dabbing at unshed tears, I continued to Newton.

My GPS led me to Gabe's apartment.

We never discussed more than the day trip, not explicitly. Our texts had gone something like this:

> Hey. I think I'm ready to talk.

Okay. Phone?

> In person. Can I come to you?

Whatever you're most comfortable with.

He gave me his address and we agreed on this date, just a few days away.

And that had been that.

Still, it was his apartment. I was going to his apartment. That had implications. I wiped sweaty hands on my jeans and left my overnight bag in the car.

He buzzed me up. A smile spreading straight into his cinnamon eyes greeted me at the open front door. "Hey."

So far, so good. I missed those eyes. Those lips. His voice melted me. But we had stuff to talk about first.

"Come in, come in. Chilly today." He took my coat, his hand lingering on my back. I didn't move away. If I'd wondered these past few months whether the spark remained, my body's response told me *heck yes*.

We talked about the weather and my drive here. Unspoken words hovered in the air like the smell of ozone before a thunderstorm. After a brief tour of his apartment—simple, functional, cozy—he suggested we go out.

I closed my eyes and took a calming breath. "How about we stay in?"

He paused in taking my coat off a hanger. His throat moved in an audible swallow as he turned to me.

"I mean, to talk," I said. I nearly lost my courage at the hope and longing in his face—the scruffy auburn-brown stubble on his chin, a dance of sunlight and shadow on the gentle creases of his cheeks, the smile lines, and a lopsided grin making my knees falter. He rubbed a hand on the back of his neck.

"Helen," he said in a bare whisper, deep and vulnerable. "I missed you. So much."

I approached him and stroked his chin. "I missed you, too." My heart hammered. I inhaled him. Something smooth, sandalwood or cedar, with a hint of vanilla. I'd missed his scent, missed his touch, missed his presence.

His phone chirped from the kitchen. He reluctantly walked over to silence it. "Reminder for today."

"Reminder?"

"Thought about taking you to the Isabella Stewart Gardner Museum. Then coffee and markets?"

He remembered. Of course he did. He was Gabe.

I bit my lower lip. Coming here had been hard enough, maybe an outing would ease us into conversations. "That'll be nice. Should we take the T?"

"We don't have to go," he said, moving in and resting his hand on my hip.

We were so close that I could brush my lips against his if I wanted to.

"No, let's go out. That's a good idea." I pulled my scarf around my neck and buttoned my long wool coat, bracing for the brisk day. I needed to start with something neutral. "I read the article you wrote. You shouldn't have—"

"I should have. It was the least I could do...for the library."

The library. A perfect conversation piece. Forget letters and apologies.

Oh, Helen, you're such a chicken.

I ignored my inner nag. "Your article was just what we needed. It's created buzz. Two news stations called the house. Interviewed us. Mom will be taking them on a tour of the library this week. It's brought this new life back to her."

"Any news with the historical commission?"

"The experts authenticated it all! The cellar, the artifacts, the journals, Alice's letters... We submitted the nomination papers. Now I'm waiting for the review board to make the final decision in March."

He squeezed my hand as we exited his apartment build-ing. "That's great! When I was in the hidden room...it felt...I can't find the right word for it. Just like it felt *special*. Knowing I was sitting in a space that was part of the Railroad was...wow, ya know. I wanted to help any way I could. I should have asked you first about writing an article, but it's all public knowledge already in your town meeting minutes. Was that okay?" He scrubbed his other hand through his hair.

"It was."

"I felt like a part of it. Instead of being an outsider looking in and writing about it, I was experiencing it. Living it. With you. And Sanders Mill has this hold on me." He paused. "You have a hold on me."

His words found purchase in my mind. I recalled him expressing how he had felt like an outsider. That not even his globetrotting could fill a void within. But my words had.

That I had.

The conversation came easier now on our way to the T.

"We can submit articles later about the historical find-ings," he said as we turned around a corner. "If you want."

We. My heart did an Olympic-sized leap. "I would like that. Thank you."

On our way to the museum, we talked more about the commission and historical finds, avoiding all talk about *the big thing*. Geesh, we were both chickens.

We made our way through the museum exhibits, chat-ting and holding hands. We fell into the rhythm I loved with him. It was comfortable. It felt right.

I sipped my chai latte as we walked around Fenway, enjoying a pleasant, albeit windy, December day. Swirls of brown leaves, the last ones to drop, flew past. Flags flapped in the breeze. I tucked my scarf in, grateful for my hat to protect my hair.

"Feels like snow," I said.

"It does."

"The flowers and art collections at the museum were as beautiful as I remembered."

"Glad you enjoyed it. I remember you saying how you liked this museum but wished you could go to Europe. Thought the museum would be an acceptable compromise for now."

For now.

I squeezed his hand as his words squeezed my heart. "A perfect alternative. I love how Isabella Stewart Gardner converted her home into a place for people to appreciate the arts. She was very particular about how she wanted it curated, and she was the first woman to build a museum in the U.S."

"I loved how she was a pioneer bringing art from all over to our country. She went against the norm. I read a book about her recently. She still seems to be a mystery to many."

We stopped by an outdoor holiday marketplace.

"Your zuke mash would sell well here at the boutique markets."

I recycled my coffee cup in a nearby bin. "Don't think I'm ready for mass production."

"Dinner out or in?"

"In?"

He shook his canvas bag with his marketplace finds. "I've got the makings for a good recipe here."

"I'll help."

He slung his arm around me, and we strolled to his place enjoying holiday lights and decorations lining streets and shops.

We prepared chicken Parmesan with a fresh marinara sauce Gabe purchased at the market, along with garlic bread, Caesar salad, and roasted asparagus. "What are you doing for Christmas?" I asked, sneaking a crisp spear off the baking sheet.

"Most years, I go to my parents' place, but this year they're visiting my brother, Corey."

"Then you should join us," I suggested. "Dan will be here. Ryan will be at the in-laws' in Portland. My dad and stepmom aren't coming north. They'll probably go to the country club to see their new friends." I scrunched my nose.

He squeezed my shoulder. "I'm sorry that he doesn't make you a priority. My dad...he's not the best either."

The tension that had crept back in dissipated with the gentle pressure of his thumb and fingers into my shoulder blade. He grazed the back of my neck with a kiss. His soft touches sent me plummeting over an edge. In a good way. I enjoyed forgetting.

We still needed to talk.

He added, "It's hard when families do their own thing, move apart. For years, we'd all gather at my parents' place—they were still at our childhood home. I miss our Sunday night dinners. As they got older, they got less tolerant of winters. Mom said the move was for Dad's arthritis." He laid out plates on the kitchen counter. He pointed to a glass cookie jar filled to the brim. "My mom sends cookies all the time. Peppermint chocolate chip cookies this week."

"Then you must come have Christmas with us. Mom loves the holidays and makes a big fuss." As I stirred the sauce, garlic and oregano teased my nose, and my stomach growled.

Gabe laughed. "Hungry?"

"I swear I've put on ten pounds since meeting you. All this eating."

He ran his fingers along my lower back, barely above my rear. "We can work it off."

I blushed, full on, and licked my lips. If I weren't starving, I'd grab his hand and have my way with him right now.

We set his kitchenette table with glasses and silverware, and he offered wine.

"Maybe a seltzer or water?"

He poured two lemon-lime seltzers for us, splashing a little. "Whoops. Butterfingers."

I wiped the spill with a dish towel. "They're good with typing." I wondered what they could do elsewhere. I stroked his hand. "I like your fingers."

He kissed the back of my hand and, with a lingering smile, pulled out a chair for me to sit.

"I hate my clumsiness, though. I mean, I am who I am, but some things don't get easier. I wish I'd had more support when I was younger. It's why I help at the Thrive Center. To make it easier for others."

I took a bite of the chicken, chewed, swallowed. "You've got a wicked toolbox of self-taught skills. I say you're doing fine. This meal is so good, by the way. Oh, and speaking of the Thrive Center—Aaron can't stop talking about how awesome you are. Thanks for connecting him with the right people. He's excited to get the program up and running soon. And your donation..." I choked up. "What you did means more than you probably know."

"I was happy to help."

Gabe's endless eyes held my gaze as I forked a bite of pasta into my mouth. What was he thinking? Ugh, or did I have oregano on my lip? I blotted my mouth with a napkin. No... This was *a look*, the kind that shot right down to my toes. I shifted in my seat.

While the after-dinner decaf brewed, hazelnut infusing the apartment air, Gabe turned on a soulful playlist of oldies. Of course, he remembered what I liked to listen to. I pointed to a stack of origami paper on his coffee table. "Want to show me how you work your magic?"

He came over and sat on the couch. "Gladly."

I nestled myself beside him, watching his fingers bend and fold—first a bird, then a 3-D heart, then a multicolored star, then a flower.

"I don't see clumsy fingers here. Now me...I can hardly do a paint-by-number with my mom." I laughed.

"It helps with my depth perception."

"Mom says the same thing about her crossword puzzles. It keeps her brain cells working."

I tried to make a simple bird. He showed me each step, our hands brushing. "Looks like a donkey?" I laughed. "Even your skilled fingers can't help my fumbling ones."

The coffee brewer gurgled as I traced my finger over his palm lines and Patsy Cline sang.

He leaned in and kissed me.

And just like that, we rekindled where we had left off months ago. His fingers traced my spine, and he drew me in closer, sucking the breath from me with the passionate movement. I loved his arms around me. Oh, so very much.

He broke for air. "Do you want to stay the weekend with me?"

"Yes."

He kissed me again with the tenderness of our very first kiss, a tickle on my lips. Hot breath fanned my face, and fingers played in my hair, sending shivers down to my curled toes. His thumb caressed my wrist and palm. I leaned into him, my lips against his in a soul-reaching dance.

He cupped my face in his hands and stared at me as if exploring my features for the first time. I got lost in the shards of green and gold in his irises. My fingers slid down his back, wanting to touch more of him.

He continued with a soft slide of fingertip along my collarbone, and my pulse raced with unbearable anticipation. He pulled me up and we swung slowly as a Roy Orbison love ballad played. Swaying, the music's rhythm and our kisses guided us to his bedroom. We kicked off our shoes on the way.

He clicked on one lamp. We kissed, touched, and moved closer to the bed.

My calves hit the bed's side rail, and I tumbled back onto a plush mattress and duvet. I laughed. "See, Gabe, you're not the only clumsy one."

"Or maybe I'm too eager," he countered, throaty.

I pulled him on top of me. He kissed my neck, his breath hot on my skin. Goose bumps shot up and raced across my neck and down an arm. The music streaming in from the living room whirred in beat with my heart.

He dripped kisses down my throat. Oh, so slowly his affections wandered—to my neck, collarbone, my chest. The man paid attention to every inch of exposed skin. I closed my eyes, relishing the sweet goodness of Gabe.

He lifted my sweater and t-shirt to continue the kisses over my belly, along the ticklish skin above my jeans' waistband, which he then pulled down. I giggled when his kisses hit a ticklish spot right on my hip bone. He licked it and my giggle turned into a moan.

His hands were indeed pure magic, but his *tongue*...

And then he stopped.

He came back up and cupped my cheeks again. "I need to give you something first."

I would take anything he gave me at this moment.

He shifted on the bed and reached toward his nightstand. Losing our physical contact left me hollow, and I sat up.

Gabe opened the top drawer and withdrew a large yellow envelope.

I clasped my hands to my chest. Lust was replaced with nerves so tightly wound, I felt I might burst.

"We've had a great day, Helen. And I...I want so much more with you, but not before giving these back. Not before I say how incredibly sorry I am for taking them. You must have felt so used and then betrayed. There's no excuse for what I did. Sorry is not good enough..." His voice got husky, and he choked up. He handed me the envelope.

I stared at it, my brain on spin cycle.

He said, painfully soft, "I had lost my muse, then found her in your letters, but in doing so, I-I didn't think. I only acted. Your words were a lifesaver to me, Helen. Your silver linings within the gloom. You gave me hope for myself. For my ability to tell another story...but that story, the foundation of it, wasn't mine. It was yours. A story I didn't ask permission to use or share. I screwed up. And I need to make up for it." He handed me another sheet of paper with something typed on it.

I closed my eyes and clutched the envelope and page to my chest as I clamped my lips to stay unbidden tears. I could hear his deep breathing, feel his warmth so close to me.

He continued, "It wasn't just about needing to find my muse. I lost *myself* for a long time. My travel writing fulfilled my hunger to see the world, experience adventure, and it paid the bills. It wasn't enough. Something else was missing." Even softer, he whispered near my ear, "Some*one* was missing. You."

As he shifted, I lifted my eyelids. Through the blur of my tears, his eyes, distraught with shame, stared back.

I peeked into the larger envelope to see five small white envelopes. I was afraid to touch them, to make it all real. He grabbed something wrapped in tissue from the nightstand and presented it to me carefully. "The dandelion. I had to put it in tissue to protect it."

I took it and slid it into the larger yellow envelope. My eyes fell upon the typed page. I read the words. "Gabe, you can't do this."

"I'll only publish it with your consent. You might not want the world to know you wrote the letters. I respect that. Ironic after what I did, I know. But if you want recognition, you deserve it, and if you want privacy, you deserve that, and you definitely deserve the choice of which you want." He took another, not entirely steady breath. "And...I can't just sit here, making money off your pain. I donated to Aaron's project, but I want to help you, Helen. Any way I can. I can donate to the Friends of the Library. Help with Mary's care. Anything."

"Gabe." I blinked tears free to flow down my face. "You don't need to...well, not all of that. But thank you. It's decent of you. I won't pretend there's no need to make up for it, or that I haven't been hurt and mad. But I don't think you're a bad person." I never had, not since we met each other in the cafe line.

"I—" Gabe closed our space, the bed creaking with his movement, and he stroked my jawline with featherlight fingertips. "I love you, Mary Helen. And will say sorry every day for the rest of my life if you need me to."

I sobbed. More than I would have liked. After a moment, I said, my voice raspy, "Gabe, you came to Sanders Mill because you fell in love with an idea, some imaginary woman. Not me..."

"No, I fell in love with the woman who wrote those letters. You. And, once I met you, I fell in love even more." He paused, his hand remaining on my cheek. "I made a very poor choice and I'm so sorry about it." A wind-soft stroke wiped away the tears dribbling down my cheeks.

"I forgive you, Gabe. I forgive you."

"Thank you." His mouth trembled, and he exhaled. Hoarse with emotion, he said, "Please let me into your heart, Helen."

"Too late."

He flinched, but I took his hand with one of mine and squeezed it. "You're already there."

His voice was a whisper, his tone more gentle than his touch had been. "I'm so sorry about Adalyn...and the baby. I'm here to listen when you're ready."

"Thank you."

I stood and gently deposited the envelope containing my letters on his dresser. On my return to the bed, I straddled his lap. Wrapping my arms around his neck, I dropped my face down to meet him, and he kissed me like he'd never kissed me before. The fire in his mouth, his tongue, his hands...

Off came my sweater and t-shirt. My chest heaved, breathless with want, with need. I lifted his flannel shirt and undershirt over his head, then put my arms back around

him. Held him so tightly. His skin against mine was elec-
trifying.

He lay back, and pulled me back with him, then sensual-
ly rolled over so that he was on top of me. Slowly—as if he
were going for the world record of slowness—he teased
my pants down.

Finally, his tongue explored my inner thigh. I shivered
with desire and propped myself up on my elbows and
stared down at wide, dark irises as he looked up at me.
His eyes expressed more than either of us ever could in
spoken or written words.

He returned to my mouth, and we kissed hard, first
each other's lips and then everywhere, driven to explore
every dip and knoll of each other's bodies. I tickled his
earlobe with my tongue as his fingertips slid inside my
panties. God, I was right about those hands. They left me
gasping.

While his fingers worked their magic, he kissed my
breasts through my lacy bra—the one that unhooked in
the front. I broke from his touch for a fleeting moment
to undo the hook. His mouth went to my nipples, and I
arched, pleasure waves shooting to every nerve ending.

Suddenly, the waves rocked me, so hard, so fast. I pant-
ed and stifled the moan with my fist.

As I lay back, basking in the shivers that shook me hard,
I heard the unzip of his jeans and him opening his bedside
drawer.

Gabe hovered over me again, propped up on his elbows.
With his jeans and boxers pulled off, my hands climbed
leisurely up his sculpted thighs to a very nice rear end.
Goose bumps prickled under my roving fingertips.

He groaned and pulled back, stroking a hand down my
cheek.

"You're so beautiful, Helen," he said through a heavy breath.

Yellow light from the bedside lamp illumined his own body. My look snagged on his crooked smile.

He kissed me again—a soft tease on my raw lips—before his mouth returned to my breasts. His kisses drove me crazy. I forgot how good this could be. It had been far, far too long! I gripped the bedspread as he slid down my panties. He dropped lower and his mouth traveled to the core of me.

His hands had nothing on his tongue.

He swept me away, ecstasy rolling in hard and fast again. My leg muscles tensed as I bit a moan. After timeless minutes of delicious torture, the agony released in a red-hot wave.

He kissed his way up along my skin.

Exhilarated and my heart pounding, I pushed his chest and rolled him onto his back. Straddling him again, this time I took him inside me as we rode the next wave of pleasure together.

Sipping decaf and snuggled against Gabe in his bed, I admired the framed photographs on the dresser and nightstand that were interspersed with more origami figures. Elephants in Africa, Ayers Rock in Australia, and a castle partly in ruins by a lake. "Where's this one?" I pointed.

"Kilchurn Castle, Scotland. I kayaked to it."

"I'm envious." I ran a finger along the black-and-white print of the elephants. I marveled at the bright color in a second photograph—a bird's-eye view of a densely populated and sprawling cityscape composed of countless orange and tan and white buildings, nestled in a lush and mountainous green valley flanked by what looked like dormant volcanoes. Maybe South America? "This one?"

"Quito, Ecuador."

"Did you take them all?"

"These, yes. Most editors use their in-house photographers for my bylines, though. They prefer my words over images. Patagonia is still on my bucket list. I have a thing for Central and South America."

"Do you miss traveling?"

"Sometimes. As inspiring as it was, I was lonely."

"Lonely?" I looked at a snowy peak of Mount Fuji.

He brushed a hand across my shoulder. "Nobody to share it with."

A trace of a sigh lodged in my throat.

I pulled off my t-shirt and drew him on top of me. "Now you do."

We stayed in bed for the remainder of the weekend.

Twenty-Seven

Gabe

Helen dabbed at small tears as she opened the Christmas gift from me. She ran a finger over the notepaper embossed with gold and teal flowers around the borders and her initials M.H.W. on the bottom.

"I love it." She squeezed me.

Having her arms wrapped around my torso felt...right.

"These will be for *addressed* letters, though. With a stamp," she added.

"Stationery is our thing," I said, waving the patterned origami paper she'd given me for Christmas.

"You ready to go?"

"Sure." I eagerly threaded the laces on my boots while Helen donned her long winter coat. "You don't think it's too early in the season?"

Helen put on her gloves and hat and knotted her new scarf. "Maybe. The icicles peak in January or February, but it's been wicked cold for December, and we've had the whole rain-freeze-thaw-refreeze thing that helps them grow. Oh, let me before we go—" She hurried outside to retrieve the newspaper beside the doormat. "It's here! The best Christmas gift." Her voice glimmered with excitement.

"Wait, I thought the book scarf was the 'best gift ever'?" I teased, toying with the purple alpaca yarn scarf I got her from Billie's boutique.

"Okay, well, second best gift." She put *The Pioneer* into my hands. "Front page."

I read the article, my pulse zigzagging all over the place. "This was all your doing, Helen."

She looked adorable with her strawberry-blonde waves poking out from her hat. I brushed my lips against her forehead in a kiss.

With a heady sigh, she pulled back. "I know it's being presumptive to have this run now, and I don't want to jinx things, but it may help people understand more at the town meeting. If I could sway voters a bit, even if the historical commission doesn't—"

"No ifs." I put two fingers over her lips. "It'll all work out." I kissed her mouth this time, the taste of the hot cocoa we just shared delicious on her tongue. I said, "It's a smart move."

"Read it to me," she asked as we made our way to the car. So, I did. I left out the "by Gabriel Dennehy" part.

"Discovery Links Sanders Mill Public Library to Underground Railroad. The Sanders Mill Public Library, built in 1860, is no stranger to history. Sanders Mill, like several towns across central Massachusetts, fell victim to the infamous June 1, 1910 tornado. Forty-three people, including Alice Foster Hadley, the second librarian of Sanders Mill, perished. The library, schoolhouse, town office, and multiple businesses were destroyed. In 1912, Joseph Hadley, grieving the loss of

his wife and hoping to continue healing in his community, dedicated twenty acres of his land to the resurrection of the library in a new building and for the creation of nature trails. To this day, the building and land remain under private ownership by his family while being publicly funded.

"The library has continuously operated under librarians who have sustained Alice's legacy of love for learning. Local artist Mary Hadley Wright was a librarian for over twenty-five years, and for the past seven years her daughter, Helen Wright, has stepped into the role. 'Tradition is important to us. So is history,' Mary said.

"Helen reiterated, 'Libraries are sources of inspiration and lifelong learning. They are both a refuge for and an asset to the community. We are a destination for those of all ages seeking connection, support, and resources, as well as a place of discovery.'

"Its newest discovery? A stop on the Underground Railroad. Historical experts have identified a root cellar on the twenty-acre Sanders Mill Public Library land as a 'station' used by people escaping slavery. The family also recovered artifacts in the cellar and in their own personal collection, such as letters written in a code used by Stationmasters. The items found in the cellar include teacups, a mug, lamp burner, comb, and glass bottles. But most intriguing was a wooden doll which historians believe belonged to a runaway slave from Worcester, ten-year-old Mabel Elizabeth. This photograph, circa 1858, shows her with two family members, and she is holding the same doll. One of Mabel Elizabeth's descendants, Angela Hoban, now lives in northern Vermont and she is ecstatic about this discovery. 'This photograph has sat on my fireplace mantel for years. My grandmother told me stories of Mabel's bravery on her escape to freedom. The close calls. The places she needed to hide for days on end. The long journey north along a route that ran parallel to the real railroad. The kindness of those helping her along the way.'

"From 1855–1862, Alice Foster and Joseph Hadley helped run this station. Mr. Hadley worked as an apprentice for another member of a notable Sanders Mill founding family, Michael Prescott. Prescott was known across Massachusetts for his innovative architectural designs, and posthumously, as an abolitionist, working with the well-known Abby Kelley Foster. It is not yet confirmed but seems very possible that Prescott worked alongside Joseph Hadley and Alice Foster to help people traveling along the Underground Railroad routes in central Massachusetts. He is the ancestor of the town's current moderator, Miriam Prescott. Though none of Michael Prescott's journals have been recovered yet, it is suspected by authenticity expert, Dr. Virgil Gavison, that Mr. Hadley used his mentor's ciphers in his own journals and in correspondence with Ms. Foster.

"Recently, the Hadley-Wright family applied for their library land to be listed as a historical landmark in the National Register program via the Massachusetts Historical Commission on behalf of the National Park Service. Gavison, a professor of American History at the University of Virginia, has been designated by the NPS as one of their lead experts on the Underground Railroad. He said, 'This discovery is promising and integral to identifying more of the network of locations in Massachusetts that contributed to the Underground Railroad. We've confirmed that Mabel Elizabeth is just one of many people who sought shelter with Mr. Hadley and Ms. Foster on their way to freedom. It just goes to show you never know what may happen at a library!'

"The Sanders Mill Public Library remains an active part of the community, hosting many meetings each month, organizing grant-funded children's programs, and creating *opportunities for youth, such as their youth council, book club, and plant sale. The library will soon announce a new mentoring program run by Aaron Murphy, a former math teacher at Prouty High School, who has spearheaded a robust tutoring program for the school district and has sought to expand the organization.*

"Due to budget cuts, the town formed a committee this year to determine the justification for keeping the library open. With its centralized location beside the conservation woodland containing impressive old-growth forest and a pond, the property is desirable to housing developers. A regional library in North Prouty has been suggested as a replacement for the one in Sanders Mill. From Mary Hadley: 'As community members come and go from the library, they're greeted by the friendly faces of volunteers and staff, notable local artwork and historical displays, open spaces and meeting rooms, countless resources and events, and the feeling of small-town Massachusetts. It would be a shame to see it bulldozed, and with it a piece of American history.'"

Helen hugged me. "Perfect. The picture of Joseph and Alice, of Mabel Elizabeth's family, the root cellar...they capture the message."

"Honest journalism at its best." I squeezed her back.

Helen absolutely glowed with happiness as she drove us to an access point on the rail trail. We parked on the side of a road and picked our way down a snowy slope in the forest and met the foot path. After walking through an underpass, we emerged into the icicle gully.

"Wow." My voice echoed while I took it all in. "I had a picture in my mind of this part of the trail from your letter, but *this*—to see it in person is just, wow." Gigantic icicles flanked us in this carved-out section of the rail trail, looking like waterfalls caught mid-flow. I ran a gloved hand along a massive frozen pillar descending from the embankment far above us. Ice dripped where the sun struck it. Droplets fed into the small streams running in channels on either side of the trail. A musical trickle came from meltwater running over the stone walls, behind the sheets of ice.

"Love it?" Helen asked, pink in her nose and cheeks. "It'll keep building up, and by February the sides are sheer walls of ice, with enormous curtains of it draping over the edges of this gorge. Icicles twice as tall as you. I wear my snow pants and heavy boots when it's that deep. Here in the shadows, the snow and icicles can stick around until spring."

In some spots, the water was frozen in round, marble-like formations. And under caps of snow, the leaves of ferns curled dormant, still green. I snapped photos with my phone. "Incredible."

Helen's ringtone sounded. She glanced at her phone before silencing it and sliding it into her coat pocket as we crunched back to the trail leading up to the overpass.

"Anything important?" I asked.

Her grin spread to her eyes. "It was Miriam."

Helen

"So, did I tell you my dad called me?" Gabe said on our walk up to the car.

"Oh?" I knew his father was a touchy subject. It's interesting how badly we both wanted to please our parents, even now, as adults. I walked in my mom's footsteps while also trying to carry her along, and he walked in the shadow of his dad's disapproval.

"Yeah, my mom told him about the library efforts. We talked for a while. I told him about the cool things we found. All the work you've done."

"We've done," I interrupted.

A small smile cracked his expression, and he said, "He's proud of me."

I squeezed his hand. "That's great, Gabe. I mean, you already do great things with your investigative articles, but I know how much it means to you to have him acknowledge that."

"Yeah. And, well, I'm almost done outlining my next book," Gabe said on our turn to the road.

My boot snagged on a surprise root under the fluffy snow. "The sequel?"

He righted me with a touch on the elbow, then scooped me into his arms. His kiss on my lips melted any uncertainty I felt about his answer.

He pulled back slowly, as if drunk from the kiss. Guess I was that good.

"Sort of," he said. "I started it as a sequel that could become a series. I was going to turn Emma and Declan into a mystery-solving duo. Each book has a new plotline following from what they discover in dead mail, be it reuniting loved ones or other intrigues."

"Sounds fun. My kind of story."

"But..." He scraped a hand over the soft bristles of his five-o'clock shadow and said, sheepishly and hinging on self-deprecating, "I'm scared I can't succeed without help. No more letters."

I bit my lower lip. "First, I have total confidence that you can write that series without other letters. However..." I kicked the idea around for a moment. "What if you can use different letters?"

"Uh, Helen, no more shady doings, remember?"

"What about Alice and Joseph's story? Based on their journals and the copies we made of their letters..."

Hope gleamed in his eyes. "It's an idea. But I would need the owner's permission first, of course."

"I think she'd be okay with it."

"Helen. Wow. Thank you." He kissed my forehead, then asked, "What if you write it with me?"

I touched my throat. "I don't write."

He leaned close and stroked my cheek.

A clump of snow fell from a nearby branch as I put my arms around him, enclosing us in a bubble of our body heat.

"You write. You snared me with your words. Consider it. How about the prologue or an epilogue? Or you can be my first reader. You can keep my facts straight, be my copyeditor, keep me honest."

I stared into his hopeful eyes for a long moment. "I'll think about it."

He unlocked the car. "In other news... A few magazine editors contacted me with offers for travel gigs this spring after my national tour."

"Oh?" My breath caught. I just got him back. Was he going to travel again?

"Thing is, I may say no."

I threaded a gloved hand in his. "Oh?"

"You could come with me," he suggested.

"I wish. I can't."

"Then down the road? Maybe a longer trip in summer after the dust settles?"

"That would be fun."

We got in the car, and I blasted the heat.

Gabe sat at the wheel, not putting it into drive. "I'm afraid to go alone, Helen."

"Why?"

"I'm superstitious about leaving. Every time I've had a girlfriend and gone away on a trip, I came home to an empty apartment or a note or text message. They didn't want to wait around for me." He bobbed his knee up and down in nervous habit, then turned to me, taking my shoulders. "I don't want that to happen again. Not with you. Not with what we have."

"If you decide to go this spring, or whenever, I'll wait for you, Gabe. I love you."

A broad smile creased his face. "I love you so much, you don't even know the half of it. You really would wait for me?"

"Yes." I lifted my chin. He caught my lips, and I returned the passion, unsure where this path of ours led, but knowing we were on it together.

Twenty-Eight

Helen

The quarterly meeting for the National Register came and went.

Crickets.

No news. I checked my email twenty times a day.

To avoid being driven out of my mind by the slothlike pace of government agencies, I kept busy with a hundred other tasks. I had the May town meeting to prepare for, after all, and had to proceed under the assumption that the National Register of Historic Places would *not* designate the library and grounds eligible.

Today, several members of the youth council hustled in and out of the downstairs rooms, carrying supplies for Aaron's space. Evans whizzed past me, two heavy boxes balanced precariously in his arms. Even though he'd been excelling with his new math tutor from the chess club, he was excited to be one of Aaron's first clients with the SPARK Tutoring program.

"Careful, Evans," I said, blowing a wisp of hair from my face, as my hands were full carrying a bulky box.

Even Harper and Brenna came. Seeing Harper in better spirits and actively engaging in a group again brought me great joy. Long months had passed without sight of her, and I'd feared the worst.

When I got a moment alone with her, I offered my apologies.

"It's okay, Miss Wright," she said, shifting from foot to foot. "I know why you denied being the writer. It sucks, what he did."

"It did. He and I, we're good now. Are you doing okay, Harper? Last time we spoke"—I searched for the words—"you weren't doing so well."

Gabe winked as he walked past, unaware of the substance of our conversation.

Harper shot a glance at the other teens helping alongside him. Two of the girls were giggling, following Gabe with their eyes. "Uh, things are better. I spoke to a different counselor, Mrs. Benway, at school, and those kids were disciplined. And I'm going to meet with one of the life coaches Mr. Murphy hired for SPARK."

"That's great, Harper. I'm here for you, too, whenever you need me."

"Thanks, Miss Wright."

At least the bullying was under control, and she was speaking to someone. She had more light to her expression and gait, and *seemed* to be in good spirits. But I knew looks could be deceiving. Had I done enough?

I caught myself from worrying too much. Things were getting better for Harper, and she knew she could talk to me—among a number of people—if she needed more help. For now, that was enough.

She spun to help Evans with a teetering stack of boxes but quickly returned. "Oh! I have something for you." She opened her shoulder bag and awkwardly handed me a stack of journals and books, their old bindings falling loose.

I ran my finger across the brown cover of the one on top. "What are these?"

A prizewinning smile brightened her expression. "Something you may need. Just don't tell my mom I was the one to give them to you."

She hurried away.

If they were what I thought they were... I gently opened one book, the creak of the old binding music to my ears. There it was—his name on the first page. Faded cursive and charts filled the next ones. Dates from the mid to late 1800s were scrawled across the tops of pages.

When Miriam called me after Gabe's article in *The Pioneer*, she was livid, claiming no such journals of Michael Prescott's existed and it was presumptuous of me to even think the library would be approved by the National Register—she had tried once, and failed, to get her own home listed—and she was going to talk to "her people" about this, and I was going down. How dare I smirch her name with this farce!

Whatever, Miriam.

Her threats no longer scared me.

It was too late to submit Michael Prescott's journals to the historical commission, but if the review board denied our nomination, these could come in handy. I needed to call Dr. Gavison tonight.

With my steps as light as a cloud, I went to Gabe, who was helping Aaron secure the sign to the wall beside the entrance door.

Smile lines joined the tired ones around Aaron's deep blue eyes. He masked a yawn and swiped his hand through his mahogany hair.

"How is Ivy?" I asked, already knowing.

"She's a night"—he yawned again—"owl."

We looked at the framed sign. SPARK Tutoring: Strive, Persist, Achieve, Reach, Know.

I hugged Aaron. "This is going to be incredible. I ran out of registration forms at the circulation desk, and we've had dozens of inquiries on the website forms."

"Adalyn would be proud, Helen," Aaron said.

Feeling it down to my bones, I agreed.

Woodcock Middle School was packed to the brim when I arrived the night of the May town meeting. I gave my name and address at registration, got my voting clicker, then waited in line to grab copies of the handout with warrant articles, motions, special descriptions, and the ad hoc Regional Library Site Plan Committee report. I'd already read them all beforehand, but there was something comforting about holding the pile of papers.

The committee had found nothing damning during their assessment of the Sanders Mill Public Library. They had evaluated our infrastructure, facilities, productivity, and impact on the community. In fact, their audit showed our activity, our life! The report painted Sanders Mill Public Library in a good light. So much for Miriam's people. Still, I was nervous. Life had shown me that things could turn on a dime.

As I expected, the Finance Committee didn't approve my budget this spring, so within Article Three, which presented all municipal budgets, was a lowballed amount for the library. One I could not function with. Hence why I proposed my request in the form of Article Seventeen.

I wove through the crowd, seeking Kayley. She waved from the bleacher section. I had two seat cushions tucked under my arms and exchanged one of them for a cup of coffee from her, glancing with a raised eyebrow at the bag in her lap. "You made popcorn?"

"You refused to sit in the front row, so we're in the nose-bleed seats. I needed my snack at least. This is going to be a good one. Plus, I'm starving. I have cocoa almonds for you."

"Hi, Helen," Aaron said from the other side of her, grabbing a handful of popcorn.

"Glad your mom could watch Ivy," I told them. "Every vote counts."

Kayley held up her clicker.

I looked down at the hundreds of folded chairs in rows on the gymnasium floor, searching for Mom.

Kayley tapped my shoulder and pointed. "There. With Coop, Nan, and Lorraine."

"Bet Chief Carter's not happy about the number of people here. We've gotta be breaking the fire code." I settled onto the cushion. A typical meeting, without any contested articles, maybe brought in two hundred voters. For a town nearing ten thousand residents, it was still a low number. Tonight looked like double or triple that at least.

"Why aren't you popping antacids?"

"Ditched them a few months ago. Feeling better."

"Look at the supporters who came."

I grimaced. "Howe's posse is over there." I shot a gaze to where they sat front and center.

"You've got half the town."

"And me," Gabe said, coming up with his friend Marco beside him. "Man, and I thought parking in the city was bad!"

I tapped the seat beside us. "Hi, Marco. I know you can't vote, but happy you're here."

"I'm glad to offer moral support at least," he said with a wink.

Gabe had told me all about Marco's involvement with the letters. In fact, the three of us had coffee the night before.

"They just sucked me in," Marco had said, his eyebrows drawn together. "Your struggles, your pain. God, it was a slap to my heart or something. I'm so sorry you went through all that, Helen. And I'm sorry I didn't toss them like I should have. I saw a buddy struggling and thought these might help him keep going."

I accepted his apology.

We had also agreed no public apology was needed from Gabe. Instead, he would donate some of his book proceeds to a local suicide awareness organization. And I could never see either Gabe or Marco be punished for what they did. I felt okay with all of it now. Maybe even grateful, sometimes, for the good parts, like bringing Gabe into my life, and the chance to revisit the letters and see how my life had changed since then.

Gabe wrapped an arm around my waist. "Good job, honey."

Yes, he had started calling me honey. I liked it.

"Nineteen articles on the warrant and we're number seventeen." I sipped the coffee, settling in for a long night. Though Kayley said she'd hijack the mic if need be, we knew it was the other town voices that needed to be heard tonight.

"Please, everyone, squeeze in, make room. We'll find space for everyone," Miriam said from the podium. "I kindly ask that if you're from out of town or not voting, please sit or stand in the section over here." She pointed to a section off to the left behind the camera crew.

An elderly woman and man came up the steps, seeking a seat. Gabe immediately stood, gave me a kiss, and said, "I'll be down there, okay?"

Marco stood, too.

They gave their spots to the couple and left.

Miriam, as moderator, began. Seated in front at long tables, representatives from the Finance Committee and Select Board flanked her along with the town clerk, town lawyer, and Craig Browning.

In her usual glowing public guise, Miriam thanked everyone for being present and reviewed the rules of a town meeting, following by asking us to stand for the pledge.

The clock moved painstakingly slow. Gabe and I texted back and forth, and it kept me composed. Articles came and went with the process of Miriam or a board member reading the motion, followed in some cases by a pre-arranged presentation by a board member or director. Then they opened the floor to commentary from citizens and the Finance Committee and Select Board. The occasional amendment would be proposed and voted upon. Then it came to voting on the main motion. It was a process, that's for sure.

Article Three, the vote to approve the municipal departments' funding and the lowballed library budget, passed without protest.

My heart sank a bit.

We slogged through other requests from departments and various town needs. Numbness traveled up my rear and lower back. Thankfully so far, nobody was proposing amendments upon amendments. That could get wild...and asinine.

Gabe texted me a yawning emoji.

"Give me some popcorn." I repositioned myself again as I took a salty hit to the taste buds. My stomach thanked me as I chased the popcorn with cocoa almonds. I whispered into Kayley's ear, "Did I tell you Prescott Realty sent me a revised offer?"

"Oh...no. Dare I ask?"

I swallowed. "Miriam proposed purchasing eighteen of the twenty acres, excluding the area around the root cellar, since it's off-limits until we get the decision from the review board. Two million bucks. There's room for at least sixty homes on the land once they clear-cut the trees. Millions of dollars of profit and a big slap on the back for Prescott Realty for brokering a deal to both 'save' the historical root cellar and build this wonderful new development." I made a gagging face.

Kayley dropped her popcorn baggie in her lap and coughed. I tapped her back as she reached for her water bottle. "That's a lot of money," she said after taking a gulp. "Double what she offered before."

I shook my head. "She knew I wouldn't take it, but I can't blame her for trying one last time. She's waiting for my funding request in Article Seventeen to be shot down here, and then I bet she offers me a quarter of that or less, knowing how desperate I'll be if the building winds up literally sitting there, unused. With no realistic budget, our hand would be forced. The historical designation, when we get it, will protect the land and building from being taken away, but I still need to pay the utilities. What if—"

"Not happening," Kayley said. "Article Seventeen will pass. They'll give you the money you need, Helen."

I was praying for a twofer: money to keep the library going, and the historical landmark designation to protect the property.

Finally, Miriam directed Nate Smith, the Planning Board representative, to read the library warrant article and motion aloud. My article requested town funds to bridge my gap between the operating budget, state aid, private donations, and endowment. He ended with, "...to see if the Town will authorize the Select Board to enter into a three-year agreement with the Sanders Mill Public Library to fund the library in the amount of $135,000 and to transfer $45,000 from Certified Free Cash for each year's funding. A two-thirds vote is necessary."

The amount was paltry in the grand scheme of things. All the other departments got their requested budgets, with only minor cuts.

Nate turned to Fred Wheeler, who said, "The Finance Committee does not recommend favorably on this motion."

I rolled my eyes so hard they might have popped out the back of my head. "Here we go," I mumbled to Kayley.

Then Nate turned to the Select Board. Frieda Hudson said, "The Select Board recommends favorably on this motion."

Wow. What? I hadn't expected that.

I watched Miriam's neutral face and posture. Had Miriam known this betrayal was going to happen and prepared for it?

Nate spoke about the purpose and findings of the ad hoc committee. Nowhere did their report claim the library was a fossil or lacking activity. We were in good standing. We had high room usage. Flourishing programs. Community opportunities. Positive feedback from the town polling they performed. An admirable vision statement and viable long-term strategic plan.

The worst this committee had to show was that a busy library was, in fact, underfunded. We stretched every last dime but were still able to provide for our patrons.

Despite this, Craig Browning boldly suggested I lay off staff at our last interdepartmental meeting. I refused. I had so few full-time staff as is.

They opened to comments.

Miriam's minion went first. "Patty Schlegel, 43 High Street. Though I appreciate the library and the continued support of knowledge, I'm opposed to this library being privately owned. If our tax dollars are going to be forked over each year to keep it afloat, the land and building should be in our hands. Why don't we sell the land and building to the town? They can't possibly need all that land." There were a few supportive cries in the crowd, along with some murmurs. She added, "We can still protect the part people are claiming is important historically. Twenty acres is a lot of land!"

Lovely Patty, the one who overheard my conversation with Kayley and told Miriam I was the letter writer inspiring Gabe's book. It was frustrating how some citizens got up to the mic and went on tangents that didn't pertain to the article being discussed. This warrant article had nothing to do with the library being privately owned. But I got where she was going—publicly owned, publicly funded...and then publicly demolished.

This was not about my ownership. This was about keeping the library funded, period.

Brett, a high school history teacher, spoke next. "Brett Watson, 613 Summer Grove Road. The library is seeking historical landmark status. This can be huge for the town! The Underground Railroad. How can we deny this gift of history? I say we approve the funding. My kids"—he paused and waved to his family in the rows of seats—"your kids, our grandkids, our grandparents...we all use this building at some point or another. Remember the ice storm ten years ago? I do. They offered a place for people to use the internet, get hot drinks, and hunker down while many of us were without power for days in record-breaking cold. And remember when they provided the space we needed for the vaccine clinic? The library has been there in the past for those seeking freedom...and those now, who need community support. Fund it."

Others spoke for and against. It went on for a while.

One man said, "If the library has to shut down, we'll still need to pay for unemployment. That's more than what they are asking for to fulfill their budget! This is a no-brainer. I fully support this motion. The library needs support."

Even old cranky pants who hated scandal and political correctness, Warren, spoke up in his gravelly voice: "I heard—"

"Name and address, please," Miriam interrupted.

"Warren Lawrence, 3 Maple Road. I heard the town wants the land to build some giant mansion-houses. Our population is nearing ten thousand. No more damn houses! They bring more kids, and then we have to pay more taxes to the school district. What about some smaller houses? What about us seniors?"

A few more shouts of *hear hear!* echoed beside him.

Howe's corner of the room grumbled, and he sent one of his stooges to the mic.

"The library needs to be fiscally responsible. They need to know when it's time to give up. Kids can get their books online. Do people really use the library anymore?"

I bit my tongue at the ignorant lout. I didn't want to waste precious popcorn by lobbing it at him. Some people would never understand that the importance of a library went beyond books, even after the ad hoc committee's findings were read in front of us all.

Soon, however, my people rallied. More came to the mic to speak in favor of the article. My neighbor, Eugene O'Connell.

Ronan Cooper.

Barb, Nan, Lorraine, Gifty, Billie, Stan.

Louie, the quiet companion of boisterous Mack, went to the mic. "Cut this crap and just vote yes."

People laughed. People clapped. Mack winked at me. Wow, Louie!

Miriam, at the front of the room, remained unruffled and professional behind her podium. Bored, even.

I dabbed at the surprised tears in my eyes.

Then sweet Evans approached the mic, accompanied by Harper and Jaxon. I had rallied the youth. They couldn't vote but they could use their voices. I wiped wetness from my cheeks with the back of my hand.

Quiet Gary, the cemetery caretaker, stepped up to the mic to voice his opinion.

Aaron shared about SPARK Tutoring. "No child should feel alone, and we strive to offer them a place of positive connection. In memory of Adalyn Foster, we wish to foster hope, foster the spark within our youth, and foster inclusivity and compassion, while providing tutoring and mentoring services and even support programs for parents. We wish for all our community to be heard, to be seen, to be acknowledged... We want to empower our next generation to lead self-directed, engaged lives. Not only will they strive, but they will thrive. To do that, we need the library."

Miriam had to bang her gavel to quiet the applause in the crowded gymnasium.

Her mother walked up to the mic and boldly turned around to face the audience instead of the board members at the front of the room. "Roberta Prescott, 11 Elm Woods. This is getting out of hand. I make a motion to terminate debate."

People murmured. No one had asked me to come up to the mic to justify my case. The people had spoken.

Miriam looked pleased to see this talk come to an end. "A motion has been made to call the question. We need a two-thirds vote to end discussion on Article Seventeen. Please grab your clickers. A yes vote means we will terminate discussion on this article."

We voted. Nearing the end of the almost three-hour meeting, I could see people fading fast.

The discussion was closed.

"Now, we need to vote on the article being considered." She repeated the motion, and said, "A two-thirds vote is required for this motion."

I clicked option one, yes, on my clicker. Kayley squeezed my hand. My heart felt like it had just run a marathon.

"Has everyone voted?" Miriam asked, watching a laptop screen. Waiting. Then she said, "Voting is closed."

We waited as Miriam read the vote count.

Her face puckered like she had bitten into a lemon, but she pasted her usual stiff expression back on in a heartbeat. "Three hundred eighty yeses, and sixty-five nos. Motion passes."

She brought the gavel down. Around the room, people applauded and cheered.

We did it!

Gabe texted me a happy face emoji. I responded with the kiss emoji.

It came as no surprise when Miriam and I found ourselves in the same area of the room at the end of the meeting. I had come down the bleachers to hug Mom and chat with a few others, and before I knew it, I was standing beside the podium.

Miriam flipped her styled, dark hair back over her shoulder with an exaggerated huff. Her hands almost curled into fists but then straightened. "I guess congratulations are in order." No acrimony hung in her plainly spoken words.

"Thanks," I said.

She twisted her lips, as if pondering her next move. Were we still playing this chess game?

"I wanted this housing development to build community."

There was the Miriam I knew, though her words lacked her usual punch. She still believed she was doing good for all. "We already have a community, Miriam."

She pressed her lips harder. But then her face softened when she spotted Harper smiling and laughing with a few friends on the bleachers. As she watched her daughter, her deep-set eyes held what I could only call maternal compassion...love.

Boldly, I said, "Harper's really found her place on the youth council. They have plans for a plant sale and another movie night Memorial Day weekend."

"Yes. She's doing well." Something flashed across her face—a smile? At me?

Miriam inhaled, opened her mouth to say something else, clamped it shut, and then just...walked off, toward Harper. The woman was the queen of diplomacy.

I watched as Miriam stood close to her daughter and laughed while talking with Harper's friends. Like, genuinely laughed at something one of the girls said. Roberta approached the group, and Miriam didn't glance her mother's way. Getting the hint, Roberta walked away and left the gymnasium.

Wow. Good for Miriam. We all had our own paths of change to walk. So maybe Miriam was on hers, too.

After another ten minutes of chatting with people—Coop, Mack and Louie, Barb—and saying goodbye to Kayley and Aaron, I muscled through the crowd of people dispersing toward the exit.

In the hallway outside the gymnasium, I found Gabe, and he gave me a huge hug and I squeaked.

"I had no doubt," he said.

I kissed him and smiled at Marco at his side. "I'll catch up with you both in a minute. I need to hit the bathroom."

I couldn't help but pause when I saw Howe approach Miriam around the corner and near the bathrooms. They were almost hidden from view. She shoved him when he came close. I couldn't hear the words but watched her mouth move in wild shapes. I imagined f-bombs falling off those lipstick-pink lips.

Good. Good for her, and Harper, and hopefully their family.

I walked through the exit of the building and to the car. When I got in the car, as if he could read my mind, Gabe said, with a wide grin, "Checkmate."

EPILOGUE

Helen

It was Memorial Day weekend, and glorious sunshine through my home office windows begged me to come outside. I nestled the pen between the pages of my journal and drew a breath as I reread the entry while running my fingers over a new piece of sea glass Dad had sent me.

Things were good. Real good. Finances were still tight, but we got the step-up raises with the passing of Article Seventeen. I had a few years of budgetary cushion at the library to hold us over, and for once, I felt like I truly had the town's support if we did fall on hard times again. Aaron's enrollment was going well, and he offered financial assistance to those who could not afford his services, thanks to Gabe's donation. Best yet, I'd gotten the email this morning from the National Park Service detailing the property's acceptance into the National Register of Historic Places. The land would be protected!

Mom was making progress these days with her health while enrolled in Dr. Boyne's clinical trial. Even Dad was making more effort. He called weekly to check on me and would chat with Mom for a few minutes. He was drawing closer to retirement and promised that she would see her share of his savings. I don't know what changed in him, but I was glad for it.

Even the Sanders Mill Historical Society had admitted their mistake in moving the Holiday Fair's venue and asked if the library could host them again.

Miriam had relaxed on her pursuits for now. Like an engaging suspense novel, one never knew when the antagonist might strike again.

Life would always have struggles, but I held hope again.

I rose from good Old Mahogany, the steadfast center of my under-renovation home office. I was finally getting the office of my dreams. Supplies to build my new shelves and rolling ladder lay scattered around the room. Coop had offered to help me with the project, and we negotiated a ridiculously low price I could pay him. He liked the work and got to see Mom more. I gave him extra jars of my soups as bonus compensation.

Leaning over my desk, I reread the salutation of my one-page letter *To Helen.*

History is more profound than what you read on the page. There is a deeper story at the heart of every tale.

You've come a long way, M.H.

You are brave, you are strong, and you are allowed to feel all the bumps of life. Grief is like a bouncing ball in a room. It starts out big and keeps hitting the walls. But with time, the ball shrinks, and hits the walls less and less. With each breath, each moment, you've allowed yourself to feel and heal and hope.

No more beating yourself up with regret.

Find the silver linings. You've done so much! You saved the library and the land. Found a historical treasure for others to share. Found love.

Allow memories to be a shining light. Let the past be the path to a future filled with hope and love. You've found ways to carry the grief without being crushed by it, to feel love without too much pain.

You will be okay. Better than that, you will thrive. Feel for what you've lost, but enjoy what you have.

Take care of YOU. And let others, too.

Continue to inspire and give hope.

Be the spark.

I closed the journal and placed it inside the desk.

I went to the kitchen, set the pitcher of tea and three glasses on a tray, and stepped through the back door. Mom waved from the garden, busy with assembling her tomato cages and stakes. Gabe wiped dirt-smeared hands on his jeans as he came over.

"I can't wait to have fingertips smelling like tomato oil again," he said, taking the glass I offered. "Think you'll let me know the zuke mash recipe now?"

"It's only passed down through family," I teased.

He gave me a wink and squeezed his free arm around my waist. "This means there's a chance someday?"

My chest expanded with a surge of love. "There's always a chance. I like a happy-ever-after."

He leaned close for a kiss. "Me, too."

ACKNOWLEDGEMENTS

So often stories begin from real-life experiences. *Letters to Nobody* is no exception. This book began its journey several years ago when my aunt shared a story with me about how she coped with the death of her mother. My aunt wrote her a "grief letter" to say goodbye and then dropped it in the mail. I was intrigued by this way of healing. I have also lost people dear to me and at times still grapple with the grieving process.

Inspired by my aunt's letter-writing, I researched what the post office does with undeliverable mail, and this fueled my curiosity. Over sixty million pieces of undeliverable mail go through the Mail Recovery Center each year in the U.S. Postal Service version of "lost and found." Wow, just wow.

I also sit on my town's Library Board of Trustees, and like many small-town departments, it has seen its fair share of fiscal growing pains. Between the anonymous grief letters and a struggling library, my idea began to take shape...and from it came *Letters to Nobody*.

I would like to thank Aunt Frances for seeding this idea. Additionally, I would like to thank Kerry for her librarian wisdom and for answering all my pesky questions, and Tyler, a former Select Board member, who provided much information on the workings of small-town government. I gleaned much by attending many town meetings. I would like to also thank history librarian Nancy for steering me toward the right information with researching the Underground Railroad. Thank you to Savannah for her guidance on understanding dyscalculia.

And, last but never least, *Letters to Nobody* would not be here without the thoughtful guidance of my beta readers (Lorraine, Keri, Jill, and Barbara); editor, Therese; and talented cover artist, Angela. Thank you, all!

About the Author

Jean has a penchant for the misunderstood, be it sharks, microbes, or wounded characters. A scientist by training, she now spends her days as an author and champion for her children. She draws from her interest in history, science, the outdoors, and her family for inspiration. She serves on the local library board of trustees and is an advocate for community, inclusion, and diversity.

A nature enthusiast who adores the national parks, Jean also writes for family-oriented travel magazines and websites. When not writing, she enjoys gardening, tackling the biggest mountains in New England, and going on adventures with her husband and children, while taking snapshots of the world around her and daydreaming about the next story. If she were stuck on a deserted island, her three essentials (besides family, food, water, shelter) would be: coffee, lip balm, and endless pink sticky notes.

Find out more about her books by visiting her website: www.jeanmgrant.com